UGLIES

SCOTT WESTERFELD

SIMON AND SCHUSTER

SIMON AND SCHUSTER
First published in Great Britain in 2006 by Simon & Schuster UK Ltd,
1st Floor, 222 Gray's Inn Road, London WC1X 8HB

This edition published in 2014

Originally published in the USA in 2005 by Simon Pulse,
an imprint of Simon & Schuster Children's Division, New York.

A CIP catalogue record for this book is available from the British Library

ISBN: 978-1-47112-394-8

10 9 8 7 6 5 4 3

Printed and bound by CPI Group (UK) Ltd, Croydon, CR0 4YY

www.simonandschuster.co.uk

www.scottwesterfeld.com

UGLIES

Also by Scott Westerfeld:

PRETTIES
SPECIALS
EXTRAS

LEVIATHAN
BEHEMOTH
GOLIATH

This novel was shaped by a series of e-mail exchanges between myself and Ted Chiang about his story "Liking What You See: A Documentary." His input on the manuscript was also invaluable.

Part I

TURNING PRETTY

Is it not good to make society full
of beautiful people?
—Yang Yuan, quoted in *The New York Times*

NEW PRETTY TOWN

The early summer sky was the color of cat vomit.

Of course, Tally thought, you'd have to feed your cat only salmon-flavored cat food for a while, to get the pinks right. The scudding clouds did look a bit fishy, rippled into scales by a high-altitude wind. As the light faded, deep blue gaps of night peered through like an upside-down ocean, bottomless and cold.

Any other summer, a sunset like this would have been beautiful. But nothing had been beautiful since Peris turned pretty. Losing your best friend sucks, even if it's only for three months and two days.

Tally Youngblood was waiting for darkness.

She could see New Pretty Town through her open window. The party towers were already lit up, and snakes of burning torches marked flickering pathways through the pleasure gardens. A few hot-air balloons pulled at their tethers against the darkening pink sky, their passengers shooting safety fireworks at other balloons and passing parasailers. Laughter and music skipped across the water like rocks thrown with just the right spin, their edges just as sharp against Tally's nerves.

Around the outskirts of the city, cut off from town by the black oval of the river, everything was in darkness. Everyone ugly was in bed by now.

Tally took off her interface ring and said, "Good night."

"Sweet dreams, Tally," said the room.

She chewed up a toothbrush pill, punched her pillows, and shoved an old portable heater—one that produced about as much warmth as a sleeping, Tally-size human being—under the covers.

Then she crawled out the window.

Outside, with the night finally turning coal black above her head, Tally instantly felt better. Maybe this was a stupid plan, but anything was better than another night awake in bed feeling sorry for herself. On the familiar leafy path down to the water's edge, it was easy to imagine Peris stealing silently behind her, stifling laughter, ready for a night of spying on the new pretties. Together. She and Peris had figured out how to trick the house minder back when they were twelve, when the three-month difference in their ages seemed like it would never matter.

"Best friends for life," Tally muttered, fingering the tiny scar on her right palm.

The water glistened through the trees, and she could hear the wavelets of a passing river skimmer's wake slapping at the shore. She ducked, hiding in the reeds. Summer was always the best time for spying expeditions. The grass was high, it was never cold, and you didn't have to stay awake through school the next day.

Of course, Peris could sleep as late as he wanted now. Just one of the advantages of being pretty.

The old bridge stretched massively across the water, its huge iron frame as black as the sky. It had been built so long ago that it held up its own weight, without any support from hoverstruts. A million years from now, when the rest of the city had crumbled, the bridge would probably remain like a fossilized bone.

Unlike the other bridges into New Pretty Town, the old bridge couldn't talk—or report trespassers, more importantly. But even silent, the bridge had always seemed very wise to Tally, as quietly knowing as some ancient tree.

Her eyes were fully adjusted to the darkness now, and it took only seconds to find the fishing line tied to its usual rock. She yanked it, and heard the splash of the rope tumbling from where it had been hidden among the bridge supports. She kept pulling until the invisible fishing line turned into wet, knotted cord. The other end was still tied to the iron framework of the bridge. Tally pulled the rope taut and lashed it to the usual tree.

She had to duck into the grass once more as another river skimmer passed. The people dancing on its deck didn't spot the rope stretched from bridge to shore. They never did. New pretties were always having too much fun to notice little things out of place.

When the skimmer's lights had faded, Tally tested the rope with her whole weight. One time it had pulled loose from the tree, and both she and Peris had swung downward, then up and out over the middle of the river before falling off, tumbling into the cold water. She smiled at the memory, realizing she would rather be on that expedition—soaking wet in the cold with Peris—than dry and warm tonight, but alone.

Hanging upside down, hands and knees clutching the knots along the rope, Tally pulled herself up into the dark framework of the bridge, then stole through its iron skeleton and across to New Pretty Town.

She knew where Peris lived from the one message he had bothered to send since turning pretty. Peris hadn't given an address, but Tally knew the trick for decoding the random-looking numbers at the bottom of a ping. They led to someplace called Garbo Mansion in the hilly part of town.

Getting there was going to be tricky. In their expeditions, Tally and Peris had always stuck to the waterfront, where vegetation and the dark backdrop of Uglyville made it easy to hide. But now Tally was headed into the center of the island, where floats and revelers populated the bright streets all night. Brand-new pretties like Peris always lived where the fun was most frantic.

Tally had memorized the map, but if she made one wrong turn, she was toast. Without her interface ring, she was invisible to vehicles. They'd just run her down like she was nothing.

Of course, Tally *was* nothing here.

Worse, she was ugly. But she hoped Peris wouldn't see it that way. Wouldn't see *her* that way.

Tally had no idea what would happen if she got caught. This wasn't like being busted for "forgetting" her ring, skipping classes, or tricking the house into playing her music louder than allowed. Everyone did that kind of stuff, and everyone got busted for it. But she and Peris had always been very careful about not getting caught on these expeditions. Crossing the river was serious business.

It was too late to worry now, though. What could they do to her, anyway? In three months she'd be a pretty herself.

Tally crept along the river until she reached a pleasure

garden, and slipped into the darkness beneath a row of weeping willows. Under their cover she made her way alongside a path lit by little guttering flames.

A pretty couple wandered down the path. Tally froze, but they were clueless, too busy staring into each other's eyes to see her crouching in the darkness. Tally silently watched them pass, getting that warm feeling she always got from looking at a pretty face. Even when she and Peris used to spy on them from the shadows, giggling at all the stupid things the pretties said and did, they couldn't resist staring. There was something magic in their large and perfect eyes, something that made you want to pay attention to whatever they said, to protect them from any danger, to make them happy. They were so . . . pretty.

The two disappeared around the next bend, and Tally shook her head to clear the mushy thoughts away. She wasn't here to gawk. She was an infiltrator, a sneak, an ugly. And she had a mission.

The garden stretched up into town, winding like a black river through the bright party towers and houses. After a few more minutes of creeping, she startled a couple hidden among the trees (it was a *pleasure* garden, after all), but in the darkness they couldn't see her face, and only teased her as she mumbled an apology and slipped away. She hadn't seen too much of them, either, just a tangle of perfect legs and arms.

Finally, the garden ended, a few blocks from where Peris lived.

Tally peered out from behind a curtain of hanging vines. This was farther than she and Peris had ever been together, and as far as her planning had taken her. There was no way to hide herself in the busy, well-lit streets. She put her fingers up to her face, felt the wide nose and thin lips, the too-high forehead and tangled mass of frizzy hair. One step out of the underbrush and she'd be spotted. Her face seemed to burn as the light touched it. What was she doing here? She should be back in the darkness of Uglyville, awaiting her turn.

But she had to see Peris, had to talk to him. She wasn't quite sure why, exactly, except that she was sick of imagining a thousand conversations with him every night before she fell asleep. They'd spent every day together since they were littlies, and now . . . nothing. Maybe if they could just talk for a few minutes, her brain would stop talking to imaginary Peris. Three minutes might be enough to hold her for three months.

Tally looked up and down the street, checking for side yards to slink through, dark doorways to hide in. She felt like a rock climber facing a sheer cliff, searching for cracks and handholds.

The traffic began to clear a little, and she waited, rubbing the scar on her right palm. Finally, Tally sighed and whispered, "Best friends forever," and took a step forward into the light.

An explosion of sound came from her right, and she leaped back into the darkness, stumbling among the vines, coming down hard on her knees in the soft earth, certain for a few seconds that she'd been caught.

But the cacophony organized itself into a throbbing rhythm. It was a drum machine making its lumbering way down the street. Wide as a house, it shimmered with the movement of its dozens of mechanical arms, bashing away at every size of drum. Behind it trailed a growing bunch of revelers, dancing along with the beat, drinking and throwing their empty bottles to shatter against the huge, impervious machine.

Tally smiled. The revelers were wearing masks.

The machine was lobbing the masks out the back, trying to coax more followers into the impromptu parade: devil faces and horrible clowns, green monsters and gray aliens with big oval eyes, cats and dogs and cows, faces with crooked smiles or huge noses.

The procession passed slowly, and Tally pulled herself back into the vegetation. A few of the revelers passed close enough that the sickly sweetness from their bottles filled her nose. A minute later, when the machine had trundled half a block farther, Tally jumped out and snatched up a discarded mask from the street. The plastic was soft in her hand, still warm from having been stamped into shape inside the machine a few seconds before.

Before she pressed it against her face, Tally realized that it was the same color as the cat-vomit pink of the sunset, with a long snout and two pink little ears. Smart adhesive flexed against her skin as the mask settled onto her face.

Tally pushed her way through the drunken dancers, out the other side of the procession, and ran down a side street toward Garbo Mansion, wearing the face of a pig.

BEST FRIENDS FOREVER

Garbo Mansion was fat, bright, and loud.

It filled the space between a pair of party towers, a squat teapot between two slender glasses of champagne. Each of the towers rested on a single column no wider than an elevator. Higher up they swelled to five stories of circular balconies, crowded with new pretties. Tally climbed the hill toward the trio of buildings, trying to take in the view through the eyeholes of her mask.

Someone jumped, or was thrown, from one of the towers, screaming and flailing his arms. Tally gulped, forcing herself to watch all the way down, until the guy was caught by his bungee jacket a few seconds before splatting. He hover-bounced in the harness a few times, laughing, before being deposited softly on the ground, close enough to Tally that she could hear nervous hiccups breaking up his giggles. He'd been as scared as Tally.

She shivered, though jumping was hardly any more dangerous than standing here beneath the looming towers. The bungee jacket used the same lifters as the hoverstruts that held the spindly structures up. If all the pretty toys somehow stopped working, just about everything in New Pretty Town would come tumbling down.

The mansion was full of brand-new pretties—the worst kind, Peris always used to say. They lived like uglies, a hundred or so together in a big dorm. But this dorm didn't have any rules. Unless the rules were Act Stupid, Have Fun, and Make Noise.

A bunch of girls in ball gowns were on the roof, screaming at the top of their lungs, balancing on the edge and shooting safety fireworks at people on the ground. A ball of orange flame bounced next to Tally, cool as an autumn wind, driving away the darkness around her.

"Hey, there's a pig down there!" someone screamed from above. They all laughed, and Tally quickened her stride toward the wide-open door of the mansion. She pushed inside, ignoring the surprised looks of two pretties on their way out.

It was all one big party, just like they always promised it would be. People were dressed up tonight, in gowns and in black suits with long coattails. Everyone seemed to find her pig mask pretty funny. They pointed and laughed, and Tally kept moving, not giving them time to do anything else. Of course, everyone was always laughing here. Unlike an ugly party, there'd never be any fights, or even arguments.

She pushed from room to room, trying to distinguish faces without being distracted by those big pretty eyes, or overwhelmed by the feeling that she didn't belong. Tally felt uglier every second she spent there. Being laughed at by everyone she met wasn't helping much. But it was better than what they'd do if they saw her real face.

Tally wondered if she would even recognize Peris. She'd only seen him once since the operation, and that was coming out of the hospital, before the swelling had subsided. But she knew his face so well. Despite what Peris always used to say, pretties didn't really all look *exactly* the same. On their expeditions, she and Peris had sometimes spotted pretties who looked familiar, like uglies they'd known. Sort of like a brother or sister—an older, more confident, *much* prettier brother or sister. One you'd be jealous of your whole life, if you'd been born a hundred years ago.

Peris couldn't have changed that much.

"Have you seen the piggy?"

"The what?"

"There's a piggy on the loose!"

The giggling voices were from the floor below. Tally

paused and listened. She was all alone here on the stairs. Apparently, pretties preferred the elevators.

"How dare she come to our party dressed like a piggy! This is white tie!"

"She's got the wrong party."

"She's got no manners, looking that way!"

Tally swallowed. The mask wasn't much better than her own face. The joke was wearing thin.

She bounded up the stairs, leaving the voices behind. Maybe they'd forget about her if she just kept moving. There were only two more floors of Garbo Mansion to go, and then the roof. Peris had to be here somewhere.

Unless he was out on the back lawn, or up in a balloon, or a party tower. Or in a pleasure garden somewhere, with someone. Tally shook away that last image and ran down the hall, ignoring the same jokes about her mask, risking glances into the rooms one by one.

Nothing but surprised looks and pointed fingers, and pretty faces. But none of them rang a bell. Peris wasn't anywhere.

"Here, piggy, piggy! Hey, there she is!"

Tally bolted up to the top floor, taking two stairs at a time. Her hard breathing had heated up the inside of the mask, her forehead sweating, the adhesive crawling as it tried to stay attached. They were following her now, a group of them, laughing and stumbling over one another up the stairs.

There wasn't any time to search this floor. Tally glanced up and down the hall. No one up here, anyway. The doors were all closed. Maybe a few pretties were actually getting their beauty sleep.

If she went up to the roof to check for Peris, she'd be trapped.

"Here, piggy, piggy!"

Time to run. Tally dashed toward the elevator, skidding to a halt inside. "Ground floor!" she ordered.

She waited, peering down the hall anxiously, panting into the hot plastic of her mask. "Ground floor!" she repeated. "Close door!"

Nothing happened.

She sighed, closing her eyes. Without an interface ring, she was nobody. The elevator wouldn't listen.

Tally knew how to trick an elevator, but it took time and a penknife. She had neither. The first of her pursuers emerged from the stairway, stumbling into the hall.

She threw herself backward against the elevator's side wall, standing on tiptoe and trying to flatten herself so they couldn't see her. More came up, huffing and puffing like typical out-of-shape pretties. Tally could watch them in the mirror at the back of the elevator.

Which meant they could also see *her* if they thought to look this way.

"Where'd the piggy go?"

"Here, piggy!"

"The roof, maybe?"

Someone stepped quietly into the elevator, looking back at the search party in bemusement. When he saw her, he jumped. "Goodness, you scared me!" He blinked his long lashes, regarding her masked face, then looked down at his own tailcoat. "Oh, dear. Wasn't this party white tie?"

Tally's breath caught, her mouth went dry. "Peris?" she whispered.

He looked at her closely. "Do I . . ."

She started to reach out, but remembered to press back

flat against the wall. Her muscles were screaming from standing on tiptoe. "It's me, Peris."

"Here, piggy, piggy!"

He turned toward the voice down the hall, raised his eyebrows, then looked back at her. "Close door. Hold," he said quickly.

The door slid shut, and Tally stumbled forward. She pulled off her mask to see him better. It was Peris: his voice, his brown eyes, the way his forehead crinkled when he was confused.

But he was so *pretty* now.

At school, they explained how it affected you. It didn't matter if you knew about evolution or not—it worked anyway. On everyone.

There was a certain kind of beauty, a prettiness that everyone could see. Big eyes and full lips like a kid's; smooth, clear skin; symmetrical features; and a thousand other little clues. Somewhere in the backs of their minds, people were always looking for these markers. No one could help seeing them, no matter how they were brought up. A million years of evolution had made it part of the human brain.

The big eyes and lips said: I'm young and vulnerable, I can't hurt you, and you want to protect me. And the rest said: I'm healthy, I won't make you sick. And no matter how you felt about a pretty, there was a part of you that thought: *If we had kids, they'd be healthy too. I* want *this pretty person. . . .*

It was biology, they said at school. Like your heart beating, you couldn't help believing all these things, not when you saw a face like this. A pretty face.

A face like Peris's.

"It's me," Tally said.

Peris took a step back, his eyebrows rising. He looked down at her clothes.

Tally realized she was wearing her baggy black expedition outfit, muddy from crawling up ropes and through gardens, from falling among the vines. Peris's suit was deep black velvet, his shirt, vest, and tie all glowing white.

She pulled away. "Oh, sorry. I won't get you muddy."

"What are you *doing* here, Tally?"

"I just—," she sputtered. Now that she was facing him, she didn't know what to say. All the imagined conversations had melted away into his big, sweet eyes. "I had to know if we were still . . ."

Tally held out her right hand, the scarred palm facing up, sweaty dirt tracing the lines on it.

Peris sighed. He wasn't looking at her hand, or into her eyes. Not into her squinty, narrow-set, indifferently brown eyes. Nobody eyes. "Yeah," he said. "But, I mean—couldn't you have waited, Squint?"

Her ugly nickname sounded strange coming from a pretty. Of course, it would be even weirder to call him Nose, as she used to about a hundred times a day. She swallowed. "Why didn't you write me?"

"I tried. But it just felt bogus. I'm so different now."

"But we're . . ." She pointed at her scar.

"Take a look, Tally." He held out his own hand.

The skin of his palm was smooth and unblemished. It was a hand that said: *I don't have to work very hard, and I'm too clever to have accidents.*

The scar that they had made together was gone.

"They took it away."

"Of course they did, Squint. All my skin's new."

Tally blinked. She hadn't thought of that.

He shook his head. "You're such a kid still."

"Elevator requested," said the elevator. "Up or down?"

Tally jumped at the machine voice.

"Hold, please," Peris said calmly.

Tally swallowed and closed her hand into a fist. "But they didn't change your blood. We shared that, no matter what."

Peris finally looked directly at her face, not flinching as she had feared he would. He smiled beautifully. "No, they didn't. New skin, big deal. And in three months we can laugh about this. Unless . . ."

"Unless what?" She looked up into his big brown eyes, so full of concern.

"Just promise me that you won't do any more stupid tricks," Peris said. "Like coming here. Something that'll get you into trouble. I want to see you pretty."

"Of course."

"So promise me."

Peris was only three months older than Tally, but, dropping her eyes to the floor, she felt like a littlie again. "All right, I promise. Nothing stupid. And they won't catch me tonight, either."

"Okay, get your mask and . . ." His voice trailed off.

She turned her gaze to where it had fallen. Discarded, the plastic mask had recycled itself, turning into pink dust, which the carpet in the elevator was already filtering away.

The two stared at each other in silence.

"Elevator requested," the machine insisted. "Up or down?"

"Peris, I promise they won't catch me. No pretty can run as fast as me. Just take me down to the—"

Peris shook his head. "Up, please. Roof."

The elevator moved.

"Up? Peris, how am I going to—"

"Straight out the door, in a big rack—bungee jackets. There's a whole bunch in case of a fire."

"You mean jump?" Tally swallowed. Her stomach did a backflip as the elevator came to a halt.

Peris shrugged. "I do it all the time, Squint." He winked. "You'll love it."

His expression made his pretty face glow even more, and Tally leaped forward to wrap her arms around him. He still felt the same, at least, maybe a bit taller and thinner. But he was warm and solid, and still Peris.

"Tally!"

She stumbled back as the doors opened. She'd left mud all over his white vest. "Oh, no! I'm—"

"Just go!"

His distress just made Tally want to hug him again. She wanted to stay and clean Peris up, make sure he looked perfect for the party. She reached out a hand. "I—"

"Go!"

"But we're best friends, right?"

He sighed, dabbing at a brown stain. "Sure, forever. In three months."

She turned and ran, the doors closing behind her.

At first no one noticed her on the roof. They were all looking down. It was dark except for the occasional flare of a safety sparkler.

Tally found the rack of bungee jackets and pulled at one. It was clipped to the rack. Her fingers fumbled, looking for a clasp. She wished she had her interface ring to give her instructions.

Then she saw the button: PRESS IN CASE OF FIRE.

"Oh, crap," she said.

Her shadow jumped and jittered. Two pretties were coming toward her, carrying sparklers.

"Who's that? What's she wearing?"

"Hey, you! This party is white tie!"

"Look at her face. . . ."

"Oh, crap," Tally repeated.

And pressed the button.

An ear-shattering siren split the air, and the bungee jacket seemed to jump from the rack into her hand. She slid into the harness, turning to face the two pretties. They leaped back as if she'd transformed into a werewolf. One dropped the sparkler, and it extinguished itself instantly.

"Fire drill," Tally said, and ran toward the edge of the roof.

Once she had the jacket around her shoulders, the strap and zippers seemed to wind around her like snakes until the plastic was snug around her waist and thighs. A green light flashed on the collar, right where she couldn't help but see it.

"Good jacket," she said.

It wasn't smart enough to answer, apparently.

The pretties playing on the roof had all gone silent and were milling around, wondering if there really was a fire. They pointed at her, and Tally heard the word "ugly" on their lips.

What was worse in New Pretty Town, she wondered? Your mansion burning down, or an ugly crashing your party?

Tally reached the edge of the roof, vaulted up onto the rail, and teetered for a moment. Below her, pretties were starting to spill out of Garbo Mansion onto the lawn and down the hill. They were looking back up, searching for smoke or flames. All they saw was her.

It was a long way down, and Tally's stomach already seemed to be in free fall. But she was thrilled, too. The shrieking siren, the crowd gazing up at her, the lights of New Pretty Town all spread out below like a million candles.

Tally took a deep breath and bent her knees, readying herself to jump.

For a split second, she wondered if the jacket would work since she wasn't wearing an interface ring. Would it hover-bounce for a nobody? Or would she just splat?

But she had promised Peris she wouldn't get caught. And the jacket was for emergencies, and there *was* a green light on. . . .

"Heads up!" Tally shouted.

And jumped.

SHAY

The siren faded behind her. It seemed like forever—or only seconds—that Tally fell, the gaping faces below becoming larger and larger.

The ground hurtled toward her, a space opening in the panicking crowd where she was going to hit. For a few moments it was just like a flying dream, silent and wonderful.

Then reality jerked at her shoulders and thighs, the webbing of the jacket cutting viciously into her. She was taller than pretty standard, she knew; the jacket probably wasn't expecting this much weight.

Tally somersaulted in the air, turning headfirst for a few terrifying moments, her face passing low enough to spot a discarded bottle cap in the grass. Then she found herself shooting upward again, completing the circle, so that the sky wheeled above her, then over and downward again, more crowd parting in front.

Perfect. She had pushed off hard enough that she was bouncing down the hill away from Garbo Mansion, the jacket carrying her toward the darkness and safety of the gardens.

Tally spun head over heels twice more, and then the jacket lowered her to the grass. She pulled randomly at straps until the garment made a hissing sound and dropped to the ground.

Her dizziness took a moment to clear as she tried to sort up from down.

"Isn't she . . . ugly?" someone asked from the edge of the crowd.

The black shapes of two firefighting hovercars zoomed past overhead, red lights flashing and sirens piercing her ears.

"Great idea, Peris," she muttered. "A false alarm." She would really be in trouble if they caught her now. She'd never even *heard* of anyone doing anything this bad.

Tally ran toward the garden.

The darkness below the willows was comforting.

Down here, halfway to the river, Tally could barely tell there was a full-scale fire alert in the middle of town. But she could see that a search was underway. More hovercars were in the air than usual, and the river seemed to be lit up extra bright. Maybe that was just a coincidence.

But probably not.

Tally made her way carefully through the trees. It was later than she and Peris had ever stayed over in New Pretty

Town. The pleasure gardens were more crowded, especially the dark parts. And now that the excitement of her escape had worn off, Tally was beginning to realize how stupid the whole idea had been.

Of course Peris didn't have the scar anymore. The two of them had only used a penknife when they'd cut themselves and held hands. The doctors used much sharper and bigger knives in the operation. They rubbed you raw, and you grew all new skin, perfect and clear. The old marks of accidents and bad food and childhood illnesses all washed away. A clean start.

But Tally had ruined Peris's starting over—showing up like some pesky littlie who's not wanted, and leaving him with the bad taste of ugly in his mouth, not to mention covered with mud. She hoped he had another vest to change into.

At least Peris hadn't seemed too angry. He'd said they'd be best friends again, once she was pretty. But the way he'd looked at her face . . . maybe that was why they separated uglies from pretties. It must be horrible to see an ugly face when you're surrounded by such beautiful people all the time. What if she'd ruined everything tonight, and Peris would always see her like this—squinty eyes and frizzy hair—even after she had the operation?

A hovercar passed overhead, and Tally ducked. She was probably going to get caught tonight, and never be turned pretty at all.

She deserved it for being so stupid.

Tally reminded herself of her promise to Peris. She was *not* going to get caught; she had to become pretty for him.

A light flashed in the corner of her vision. Tally crouched and peered through the hanging willow leaves.

A safety warden was in the park. She was a middle pretty, not a new one. In the firelight, the handsome features of the second operation were obvious: broad shoulders and a firm jaw, a sharp nose and high cheekbones. The woman carried the same unquestionable authority as Tally's teachers back in Uglyville.

Tally swallowed. New pretties had their own wardens. There was only one reason why a middle pretty would be here in New Pretty Town: The wardens were looking for someone, and they were serious about finding him or her.

The woman flashed her light at a couple on a bench, illuminating them for the split second it took to confirm that they were pretty. The couple jumped, but the warden chuckled and apologized. Tally could hear her low, sure voice, and saw the new pretties relax. Everything had to be okay if she said it was.

Tally felt herself wanting to give up, to throw herself on the wise mercy of the warden. If she just explained, the warden would understand and fix everything. Middle pretties always knew what to do.

But she had promised Peris.

Tally pulled back into the darkness, trying to ignore the horrible feeling that she was a spy, a sneak, for not surrendering to the woman's authority. She moved through the brush as fast as she could.

Close to the river, Tally heard a noise in front of her. A dark form was outlined in river lights before her. Not a couple, a lone figure in the dark.

It had to be a warden, waiting for her in the brush.

Tally hardly dared breathe. She had frozen in midcrawl, her weight all poised on one knee and one muddy hand. The warden hadn't seen her yet. If Tally waited long enough, maybe the warden would move on.

She waited, motionless, for endless minutes. The figure

didn't budge. They must know that the gardens were the only dark way in and out of New Pretty Town.

Tally's arm started to shake, the muscles complaining about staying frozen for so long. But she didn't dare let her weight settle onto the other arm. The snap of a single twig would give her away.

She held herself still, until all her muscles were screaming. Maybe the warden was just a trick of the light. Maybe this was all in her imagination.

Tally blinked, trying to make the figure disappear.

But it was still there, clearly outlined by the rippling lights of the river.

A twig popped under her knee—Tally's aching muscles had finally betrayed her. But the figure *still* didn't move. He or she must have heard. . . .

The warden was being kind, waiting for her to give herself up. Letting her surrender. The teachers did that at school, sometimes. Made you realize that you couldn't escape, until you confessed everything.

Tally cleared her throat. A small, pathetic sound. "I'm sorry," she said.

The figure let out a sigh. "Oh, phew. Hey, that's okay. I must have scared you, too." The girl leaned forward, grimacing as if she was also sore from remaining still so long. Her face caught the light.

She was ugly too.

Her name was Shay. She had long dark hair in pigtails, and her eyes were too wide apart. Her lips were full enough, but she was even skinnier than a new pretty. She'd come over to New Pretty Town on her own expedition, and had been hiding here by the river for an hour. "I've never seen anything like this," she whispered. "There's wardens and hovercars everywhere!"

Tally cleared her throat. "I think it's my fault."

Shay looked dubious. "How'd you manage that?"

"Well, I was up in the middle of town, at a party."

"You crashed a party? That's crazy!" Shay said, then lowered her voice back to a whisper. "Crazy, but awesome. How'd you get in?"

"I was wearing a mask."

"Wow. A pretty mask?"

"Uh, more like a pig mask. It's a long story."

Shay blinked. "A pig mask. Okay. So let me guess, someone blew your house down?"

"Huh? No. I was about to get caught, so I kind of . . . set off a fire alarm."

"Nice trick!"

Tally smiled. It was actually a pretty good story, now that she had someone to tell it to. "And I was trapped up on the roof, so I grabbed a bungee jacket and jumped off. I hover-bounced halfway here."

"No way!"

"Well, part of the way here, anyhow."

"Pretty awesome." Shay smiled, then her face went serious. She bit at one of her fingernails, which was one of those bad habits that the operation cured. "So, Tally, were you at this party . . . to see someone?"

It was Tally's turn to be impressed. "How'd you figure that out?"

Shay sighed, looking down at her ragged nails. "I've got friends too, over here. I mean, they *were* friends. Sometimes I spy on them." She looked up. "I was always the youngest, you know? And now—"

"You're all alone."

Shay nodded. "It's sounds like you did more than spy, though."

"Yeah. I kind of said hello."

"Wow, that's crazy. Your boyfriend or something?"

Tally shook her head. Peris had gone with other girls, and Tally had dealt with it and tried to do the same, but their friendship had always been the main thing in both their lives. Not anymore, apparently.

"If he'd been my boyfriend, I don't think I could have done it, you know? I wouldn't have wanted him to see my face. But because we're friends, I thought maybe . . ."

"Yeah. So how'd it go?"

Tally thought for a second, looking out at the rippling water. Peris had been so pretty, and grown-up looking, and he'd said they'd be friends again. Once Tally was pretty too . . . "Basically, it sucked," she said.

"Thought so."

"Except getting away. That part was very cool."

"Sounds like it." Tally heard the smile in Shay's voice. "Very tricky."

They were silent for a moment as a hovercar went over.

"But you know, we haven't totally gotten away yet," Shay said. "Next time you're going to pull a fire alarm, let me know ahead of time."

"Sorry about getting you trapped here."

Shay looked at her and frowned. "Not that. I just meant if I'm going to have to do the running-away part, I might as well get in on the fun."

Tally laughed softly. "Okay. Next time, I'll let you know."

"Please do." Shay scanned the river. "Looks a little clearer now. Where's your board?"

"My what?"

Shay pulled a hoverboard from under a bush. "You've got a board, right? What'd you do, swim over?"

"No, I . . . hey, wait. How'd you get a hoverboard to take you across the river?" Anything that flew had minders all over it.

Shay laughed. "That's the oldest trick in the book. I figured you'd know all about it."

Tally shrugged. "I don't board much."

"Well, this one'll take both of us."

"Wait, shhh."

Another hovercar had come into view, cruising down the river just above the height of the bridges.

Tally waited for a count of ten after it had passed before she spoke. "I don't think it's a good idea, flying back."

"So how *did* you get over?"

"Follow me." Tally rose from her crouch onto hands and knees, and crawled a bit ahead. She looked back. "Can you carry that thing?"

"Sure. It doesn't weigh much." Shay snapped her fingers, and the hoverboard drifted upward. "Actually, it doesn't weigh *anything,* unless I tell it to."

"That's handy."

Shay started to crawl, the board bouncing along behind her like a littlie's balloon. Tally couldn't see any string, though. "So, where're we going?" Shay asked.

"I know a bridge."

"But it'll tattle."

"Not this one. It's an old friend."

WIPE OUT

Tally fell off. Again.

The spill didn't hurt so much, this time. The moment her feet slipped off the hoverboard, she'd relaxed, the way Shay kept telling her to. Spinning out wasn't much worse than having your dad swing you around by the wrists when you were little.

If your dad happened to be a superhuman freak and was trying to pull your arms out of their sockets.

But the momentum had to go somewhere, Shay had explained. And around in circles was better than into a tree. Here in Cleopatra Park there were plenty of those.

After a few rotations, Tally found herself being lowered to the grass by her wrists, dizzy but in one piece.

Shay cruised up, banking her hoverboard to an elegant stop as if she'd been born on one.

"That looked a little better."

"It didn't *feel* any better." Tally pulled off one crash bracelet and rubbed her wrist. It was turning red, and her fingers felt weak.

The bracelet was heavy and solid in her hand. Crash bracelets had to have metal inside, because they worked on magnets, the way the boards did. Whenever Tally's feet slipped, the bracelets got all hovery and caught her fall, like some friendly giant plucking her from danger and swinging her to a halt.

By her wrists. Again.

Tally pulled the other bracelet off and rubbed.

"Don't give up. You almost made it!"

Tally's board cruised back on its own, nuzzling at her

ankles like an apologetic dog. She crossed her arms and rubbed her shoulders. "I almost got snapped in two, you mean."

"Never happens. I've spilled more times than a glass of milk on a roller coaster."

"On a *what*?"

"Never mind. Come on, one more try."

Tally sighed. It wasn't just her wrists. Her knees ached from banking hard, whipping through turns so quickly that her body seemed to weigh a ton. Shay called that "high gravity," which happened every time a fast-moving object changed direction.

"Hoverboarding *looks* so fun, like being a bird. But actually doing it is hard work."

Shay shrugged. "Being a bird's probably hard work too. Flapping your wings all day, you know?"

"Maybe. Does it get any better?"

"For birds? I don't know. On a board? Definitely."

"I hope so." Tally pulled her bracelets on and stepped onto the hoverboard. It bobbed a little as it adjusted to her weight, like the bounce of a diving board.

"Check your belly sensor."

Tally touched her belly ring, where Shay had clipped the little sensor. It told the board where Tally's center of gravity was, and which way she was facing. The sensor even read her stomach muscles, which, it turned out, hoverboarders always clenched in anticipation of turns. The board was smart enough to gradually learn how her body moved. The more Tally rode, the more it would keep itself under her feet.

Of course, Tally had to learn too. Shay kept saying that if your feet weren't in the right place, the smartest board in the world couldn't keep you on. The riding surface was all knobbly for traction, but it was amazing how easy it was to slip off.

The board was oval-shaped, about half as long as Tally was tall, and black with the silver spots of a cheetah—the only animal in the world that could run faster than a hoverboard could fly. It was Shay's first board, and she'd never recycyled it. Until today, it had hung on the wall above her bed.

Tally snapped her fingers, bent her knees as she rose into the air, then leaned forward to pick up speed.

Shay cruised along just above her, staying a little behind.

The trees started to rush by, whipping Tally's arms with the sharp stings of evergreen needles. The board wouldn't let her crash into anything solid, but it didn't get too concerned about twigs.

"Extend your arms. Keep your feet apart!" Shay yelled for the thousandth time. Tally nervously scooted her left foot forward.

At the end of the park, Tally leaned to her right, and the board pulled into a long, steep turn. She bent her knees, growing heavy as she cut back toward where they'd started.

Now Tally was rushing toward the slalom flags, crouching as she drew closer. She could feel the wind drying her lips, lifting her ponytail up.

"Oh, boy," she whispered.

The board raced past the first flag, and she leaned hard right, her arms all the way out now for balance.

"Switch!" cried Shay. Tally twisted her body to bring the board under her and across, cutting around the next flag. Once it was past, she twisted again.

But her feet were too close together. Not again! Her shoes slipped across the surface of the board. "No!" she cried, clenching her toes, cupping the air with her palms, anything to keep herself on board. Her right shoe slid toward the board's edge until her toes were silhouetted against the trees.

The trees! She was almost sideways, her body parallel with the ground.

The slalom flag zoomed past, and suddenly, it was over. The board swung back under Tally as her course straightened out again.

She'd made the turn!

Tally spun to face Shay. "I did it!" she cried.

And fell.

Confused by her spin, the board had tried to execute a turn, and dumped her. Tally relaxed as her arms jerked straight and the world spun around her. She was laughing as she descended to the grass, dangling by her bracelets.

Shay was also laughing. "*Almost* did it."

"No! I got around the flags. You saw!"

"Okay, okay. You made it." Shay laughed, stepping off onto the grass. "But don't dance around like that afterward. It's not cool, Squint."

Tally stuck out her tongue. In the last week, Tally had learned that Shay only used her ugly nickname as a put-down. Shay insisted they call each other by their real names most of the time, which Tally had quickly gotten used to. She liked it, actually. Nobody but Sol and Ellie—her parents—and a few stuck-up teachers had ever called her "Tally" before.

"Whatever you say, Skinny. That was great."

Tally collapsed on the grass. Her whole body ached,

every muscle exhausted. "Thanks for the lesson. Flying's the best."

Shay sat down close by. "Never bored on a hoverboard."

"This is the best I've felt since . . ." Tally didn't say his name. She looked up into the sky, which was a glorious blue. A perfect sky. They hadn't gotten started until late afternoon. Above, a few high clouds were already showing hints of pink, even though sunset was hours off.

"Yeah," Shay agreed. "Me too. I was getting sick of hanging out alone."

"So how long you got?"

Shay answered instantly. "Two months and twenty-six days."

Tally was stunned for a moment. "Are you sure?"

"'Course I'm sure."

Tally felt a big, slow smile roll across her face, and she fell back onto the grass, laughing. "You've got to be kidding. We've got the same birthday!"

"No way."

"Yeah, way. It's perfect. We'll both turn pretty together!"

Shay was silent for a moment. "Yeah, I guess."

"September ninth, right?"

Shay nodded.

"That is so cool. I mean, I don't think I could stand to lose another friend. You know? We don't have to worry about one of us abandoning the other. Not for a single day."

Shay sat up straight, her smile gone. "I wouldn't do that, anyway."

Tally blinked. "I didn't say you would, but . . ."

"But what?"

"But when you turn, you go over to New Pretty Town."

"So? Pretties are allowed to come back over here, you know. Or write."

Tally snorted. "But they don't."

"I would." Shay looked out over the river at the spires of the party towers, placing a thumbnail firmly between her teeth.

"So would I, Shay. I'd come see you."

"Are you sure?"

"Yeah. Really."

Shay shrugged, and lay back down to stare up at the clouds. "Okay. But you're not the first person to make that promise, you know."

"Yeah, I do know."

They were silent for a moment. Clouds rolled slowly across the sun, and the air grew cool. Tally thought of Peris, and tried to remember the way he used to look back when he was Nose. Somehow, she couldn't recall his ugly face anymore. As if those few minutes of seeing him pretty had wiped out a lifetime of memories. All she could see now was pretty Peris, those eyes, that smile.

"I wonder why they never come back," Shay said. "Just to visit."

Tally swallowed. "Because we're so ugly, Skinny, that's why."

FACING THE FUTURE

"Here's option two." Tally touched her interface ring, and the wallscreen changed.

This Tally was sleek, with ultrahigh cheekbones, deep green catlike eyes, and a wide mouth that curled into a knowing smile.

"That's, uh, pretty different."

"Yeah. I doubt it's even legal." Tally tweaked the eye-shape parameters, pulling the arch of the eyebrows down almost to normal. Some cities allowed exotic operations—for new pretties only—but the authorities here were notoriously conservative. She doubted a doctor would give this morpho a second glance, but it was fun to push the software to its limits. "You think I look too scary?"

"No. You look like a real pussycat." Shay giggled. "Unfortunately, I mean that in the literal, dead-mouse-eating sense."

"Okay, moving right along."

The next Tally was a much more standard morphological model, with almond-shaped brown eyes, straight black hair with long bangs, the dark lips set to maximum fullness.

"Pretty generic, Tally."

"Oh, come on! I worked on this one for a long time. I think I'd look great this way. There's a whole Cleopatra thing going on."

"You know," Shay said, "I read that the real Cleopatra wasn't even that great-looking. She seduced everyone with how clever she was."

"Yeah, right. And you've seen a picture of her?"

"They didn't have cameras back then, Squint."

"Duh. So how do you know she was ugly?"

"Because that's what historians wrote at the time."

Tally shrugged. "She was probably a classic pretty and they didn't even know it. Back then, they had weird ideas about beauty. They didn't know about biology."

"Lucky them." Shay stared out the window.

"So, if you think all my faces are so crappy, why don't you show me some of yours?" Tally cleared the wallscreen and leaned back on the bed.

"I can't."

"You can dish it out, but you can't take it, huh?"

"No, I mean I just can't. I never made one."

Tally's jaw dropped. Everyone made morphos, even littlies, too young for their facial structure to have set. It was a great waste of a day, figuring out all the different ways you could look when you finally became pretty.

"Not even one?"

"Maybe when I was little. But my friends and I stopped doing that kind of stuff a long time ago."

"Well." Tally sat up. "We should fix that right now."

"I'd rather go hoverboarding." Shay tugged anxiously under her shirt. Tally figured that Shay slept with her belly sensor on, hoverboarding in her dreams.

"Later, Shay. I can't believe you don't have a single morph. *Please*."

"It's stupid. The doctors pretty much do what they want, no matter what you tell them."

"I know, but it's *fun*."

Shay made a big point of rolling her eyes, but finally nodded. She dragged herself off the bed and plopped down in front of the wallscreen, pulling her hair back from her face.

Tally snorted. "So you *have* done this before."

"Like I said, when I was a littlie."

"Sure." Tally turned her interface ring to bring up a menu on the wallscreen, and blinked her way through a set of eyemouse choices. The screen's camera flickered with laser light, and a green grid sprang up on Shay's face, a field of tiny squares imposed across the shape of her cheekbones, nose, lips, and forehead.

Seconds later, two faces appeared on the screen. Both of them were Shay, but there were obvious differences: One looked wild, slightly angry; the other had a slightly distant expression, like someone having a daydream.

"It's weird how that works, isn't it?" Tally said. "Like two different people."

Shay nodded. "Creepy."

Ugly faces were always asymmetrical; neither half looked exactly like the other. So the first thing the morpho software did was take each side of your face and double it, like holding a mirror right down the middle, creating two examples of perfect symmetry. Already, both of the symmetrical Shays looked better than the original.

"So, Shay, which do you think is your good side?"

"Why do I have to be symmetrical? I'd rather have a face with two different sides."

Tally groaned. "That's a sign of childhood stress. No one wants to look at that."

"Gee, I wouldn't want to look stressed," Shay snorted, and pointed at the wilder-looking face. "Okay, whatever. The right one's better, don't you think?"

"I *hate* my right side. I always start with the left."

"Yeah, well, I happen to like my right side. Looks tougher."

"Okay. You're the boss."

Tally blinked, and the right-side face filled the screen.

"First, the basics." The software took over: The eyes gradually grew, reducing the size of the nose between them, Shay's cheekbones moved upward, and her lips became a tiny bit fuller (they were already almost pretty-sized). Every blemish disappeared, her skin turning flawlessly smooth. The skull moved subtly under the features, the angle of her forehead tilting back, her chin becoming more defined, her jaw stronger.

When it was done, Tally whistled. "Wow, that's pretty good already."

"Great," Shay groaned. "I totally look like every other new pretty in the world."

"Well, sure, we just got started. How about some hair on you?" Tally blinked through menus quickly, picking a style at random.

When the wallscreen changed, Shay fell over on the floor in a fit of giggles. The high hairdo towered over her thin face like dunce cap, the white-blond hair utterly incongruous with her olive skin.

Tally could hardly manage to speak through her own laughter. "Okay, maybe not that." She flipped through more styles, settling on basic hair, dark and short. "Let's get the face right first."

She tweaked the eyebrows, making their arch more dramatic, and added roundness to the cheeks. Shay was still too skinny, even after the morpho software had pulled her toward the average.

"And maybe a bit lighter?" Tally took the shade of the skin closer to baseline.

"Hey, Squint," Shay said. "Whose face is this, anyway?"

"Just playing," Tally said. "You want to take a shot?"

"No, I want to go hoverboarding."

"Sure, great. But first let's get this right."

"What do you mean 'get it right,' Tally? Maybe I think my face is already right!"

"Yeah, it's great." Tally rolled her eyes. "For an ugly."

Shay scowled. "What, can't you stand me? Do you need to get some picture into your head so you can imagine it instead of my face?"

"Shay! Come on. It's just for fun."

"Making ourselves feel ugly is not fun."

"We *are* ugly!"

"This whole game is just designed to make us hate ourselves."

Tally groaned and flopped back onto her bed, glaring up at the ceiling. Shay could be so weird sometimes. She always had a chip on her shoulder about the operation, like someone was *making* her turn sixteen. "Right, and things were so great back when everyone was ugly. Or did you miss that day in school?"

"Yeah, yeah, I know," Shay recited. "Everyone judged everyone else based on their appearance. People who were taller got better jobs, and people even voted for some politicians just because they weren't quite as ugly as everybody else. Blah, blah, blah."

"Yeah, and people killed one another over stuff like having different skin color." Tally shook her head. No matter how many times they repeated it at school, she'd never really quite believed that one. "So what if people look more alike now? It's the only way to make people equal."

"How about making them smarter?"

Tally laughed. "Fat chance. Anyway, it's just to see what you and I will look like in only . . . two months and fifteen days."

"Can't we just wait until then?"

Tally closed her eyes, sighing. "Sometimes I don't think I can."

"Well, tough luck." She felt Shay's weight on the bed

and a light punch on her arm. "Hey, might as well make the best of it. Can we go hoverboarding now? Please?"

Tally opened her eyes and saw that her friend was smiling. "Okay: hoverboard." She sat up and glanced at the screen. Even without much work, Shay's face was already welcoming, vulnerable, healthy . . . pretty. "Don't you think you're beautiful?"

Shay didn't look, just shrugged. "That's not me. It's some committee's idea of me."

Tally smiled and hugged her.

"It will be you, though. *Really* you. Soon."

PRETTY BORING

"I think you're ready."

Tally cruised to a stop—right foot down, left foot up, bend the knees.

"Ready for what?"

Shay drifted slowly past, letting the breeze tug her along. They were as high up and far out as hoverboards would go, just above treetop level, at the edge of town. It was amazing how quickly Tally had gotten used to being up high, with nothing but a board and bracelets between her and a long fall.

The view from up here was fantastic. Behind them the spires of New Pretty Town rose from the center of town, and around them was the greenbelt, a swath of forest that separated the middle and the late pretties from the youngsters. Older generations of pretties lived out in the suburbs, hidden by the hills, in rows of big houses separated by strips of private garden for their littlies to play in.

Shay smiled. "Ready for a night ride."

"Oh. Look, I don't know if I want to cross the river again," Tally said, remembering her promise to Peris. She and Shay had shown each other a lot of tricks over the last three weeks, but they hadn't been back into New Pretty Town since the night they'd met. "Until we get turned, of course. After last time, the wardens are probably all—"

"I wasn't talking about New Pretty Town," Shay interrupted. "That place is boring, anyway. We'd have to sneak around all night."

"Okay. You mean just board around Uglyville."

Shay shook her head, still coasting gradually away on the breeze.

Tally shifted her weight on the board uncomfortably. "Where else is there?"

Shay put her hands in her pockets and spread her arms, turning her dorm's team jacket into a sail. The breeze pulled her farther away from Tally. By reflex, Tally tipped her toes forward so that her board would keep up.

"Well, there's out there." Shay nodded at the open land before them.

"The suburbs? That's dullsville."

"Not the burbs. Past them." Shay slid her feet in opposite directions, to the very edges of the board. Her skirt caught the cool evening wind, which tugged her away even faster. She was drifting toward the outer edge of the greenbelt. Off-limits.

Tally planted her feet and dipped the board, and pulled up next to her friend. "What do you mean? Outside the city completely?"

"Yeah."

"That's crazy. There's nothing out there."

"There's plenty out there. Real trees, hundreds of years old. Mountains. And the ruins. Ever been there?"

Tally blinked. "Of course."

"I don't mean on a school trip, Tally. You ever been there at night?"

Tally brought her board to a sharp halt. The Rusty Ruins were the remains of an old city, a hulking reminder of back when there'd been way too many people, and everyone was incredibly stupid. And ugly. "No way. Don't tell me you have."

Shay nodded.

Tally's mouth dropped open. "That's impossible."

"You think you're the only one who knows good tricks?"

"Well, maybe I believe you," Tally said. Shay had that look on her face, the one Tally had learned to watch out for. "But what if we get busted?"

Shay laughed. "Tally, there's nothing out there, like you just said. Nothing and no one to bust us."

"Do hoverboards even work out there? Does anything?"

"Special ones do, if you know how to trick them, and where to ride. And getting past the burbs is easy. You take the river the whole way. Farther upstream it's white water, too rough for skimmers."

Tally's mouth dropped open again. "You really have done this before."

A gust of wind billowed in Shay's jacket, and she slid farther away, still smiling. Tally had to lean her board into motion again to stay within earshot. A treetop brushed her ankles as the ground below them started to rise.

"It'll be really fun," Shay called.

"Sounds too risky."

"Come on. I've been wanting to show you this since we met. Since you told me you crashed a pretty party—and pulled a fire alarm!"

Tally swallowed, wishing she'd told the whole truth about that night—about how it had all just sort of *happened*. Shay seemed to think she was the world's biggest daredevil now. "Well, I mean, that alarm thing was partly an accident. Kind of."

"Yeah, sure."

"I mean, maybe we should wait. It's only a couple of months now."

"Oh, that's right," Shay said. "A couple of months and we'll be stuck inside the river. Pretty and boring."

Tally snorted. "I don't think it's exactly boring, Shay."

"Doing what you're supposed to do is *always* boring. I can't imagine anything worse than being required to have fun."

"I can," Tally said quietly. "Never having any."

"Listen, Tally, these two months are our last chance to do anything really cool. To be ourselves. Once we turn, it's new pretty, middle pretty, late pretty." Shay dropped her arms, and her board stopped drifting. "Then dead pretty."

"Better than dead ugly," Tally said.

Shay shrugged and opened her jacket into a sail again. They weren't far from the edge of the greenbelt now. Soon Shay would get a warning. Then her board would tattle.

"Besides," Tally argued, "just because we get the operation doesn't mean we can't do stuff like this."

"But pretties never do, Tally. Never."

Tally sighed, tipping her feet again to follow. "Maybe that's because they have better stuff to do than kid tricks. Maybe partying in town is better than hanging out in a bunch of old ruins."

Shay's eyes flashed. "Or maybe when they do the operation—when they grind and stretch your bones to the right shape, peel off your face and rub all your skin away, and stick in plastic cheekbones so you look like everybody else—maybe after going through all that you just aren't very interesting anymore."

Tally flinched. She'd never heard the operation described that way. Even in bio class, where they went into the details, it didn't sound that bad. "Come on, we won't even know it's happening. You just have pretty dreams the whole time."

"Yeah, sure."

A voice came into Tally's head: *"Warning, restricted area."* The wind was turning cold as the sun dropped.

"Come on, Shay, let's go back down. It's almost dinner."

Shay smiled and shook her head, and pulled off her interface ring. Now she wouldn't hear the warnings. "Let's go tonight. You can ride almost as well as me now."

"Shay."

"Do this with me. I'll show you a roller coaster."

"What's a—"

"Second warning. Restricted area."

Tally stopped her board. "If you keep going, Shay, you'll get busted and we won't be doing anything tonight."

Shay shrugged as the wind tugged her farther away.

"I just want to show you something that's my idea of fun, Tally. Before we go all pretty and only get to have everybody else's idea of fun."

Tally shook her head, wanting to say that Shay had already taught her how to hoverboard, the coolest thing she'd ever learned. In less than a month she'd come to feel like they were best friends. Almost like when she'd met Peris as a littlie, and they'd known instantly they'd be together forever. "Shay . . ."

"Please?"

Tally sighed. "Okay."

Shay dropped her arms and dipped her toes to bring the board to a halt. "Really? Tonight?"

"Sure. Rusty Ruins it is."

Tally told herself to relax. It wasn't that big a deal, really. She broke rules all the time, and everyone went to the ruins once a year on school trips. It couldn't be dangerous or anything.

Shay zoomed back from the edge of the belt, swooping up beside Tally to put her arm around her. "Wait until you see the river."

"You said it's got white water?"

"Yeah."

"Which is what?"

Shay smiled. "It's water. But much, much better."

RAPIDS

"Good night."

"Sleep tight," replied the room.

Tally pulled on a jacket, clipped her sensor to her belly ring, and opened the window. The air was still, the river so flat that she could make out every detail of the city skyline mirrored in it. It looked like the pretties were having some sort of event. She could hear the roar of a huge crowd across the water, a thousand cheers rising and falling together. The party towers were dark under the almost full moon, and the fireworks all shimmering hues of blue, climbing so high that they exploded in silence.

The city had never looked so far away.

"I'll see you soon, Peris," she said quietly.

The roof tiles were slick with a late evening rain. Tally climbed carefully to the corner of the dorm where it was brushed by an old sycamore tree. The handholds in its branches felt solid and familiar, and she descended quickly into the darkness behind a recycler.

When she'd cleared the dormitory grounds, Tally looked back. The pattern of shadows that led away from the dorm seemed so convenient, almost intentional. As if uglies were supposed to sneak out every once in a while.

Tally shook her head. She was starting to think like Shay.

They met at the dam, where the river split in two to encircle New Pretty Town. Tonight, there weren't any river skimmers out to disturb the darkness, and Shay was practicing moves on her board when Tally walked up.

"Should you be doing that here in town?" Tally called over the roar of water rushing through the dam's gates.

Shay danced, shifting her weight back and forth on the floating board, dodging imaginary obstacles. "I was just making sure it worked. In case you were worried."

Tally looked at her own board. Shay had tricked the safety governor so it wouldn't tattle when they flew at night, or crossed the boundary out of town. Tally wasn't so much worried about it squealing on them as whether it would fly at all. Or let her fly into a tree. But Shay's board seemed to be hovering just fine.

"I boarded all the way here, and nobody's come to get me," Shay said.

Tally dropped her board to the ground. "Thanks for making sure. I didn't mean to be so wimpy about this."

"You weren't."

"Yeah, I was. I should tell you something. That night, when you met me, I kind of promised my friend Peris I wouldn't take any big risks. You know, in case I really got in trouble, and they got really mad."

"Who cares if they get mad? You're almost sixteen."

"But what if they get mad enough that they won't make me pretty?"

Shay stopped bouncing. "I've never heard of that happening."

"I guess I haven't either. But maybe they wouldn't tell us if it had. Anyway, Peris made me promise to take it easy."

"Tally, do you think maybe he just said that so you wouldn't come around again?"

"Huh?"

"Maybe he made you promise to take it easy so you wouldn't bother him anymore. To make you afraid to go to New Pretty Town again."

Tally tried to answer, but her throat was dry.

"Listen, if you don't want to come, that's fine," Shay said. "I mean it, Squint. But we're not going to get caught. And if we do, I'll take the blame." She laughed. "I'll tell them I kidnapped you."

Tally stepped onto her board and snapped her fingers. When she reached Shay's eye level she said, "I'm coming. I said I would."

Shay smiled and took Tally's hand for a second,

squeezing. "Great. It's going to be fun. Not new pretty fun—the real kind. Put these on."

"What are they? Night vision?"

"Nope. Goggles. You're going to love the white water."

They hit the rapids ten minutes later.

Tally had lived her whole life within sight of the river. Slow-moving and dignified, it defined the city, marking the boundary between worlds. But she'd never realized that a few kilometers upstream from the dam, the stately band of silver became a snarling monster.

The churning water really was white. It crashed over rocks and through narrow channels, catapulted up into moonlit sprays, split apart, rejoined, and dropped down into boiling cauldrons at the bottom of steep falls.

Shay was skimming just above the torrent, so low that she lifted a wake every time she banked. Tally followed at what she guessed was a safe distance, hoping her tricked-up board was still reluctant to crash into the darkness-cloaked rocks and tree branches. The forest to either side was a black void full of wild and ancient trees, nothing like the generic carbon-dioxide suckers that decorated the city. The moonlit clouds above glowed through their branches like a ceiling of pearl.

Every time Shay screamed, Tally knew she was about to follow her friend through a wall of spray leaping up from the maelstrom. Some shone like white lace curtains in the moonlight, but others struck unexpectedly from the darkness. Tally also found herself crashing through the arcs of cold water rising from Shay's board when it dipped or banked, but at least she knew when a turn was coming.

The first few minutes were sheer terror, her teeth

clenched so hard that her jaw ached, her toes curled up inside her special new grippy shoes, her arms and even fingers spread wide for balance. But gradually Tally grew accustomed to the darkness, the roar of water below, the unexpected slap of cold spray against her face. It was wilder, and faster, and farther than she'd ever flown before. The river wound into the dark forest, cutting its serpentine route into the unknown.

Finally, Shay waved her hands and pulled up, the back of her board dipping low into the water. Tally climbed to avoid the wake, spinning her board in a tight circle to bring it to a smooth halt.

"Are we there?"

"Not quite. But look." Shay pointed back the way they'd come.

Tally gasped as she took in the view. The distant city was a bright coin nestled in darkness, the fireworks of New Pretty Town the barest cold-blue shimmer. They must have climbed a long way up; Tally could see patches of moonlight rolling slowly across the low hills around the city, pushed along by the light wind that barely tugged at the clouds.

She'd never been beyond the city limits at night, had never seen it lit up like this from afar.

Tally pulled off her spattered goggles and took a deep breath. The air was full of sharp smells, evergreen sap and wildflowers, the electric smell of churning water.

"Nice, huh?"

"Yeah," Tally panted. "Much better than sneaking around New Pretty Town."

Shay grinned happily. "I'm really glad you think so. I've been wanting to come out here so bad, but not alone. You know?"

Tally looked at the surrounding forest, trying to peer into the black spaces between the trees. This was really the wild, where anything could be hidden, not a place for human beings. She shivered at the thought of being there alone. "Where to now?"

"Now we walk."

"Walk?"

Shay eased her board to the shore and stepped off. "Yeah, there's a vein of iron about half a kilometer that way. But nothing between here and there."

"What are you talking about?"

"Tally, hoverboards work on magnetic levitation, right? So there's got to be some kind of metal around or they don't hover."

"I guess so. But in town—"

"In town, there's a steel grid built into the ground, no matter where you go. Out here, you have to be careful."

"What happens if your board can't hover anymore?"

"It falls down. And your crash bracelets don't work either."

"Oh." Tally stepped from her board and held it under one arm. All her muscles were sore from the wild ride here. It was good to be on solid ground. The rocks felt reassuringly the-opposite-of-hovery under her shakey legs.

After a few minutes' walking, though, the board started to grow heavy. By the time the noise of the river had faded to a dull roar behind them, it felt like a plank of oak under her arm.

"I didn't know these things weighed so much."

"Yeah, this is what a board weighs when it's not hovering. Out here, you find out that the city fools you about how things really work."

The sky was getting cloudier, and in the darkness the cold seemed more intense. Tally hoisted the board up to get a better grip, wondering if it was going to rain. She was already wet enough from the rapids. "I kind of like being fooled about some things."

After a long scramble through the rocks, Shay broke the silence. "This way. There's a natural vein of iron underground. You can feel it in your crash bracelets."

Tally held out one hand and frowned, unconvinced. But after another minute she felt a faint tugging in her bracelet, like a ghost pulling her forward. Her board started to lighten, and soon she and Shay had hopped on again, coasting over a ridge and down into a dark valley.

Onboard, Tally found the breath to ask a question that had been bugging her. "So if hoverboards need metal, how do they work on the river?"

"Panning for gold."

"What?"

"Rivers come from springs, which come from inside mountains. The water brings up minerals from inside the earth. So there's always metals at the bottom of rivers."

"Right. Like when people used to pan for gold?"

"Yeah, exactly. But, actually, boards prefer iron. All that glitters is not hovery."

Tally frowned. Shay sometimes talked in a mysterious way, like she was quoting the lyrics of some band no one else listened to.

She almost asked, but Shay came to a sudden halt and pointed downward.

The clouds were breaking, and moonlight shot through them to fall across the floor of the valley. Hulking towers rose up, casting jagged shadows, their human-made shapes obvious against the plain of treetops rippling in the wind.

The Rusty Ruins.

THE RUSTY RUINS

A few blank windows stared down on them in silence from the husks of the giant buildings. Any glass had long since shattered, any wood had rotted, and nothing remained but metal frames, mortar, and stone crumbling in the grip of invading vegetation. Looking down at the black, empty doorways, Tally's skin crawled with the thought of descending to peer into one.

The two friends slid between the ruined buildings, riding high and silent as if not to disturb the ghosts of the dead city. Below them the streets were full of burned-out cars squeezed together between the looming walls. Whatever had destroyed this city, the people had tried to escape it. Tally remembered from her last school trip to the ruins that their cars couldn't hover. They just rolled along on rubber wheels. The Rusties had been stuck down in these streets like a horde of rats trapped in a burning maze.

"Uh, Shay, you're pretty sure our boards aren't suddenly going to conk out, right?" she called softly.

"Don't worry. Whoever built this city loved to waste metal. They aren't called the Rusty Ruins because some guy called Rusty discovered them."

Tally had to agree. Every building sported jagged spurs of metal sticking from its broken walls, like bones jutting from a long-dead animal. She remembered that the Rusties didn't use hoverstruts; every building was squat, crude, and massive, and needed a steel skeleton to keep it from falling down.

And some of them were so *huge*. The Rusties didn't put their factories underground, and they all worked together like bees in a hive instead of at home. The smallest ruin here was bigger than the biggest dorm in Uglyville, bigger even than Garbo Mansion.

Seeing them now, at night, the ruins felt much more real to Tally. On school trips, the teachers always made the Rusties out to be so stupid. You almost couldn't believe people lived like this, burning trees to clear land, burning oil for heat and power, setting the atmosphere on fire with their weapons. But in the moonlight she could imagine people scrambling over flaming cars to escape the crumbling city, panicking in their flight from this untenable pile of metal and stone.

Shay's voice pulled Tally from her reverie. "Come on, I want to show you something."

Shay cruised to the edge of the buildings, then out over the trees.

"Are you sure we can—"

"Look down."

Below, Tally saw metal glinting through the trees.

"The ruins are much bigger than they let on," Shay said. "They just keep that part of the city standing for school trips and museum stuff. But it goes on forever."

"With lots of metal?"

"Yeah. Tons. Don't worry, I've flown all over the place."

Tally swallowed, keeping an eye out for signs of ruin below, glad that Shay was moving at a nice, slow speed.

*

A shape emerged from the forest, a long spine that rose and fell like a frozen wave. It led away from them, off into the darkness.

"Here it is."

"Okay, but what is it?" Tally asked.

"It's called a roller coaster. Remember, I told you I'd show you one."

"It's pretty. But what's it for?"

"For having fun."

"No way."

"Yeah, way. Apparently, the Rusties did have some fun. It's like a track. They would stick ground cars to it and go as fast as they could. Up, down, around in circles. Like hoverboarding, without hovering. And they made it out of some really unrusty kind of steel—for safety, I guess."

Tally frowned. She'd only imagined the Rusties working in the giant stone hives and struggling to escape on that last, horrible day. Not having fun.

"Let's do it," Shay said. "Let's roller coaster."

"How?"

"On your board." Shay turned to Tally and said seriously, "But you've got to go fast. It's dangerous unless you're really moving."

"Why?"

"You'll see."

Shay turned away and sped down the roller coaster, flying just above the track. Tally sighed and leaned hard after her. At least the thing was metal.

It also turned out to be a great ride. It was like a hoverboard course made solid, complete with tight, banked turns, sharp climbs followed by long drops, even loops that took Tally upside down, her crash bracelets activating to keep her on board. It was amazing what good shape it was in. The Rusties must have built it out of something special, just as Shay had said.

The track went much higher than a hoverboard could go on its own. On the roller coaster, hoverboarding really was like being a bird.

It wound around in a wide, slow arc, circling back toward where they'd started. The final approach began with a huge climb.

"Take this part fast!" Shay shouted over her shoulder as she zoomed ahead.

Tally followed at top speed, rocketing up the spindly track. She could see the ruins in the distance: broken, black spires against the trees. And behind them, a moonlit glimmer that might have been the sea. This *was* really high!

She heard a scream of pleasure as she reached the top. Shay had disappeared. Tally leaned forward to speed up.

Suddenly, the board dropped out from under her. It simply fell away from her feet, leaving her flying through midair. The track below her had disappeared.

Tally clenched her fists, waiting for the crash bracelets to kick in and haul her up by her wrists. But they had become as useless as the board, just heavy strips of steel dragging her toward the ground. "Shay!" she screamed as she fell into blackness.

Then Tally saw the framework of the roller coaster ahead. Only a short segment was missing.

Suddenly, the crash bracelets pulled her upward, and she felt the solid surface of the hoverboard coming up from under her feet. Her momentum had carried her to the other side of the gap! The board must have sailed along with her, just below her feet for those terrifying seconds of free fall.

She found herself cruising down the track, to where Shay was waiting at the bottom. "You're insane!" she shouted.

"Pretty cool, huh?"

"No!" Tally yelled. "Why didn't you tell me it was *broken*?"

Shay shrugged. "More fun that way?"

"More *fun*?" Her heart was beating fast, her vision strangely clear. She was full of anger and relief and . . . joy. "Well, kind of. But you *suck*!"

Tally stepped from the board and walked across the grass on rubbery legs. She found a broken stone big enough to sit on, and lowered herself shakily onto it.

Shay jumped off her board. "Hey, sorry."

"That was horrible, Shay. I was *falling*."

"Not for long. Like, five seconds. I thought you said you'd bungee jumped off a building."

Tally glared at Shay. "Yeah, I did, but I *knew* I wasn't going to splat."

"True. But, you see, the first time someone showed me the roller coaster, they didn't tell me about the gap. And I thought it was pretty cool, finding out that way. Best time's the first time. I wanted you to feel it too."

"You thought falling was *cool*?"

"Well, maybe at first I was pretty angry. Yeah, I definitely was." Shay smiled broadly. "But I got over it."

"Give me a second on that one, Skinny."

"Take your time."

Tally's breathing slowed, and her heart gradually stopped trying to beat its way out of her chest. But her brain stayed as clear as it had for those seconds of free fall, and she found herself wondering who had found the roller coaster first, and how many other uglies had come here since. "Shay, who showed you all this? "

"Friends, older than me. Uglies like us, who try to figure out how stuff works. And how to trick it."

Tally looked up at the ancient, serpentine shape of the roller coaster, the vines crawling up its framework. "I wonder how long uglies have been coming here."

"Probably a long time. You pass along stuff. You know, one person figures out how to trick their board, the next finds the rapids, the next makes it to the ruins."

"Then somebody gets brave enough to jump the gap in the roller coaster." Tally swallowed. "Or jumps it accidentally."

Shay nodded. "But they all get turned pretty in the end."

"Happy ending," Tally said.

Shay shrugged.

"How do you know it's called a 'roller coaster,' anyway? Did you look it up somewhere?"

"No," Shay said. "Someone told me."

"But how'd they know?"

"This guy knows a lot of stuff. Tricks, stuff about the ruins. He's really cool."

Something about Shay's voice made Tally turn and take her hand. "But he's pretty now, I guess."

Shay pulled away and bit a fingernail. "No. He's not."

"But I thought all your friends—"

"Tally, will you make me a promise? A real promise."

"Sure, I guess. What kind of promise?"

"You can never tell anyone what I'm about to show you."

"It doesn't involve free fall, does it?"

"No."

"Okay. I swear." Tally held up her hand with the scar she and Peris had made. "I'll never tell anyone."

Shay looked into her eyes for a moment, searching hard, then nodded. "All right. There's someone I want you to meet. Tonight."

"Tonight? But we won't get back into town until—"

"He's not in town." Shay smiled. "He's out here."

WAITING FOR DAVID

"This is a joke, right?"

Shay didn't answer. They were back in the heart of the ruins, in the shadow of the tallest building around. She was staring up at it with a puzzled expression on her face. "I think I remember how to do this," she said.

"Do what?"

"Get up there. Yeah, here it is."

Shay eased her board forward, ducking to pass through a gap in the crumbling wall.

"Shay?"

"Don't worry. I've done this before."

"I think I already had my initiation for tonight, Shay." Tally wasn't in the mood for another one of Shay's jokes. She was tired, and it was a long way back to town. And she had cleanup duty tomorrow at her dorm. Just because it was summer didn't mean she could sleep all day.

But Tally followed Shay through the gap. Arguing would probably take longer.

They rose straight into the air, the boards using the metal skeleton of the building to climb. It was creepy being inside, looking out of the empty windows at the ragged shapes of other buildings. Like being a Rusty ghost watching as its city crumbled over the centuries.

The roof was missing, and they emerged to a spectacular view. The clouds had all disappeared, and moonlight brought the ruins into sharp relief, the buildings like rows of broken teeth. Tally saw that it really had been the ocean she'd glimpsed from the roller coaster. From up here, the water shone like a pale band of silver in the moonlight.

Shay pulled something from her shoulder pack and tore it in half.

The world burst into flame.

"Ow! Blind me, why don't you!" Tally cried, covering her eyes.

"Oh, yeah. Sorry." Shay held the safety sparkler at arm's length. It crackled to full strength in the silence of the ruins, casting flickering shadows through the interior of the ruin. Shay's face looked monstrous in the glare, and sparks floated downward to be lost in the depths of the wrecked building.

Finally, the sparkler ran out. Tally blinked, trying to clear the spots from before her eyes. Her night vision ruined, she could hardly see anything except the moon in the sky.

She swallowed, realizing that the sparkler would have been seen from anywhere in the valley. Maybe even out to sea. "Shay, was that a signal?"

"Yeah, it was."

Tally looked down. The dark buildings below were filled with phantom flickers of light, echoes of the sparkler burned into her eyes. Suddenly very aware of how blind she was, Tally felt a drop of cold sweat creep down her spine. "Who are we meeting, anyway?"

"His name's David."

"David? That's a weird name." It sounded made up, to Tally. She decided again that this was all a joke. "So he's just going to show up here? This guy doesn't really live in the ruins, does he?"

"No. He lives pretty far away. But he might be close by. He comes here sometimes."

"You mean, he's from another city?"

Shay looked at her, but Tally couldn't read her expression in the darkness. "Something like that."

Shay returned her gaze to the horizon, as if looking for a signal in answer to her own. Tally wrapped herself in her jacket. Standing still, she began to realize how cold it had become. She wondered how late it was. Without her interface ring, she couldn't just ask.

The almost full moon was descending in the sky, so it had to be past midnight, Tally remembered from astronomy. That was one thing about being outside the city: It made all that nature stuff they taught in school seem a lot more useful. She remembered now how rainwater fell on the mountains, and soaked into the ground before bubbling up full of minerals. Then it made its way back to the sea, cutting rivers and canyons into the earth over the centuries. If you lived out here, you could ride your hoverboard along the rivers, like in the really old days before the Rusties, when the not-as-crazy pre-Rusties traveled around in small boats made from trees.

Her night vision gradually returned, and she scanned the horizon. Would there really be another flare out there, answering Shay's? Tally hoped not. She'd never met anyone from another city. She knew from school that in some cities they spoke other languages, or didn't turn pretty until they were eighteen, and other weird stuff like that. "Shay, maybe we should head home."

"Let's wait a while longer."

Tally bit her lip. "Look, maybe this David isn't around tonight."

"Yeah, maybe. Probably. But I was hoping he'd be here." She turned to face Tally. "It would be really cool if you met him. He's . . . different."

"Sounds like it."

"I'm not making this up, you know."

"Hey, I believe you," Tally said, although with Shay, she was never totally sure.

Shay turned back to the horizon, chewing on a fingernail. "Okay, I guess he's not around. We can go, if you want."

"It's just that it's really late, and a long way back. And I've got cleanup tomorrow."

Shay nodded. "Me too."

"Thanks for showing me all this, Shay. It was all really incredible. But I think one more cool thing would kill me."

Shay laughed. "The roller coaster didn't kill you."

"Just about."

"Forgive me for that yet?"

"I'll let you know, Skinny."

Shay laughed. "Okay. But remember not to tell anyone about David."

"Hey, I promised. You can trust me, Shay. Really."

"All right. I do trust you, Tally." She bent her knees, and her board started to descend.

Tally took one last look around, taking in the ruins splayed out below them, the dark woods, the pearly strip of river stretching toward the glowing sea. She wondered if there was anyone out there, really, or if David was just some story that uglies made up to scare one another.

But Shay didn't seem scared. She seemed genuinely

disappointed that no one had answered her signal, as if meeting David would have been even better than showing off the rapids, the ruins, and the roller coaster.

Whether he was real or not, Tally thought, David was very real to Shay.

They left through the gap in the wall and flew to the outskirts of the ruins, then followed the vein of iron up out of the valley. At the ridge, the boards started to stutter, and they stepped off. Tired as Tally was, carrying the board didn't seem so impossible this time. She had stopped thinking of it as a toy, like a littlie's balloon. The hoverboard had become something more solid, something that obeyed its own rules, and that could be dangerous, too.

Tally figured that Shay was right about one thing: Being in the city all the time made everything fake, in a way. Like the buildings and bridges held up by hoverstruts, or jumping off a rooftop with a bungee jacket on, nothing was quite real there. She was glad Shay had taken her out to the ruins. If nothing else, the mess left by the Rusties proved that things could go terribly wrong if you weren't careful.

Close to the river the boards lightened up, and the two of them jumped on gratefully.

Shay groaned as they got their footing. "I don't know about you, but I'm not taking another step tonight."

"That's for sure."

Shay leaned forward and eased her board out onto the river, wrapping her dorm jacket around her shoulders against the spray of the rapids. Tally turned to take one last look back. With the clouds gone, she could just see the ruins from here.

She blinked. There seemed to be the barest flicker

coming from over where the roller coaster had been. Maybe it was just a trick of the light, a reflection of moonlight from some exposed piece of unrusted metal. "Shay?" she said softly.

"You coming or what?" Shay shouted over the roar of the river.

Tally blinked again, but couldn't make out the flicker anymore. In any case, they were too far away. Mentioning it to Shay would only make her anxious to go back. There was no way Tally was making the hike again.

And it probably was nothing.

Tally took a deep breath and shouted, "Come on, Skinny. Race you!" She urged her board onto the river, cutting into the cold spray and for a moment leaving a laughing Shay behind.

FIGHT

"Look at them all. What dorks."

"Did we ever look like that?"

"Probably. But just because we were dorks doesn't mean they're not."

Tally nodded, trying to remember what being twelve was like, what the dorm had looked like on her first day there. She remembered how intimidating the building had seemed. Much bigger than Sol and Ellie's house, of course, and bigger than the huts that littlies went to school in, one teacher and ten students to each one.

Now the dorm seemed so small and claustrophobic.

Painfully childish, with its bright colors and padded stairs. So boring during the day and easy to escape at night.

The new uglies all stuck together in a tight group, afraid to stray too far from their guide. Their ugly little faces peered up at the dorm's four-story height, their eyes full of wonder and terror.

Shay pulled her head back in through the window. "This is going to be so fun."

"It'll be one orientation they won't forget."

Summer was over in two weeks. The population of Tally's dorm had been steadily dropping for the last year as seniors turned sixteen. It was almost time for a new batch to take their place. Tally watched the last few uglies make their way inside, gawky and nervous, unkempt and uncoordinated. Twelve was definitely the turning point, when you changed from a cute littlie into an oversize, under-educated ugly.

It was a stage of life she was glad to be leaving behind.

"You sure this thing is going to work?" Shay asked.

Tally smiled. It wasn't often that Shay was the cautious one. She pointed at the collar of the bungee jacket. "You see that little green light? That means it's working. It's for emergencies, so it's always ready to go."

Shay's hand slipped under the jacket to pull at her belly sensor, which meant she was nervous. "What if it knows there's no real emergency?"

"It's not that smart. You fall, it catches you. No tricks necessary."

Shay shrugged and put it on.

They'd borrowed the jacket from the art school, the tallest building in Uglyville. It was a spare from the basement, and they hadn't even had to trick the rack to get it free. Tally definitely didn't want to get caught messing around with fire alarms, in case the wardens connected her to a certain incident in New Pretty Town back at the beginning of summer.

Shay pulled an oversize basketball jersey over the bungee jacket. It was in her dorm's colors, and none of the teachers here knew her face very well. "How's that look?"

"Like you've gained weight. It suits you."

Shay scowled. She hated being called Stick Insect, or Pig-Eyes, or any of the other things uglies called one another. Shay sometimes claimed that she didn't care if she ever got the operation. It was crazy talk, of course. Shay wasn't exactly a *freak*, but she was hardly a natural-born pretty. There'd only been about ten of those in all of history, after all. "Do *you* want to do the jump, Squint?"

"I have both been there and done that, Shay, before I even met you. And you're the one who had this brilliant idea."

Shay's scowl faded into a smile. "It is brilliant, isn't it?"

"They'll never know what hit them."

They waited until the new uglies were in the library, scattered around the worktables to watch some orientation video. Shay and Tally lay on their stomachs on the top floor of the stacks, where the dusty old paper books were stored, peering through the guardrails down at the group. They waited for the tour leader to quiet the chattering uglies.

"This is almost too easy," Shay said, penciling a pair of fat, black eyebrows over her own.

"Easy for you. You'll be out the door before anyone knows what's happened. I've got to make it all the way down the stairs."

"So what, Tally? What are they going to do if we get caught?"

Tally shrugged. "True." But she pulled on her mousy brown wig anyway.

Over the summer, as the last few seniors turned sixteen and pretty, the tricks had grown worse and worse. But nobody ever seemed to get punished, and Tally's promise to Peris seemed ages ago. Once she was pretty, nothing she'd done in this last month would matter. She was anxious to leave it all behind, but not without a big finish.

Thinking of Peris, Tally stuck on a big plastic nose. They'd raided the drama room at Shay's dorm the night before and were loaded with disguises. "Ready?" she asked. Then she giggled at the nasal twang the fake nose gave her voice.

"Hang on." Shay grabbed a big, fat book from the shelf. "Okay, showtime."

They stood up.

"Give me that book!" Tally shouted at Shay. "It's mine!"

She heard the uglies below fall silent, and had to resist looking down to see their upturned faces.

"No way, Pignose! I checked it out first."

"Are you kidding, Fattie? You can't even read!"

"Oh, yeah? Well, read *this*!"

Shay swung the book at Tally, who ducked. She snatched it away and swung back, catching Shay solidly on her upraised forearms. Shay rolled back at the impact, spinning over the railing.

Tally leaned forward, watching wide-eyed as Shay tumbled down toward the library's main floor, three stories below. The new uglies screamed in unison, scattering away from the flailing body plummeting toward them.

A second later the bungee jacket activated, and Shay bobbed back up in midair, laughing maniacally at the top of her lungs. Tally waited another moment, watching the uglies' horror dissolve into confusion as Shay bounced again, then righted herself on one of the tables and headed for the door.

Tally dropped the book and dashed for the stairs, leaping a flight at a time until she reached the back exit of the dorm.

"Oh, that was perfect!"

"Did you see their faces?"

"Not actually," Shay said. "I was kind of busy watching the floor coming at me."

"Yeah, I remember that from jumping off the roof. It does catch your attention."

"Speaking of faces, love the nose."

Tally giggled, pulling it off. "Yeah, no point in being uglier than usual."

Shay's face clouded. She wiped off an eyebrow, then looked up sharply. "You're not ugly."

"Oh, come on, Shay."

"No, I mean it." She reached out and touched Tally's real nose. "Your profile is great."

"Don't be weird, Shay. I'm an ugly, you're an ugly. We will be for two more weeks. It's no big deal or anything." She laughed. "You, for example, have one giant eyebrow and one tiny one."

Shay looked away, stripping off the rest of her disguise in silence.

They were hidden in the changing rooms beside the sandy beach, where they'd left their interface rings and a spare set of clothes. If anyone asked, they'd say they were swimming the whole time. Swimming was a great trick. It hid your body-heat signature, involved changing clothes, and was a perfect excuse for not wearing your interface ring. The river washed away all crimes.

A minute later they splashed out into the water, sinking the disguises. The bungee jacket would go back to the art school basement that night.

"I'm serious, Tally," Shay said once they were out in the water. "Your nose isn't ugly. I like your eyes, too."

"My eyes? Now you're totally crazy. They're way too close together."

"Who says?"

"Biology says."

Shay splashed a handful of water at her. "You don't believe all that crap, do you—that there's only one way to look, and everyone's programmed to agree on it?"

"It's not about believing, Shay. You just *know* it. You've seen pretties. They look . . . wonderful."

"They all look the same."

"I used to think that too. But when Peris and I would go into town, we'd see a lot of them, and we realized that pretties do look different. They look like themselves. It's just a lot more subtle, because they're not all freaks."

"We're not freaks, Tally. *We're* normal. We may not be gorgeous, but at least we're not hyped-up Barbie dolls."

"What kind of dolls?"

She looked away. "It's something David told me about."

"Oh, great. David again." Tally pushed away and floated on her back, looking up at the sky and wishing this conversation would end. They'd been out to the ruins a few more times, and Shay always insisted on setting off a sparkler, but David had never showed. The whole thing gave Tally the creeps, waiting around in the dead city for some guy who didn't seem to exist. It was great exploring out there, but Shay's obsession with David had started to sour it for Tally.

"He's real. I've met him more than once."

"Okay, Shay, David's real. But so is being ugly. You can't change it just by wishing, or by telling yourself that you're pretty. That's why they invented the operation."

"But it's a trick, Tally. You've only seen pretty faces your whole life. Your parents, your teachers, everyone over sixteen. But you weren't *born* expecting that kind of beauty in everyone, all the time. You just got programmed into thinking anything else is ugly."

"It's not programming, it's just a natural reaction. And more important than that, it's fair. In the old days it was all random—some people *kind* of pretty, most people ugly all their lives. Now everyone's ugly . . . until they're pretty. No losers."

Shay was silent for a while, then said, "There are losers, Tally."

Tally shivered. Everyone knew about uglies-for-life, the few people for whom the operation wouldn't work. You didn't see them around much. They were allowed in public, but most of them preferred to hide. Who wouldn't? Uglies might look goofy, but at least they were young. *Old* uglies were really unbelievable.

"Is that it? Are you worried about the operation not working? That's silly, Shay. You're no freak. In two weeks you'll be as pretty as anyone else."

"I don't want to be pretty."

Tally sighed. This again.

"I'm sick of this city," Shay continued. "I'm sick of the rules and boundaries. The last thing I want is to become some empty-headed new pretty, having one big party all day."

"Come on, Shay. They do all the same stuff we do: bungee jump, fly, play with fireworks. Only they don't have to sneak around."

"They don't have the imagination to sneak around."

"Look, Skinny, I'm with you," Tally said sharply. "Doing tricks is great! Okay? Breaking the rules is fun! But eventually you've got to do something besides being a clever little ugly."

"Like being a vapid, boring pretty?"

"No, like being an adult. Did you ever think that when you're pretty you might not *need* to play tricks and mess things up? Maybe just being ugly is why uglies always fight and pick on one another, because they aren't happy with who they are. Well, I want to be happy, and looking like a real person is the first step."

"I'm not afraid of looking the way I do, Tally."

"Maybe not, but you are afraid of growing up!"

Shay didn't say anything. Tally floated in silence, looking up at the sky, barely able to see the clouds through her anger. She wanted to be pretty, wanted to see Peris again. It seemed like forever since she'd talked to him, or to anyone else except Shay. She was sick of this whole ugly business, and just wanted it to end.

A minute later, she heard Shay swimming for shore.

LAST TRICK

It was strange, but Tally couldn't help feeling sad. She knew she'd miss the view from this window.

She'd spent the last four years looking out at New

Pretty Town, wanting nothing more than to cross the river and not come back. That's probably what had tempted her through the window so many times, learning every trick she could to sneak closer to the new pretties, to spy on the life she would eventually have.

But now that the operation was only a week away, time seemed to be moving too fast. Sometimes, Tally wished that they could do the operation gradually. Get her squinty eyes fixed first, then her lips, and cross the river in stages. Just so she wouldn't have to look out the window one last time and know she'd never see this view again.

Without Shay around, things felt incomplete, and she'd spent even more time here, sitting on her bed and staring at New Pretty Town.

Of course, there wasn't much else to do these days. Everyone in the dorm was younger than Tally now, and she'd already taught all of her best tricks to the next class. She'd watched every movie her wallscreen knew about ten times, all the way back to some old black-and-white ones in an English she could barely understand. There was no one to go to concerts with, and dorm sports were boring to watch now that she didn't know anyone on the teams. All the other uglies looked at her enviously, but no one saw much point in making friends. Probably it was better to get the operation over with all at once. Half the time, she wished the doctors would just kidnap her in the middle of the night and do it. She could imagine a lot worse things than waking up pretty one morning. They said at school that they could make the operation work on fifteen-year-olds now. Waiting until sixteen was just a stupid old tradition.

But it was a tradition nobody questioned, except the occasional ugly. So Tally had a week to go, alone, waiting.

Shay hadn't talked to her since their big fight. Tally had tried to write a ping, but working it all out on-screen just made her angry again. And it didn't make much sense to sort it out now. Once they were both pretty, there wouldn't be anything to fight about anymore. And even if Shay still hated her, there was always Peris and all their old friends, waiting across the river for her with their big eyes and wonderful smiles.

Still, Tally spent a lot of time wondering what Shay was going to look like pretty, her skin-and-bones body all filled out, her already full lips perfected, and the ragged fingernails gone forever. They'd probably make her eyes a more intense shade of green. Or maybe one of the newer colors—violet, silver, or gold.

"Hey, Squint!"

Tally jumped at the whisper. She peered into the darkness and saw a form scuttling toward her across the roof tiles. A smile broke onto her face. "Shay!"

The silhouette paused for a moment.

Tally didn't even bother to whisper. "Don't just stand there. Come in, stupid!"

Shay crawled into the window, laughing, as Tally gathered her into a hug, warm and joyful and solid. They stepped back, still holding each other's hands. For a moment, Shay's ugly face looked perfect.

"It's so great to see you."

"You too, Tally."

"I missed you. I wanted to—I'm so sorry about—"

"No," Shay interrupted. "You were right. You made me think. I was going to write you, but it was all . . ." She sighed.

Tally nodded, squeezing Shay's hands. "Yeah. It sucked."

They stood in silence for a moment, and Tally glanced past her friend out the window. Suddenly, the view of New Pretty Town didn't seem so sad. It looked bright and tempting, as if all the hesitation had drained out of her. The open window was exciting again. "Shay?"

"Yeah?"

"Let's go somewhere tonight. Do some major trick."

Shay laughed. "I was kind of hoping you'd say that."

Tally noticed the way Shay was dressed. She was wearing serious trick-wear: all black clothes, hair tied back tight, a knapsack over one shoulder. She grinned. "Already got a plan, I see. Great."

"Yeah," Shay said softly. "I've got a plan."

She walked over to Tally's bed, unslinging the knapsack from her shoulder. Her footsteps squeaked, and Tally smiled when she saw that Shay was wearing grippy shoes. Tally hadn't been on a hoverboard in days. Flying alone was all the hard work and only half the fun.

Shay dumped the contents of the knapsack out onto the bed, and pointed. "Position-finder. Firestarter. Water purifier." She picked up two shiny wads the size of sandwiches. "These pull out into sleeping bags. And they're really warm inside."

"Sleeping bags? Water purifier?" Tally exclaimed. "This must be some kind of awesome multiday trick. Are we going all the way to the sea or something?"

Shay shook her head. "Farther."

"Uh, cool." Tally kept her smile on her face. "But we've only got six days till the operation."

"I know what day it is." Shay opened a waterproof bag and spilled its contents alongside the rest. "Food for two weeks—dehydrated. You just drop one of these into the purifier and add water. Any kind of water." She giggled. "The purifier works so well, you can even pee in it."

Tally sat down on the bed, reading the labels on the food packs. "Two weeks?"

"Two weeks for two people," Shay said carefully. "Four weeks for one."

Tally didn't say anything. Suddenly, she couldn't look at the stuff on the bed, or at Shay. She stared out the window, at New Pretty Town, where the fireworks were starting.

"But it won't take two weeks, Tally. It's much closer."

A plume of red soared up in the middle of town, tendrils of fireworks drifting down like the leaves of a giant willow tree. "What won't take two weeks?"

"Going to where David lives."

Tally nodded, and closed her eyes.

"It's not like here, Tally. They don't separate everyone, uglies from pretties, new and middle and late. And you can leave whenever you want, go anywhere you want."

"Like where?"

"Anywhere. Ruins, the forest, the sea. And . . . you never have to get the operation."

"You *what*?"

Shay sat next to her, touching Tally's cheek with one finger. Tally opened her eyes. "We don't have to look like everyone else, Tally, and act like everyone else. We've got a choice. We can grow up any way we want."

Tally swallowed. She felt like speech was impossible, but knew she had to say something. She forced words from her dry throat. "Not be pretty? That's crazy, Shay. All the times you talked that way, I thought you were just being stupid. Peris always said the same stuff."

"I *was* just being stupid. But when you said I was afraid of growing up, you really made me think."

"*I* made you think?"

"Made me realize how full of crap I was. Tally, I've got to tell you another secret."

Tally sighed. "Okay. I guess it can't get any worse."

"My older friends, the ones I used to hang out with before I met you? Not all of them wound up pretty."

"What do you mean?"

"Some of them ran away, like I am. Like I want us to."

Tally looked into Shay's eyes, searching for some sign that this was all a joke. But the intense look on her face held firm. She was dead serious.

"You know someone who actually ran away?"

Shay nodded. "I was supposed to go too. We had it all planned, about a week before the first of us turned sixteen. We'd already stolen survival gear, and told David that we were coming. It was all set up. That was four months ago."

"But you didn't . . ."

"Some of us did, but I chickened out." Shay looked out the window. "And I wasn't the only one. A couple of the others stayed and turned pretty instead. I probably would have too, except I met you."

"Me?"

"All of a sudden I wasn't alone anymore. I wasn't afraid to go back out to the ruins, to look for David again."

"But we never . . ." Tally blinked. "You finally found him, didn't you?"

"Not until two days ago. I've been out every night since we . . . since our fight. After you said I was afraid to grow up, I realized you were right. I'd chickened out once, but I didn't have to again."

Shay grasped Tally's hand, and waited until their eyes were locked. "I want you to come, Tally."

"No," Tally said without thinking. Then she shook her head. "Wait. How come you never *told* me any of this before?"

"I wanted to, except you would have thought I was crazy."

"You *are* crazy!"

"Maybe. But not that way. That's why I wanted you to meet David. So you'd know that it's all real."

"It doesn't seem real. I mean, what is this place you're talking about?"

"It's just called the Smoke. It's not a city, and nobody's in charge. And nobody's pretty."

"Sounds like a nightmare. And how do you get there, walk?"

Shay laughed. "Are you kidding? Hoverboards, like always. There are long-distance boards that recharge on solar, and the route's all worked out to follow rivers and stuff. David does it all the time, as far as the ruins. He'll take us to the Smoke."

"But how do people *live* out there, Shay? Like the Rusties? Burning trees for heat and burying their junk everywhere? It's wrong to live in nature, unless you want to live like an animal."

Shay shook her head and sighed. "That's just school-talk, Tally. They've still got technology. And they're not like the Rusties, burning trees and stuff. But they don't put a wall up between themselves and nature."

"And everyone's ugly."

"Which means no one's ugly."

Tally managed to laugh. "Which means no one's *pretty*, you mean."

They sat in silence. Tally watched the fireworks, feeling

a thousand times worse than she had before Shay had appeared at the window.

Finally, Shay said the words Tally had been thinking. "I'm going to lose you, aren't I?"

"You're the one who's running away."

Shay brought her fists down onto her knees. "It's all my fault. I should've told you earlier. If you'd had more time to get used to the idea, maybe . . ."

"Shay, I never would have gotten used to the idea. I don't want to be ugly all my life. I want those perfect eyes and lips, and for everyone to look at me and gasp. And for everyone who sees me to think *Who's that?* and want to get to know me, and listen to what I say."

"I'd rather *have* something to say."

"Like what? 'I shot a wolf today and ate it'?"

Shay giggled. "People don't eat wolves, Tally. Rabbits, I think, and deer."

"Oh, gross. Thanks for the image, Shay."

"Yeah, I think I'll stick to vegetables and fish. But it's not about camping out, Tally. It's about becoming what I want to become. Not what some surgical committee thinks I should."

"You're still yourself on the inside, Shay. But when you're pretty, people pay more attention."

"Not everyone thinks that way."

"Are you sure about that? That you can beat evolution by being smart or interesting? Because if you're wrong . . . if you don't come back by the time you're twenty, the operation won't work as well. You'll look wrong, forever."

"I'm not coming back. Forever."

Tally's voice caught, but she forced herself to say it: "And I'm not going."

*

They said good-bye under the dam.

Shay's long-range hoverboard was thicker, and glimmered with the facets of solar cells. She'd also stashed a heated jacket and hat under the bridge. Tally guessed that winters at the Smoke were cold and miserable.

She couldn't believe her friend was really going.

"You can always come back. If it sucks."

Shay shrugged. "None of my friends has."

The words gave Tally a creepy feeling. She could think of a lot of horrible reasons to explain why no one had come back. "Be careful, Shay."

"You too. You're not going to tell anyone about this, right?"

"Never, Shay."

"You swear? No matter what?"

Tally raised her scarred palm. "I swear."

Shay smiled. "I know. I just had to ask again before I . . ." She pulled out a piece of paper and handed it to Tally.

"What's this?" Tally opened it up and saw a scrawl of letters. "When did you learn to write by hand?"

"We all learned while we were planning to leave. It's a good idea if you don't want minders sniffing your diary. Anyway, that's for you. I'm not supposed to leave any record of where I'm going, so it's in code, kind of."

Tally frowned, reading the first line of slanted words. "'Take the coaster straight past the gap'?"

"Yeah. Get it? Only you could figure it out, in case someone finds it. You know, if you ever want to follow me."

Tally started to say something, but couldn't. She managed to nod.

"Just in case," Shay said.

She jumped onto her board and snapped her fingers, securing her knapsack over both shoulders. "Good-bye, Tally."

"Bye, Shay. I wish . . ."

Shay waited, bobbing just a bit in the cool September wind. Tally tried to imagine her growing old, wrinkled, gradually ruined, all without ever having been truly beautiful. Never learning how to dress properly, or how to act at a formal dance. Never having anyone look into her eyes and be simply overwhelmed.

"I wish I could have seen what you would look like. Pretty, I mean."

"Guess you'll just have to live with remembering my face this way," Shay said.

Then she turned and her hoverboard climbed away toward the river, and Tally's next words were lost on the roar of the water.

OPERATION

When the day came, Tally waited for the car alone.

Tomorrow, when the operation was all over, her parents would be waiting outside the hospital, along with Peris and her other older friends. That was the tradition. But it seemed strange that there was no one to see her off on this end. No one said good-bye except a few uglies passing by. They looked so young to her now, especially the just-arrived new class, who gawked at her like she was an old pile of dinosaur bones.

She'd always loved being independent, but now Tally felt like the last littlie to be picked up from school, abandoned and alone. September was a crappy month to be born.

"You're Tally, right?"

She looked up. It was a new ugly, awkwardly exploding into unfamiliar height, tugging at his dorm uniform like it was already too tight.

"Yeah."

"Aren't you the one who's going to turn today?"

"That's me, Shorty."

"So how come you look so sad?"

Tally shrugged. What could this half-littlie, half-ugly understand, anyway? She thought about what Shay had said about the operation.

Yesterday they'd taken Tally's final measurements, rolling her all the way through an imaging tube. Should she tell this new ugly that sometime this afternoon, her body was going to be opened up, the bones ground down to the right shape, some of them stretched or padded, her nose cartilage and cheekbones stripped out and replaced with programmable plastic, skin sanded off and reseeded like a soccer field in spring? That her eyes would be laser-cut for a lifetime of perfect vision, reflective implants inserted under the iris to add sparkling gold flecks to their indifferent brown? Her muscles all trimmed up with a night of electrocize and all her baby fat sucked out for good? Teeth replaced with ceramics as strong as a suborbital aircraft wing, and as white as the dorm's good china?

They said it didn't hurt, except the new skin, which felt like a killer sunburn for a couple of weeks.

As the details of the operation buzzed around in her head, she could imagine why Shay had run away. It did seem like a lot to go through just to look a certain way. If only people were smarter, evolved enough to treat everyone the same even if they looked different. Looked ugly.

If only Tally had come up with the right argument to make her stay.

The imaginary conversations were back, but much worse than they had been after Peris had left. A thousand times she'd fought with Shay in her head—long, rambling discussions about beauty, biology, growing up. All those times out in the ruins, Shay had made her points about uglies and pretties, the city and the outside, what was fake and what was real. But Tally had never once realized her friend might actually run away, giving up a life of beauty, glamour, elegance. If only she'd said the right thing. *Any*thing.

Sitting here, she felt as if she'd hardly tried.

Tally looked the new ugly in the eye. "Because it all comes down to this: Two weeks of killer sunburn is worth a lifetime of being gorgeous."

The kid scratched his head. "Huh?"

"Something I should have said, and didn't. That's all."

The hospital hovercar finally came, settling onto the school grounds so lightly that it hardly disturbed the fresh-mown grass.

The driver was a middle pretty, radiating confidence and authority. He looked so much like Sol that Tally almost called her father's name.

"Tally Youngblood?" he said.

Tally had already seen the flash of light that had read her eye-print, but she said, "Yes, that's me," anyway. Something about the middle pretty made it hard to be flippant. He was wisdom personified, his manner so serious and formal that Tally found herself wishing she had dressed up.

"Are you ready? Not taking much."

Her duffel bag was only half-full. Everyone knew that new pretties wound up recycling most of the stuff they brought over the river, anyway. She'd have all new clothes, of course, and all the new pretty toys she wanted. All she'd really kept was Shay's handwritten note, hidden among a bunch of random crap. "Got enough."

"Good for you, Tally. That's very mature."

"That's me, sir."

The door closed, and the car took off.

The big hospital was on the bottom end of New Pretty Town. It was where everyone went for serious operations: littlies, uglies, even late pretties from way out in Crumblyville coming in for life-extension treatments.

The river was sparkling under a cloudless sky, and Tally allowed herself to be swept away by the beauty of New Pretty Town. Even without the nighttime lights and fireworks, the city's surfaces shone with glass and metal, the unlikely spindles of party towers casting thin shadows across the island. It was so much more vibrant than the Rusty Ruins, Tally suddenly saw. Not as dark and mysterious, perhaps, but more alive.

It was time to stop sulking about Shay. Life was going to be one big party from now on, full of beautiful people. Like Tally Youngblood.

The hovercar descended onto one of the red *X*s on the hospital roof, and Tally's driver escorted her inside, taking her to a waiting room. An orderly looked up Tally's name, flashed her eye again, and told her to wait.

"You'll be okay?" the driver asked.

She looked up into his clear, soft eyes, wanting him to stay. But asking him to wait with her didn't seem very mature. "No, I'm fine. Thanks." He smiled and went away.

No one else was in the waiting room. Tally settled back and counted the tiles on the ceiling. As she waited, the conversations with Shay in her head came back again, but they weren't so troubling here. It was too late for second thoughts now.

Tally wished there was a window to look out onto New Pretty Town. She was so close now. She imagined tomorrow night, her first night pretty, dressed in new and wonderful clothes (her dorm uniforms all shoved down the recycler), looking out from the top of the highest party tower she could find. She would watch as lights-out fell across the river, bedtime for Uglyville, and know that she still had all night with Peris and her new friends, all the beautiful people she would meet.

She sighed.

Sixteen years. Finally.

Nothing happened for a long hour. Tally drummed her fingers, wondering if they always kept uglies waiting this long.

Then the man came.

He looked strange, unlike any pretty Tally had ever seen. He was definitely of middle age, but whoever had done his operation had botched it. He was beautiful, without a doubt, but it was a terrible beauty.

Instead of wise and confident, the man looked cold, commanding, intimidating, like some regal animal of prey. When he walked up, Tally started to ask what was going on, but a glance from him silenced her.

She had never met an adult who affected her this way. She always felt respect when face-to-face with a middle or late pretty. But in the presence of this cruelly beautiful man, respect was saturated with fear.

The man said, "There's a problem with your operation. Come with me."

She went.

SPECIAL CIRCUMSTANCES

This hovercar was larger, but not as comfortable.

The trip was much less pleasant than Tally's first ride that day. The strange-looking man flew with an aggressive impatience, dropping like a rock to cut between flight lanes, banking as steeply as a hoverboard with every turn. Tally had never been airsick before, but now she clutched the seat restraints, her knuckles white and eyes fixed on the solid ground below. She caught one last glimpse of New Pretty Town receding behind them.

They headed downriver, across Uglyville, over the greenbelt and farther out to the transport ring, where the factories stuck their heads aboveground. Beside a huge, misshapen hill, the car descended into a complex of rectangular buildings, as squat as ugly dorms and painted the color of dried grass.

They landed with a painful bump, and the man led her into one of the buildings, and down into a murk of yellow-brown hallways. Tally had never seen so much space painted in such putrid colors, as if the building were designed to make its occupants vaguely nauseated.

There were more people like the man.

They were all dressed in formals, raw silks in black and gray, and their faces had the same cold, hawkish look. Both the men and women were taller than pretty standard, and more powerfully built, their eyes as pale as an ugly's. There were a few normal people as well, but they faded into insignificance next to the predatory forms moving gracefully through the halls.

Tally wondered if this was someplace where people were taken when their operations went wrong, when beauty turned cruel. Then why was she here? She hadn't even had the operation yet. Tally swallowed. What if these terrible pretties had been made this way intentionally? When they had measured her yesterday, had they determined that she would never fit the vulnerable, doe-eyed pretty mold? Maybe she'd already been chosen to be remade for this strange, other world.

The man stopped outside a metal door, and Tally halted behind him. She felt like a littlie again, jerked along by a minder on an invisible string. All her ugly senior's confidence had evaporated the moment she'd seen him back at the hospital. Four years of tricks and independence gone.

The door flashed his eye and opened, and he pointed for her to go in. Tally realized he hadn't said a word since collecting her at the hospital. She took a deep breath, which made the paralyzed muscles in her chest flinch with pain, and managed to croak, "Say please."

"Inside," was his answer.

Tally smiled, silently declaring a small victory that she had made him speak again, but she did as she was told.

"I'm Dr. Cable."

"Tally Youngblood."

Dr. Cable smiled. "Oh, I know who you are."

The woman was a cruel pretty. Her nose was aquiline, her teeth sharp, her eyes a nonreflective gray. Her voice had the same slow, neutral cadence as a bedtime book. But it hardly made Tally sleepy. An edge was hidden in the voice, like a piece of metal slowly marking glass.

"You have a problem, Tally."

"I had kind of guessed that, uh . . ." It was strange, not knowing the woman's first name.

"Dr. Cable will do."

Tally blinked. She'd never called anyone by their last name in her life.

"Okay, Dr. Cable." She cleared her throat and managed to say more, in a dry voice. "My problem right now is that I don't know what's going on. So . . . why don't you tell me?"

"What do you think's going on, Tally?"

Tally closed her eyes, taking a rest from the sharp angles of the woman's face. "Well, that bungee jacket *was* a spare, you know, and we did put it back on the recharge pile."

"This isn't about some ugly-trick."

She sighed and opened her eyes. "No, I didn't think so."

"This is about a friend of yours. Someone missing."

Of course. Shay's disappearing trick had gone too far, leaving Tally to explain. "I don't know where she is."

Dr. Cable smiled. Only her top teeth showed when she did. "But you do know something."

"Who are you, anyway?" Tally blurted. "Where am I?"

"I'm Dr. Cable," the woman said. "And this is Special Circumstances."

First Dr. Cable asked her a lot of questions. "You didn't know Shay long, did you?"

"No. Just this summer. We were in different dorms."

"And you didn't know any of her friends?"

"No. They were all older than her. They'd already turned."

"Like your friend Peris?"

Tally swallowed. How much did this woman know about her? "Yeah. Like Peris and me."

"But Shay's friends didn't wind up pretty, did they?"

Tally took a slow breath, remembering her promise to Shay. She didn't want to lie, though. Dr. Cable would know if she did, Tally was sure. She was in enough trouble already. "Why wouldn't they?"

"Did she tell you about her friends?"

"We didn't talk about stuff like that. We just hung out. Because . . . it hurt being alone. We were just into playing tricks."

"Did you know she'd been in a gang?"

Tally looked up into Dr. Cable's eyes. They were almost as big as a normal pretty's, but they angled upward like a wolf's.

"A gang? How do you mean?"

"Tally, did you and Shay ever go to the Rusty Ruins?"

"Everyone does."

"But did you ever *sneak out* to the ruins?"

"Yeah. A lot of people do."

"Did you ever meet anyone there?"

Tally bit her lip. "What's Special Circumstances?"

"Tally." The edge in her voice was suddenly sharp as a razor blade.

"If you tell me what Special Circumstances is, I'll answer you."

Dr. Cable sat back. She folded her hands and nodded.

"This city is a paradise, Tally. It feeds you, educates you, keeps you safe. It makes you pretty."

Tally couldn't help looking up hopefully at this.

"And our city can stand a great deal of freedom, Tally. It gives youngsters room to play tricks, to develop their creativity and independence. But occasionally bad things come from *outside* the city."

Dr. Cable narrowed her eyes, her face becoming even more like a predator's. "We exist in equilibrium with our environment, Tally, purifying the water that we put back in the river, recycling the biomass, and using only power drawn from our own solar footprint. But sometimes we can't purify what we take in from the outside. Sometimes there are threats from the environment that must be faced."

She smiled. "Sometimes there are Special Circumstances."

"So, you guys are like minders, but for the whole city."

Dr. Cable nodded. "Other cities sometimes pose a challenge. And sometimes those few people who live outside the cities can make trouble."

Tally's eyes widened. *Outside* the cities? Shay had been telling the truth—places like the Smoke really existed.

"It's your turn to answer my question, Tally. Did you ever meet anyone in the ruins? Someone not from this city? Not from any city?"

Tally grinned. "No. I never did."

Dr. Cable frowned, her eyes darting downward for a second, checking something. When they returned to Tally, they had grown even colder. Tally smiled again, certain now that Dr. Cable knew when she was telling the truth. The room must be reading her heartbeat, her sweat, her pupil dilation. But Tally couldn't tell what she didn't know.

The razor blade slid back into the woman's voice. "Don't play games with me, Tally. Your friend Shay will never thank you for it, because you'll never see her again."

The thrill of her small victory disappeared, and Tally felt her smile fade.

"Six of her friends disappeared, Tally, all at once. None of them has ever been found. Another two who were meant to join them chose not to throw their lives away, however, and we discovered a little about what had happened to the others. They didn't run away on their own. They were tempted by someone from outside, someone who wanted to steal our cleverest little uglies. We realized that this was a special circumstance."

One word sent ice down Tally's spine. Had Shay really been *stolen*? What did Shay or any ugly really know about the Smoke?

"We've been watching Shay since then, hoping she might lead us to her friends."

"So why didn't you . . . ," Tally blurted out. "You know, *stop* her!"

"Because of you, Tally."

"Me?"

Dr. Cable's voice softened. "We thought she had made a friend, a reason to stay here in the city. We thought she'd be okay."

Tally could only close her eyes and shake her head.

"But then Shay disappeared," Dr. Cable continued. "She turned out to be trickier than her friends. You taught her well."

"*I* did?" Tally cried. "I don't know any more tricks than most uglies."

"You underestimate yourself," Dr. Cable said.

Tally turned away from the vulpine eyes, shut out the razor-blade voice. This was *not* her fault. She had decided to stay here in the city, after all. She wanted to become pretty. She'd even tried to convince Shay.

But failed.

"It's not my fault."

"Help us, Tally."

"Help you what?"

"Find her. Find them all."

She took a deep breath. "What if they don't want to be found?"

"What if they do? What if they were lied to?"

Tally tried to remember Shay's face that last night, how hopeful she had been. She'd wanted to leave the city as much as Tally wanted to be pretty. However stupid the choice seemed, Shay had made it with her eyes open, and had respected Tally's choice to stay.

Tally looked up at Dr. Cable's cruel beauty, at the puke-yellow-brown of the walls. She remembered all the tricks Special Circumstances had played on her today—how they'd kept her waiting for an hour in the hospital, waiting and thinking she would soon be pretty, the brutal flight here, and all the cruel faces in the halls—and she decided. "I can't help you," Tally said. "I made a promise."

Dr. Cable bared her teeth. This time, it wasn't even a mockery of a smile. The woman became nothing but a monster, vengeful and inhuman. "Then I'll make you a promise too, Tally Youngblood. Until you do help us, to the very best of your ability, you will never be pretty."

Dr. Cable turned away.

"You can die ugly, for all I care."

The door opened. The scary man was outside, where he'd been waiting all along.

UGLY FOR LIFE

They must have forewarned the minders about her return. All the other uglies were gone, off on some unscheduled school trip. But they hadn't found out in time to save her stuff. When Tally reached her old room, she saw that everything had been recycled. Clothes, bedding, furniture, the pictures on the wallscreen—it had all reverted back to Generic Ugly. It even looked as if somebody else had been briefly moved in, then out again, leaving a strange drink can in the fridge.

Tally sat down on the bed, too stunned to cry. She knew she would start bawling soon, probably losing it at the worst possible time and place. Now that the encounter with Dr. Cable was over, her anger and defiance were fading, and there was nothing left to sustain her. Her stuff was gone, her future was gone, only the view out the window remained.

She sat and stared, having to remind herself every few minutes that it had all really happened: the cruel pretties, the strange buildings on the edge of town, the terrible ultimatum from Dr. Cable. Tally felt as if some wild trick had gone horribly wrong. A weird and horrible new reality had opened up, devouring the world she knew and understood.

All she had left was the small duffel bag she'd packed for the hospital. She couldn't even remember carrying it all the way back here. Tally pulled out the few clothes, which she'd shoved in at random, and found Shay's note.

She read it, looking for clues.

Take the coaster straight past the gap,
until you find one that's long and flat.
Cold is the sea and watch for breaks.
At the second make the worst mistake.
Four days later take the side you despise,
and look in the flowers for fire-bug eyes.
Once they're found, enjoy the flight.
Then wait on the bald head until it's light.

Hardly any of it made sense to her, only bits and pieces. Shay had obviously meant to hide the meaning from anyone else reading it, using references only the two of them would understand. Her paranoia made a lot more sense now. Having met Dr. Cable, Tally could see why David wanted to keep his city—or camp, or whatever it was—a secret.

As Tally held the note, she realized that it was what Dr. Cable had wanted. The woman had been sitting across the room from the letter the whole time, but they'd never bothered to search her. That meant that Tally had kept Shay's secret, and that she still had something to bargain with.

It also meant that Special Circumstances could make mistakes.

Tally saw the other uglies come back in before lunchtime. As they filed off the school transport, all of them craned their necks to look up at her window. A few pointed before she ducked back into the shadows. Minutes later Tally could hear kids in the hall outside, growing silent as they passed her door. A few even giggled, as new uglies always did when tried to keep quiet.

Were they *laughing* at her?

Her rumbling stomach reminded Tally that she hadn't eaten breakfast, or dinner the night before. You weren't supposed to have food or water for sixteen hours before the operation. She was starving.

But she stayed in her room until lunch was over. She couldn't face a cafeteria full of uglies watching her every move, wondering what she had done to deserve her still-ugly face. When she couldn't stand her hunger anymore, Tally stole upstairs to the roof deck, where they put out leftovers for whoever wanted them.

A few uglies saw her in the hall. They clammed up and stood aside as Tally passed, as if she were contagious. What had the minders told them? Tally wondered. That she'd pulled one too many tricks? That she was inoperable, an ugly-for-life? Or just that she was a Special Circumstance?

Everywhere she went, eyes looked away, but it was the most *visible* she'd ever felt.

A plate was set out for her on the roof deck, sealed in plastic wrap, her name stuck to it. Someone had noticed that she hadn't eaten. And, of course, everyone would realize that she was in hiding.

The sight of the plate of food, wilted and solitary, made the suppressed tears well up in her eyes. Tally's throat burned as if she'd swallowed something sharp, and it was all she could do to get back to her room before she burst into loud, jagged sobs.

When she got there, Tally found that she hadn't forgotten to bring the plate. She ate while she cried, tasting the salt of her tears in every bite.

*

Her parents came by about an hour later.

Ellie swept in first, gathering Tally into a hug that emptied her lungs and lifted her feet off the ground. "Tally, my poor baby!"

"Now don't injure the girl, Ellie. She's had a tough day."

Even without oxygen, it felt good inside the crushing embrace. Ellie always smelled just right, like a mom, and Tally always felt like a littlie in her arms. Released after what was probably a solid minute, but still too soon, Tally stepped back, hoping that she wouldn't cry again. She looked at her parents sheepishly, wondering what they must be thinking. She felt like a total failure. "I didn't know you guys were coming."

"Of course we came," Ellie said.

Sol shook his head. "I've never heard of anything like this happening. It's ridiculous. And we'll get to the bottom of it, don't you worry!"

Tally felt a weight lift from her shoulders. Finally there was someone else on her side. Her father's middle-pretty eyes twinkled with calm certainty. There was no question that he would sort everything out.

"What did they tell you?" Tally asked.

Sol gestured, and Tally sat down on the bed. Ellie settled beside her while he paced back and forth across the small room.

"Well, they told us about this Shay girl. Sounds like she's a lot of trouble."

"Sol!" Ellie interrupted. "The poor girl's missing."

"Sounds like she wants to be missing."

Her mother pursed her lips in silence.

"It's not her fault, Sol," Tally said. "She just didn't want to turn pretty."

"So, she's an independent thinker. Fine. But she should have had better sense than to drag someone else down with her."

"She didn't drag me anywhere. I'm right here." Tally looked out the window at the familiar view of New Pretty Town. "Where I'll be forever, apparently."

"Now, now," Ellie said. "They said that once you've helped them find this Shay girl, everything should go ahead as normal."

"It won't make any difference if the operation happens a few days late. It'll be a great story when you're old." Sol chuckled.

Tally bit her lip. "I don't think I can help them."

"Well, you just do your best," Ellie said.

"But I can't. I mean, I promised Shay that I wouldn't tell anyone her plans."

They were silent for a moment.

Sol sat down, taking one of her hands in his. They felt so warm and strong, almost as wrinkled as a crumbly's from days spent working in his wood shop. Tally realized that she hadn't visited her parents since the week of summer break, when she'd mostly been anxious to get back to hanging out with Shay full-time. But it was good to see them now.

"Tally, we all make promises when we're little. That's part of being an ugly—everything's exciting and intense and important, but you have to grow out of it. After all, you don't owe this girl anything. She's done nothing but cause you trouble."

Ellie took her other hand. "And you'll only be helping her, Tally. Who knows where she is now and what's happening to her? I'm surprised you let her run off like that. Don't you know how dangerous it is out there?"

Tally found herself nodding. Looking into Sol's and Ellie's faces, everything seemed so clear. Maybe cooperating with Dr. Cable would really be helping Shay, and would set things back on course for herself. But the thought of Dr. Cable made her wince. "You should have seen these people. The ones investigating Shay? They look like . . ."

Sol laughed. "I guess it would be a bit of a shock at your age, Tally. But of course we old folks know all about Special Circumstances. They may be tough, but they're just doing their jobs, you know. It's a tough world out there."

Tally sighed. Maybe her reluctance was just because the cruel pretties had scared her so much. "Have you ever met them? I couldn't believe the way they looked."

Ellie furrowed her brow. "Well, I can't say I've actually *met* one."

Sol frowned, then broke into a laugh. "Well, you wouldn't *want* to meet one, Ellie. And Tally, if you do the right thing now, you probably won't ever meet one again. That sort of business is something we can all do without."

Tally looked at her father, and for a moment she saw something other than wisdom and confidence in his expression. It was almost too easy the way Sol laughed off Special Circumstances, dismissing everything that went on outside the city. For the first time in her life, Tally found herself listening to a middle pretty without being completely reassured, a realization that made her dizzy. And she couldn't shake the thought that Sol knew nothing about the outside world Shay had fled to.

Maybe most people just didn't *want* to know. Tally had

been taught all about the Rusties and early history, but at school they never said a single thing about people living outside the cities right now, people like David. Until she'd met Shay, Tally had never thought about it either.

But she couldn't dismiss the whole thing the way her father had.

And she had made Shay a solemn promise. Even if she was just an ugly, a promise was a promise. "Guys, I'm going to have to think about this."

For a moment, an awkward silence filled the room. She'd said something they hadn't expected.

Then Ellie laughed and patted her hand. "Well, of course you do, Tally."

Sol nodded, back in command. "We know you'll do the right thing."

"Sure. But in the meantime," Tally said, "maybe I could come home with you?"

Her parents shared another look of surprise.

"I mean, it's really weird being here now. Everyone knows that I . . . I'm not scheduled for classes anymore, so it would just be like coming home for autumn break, but a little early."

Sol recovered first, and patted her shoulder. "Now, Tally, don't you think it would be even stranger for you out in Crumblyville? I mean, there's no other kids out there this time of year."

"You're much better off here with the other children, darling," Ellie added. "You're only a few months older than some of them. And goodness, we don't have your room ready at all!"

"I don't care. Nothing could be worse than this," Tally said.

"Oh, just order up some more clothes, and get that wallscreen back the way you want it," Sol said.

"I didn't mean the room—"

"In any case," Ellie interrupted, "why make a fuss? This'll all be over in no time. Just have a nice chat with Special Circumstances, tell them everything, and you'll be headed where you really want to be."

They all looked out the window at the towers of New Pretty Town.

"I guess so."

"Sweetheart," Ellie said, patting her leg, "what other choice do you have?"

PERIS

During the daytime, she hid in her room.

Going anywhere else was pure torture. The uglies in her own dorm treated her like a walking disease, and anyone else who recognized her sooner or later asked, "Why aren't you pretty yet?"

It was strange. She'd been an ugly for four years, but a few extra days had brought home to her exactly what the word really meant. Tally peered into her mirror all day, noting every flaw, every deformity. Her thin lips pursed with unhappiness. Her hair grew even frizzier because she kept running her hands through it in frustration. A trio of zits exploded across her forehead, as if marking the days since her sixteenth birthday. Her watery, too-small eyes glared back at her, full of anger.

Only at night could she escape from the tiny room, the nervous stares, her own ugly face.

She fooled the minders and climbed out as usual, but she didn't feel much like any real tricks. There was no one to visit, no one to play a prank on, and the idea of crossing the river was too painful to consider. She had gotten a new hoverboard, and tricked it up like Shay had taught her, so at least she could fly at night.

But flying didn't feel the same. She was alone, it was getting cold at night, and no matter how fast she flew, Tally was trapped, and she knew it.

The fourth night in ugly exile she took her board up into the greenbelt, staying at the edge of town. She whipped it back and forth past the dark columns of tree trunks, shooting through them at top speed, so fast that her hands and face collected dozens of scratches from the branches blurring by.

After a few hours' flying had worn away some of her anguish, Tally had a happy realization: This was the best she'd ever ridden; she was almost as good as Shay now. Never once did the board dump her for getting too close to a tree, and her shoes held on to its grippy surface like they were glued there. She worked up a sweat even in the autumn chill, riding until her legs were tired, her ankles aching, her arms sore from being spread out like wings guiding her through the dark forest. If she rode this hard all night, Tally thought, maybe tomorrow she could sleep the hideous daylight away.

She flew until exhaustion forced her home.

When she crawled back into her room at dawn, someone was waiting there.

"Peris!"

His features burst into a radiant smile, big eyes flashing

beautifully in the early light. But when he looked closer, his expression changed. "What happened to your face, Squint?"

Tally blinked. "Haven't you heard? They didn't do the—"

"Not that." Peris reached up and touched her cheek, which smarted under his fingertips. "You look like you've been juggling cats all night."

"Oh, yeah." Tally ran her fingers through her hair, and rummaged through a drawer. She pulled a medspray out, closed her eyes, and squirted herself in the face.

"Ow!" she yelped in the few seconds before the anesthetic kicked in. She sprayed her scratched hands as well. "Just a little midnight hoverboarding."

"A little past midnight, don't you think?"

Out the window, the sun was just beginning to turn the towers of New Pretty Town pink. Cat-vomit pink. She looked at Peris, exhausted and confused. "How long have you been here?"

He shifted uncomfortably in her window chair. "Long enough."

"Sorry. I didn't know you were coming."

He raised his eyebrows in beautiful anguish. "Of course I came. The moment I figured out where you were, I came."

Tally turned away, unlacing her grippy shoes as she collected herself. She'd felt so abandoned since her birthday, it had never occurred to her that Peris would want to see her, especially not here in Uglyville. But here he was, worried, anxious, lovely.

"It's good to see you," she said, feeling tears come into her eyes. They were red and puffy most of the time these days.

He beamed up at her. "You too."

The thought of what she must look like was too much.

Tally collapsed onto the bed, covering her face with her hands and sobbing. Peris sat next to her and held her for a while as she cried, then wiped her nose and sat her up. "Look at you, Tally Youngblood."

She shook her head. "Please don't."

"You're an absolute mess."

Peris found a brush and ran it through her hair. She couldn't meet his eyes, and stared at the floor.

"So, do you always go hoverboarding in a blender?"

She shook her head, lightly touching the scratches on her face. "Just tree branches. At high speed."

"Oh, so getting yourself killed is your next brilliant trick. I guess that would just about top your current one."

"My current what?"

Peris rolled his eyes. "This whole trick where you haven't turned pretty yet. Very mysterious."

"Yeah. Some trick."

"When did *you* get modest, Squint? All my friends are fascinated."

She turned her puffy eyes to her friend, trying to figure out if he was kidding.

"I mean, I already told everyone about you after that fire alarm thing, but they're *really* dying to meet you now," he continued. "There's even a rumor that Special Circumstances is involved."

Tally blinked. Peris was serious.

"Well, that's true," she said. "They're the reason I'm still ugly."

Peris's big eyes widened even more. "Really? That is so bubbly!"

She sat up and frowned. "Did *everyone* know about them but me?"

"Well, I had no idea what anyone was talking about. Apparently, Specials are like gremlins; you blame them when anything weird happens. Some people think they're totally bogus, and no one I know has actually *seen* a Special."

Tally sighed. "Just my luck, I guess."

"So they're real?" Peris lowered his voice to a whisper. "Do they really look different? You know, *not* pretty."

"It's not that they're not pretty, Peris. But they're really . . ." Tally looked at him, gorgeous and hanging on every word. It felt so perfect to be sitting next to him, talking and touching, as if they'd never been apart. She smiled. "They're just not as pretty as you."

He laughed. "You'll have to tell me all about it. But don't you dare tell anyone else. Not yet. Everyone's going to be so intrigued. We can throw a big party when you get yourself prettied up."

She tried to smile. "Peris . . ."

"I know, you're probably not supposed to talk about it. But once you're across the river, just drop a few hints about Special-you-know-what and you'll get invited to all the parties! Just make sure you take me with you." He leaned closer. "There's even a rumor that all the bubbly jobs go to people who had tricky records as kids. But that's years from now. The main thing is to get you pretty already."

"But, Peris," she said, her stomach starting to hurt. "I don't think I'll . . ."

"You'll love it, Tally. Being pretty's the best thing ever. And I'll enjoy it about a million times more once you're there with me."

"I can't."

He frowned. "Can't what?"

Tally looked up at Peris, clutching his hand. "You see, they want me to tattle on a friend of mine. Someone I got to know really well. After you left."

"Tattle? Don't tell me this is all about some ugly-trick."

"Sort of."

"So, tattle away. How big a deal can it be?"

Tally turned away. "It's important, Peris. It's more than a trick. I made my friend a promise that I'd keep a secret for her."

His eyes narrowed, and for a moment he looked like the old Peris: serious, thoughtful, even a little bit unhappy. "Tally, you made me a promise too."

She swallowed and stared back at him. His eyes shone with tears.

"You promised you wouldn't do anything stupid, Tally. That you'd be with me soon. That we'd be pretty together."

She touched the scar on her palm, still there, even though Peris's had been rubbed away. He reached over and held her hand. "Best friends forever, Tally."

She knew that if she looked into his eyes again, it would be all over. One glance, and her resistance would evaporate. "Best friends forever?" she said.

"Forever."

She took a deep breath and let herself stare into his eyes. He looked so sad, so vulnerable and wounded. So perfect. Tally imagined herself by his side, just as beautiful, spending every day doing nothing but talking and laughing and having fun.

"You'll keep your promise, Tally?"

A shudder of exhaustion and relief went through her. She had it now, an excuse to break her vow. She'd made that promise to Peris, just as real, before she'd ever met Shay.

She had known him for years, and Shay for only a few months.

And Peris was right here, not out in some strange wilderness, and was looking at her with those eyes . . .

"Of course."

"Really?" He smiled, and it was as bright as the day-break outside.

"Yeah." The words came out so easily. "I'll be there as soon as I can. I promise."

He sighed and hugged her tight, rocking her softly. Tears rose up in her again.

Peris finally released her, and looked out at the sunny day.

"I should go." He waved at the door. "You know, before the . . . thingies . . . all wake up."

"Of course."

"It's almost past my bedtime, and you've got a big day ahead of you."

Tally nodded. She'd never felt so exhausted. Her muscles ached, and her face and hands had started stinging again. But she was overwhelmed with relief. This nightmare had begun three months ago, when Peris went across the river. And soon it would end.

"Okay, Peris. I'll see you soon. As soon as possible."

He hugged her again, kissed her salty, scratched cheeks, and whispered, "Maybe in just a couple of days. I'm so excited!"

He said good-bye and left, checking both ways down the corridor before departing. Tally looked out the window for another glance at Peris, and realized that a hovercar was waiting for him below. Pretties really did get whatever they wanted.

Tally wanted nothing more than to fall asleep, but acting on her decision couldn't wait. She knew that with Peris gone, the doubts would come back again and haunt her. She couldn't stand another day like this, not knowing if her ugly purgatory would ever end. And she'd promised Peris she'd be with him as soon as possible.

"I'm sorry, Shay," Tally said quietly.

Then she picked up her interface ring from where it had lain on the bedside table all night, and slipped it on. "Message to Dr. Cable, or whomever," she said to it. "I'll do what you want. Just let me sleep for a while. Message over."

Tally sighed, and let herself fall back onto the bed. She knew she should spray her scratches again before passing out, but the thought of moving made her whole body ache. A few dozen scratches wouldn't keep her from sleeping today. Nothing would.

Seconds later, the room spoke. "Reply from Dr. Cable: A car will be sent for you, arriving in twenty minutes."

"No," she mumbled, but realized that it would be useless to argue. Special Circumstances would come, they would wake her up, they would take her.

Tally decided to try for a few minutes of sleep. It would be better than nothing.

But for the next twenty minutes, she never once shut her eyes.

INFILTRATOR

The cruel pretties seemed even more unearthly to exhausted eyes. Tally felt like a mouse in a cage full of hawks, just waiting for one to swoop down and take her. The trip in the hovercar had been even more sickening this time.

She focused on the nausea eating away at her stomach, trying to forget why she was here. As Tally and her escort made their way down the hall, she tried to pull herself together, tucking in her shirt and tugging at her hair.

Dr. Cable certainly didn't look like she'd just gotten up. Tally tried without success to imagine what a tousled Dr. Cable would look like. Her darting, metal-gray eyes hardly seemed as if they would ever close long enough to sleep.

"So, Tally. You've reconsidered."

"Yes."

"And you'll answer all our questions now? Honestly and of your own free will?"

Tally snorted. "You're not giving me a choice."

Dr. Cable smiled. "We always have choices, Tally. You've made yours."

"Great. Thanks. Look, just ask your questions."

"Certainly. First of all, what on earth happened to your face?"

Tally sighed, one hand touching the scratches. "Trees."

"Trees?" Dr. Cable raised an eyebrow. "Very well. On a more important subject, what did you and Shay talk about the last time you saw her?"

Tally closed her eyes. This was it, the moment when she would break her vow to Shay. But a small voice in her exhausted brain reminded her that she was also keeping a promise. Now she could finally join Peris.

"She talked about going away. Running away with someone called David."

"Ah, yes, the mysterious David." Dr. Cable leaned back. "And did she say where she and David were going?"

“A place called the Smoke. Like a city, only smaller. And no one was in charge there, and no one was pretty.”

“And did she say where it was?”

“No, she didn’t, not really.” Tally sighed and pulled Shay’s crumpled note from her pocket. “But she left me these directions.”

Dr. Cable didn’t even look at the note. Instead, she pushed a piece of paper from her side of the desk over to Tally’s. Through bleary eyes, Tally saw that it was a 3-D copy of the note, perfect down to the slight incisions of Shay’s labored penmanship on the paper.

“We took the liberty of making a copy of that the first time you were here.”

Tally glared at Dr. Cable, realizing she’d been duped. “Then why do you need me? I don’t know anything more than what I just said. I didn’t ask her to tell me any more. And I didn’t go with her, because I just . . . wanted . . . to be *pretty*!” A lump rose in her throat, but Tally decided that under no circumstances—special or not—was she going to cry in front of Dr. Cable.

“I’m afraid that we find the instructions on the note rather cryptic, Tally.”

“You and me both.”

Dr. Cable’s hawk-eyes narrowed. “They seem to be designed to be read by someone who knows Shay quite well. By you, perhaps.”

“Yeah, well, I get some of it. But after the first couple of lines, I’m lost.”

“I’m sure it’s very difficult. Especially after a long night of . . . trees. I still think you can help us, however.”

Dr. Cable opened a small briefcase on the desk between them. Tally’s tired brain struggled to make sense of the objects in the case. A firestarter, a crumpled sleeping bag . . .

"Hey, that's like the survival stuff that Shay had."

"That's right, Tally. These ranger kits go missing every so often. Usually just about the same time that one of our uglies disappears."

"Well, mystery solved. Shay was all ready to travel to the Smoke with a bunch of that stuff."

"What else did she have?"

Tally shrugged. "A hoverboard. A special one, with solar."

"Of course a hoverboard. What is it about those things and miscreants? And what did Shay plan to eat, do you suppose?"

"She had food in packets. Dehydrated."

"Like this?" Dr. Cable produced a silvery food pack.

"Yeah. She had enough for four weeks." Tally took a deep breath. "Two weeks, if I'd gone along. More than enough, she said."

"Two weeks? Not so very far." Dr. Cable pulled a black knapsack from beside her desk and started to pack the various objects into it. "You might just make it."

"Make it? Make *what*?"

"The trip. To the Smoke."

"Me?"

"Tally, only you can understand these directions."

"I told you: I don't know what they mean!"

"But you will, once you're on the journey. And if you're . . . properly motivated."

"But I already told you everything you wanted to know. I gave you the note. You promised!"

Dr. Cable shook her head. "My promise, Tally, was that

you wouldn't be pretty until you helped us to the very best of your ability. I have every confidence that this is within your ability."

"But why me?"

"Listen carefully, Tally. Do you really think that this is the first time we've been told about David? Or the Smoke? Or found some scrawled directions about how to get there?"

Tally flinched at the razor-blade voice, turning away from the anger on the woman's cruel face. "I don't know."

"We've seen all this before. But whenever we go ourselves, we find nothing. Smoke, indeed."

The lump had return to Tally's throat. "So how am I supposed to find anything?"

Dr. Cable pulled the copy of Shay's note toward herself. "This last line, where it says to 'wait on the bald head,' clearly refers to a rendezvous point. You go there, you wait. Sooner or later, they'll pick you up. If I send a hovercar full of Specials, your friends will probably be a bit suspicious."

"You mean, you want me to go *alone*?"

Dr. Cable took a deep breath, a disgusted look on her face. "This isn't very complicated, Tally. You have had a change of heart. You have decided to run away, following your friend Shay. Just another ugly escaping the tyranny of beauty."

Tally looked up at the cruel face through a prism of gathering tears. "And then what?"

Dr. Cable pulled another object from the briefcase, a necklace with a little heart pendant. She pressed on its sides, and the heart clicked open. "Look inside."

Tally held the tiny heart up to her eye. "I can't see anything . . . ow!"

The pendant had flashed, blinding her for a moment. The heart made a little beep.

"The finder will only respond to your eye-print, Tally. Once it's activated, we'll be there within a few hours. We can travel very quickly." Cable dropped the necklace onto the desk. "But don't activate it until you're in the Smoke. This has taken us some time to set up. I want the real thing, Tally."

Tally blinked away the afterimage of the flash, trying to force her exhausted brain to think. She realized now that this had never been simply a matter of answering questions. They had always wanted her as a spy, an infiltrator. She wondered just how long this had been planned. How many times had Special Circumstances tried to get an ugly to work for them before? "I can't do this."

"You can, Tally. You must. Think of it as an adventure."

"Please. I've never even spent the whole night outside the city. Not alone."

Dr. Cable ignored the sob that had cut through Tally's words. "If you don't agree right now, I'll find someone else. And you'll be ugly forever."

Tally looked up, trying to see through the tears that were flowing freely now, to peer past Dr. Cable's cruel mask and find the truth. It was there in her dull, metal-gray eyes, a cold, terrible surety unlike anything a normal pretty could ever convey. Tally realized that the woman meant what she said.

Either Tally infiltrated the Smoke and betrayed Shay, or she'd be an ugly for life.

"I have to think."

"Your story will be that you ran away the night before your birthday," Dr. Cable said. "That means you've already got to make up for four lost days. Any more delays, and they won't believe you. They'll guess what happened. So decide now."

"I can't. I'm too tired."

Dr. Cable pointed at the wallscreen, and an image appeared. Like a mirror, but in close-up, it showed Tally as she looked right now: puffy-eyed and disheveled, exhaustion and red scratches marking her face, her hair sticking out in all directions, and her expression turning horrified as she beheld her own appearance.

"That's you, Tally. Forever."

"Turn it off . . ."

"Decide."

"Okay, I'll do it. Turn it off."

The wallscreen went dark.

Part II

THE SMOKE

There is no excellent beauty that hath not some strangeness in the proportion.
—Francis Bacon, *Essays, Civil and Moral*, "Of Beauty"

LEAVING

Tally left at midnight.

Dr. Cable had demanded that no one be told about her mission, even the dorm minders. It was fine if Peris spread rumors—no one believed the gossip of new pretties, anyway. But not even her parents would be officially informed that Tally had been forced to run away. Except for her little heart pendant, she was on her own.

She slipped out the usual way, out the window and down behind the recycler. Her interface ring remained on the bedside table, and Tally carried nothing but the survival knapsack and Shay's note. She almost forgot her belly sensor, but clipped it on just before she left. The moon was about half-full and growing. At least she'd have some light as she traveled.

A special long-range hoverboard was waiting under the dam. It hardly moved when she stepped on. Most boards gave a little as they adjusted to a rider's weight, bouncing like a diving board, but this one was absolutely firm. She snapped her fingers, and it rose under her, steady as concrete under her feet.

"Not bad," she said, then bit her lip. Since Shay had run away ten days ago, she'd started talking to herself. That wasn't a good sign. She was going to be completely alone for at least a few days now, and the last thing she needed was more imaginary conversations.

The board eased forward smoothly, climbing the embankment to the top of the dam. Once on the river, Tally pushed it faster, leaning forward until the river was a shining blur beneath her feet. The board didn't seem to have a speed governor—no safety warning sounded. Perhaps its only limits were the open space in front of her, metal in the ground below, and Tally's feet staying on board.

Speed was everything if she was going to make up for the last four days in limbo. If Tally showed up too long after her birthday, Shay might realize that her operation had been delayed. From there, she might guess that Tally wasn't an ordinary runaway.

The river passed beneath her faster and faster, and she reached the rapids in record time. Drops of spray stung like hailstones when she hit the first falls, and Tally leaned back to slow herself a bit. Still, she was taking the rapids faster than she ever had before.

Tally realized that this hoverboard was no ugly toy. It was the real thing. On its front end a half circle of lights glowed, giving feedback from the board's metal detector, which constantly searched ahead to see if there was enough iron in the ground to stay aloft. The lights stayed on solidly as she climbed the rapids, and Tally hoped that Shay was right about metal deposits being found in every river. Otherwise, this could be a very long trip.

Of course, at this speed she wouldn't have time to stop if the lights suddenly went out. Which would make it a very short trip.

But the lights stayed on, and Tally's nerves were soothed by the roar of white water, the cold slap of spray in her face, the thrill of bending her body through curve after curve in the moon-speckled darkness. The board was smarter than her old one, learning her moves in a matter of minutes. It was like graduating from a tricycle to a motorbike: scary, but thrilling.

Tally wondered if the route to the Smoke had a lot of rapids to ride. Maybe this really would be an adventure. Of course, at the end of the journey there would only be betrayal. Or worse, she would discover that Shay's trust in David had been misplaced, which could mean . . . anything. Probably something horrible.

She shivered, deciding not to think about that possibility again.

When Tally reached the turnoff, she slowed and turned the board around, taking a last look at the city. It shone brilliantly in the dark valley, so distant that she could blot it out with one hand. In the clear night air, Tally could make out individual fireworks unfolding like bright flowers, everything in perfect miniature. The wild around her seemed so much larger, the churning river full of power, the forest huge with the secrets hidden in its black depths.

She allowed herself a long stare at the city lights before she stepped onto shore, wondering when she would see her home again.

On the trail, Tally wondered how often she'd have to walk. The trip up the rapids had been the fastest she had ever flown, even quicker than the Special Circumstances hovercar dodging through city traffic. After that rush of speed, carrying the knapsack and board felt like being turned into a slug.

But soon enough the Rusty Ruins appeared below, and

the board's metal detector guided Tally to the natural vein of iron. She rode it down toward the crumbling towers, her nerves growing jumpy as the ruins rose up to blot out the half-moon. The broken buildings surrounded her, the scorched and silent cars passing below. Peering through the empty windows made her feel how alone she was, a solitary wanderer in an empty city.

"Take the coaster straight past the gap," she said aloud, an incantation to keep away any Rusty ghosts. At least that much of the note was crystal clear: The "coaster" had to be the roller coaster.

When the towering ruins gave way to flatter ground, Tally opened up the hoverboard. Reaching the roller coaster, she took the entire circuit at full speed. Maybe "straight past the gap" was the only important part of the clue, but Tally had decided to treat the note like a magic spell. Leaving out any part might make the whole thing meaningless.

And it felt good to ride fast and hard again, leaving the ghosts of the Rusty Ruins behind. As she whipped around tight turns and down steep descents, the world whirling around her, Tally felt like something caught in the wind, not knowing which direction the journey would ultimately take her.

A few seconds before she took the jump across the gap, the metal-detector lights winked out. The board dropped away, and her stomach seemed to go with it, leaving a hollow feeling inside. Her suspicion had proved right—at top speed, there hadn't been much warning.

Tally flew through the air in the silent darkness, the rush of her passage the only sound. She remembered her first time across the gap, how angry she'd been. A few days later it had turned into a joke between them, typical ugly stuff. But now Shay had done it again, disappearing like the track below, leaving Tally in free fall.

A count of five later, the lights flickered on, and the crash bracelets steadied her as the board reactivated, rising smoothly up under her feet with reassuring solidness. At the bottom of the hill the track turned, climbing into a steep corkscrew of turns. But Tally slowed and kept going ahead, murmuring, "straight past the gap."

The ruins continued under her feet. Out here they were almost completely submerged, only a few shapeless masses rising through the grasp of vegetation. But the Rusties had built solidly, in love with their wasteful skeletons of metal. The lights on the front of her board stayed bright.

"Until you find one that's long and flat," Tally said to herself. She had memorized the note backward and forward, but repeating the words hadn't made their meaning any clearer.

"One *what*?" was the question. A roller coaster? A gap? The first would be silly. Where would be the point of a long, flat roller coaster? A long, flat gap? Maybe that would describe a canyon, complete with a handy river at the bottom. But how could a canyon be flat?

Maybe "one" meant a one, like the number. Should she be looking for something that looked like a one? But a one was just a straight line, anyway, kind of long and flat already. So was *I*, the Roman numeral for one, except for the crossbars on top and bottom. Or the dot on the top if it was a small *i*.

"Thanks for the great clue, Shay," Tally said aloud. Talking to herself didn't seem like such a bad idea there in the outer ruins, where the relics of the Rusties struggled against the grip of creeping plants. Anything was better than ghostly silence. She passed concrete plains, vast expanses cracked by thrusting grasses. The windows of fallen walls stared up at her, sprouting weeds as if the earth had grown eyes.

She scanned the horizon, looking for clues. There was nothing long and flat that she could see. Peering down at the ground passing below, Tally could hardly make out anything in the weed-choked darkness. She might zoom right past whatever the clue referred to and not even know it, and have to retrace her path in daylight. But how would she know when she'd gone too far? "Thanks, Shay," she repeated.

Then she spotted something on the ground, and stopped.

Through the shroud of weeds and rubble, geometrical shapes had appeared—a series of rectangles in a line. She lowered the board and saw that below her was a track with metal rails and wooden crossbars—like the roller coaster, but much bigger. And it went in a straight line, as far as she could see.

"Take the coaster straight past the gap, until you find one that's long and flat."

This thing was a roller coaster, but long and flat.

"But what's it *for*?" she wondered aloud. What fun was a roller coaster without any turns or climbs?

She shrugged. However the Rusties got their kicks, this was perfect for a hoverboard. The track stretched off in two directions, but it was easy enough to tell which one to take. One led back the way she'd come, toward the center of the ruins. The other headed outward, northward and angling toward the sea.

"Cold is the sea," she quoted from the next line of Shay's note, and wondered how far north she was going.

Tally brought the hoverboard up to speed, pleased that she'd found the answer. If all of Shay's little riddles were this easy to solve, this whole trip was going to a breeze.

SPAGBOL

She made good time that night.

The track zoomed along beneath her, tracing slow arcs around hills, crossing rivers on crumbling bridges, always headed toward the sea. Twice it took her through other Rusty ruins, smaller towns further along in their disintegration. Only a few twisted shapes of metal remained, rising above the trees like skeletal fingers grasping at the air. Burned-out groundcars were everywhere, choking the streets out of town, twisted together in the collisions of the Rusties' last panic.

Near the center of one ruined town, she discovered what the long, flat roller coaster was all about. In a nest of tracks tangled up like a huge circuit board, she found a few rotting roller-coaster cars, huge rolling containers full of Rusty stuff, unidentifiable piles of rust and plastic. Tally remembered now that Rusty cities weren't self-sufficient, and were always trading with one another, when they weren't fighting over who had more stuff. They must have used the flat roller coaster to move trade from town to town.

As the sky began to grow light, Tally heard the sound of the sea in the distance, a faint roar coming from across the horizon. She could smell salt in the air, which brought back memories of going to the ocean with Ellie and Sol as a littlie.

"Cold is the sea and watch for breaks," Shay's note read. Soon, Tally would be able to see the waves breaking on the shore. Maybe she was close to the next clue.

Tally wondered how much time she'd made up with her new hoverboard. She increased its speed, wrapping her dorm jacket around herself in the predawn chill. The track was slowly climbing now, cutting through formations of chalky rock. She remembered white cliffs towering over the ocean, swarming with seabirds nesting in high caves.

Those camping trips with Sol and Ellie felt as if they'd happened a hundred years ago. She wondered if there was some operation that could make her back into a littlie again, forever.

Suddenly, a gap opened up in front of Tally, spanned by a crumbling bridge. An instant later she saw that the bridge didn't make it all the way across, and there was no river full of metal deposits beneath it to catch her. Just a precipitous drop to the sea.

Tally spun her board sideways into a skid. Her knees bent under the force of braking, her grippy shoes squealing as they slipped across the riding surface, her body turning almost parallel to the ground.

But the ground was gone.

A deep chasm opened up under her, a fissure cut into the cliffs by the sea. Boiling waves crashed into the narrow channel, their whitecaps glowing in the darkness, their hungry roars reaching her ears. The board's metal-detector lights flickered out one by one as Tally left the splintered end of the iron bridge behind.

She felt the board lose purchase, slipping downward.

A thought flashed through her mind: If she jumped now, she could make a grab for the end of the broken bridge. But then the hoverboard would tumble into the chasm behind her, leaving her stranded.

The board finally halted in its slide out into midair, but Tally was still descending. The last fingers of the crumbling bridge were *above* her now, out of reach. The board inched downward, metal-detector lights flickering off one by one as the magnets lost their grip. She was too heavy. Tally slipped off the knapsack, ready to hurl it down. But how could she survive without it? Her only choice would be to return to the city for more supplies, which would lose two more days. A cold wind off the ocean blew up the chasm, goose-pimpling her arms like the chill of death.

But the breeze buoyed the hoverboard, and for a moment she neither rose nor fell. Then the board started to slip downward again. . . .

Tally thrust her hands into the pockets of her jacket and spread her arms, making a sail to catch the wind. A stronger gust struck, lifting her slightly, taking some weight off the board, and one of the metal-detector lights flickered stronger.

Like a bird with outstretched wings, she began to rise.

The lifters gradually regained purchase on the track, until the hoverboard had brought her level with the broken end of the bridge. She coaxed it carefully back over the cliff's edge, a huge shiver passing through her body as the board passed over solid ground. Tally stepped off, legs shaking.

"Cold is the sea and watch for *breaks,*" she said hoarsely. How could she have been so stupid, speeding up just when Shay's note said to be careful?

Tally collapsed onto the ground, suddenly dizzy and

tired. Her mind replayed the chasm opening up, the waves below smashing indifferently against the jagged rocks. *She* could have been down there, battered again and again until there was nothing left.

This was the wild, she reminded herself. Mistakes had serious consequences.

Even before Tally's heart had stopped pounding, her stomach growled.

She reached into her knapsack for the water purifier, which she'd filled at the last river, and emptied the muck-trap. A spoonful of brown sludge that it had filtered from the water glopped out. "Eww," she said, opening the top to peer in. It looked clear, and smelled like water.

She took a much needed drink, but saved most to make dinner, or breakfast, whatever it was. Tally planned to do most of her traveling at night, letting the hoverboard recharge in sunlight, wasting no time.

Reaching into the waterproof bag, she pulled out a food packet at random. "'SpagBol,'" she read from the label, and shrugged. Unwrapped, it looked and felt like a finger-size knot of dried yarn. She dropped it into the purifier, which made burbling noises as it came to a boil.

When Tally glanced out at the glowing horizon, her eyes opened wide. She'd never seen dawn from outside the city before. Like most uglies, she was rarely up early enough, and in any case the horizon was always hidden behind the skyline of New Pretty Town. The sight of a real sunrise amazed her.

A band of orange and yellow ignited the sky, glorious and unexpected, as spectacular as fireworks, but changing at a stately, barely perceptible pace. That's how things were out here in the wild, she was learning. Dangerous or beautiful. Or both.

The purifier *pinged*. Tally opened the top and looked inside. It was noodles with a red sauce, with small kernels of soymeat, and it smelled delicious. She looked at the label again. "SpagBol . . . spaghetti Bolognese!"

She found a fork in the knapsack and ate hungrily. With the sunrise warming her and the crash of the sea rumbling below, it was the best meal she'd had for ages.

The hoverboard still had some charge left, so after breakfast she decided to keep moving. She reread the first few lines of Shay's note:

> Take the coaster straight past the gap,
> until you find one that's long and flat.
> Cold is the sea and watch for breaks.
> At the second make the worst mistake.

If "the second" meant a second broken bridge, Tally wanted to run into it in daylight. If she'd spotted the gap a split second later, she would have ended up so much SpagBol at the bottom of the cliffs.

But her first problem was getting across the chasm. It was much wider than the gap in the roller coaster, definitely too far to jump. Walking looked like the only way around. She hiked inland through the scrubby grass, her legs grateful for a stretch after the long night on board. Soon the chasm closed, and an hour later she had hiked back up the other side.

Tally flew much slower now, eyes fixed ahead, daring only an occasional glimpse at the view around her.

Mountains rose up on her right, tall enough that snow capped their tops even in the early autumn chill. Tally had always thought of the city as huge, a whole world in itself, but the scale of everything out here was so much grander. And so beautiful. She could see why people used to live out in nature, even if there weren't any party towers or mansions. Or even dorms.

The thought of home, however, reminded Tally how much her sore muscles would love a hot bath. She imagined a giant bathtub, like they had in New Pretty Town, with whirlpool jets and a big packet of massage bubbles dissolving in it. She wondered if the water purifier could boil enough water to fill a tub, in the unlikely event that she found one. How did they bathe in the Smoke? Tally wondered what she'd smell like when she arrived, after days without a bath. Was there soap in the survival kit? Shampoo? There certainly weren't any towels. Tally had never realized how much *stuff* she'd needed before.

The second break in the track came up after another hour: a crumbling bridge over a river that snaked down from the mountains.

Tally came to a controlled stop and peered over the edge. The drop wasn't as bad as the first chasm, but it was still deep enough to be deadly. Too wide to jump. Hiking around it would take forever. The river gorge stretched away, with no easy way down in sight.

"At the second make the worst mistake," she murmured.

Some clue. Anything she did right now would be a mistake. Her brain was too tired to handle this, and the board was short on power, anyway.

Midmorning, it was time to sleep.

But first she had to unfold the hoverboard. The Special who'd instructed her had explained that it needed as much surface area in the sun as possible while it recharged. She pulled the release tabs, and it came apart. It opened like a book in her hands, becoming two hoverboards, then each of those opened up, and then those, unfolding like a string of paper dolls. Finally, Tally had eight hoverboards connected side-to-side, twice as wide as she was tall, no thicker than a stiff sheet of paper. The whole thing fluttered in the stiff ocean breeze like a giant kite, though the board's magnets kept it from blowing away.

Tally laid it flat, stretched out in the sun, where its metallic surface turned jet black as it drank in solar energy. In a few hours it would be charged up and ready to ride again. She just hoped it would go back together as easily as it had pulled apart.

Tally pulled out her sleeping bag, yanked it out of its pack, and wriggled inside, still in her clothes. "Pajamas," she added to her list of things she missed about the city.

She made a pillow of her jacket, struggled out of her shirt, and covered her head with it. She could already feel a hint of burn on her nose, and realized she had forgotten to stick on a sunblock patch after daybreak. Perfect. A little red and flaking skin should go quite nicely with the scratches on her ugly face.

Sleep didn't come. The day was getting warm, and it felt weird lying there in the open. The cries of seabirds rang in her head. Tally sighed and sat up. Maybe if she had a little more to eat.

She pulled out food packets one by one. The labels read:

SpagBol
SpagBol
SpagBol
SpagBol
SpagBol . . .

Tally counted forty-one more packets, enough for three SpagBols a day for two weeks. She leaned back and closed her eyes, suddenly exhausted. "Thank you, Dr. Cable."

A few minutes later, Tally was asleep.

THE WORST MISTAKE

She was flying, skimming the ground with no track under her, not even a hoverboard, keeping herself aloft by sheer willpower and the wind in her outspread jacket. She skirted the edge of a massive cliff that overlooked a huge, black ocean. A flock of seabirds pursued her, their wild screams beating at her ears like Dr. Cable's razor-edged voice.

Suddenly, the stony cliffs beneath her cracked and fissured. A huge rift opened up, the ocean rushing in with a roar that drowned the seabirds' cries. She found herself tumbling through the air, falling down toward the black water.

The ocean swallowed her, filling her lungs, freezing her heart so that she couldn't cry out. . . .

"No!" Tally shouted, sitting bolt upright.

A cold wind off the sea struck her face, clearing her head. Tally looked around, realizing that she was up on the cliffs, tangled in her sleeping bag. Tired, hungry, and desperate to pee, but not falling into oblivion.

She took a deep breath. The seabirds still cried around her, but in the distance.

That last dream had been only one of many falling nightmares.

Night was coming, the sun setting over the ocean, turning the water bloodred. Tally pulled her shirt and jacket on before daring to emerge from the sleeping bag. The temperature seemed to be dropping by the minute, the light fading before her eyes. She hurried to get ready to go.

The hoverboard was the tricky part. Its unfolded surface had gotten wet, covered with a fine layer of ocean spray and dew. Tally tried to wipe it off with her jacket sleeve, but there was too much water and not enough jacket. The wet board folded up easily enough, but it felt too heavy when she was done, as if the water was still trapped between the layers. The board's operation light turned yellow, and Tally looked closely. The sides of the board were gradually oozing the water away. "Fine. Gives me time to eat."

Tally pulled out a packet of SpagBol, then realized that her purifier was empty. The only ready source of water was at the bottom of the cliff, and there was no way down. She wrung out her wet jacket, which produced a few good *squooshes,* then scraped off handfuls of the water oozing from the board until the purifier was half-full. The result was a dense, overspiced SpagBol that required lots of chewing.

By the time she was done with the unhappy meal, the board's light had turned green.

"Okay, ready to go," Tally said to herself. But where? She stood still, pondering, one foot on the board and one on the ground.

Shay's note read, "At the second make the worst mistake."

Making a mistake shouldn't be that hard. But what was the *worst* mistake? She'd almost killed herself once today already.

Tally remembered her dream. Falling into the gorge would count as a pretty bad mistake. She stepped onto the board and edged it to the crumbling end of the bridge, looking down to where the river met the sea far below.

If she climbed down, her only possible path would be to follow the river upstream. Maybe that's what the clue meant. But the steep cliff showed no obvious path, not even a handhold.

Of course, a vein of iron in the cliff might carry her down safely. Her eyes scanned the walls of the gorge, searching for the reddish color of iron. A few spots looked promising, but in the growing darkness, she couldn't be certain.

"Great." Tally realized that she'd slept too long. Waiting for dawn would be twelve hours lost, and she didn't have any more water.

The only other option was to hike upriver atop the cliff. But it might be days before she reached a place to climb down. And how would she see it at night?

She had to make up time, not blunder around in the dark.

Tally swallowed, coming to a decision. There had to be a way down on her board. Maybe she was making a mistake, but that's what the clue called for. She edged the board off the bridge until it began to lose purchase. It slipped down the cliffside, descending faster as it left the metal of the track behind.

Tally's eye searched desperately for any sign of iron in the cliff. She eased the board forward, bringing it closer to the wall of stone, but saw nothing. A few of the board's metal-detector lights flickered out. Any lower, and she was going to fall.

This wasn't going to work. Tally snapped her fingers. The board slowed for a second, trying to climb, but then shivered and continued to descend.

Too late.

Tally spread her jacket, but the air in the gorge was still. She spotted a rusty-looking streak in the wall of stone and coaxed the board closer, but it turned out to be just a slimy smear of lichen. The board slipped downward faster and faster, the metal-detector lights flickering out one by one.

Finally, the board went dead.

Tally realized that this mistake might be her last.

She fell like a rock, down toward the crashing waves. Just like in the dream, her voice felt choked by a freezing hand, as if her lungs were already filled with water. The board tumbled below her, spinning like a falling leaf.

Tally closed her eyes, waiting for the shattering impact of cold water.

Suddenly, something grabbed her by the wrists and yanked her up cruelly, spinning her in the air. Her shoulders screamed with pain, and she spun once all the way around like a gymnast on the rings.

Tally opened her eyes and blinked. She was being lowered onto the hoverboard, which waited rock-steady just above the water.

"What the . . . ?" she wondered aloud. Then, as her feet came to rest, Tally realized what had happened.

The river had caught her. It had been dumping metal deposits there for centuries, or however long rivers lasted, and the board's magnets had found purchase just in time.

"Saved, more or less," Tally muttered. She rubbed her shoulders, which ached from being caught by the crash bracelets, and wondered how far you had to fall before the bracelets would rip your arms out of their sockets.

But she'd made it down. The river stretched out in front of her, winding its way into the snowcapped mountains. Tally shivered in the ocean breeze and pulled her soggy jacket tighter around her.

"'Four days later take the side you despise,'" she quoted Shay's note. "Four days. Might as well get started."

After her first sunburn, Tally stuck a sunblock patch onto her skin every morning at dawn. But even with only a few hours in the sun each day, her already brown arms gradually deepened in color.

SpagBol never again tasted as good as it had that first time on the cliffs. Tally's meals ranged from decent to odious. The worst were SpagBol breakfasts, around sunset, when the mere thought of more noodles made her never want to eat again. She almost wished she would run out of the stuff and be forced to either catch a fish and cook it, or simply starve, losing her ugly-fat the hard way.

What Tally really dreaded was running out of toilet paper. Her only roll was already half-gone, and she rationed it strictly now, counting the sheets. And every day, she smelled a little worse.

On the third day up the river, she decided to take a bath.

Tally awoke, an hour before sunset as usual, feeling sticky inside the sleeping bag. She'd washed her clothes that morning and left them to dry on a rock. The thought of getting into clean clothes with dirty skin made her flesh crawl.

The water in the river was fast-moving, and left almost nothing in the muck-trap of the purifier, which meant it was clean. It was icy cold, though, probably fed by melting snow in the approaching mountains. Tally prayed it would be slightly less freezing late in the day, after the sun had had a chance to warm it up.

The survival kit did have soap, it turned out—a few disposable packets tucked into a corner of the knapsack. Tally clenched one in her hand as she stood at the edge of the river, wearing nothing but the sensor clipped to her belly ring, shivering in the cool breeze.

"Here we go," she said, trying to keep her teeth from chattering.

She put one foot in and jumped back from the icy streak of agony that shot into her leg. Apparently, there would be no easing slowly into the water. She had to take a running jump.

Tally walked along the riverbank, searching for a good place to leap in, slowly gathering her courage. She realized she'd never been naked outside before. In the city, everywhere outdoors was public, but she hadn't seen another human face for days. The world seemed to belong to her. Even in the cool air, the sun felt wonderful on her skin.

She clenched her teeth and faced the river. Standing here pondering the wild wasn't going to get her clean. Just a few steps and a leap, and gravity would do the rest.

She counted down from five, then counted down from ten, neither of which worked. Then she realized that she was getting cold just standing there.

Finally, Tally jumped.

The freezing water closed like a fist around her. It paralyzed every muscle, turning her hands into shivering claws.

For a moment, Tally wondered how she would make it back to shore. Maybe she would just expire here, slipping under the icy water forever.

She took a deep, shuddering breath, reminding herself that the people before the Rusties must have taken baths in freezing streams all the time. Tally clenched her teeth to stop them chattering, and dipped her head under the water and out, whipping wet hair onto her back.

A few moments later an unlikely kernel of warmth ignited in her stomach, as if the icy water had activated some secret reserve of energy within her body. Her eyes opened wide, and she found herself whooping with excitement. The mountains, towering above her after three nights' travel inland, seemed suddenly crystal clear, their snowy peaks catching the last rays of the setting sun. Tally's heart pounded fiercely, her blood spreading unexpected warmth throughout her body.

But the burst of energy was burning quickly. She fumbled the soap packet open, squishing it between her fingers, across her skin, and into her hair. Another dunking and she was ready to get out.

Looking back at the shore, Tally realized that she'd been carried away from her camp by the river's current. She swam a few strokes upstream, then trudged toward the rocky shore.

Waist-high in the water, already shivering from the breeze on her wet body, Tally heard something that made her heart freeze.

Something was coming. Something big.

THE SIDE YOU DESPISE

Thunder came from the sky, like a giant drum beating fiercely and fast, forcing its way into her head and chest. It seemed to rattle the whole horizon, making the surface of the river shimmer with every thud.

Tally crouched low in the water, sinking to her neck just before the machine appeared.

It came from the direction of the mountains, flying low and kicking up dust in a dozen separate windstorms in its wake. It was much bigger than a hovercar, and a hundred times louder. Apparently without magnets, it beat the air into submission with a half-invisible disk shimmering in the sun.

When the machine reached the river, it banked into a turn. Its passage churned the water, sending out circular waves as if some huge stone were skimming across the surface. Tally saw people inside, looking down at her camp. The unfolded hoverboard pitched in the windstorm, its magnets fighting to keep it on the ground. Her knapsack disappeared in the dust, and she saw clothing, the sleeping bag, and packets of SpagBol scattering in the machine's wake.

Tally sank lower into the frantic water, struck by the thought that she would be left here, naked and alone, with nothing. She was already half frozen.

But the machine dipped forward, just like a hoverboard, and moved on. It headed toward the sea, vanishing as quickly as it had appeared, leaving her ears pounding and the river's surface boiling.

Tally crept out shivering. Her body felt ice cold, her

fingers barely able to clench into a fist. She made her way back to her camp, grasping clothes to her body, putting them on before the setting sun could dry her. She sat and wrapped her arms around herself until the shaking stopped, glancing fearfully at the red horizon every few seconds.

The damage was less than she'd feared. The hoverboard's operation light was green, and her knapsack, dusty but unharmed. After a search for SpagBol and a count of the remaining packets, Tally found that she had lost only two. But the sleeping bag was shredded. Something had chopped it to pieces.

Tally swallowed. There was nothing left of the bag bigger than a handkerchief. What if she had been in it when the machine had come?

She folded the hoverboard quickly and packed everything away. The board was ready to go almost instantly. At least the strange machine's windstorm had dried it off.

"Thanks a lot," Tally said as she stepped on, leaning forward as the sun began to set. She was anxious to leave the campsite behind her as quickly as possible, in case they came back.

But who were they? The flying machine had been just like what Tally imagined when her teachers had described Rusty contraptions: a portable tornado crashing along, destroying everything in its path. Tally had read about aircraft that shattered windows as they flew past, armored war vehicles that could drive straight through a house.

But the Rusties had been gone a long time. Who would be stupid enough to rebuild their insane machines?

Tally rode into the growing darkness, her eyes peeled for any signs of the next clue—"Four days later take the side you despise"—and for whatever other surprises the night would bring.

One thing was certain now: She wasn't alone out here.

Later that night, the river branched in two.

Tally cruised to a halt, surveying the junction. One of the branches was clearly larger, the other more like a broad stream. A "tributary," she remembered, was the name for a small river that fed into a larger one.

Probably she should just stay on the main river. But she'd been traveling for just three days, and her hoverboard was a lot faster than most. Maybe it was time for the next clue.

"Four days later take the side you despise," Tally muttered.

She peered at the two rivers in the light from the moon, which was almost full now. Which river did she despise? Or which one would Shay *think* she despised? They both looked pretty ordinary to her. She squinted into the distance. Maybe one led toward something despicable that would be visible in daylight.

But waiting would mean losing a night's travel, and sleeping in the cold and dark without a sleeping bag.

Tally reminded herself that the clue might not be about this junction. Maybe she should just stay on the big river until something more obvious came up. Why would Shay call the two rivers "sides," anyway? If she'd meant this junction, wouldn't it be "take the direction you despise"?

"The side you despise," Tally mumbled, remembering something.

Her fingers went to her face. When she had showed Shay her pretty morphos, Tally had mentioned how she always started by doubling her left side—that she had always hated the right side of her face. Which was exactly the sort of thing that Shay would remember.

Was this Shay's way of telling her to take a right?

Branching to the right was the smaller river, the tributary. The mountains were closer in that direction. Maybe she was drawing near the Smoke.

She stared at the two rivers in the darkness, one big and one small, and remembered Shay saying that pretty symmetry was silly, because she'd rather have a face with two different sides.

Tally hadn't realized it at the time, but that had been an important conversation for Shay, the first time she had talked about wanting to stay ugly. If only Tally had noticed at the time, maybe she could have talked Shay out of running away. And they'd both be in a party tower right now, together and pretty.

"Right it is." Tally sighed, and eased her board onto the smaller river.

By the time the sun rose, Tally knew she had made the right choice.

As the tributary climbed its way into the mountains, the fields around her filled with flowers. Soon the brilliant white bonnets were as thick as grass, driving every other color from the landscape. In the dawn light, it was as if the earth were glowing from within.

"'And look in the flowers for fire-bug eyes,'" Tally said to herself, wondering if she should get off the board. Maybe there was some kind of bug with fiery eyes she should be looking for.

She drifted to shore and stepped off.

The flowers came right up to the edge of the water. Tally knelt to inspect one closely. The five long white petals curved delicately up from the stem and around its mouth, which contained just a hint of yellow deep inside. One of the petals below the mouth was longer, arching down almost to the ground. Motion caught her eye, and she spotted a small bird hovering among the flowers, flitting from one to the next to alight on the longest petal, thrusting its beak into one after another.

"They're so beautiful," she said. And there were so many of them. She wanted to lie down in the flowers and sleep.

But she couldn't see anything that might be "fire-bug eyes." Tally stood, scanning the horizon. Nothing met her gaze but hills, blinding white with flowers, and the glimmering river climbing up into the mountains. It all looked so peaceful, a different world from the one that the flying machine had shattered last night.

She stepped back on the board and continued, slower now as she looked carefully for whatever might fit Shay's clue, remembering to stick on a sunblock patch as the sun rose higher.

The river climbed higher into the hills. From up there, Tally saw bare stretches among the flowers, expanses of dry, sandy earth. The patchy landscape was a strange sight, like a beautiful painting that someone had taken sandpaper to.

She got off her board several times to inspect the flowers, looking for insects or anything else that might match the words "fire-bug eyes." But as the day wore on, nothing made sense.

By the time noon approached the tributary was gradually growing smaller. Sooner or later, she would reach its source, a mountain spring or melting snowdrift, and then she'd have to walk. Tired after the long night, she decided to make camp.

Her eyes scanned the sky, wondering if any more of the Rusty flying machines were around. The idea of another one crashing into her in her sleep terrified her. Who knew what the people inside the thing wanted? If she hadn't been hidden in the water the night before, what would they have done with her?

One thing was certain: The shiny solar cells of the hoverboard would be obvious from the air. Tally checked the charge; more than half remained thanks to her slow speed and the bright sun now overhead. She unfolded the hoverboard, but only halfway, and hid it among the tallest flowers she could find. Then she hiked to the top of a nearby hill. From up there Tally could keep her eye on the hoverboard, and hear and see anything approaching from the air. She decided to repack her knapsack before she went to sleep, so she could bolt at a moment's notice.

It was the best she could do.

After a mildly revolting packet of SpagBol, Tally curled up in a spot where the white flowers were tall enough to hide her. The breeze stirred their long stalks, and shadows danced on her closed eyelids.

Tally felt strangely exposed without her sleeping bag, lying there in her clothes, but the warm sun and the long night's travel put her quickly to sleep.

When she awoke, the world was on fire.

FIRESTORM

At first there was a sound like a roaring wind in her dreams.

Then a tearing noise filled the air, the crackle of dry brush inflamed, and the smell of smoke swept over Tally, bringing her suddenly and completely awake.

Billowing clouds of smoke surrounded her, blotting out the sky. A ragged wall of flame moved through the flowers, giving off a wave of blistering heat. She grabbed her knapsack and stumbled down the hill away from the fire.

Tally had no idea in which direction the river lay. Nothing was visible through the dense clouds. Her lungs fought for air in the foul brown smoke.

Then she spotted a few rays from the setting sun breaching the billows, and she oriented herself. The river was back toward the flame, on the other side of the hill.

Tally retraced her path to the top of the hill and peered down through the smoke. The fire was growing stronger. Fingers of it shot up the hill, leaping from one beautiful flower to another, leaving them scorched and black. Tally caught the glimmer of the river through the smoke, but the heat pushed her back.

She stumbled down the other side again, coughing and spitting, one thought in her mind: Was her hoverboard already engulfed in flames?

Tally had to get to the river. The water was the only place safe from the rampaging fire. If she couldn't go over the hill, maybe she could go around.

She descended the slope at full tilt. There were a few spots burning on this side, but nothing like the galloping flame behind her. She reached level ground and made her way around the base of the hill, crouching low to the ground to duck under the smoke.

Halfway around, she reached a blackened patch where the fire had already passed. The brittle stems of flowers crunched under her shoes, and the heat coming off the scorched earth stung her eyes.

Her footsteps ignited with flame as she ran through the blackened flowers, like stabbing a poker into a slumbering fire. She felt her eyes drying, her face blistering.

Moments later, Tally spotted the river. The fire stretched in an unbroken wall across the opposite shore, a roaring wind pressing at its back and sending embers flying across to alight on the near side. A rolling billow of smoke surged toward her, choking and blinding her until it passed.

When her eyes could open again, Tally spotted the shiny solar surface of her hoverboard. She ran toward it, ignoring the burning flowers in her path.

The board seemed untouched by the flame, protected by good luck and the layer of dew it collected every nightfall.

She quickly folded the board and stepped onto it, not waiting for the yellow light to turn green. The heat had mostly dried it already, and it rose into the air at her command. Tally took the board over the river, just above the water, and skimmed her way upstream, looking for a break in the wall of fire to her left.

Her grippy shoes were ruined, their soles cracked like sunbaked mud, so she flew slowly, scooping up handfuls of water to soothe her burning face and arms.

A noise thundered to life on Tally's left, unmistakable even above the roar of the fire. She and the board were caught in a sudden wind, shoved back toward the other shore. Tally leaned hard against it and stuck a foot into the water to slow the board. She clung tightly with both hands, desperately fighting being thrown into the river.

The smoke suddenly cleared, and a familiar shape loomed out of the darkness. It was the flying machine, its thundering beat now obvious above the raging fire. Sparks jumped across the river as the machine's windstorm stirred the fire to a new intensity.

What were they *doing*? she wondered. Didn't they realize they were spreading the fire?

Her question was answered a moment later when a gout of flame shot from the machine, squirting across the river to ignite another patch of flowers.

They had set the fire, and were driving it on in every way they could.

The flying machine thundered closer, and she glimpsed an inhuman face staring at her from the pilot seat. She turned her board to fly away, but the machine lifted up into the air, passing right over her, and suddenly the wind was too great.

Tally pitched off and into the water. Her crash bracelets caught for a moment, holding her up above the waves, but then the wind caught the hoverboard, much lighter without her on it, and spun it away like a leaf.

She sank into the deep water in the middle of the river, knapsack and all.

It was cool and quiet under the waves.

For a few endless moments, Tally felt only relief to have escaped the searing wind, the thundering machine, the blistering heat of the firestorm. But the weight of the crash bracelets and knapsack pulled her down fast, and panic welled up in her pounding chest.

She thrashed in the water, climbing up toward the flickering lights of the surface. Her wet clothes and gear dragged at her, but just as her lungs were about to burst, she broke the surface into the maelstrom. Tally gulped a few breaths of smoky air, then was slapped in the face by a wave. She coughed and sputtered, struggling to stay afloat.

A shadow passed over her, blacking out the sky. Then her hand struck something—a familiar grippy surface. . . .

Her hoverboard had come back to her! Just the way it always did when she spilled. The crash bracelets lifted her up until she could grab on to it, her fingers clinging to its knobbly surface as she gasped for air.

A high-pitched whine came from the nearby shore. Tally blinked away water from her eyes and saw that the Rusty machine had landed. Figures were jumping from the machine, spraying white foam at the ground as they crashed through the burning flowers and into the river. They were headed for her.

She struggled to climb onto the board.

"Wait!" the nearest figured called.

Tally rose shakily to her feet, trying to keep steady on the wet surface of the board. Her hard-baked shoes were slippery, and her sodden knapsack seemed to weigh a ton. As she leaned forward, a gloved hand reached up to grab the front of the board. A face came up from the water, wearing some sort of mask. Huge eyes stared up at her.

She stomped at the hand, crunching the fingers. They slipped off, but her weight was thrown too far forward, and the board tipped its nose into the water.

Tally tumbled into the river again.

Hands grabbed at her, pulling her away from the hoverboard. She was hoisted out of the water and onto a broad shoulder. She caught glimpses of masked faces: huge, inhuman eyes staring at her unblinkingly.

Bug eyes.

BUG EYES

They pulled her to the shore and out of the water, hauling her to the flying machine.

Tally's lungs felt full of water and smoke. She could hardly take a breath without a wracking cough shaking her whole body.

"Put her down!"

"Where the hell did she come from?"

"Give her some oh-two."

They flopped Tally onto her back on the ground, which was thick with the white foam. The one who'd carried her pulled off his bug-eyed mask, and Tally blinked.

He was a pretty. A new pretty, every bit as beautiful as Peris.

The man plunged the mask over her face. Tally fought weakly for a moment, but then cold, pure air surged into her lungs. Her head grew light as she gratefully sucked it down.

He pulled the mask off. "Not too much. You'll hyperventilate."

She tried to speak but could only cough.

"It's getting bad," another figure said. "Jenks wants to take her back up."

"Jenks can wait."

Tally cleared her throat. "My board."

The man smiled beautifully and glanced up. "It's headed over. Hey! Somebody stick that thing to the chopper! What's your name, kid?"

"Tally." Cough.

"Well, Tally, are you ready to move? The fire won't wait."

She cleared her throat and coughed again. "I guess so."

"Okay, come on." The man helped her up and pulled her toward the machine. She found herself pushed inside, where the noise was much less, crowded into the back with three others in bug-eyed masks. A door slammed shut.

The machine rumbled, and then Tally felt it lift from the ground. "My board!"

"Relax, kid. We got it." The woman pulled her mask off. She was another young pretty.

Tally wondered if these were the people in the clue. The "fire-bug eyes." Was she supposed to be looking for *them*?

"Is she going to make it?" a voice popped through the cabin.

"She'll live, Jenks. Make the usual detour, and work the fire a little on the way home."

Tally looked down as the machine climbed. Their flight followed the course of the river, and she saw the fires spreading across to the other shore, driven by the wind of its passage. Occasionally, the craft would shoot out a gout of flame.

She looked at the faces of the crew. For new pretties, they seemed so determined, so focused on their task. But their actions were madness. "What are you guys doing?" she said.

"A little burning."

"I can see that. But *why*?"

"To save the world, kid. But hey, we're real sorry about your getting in the way."

They called themselves rangers.

The one who'd pulled her from the river was called Tonk. They all spoke with an accent, and came from a city Tally had never heard of.

"It's not too far from here," Tonk said. "But we rangers spend most of our time out in the wild. The fire helicopters are based in the mountains."

"The fire *whats*?"

"Helicopters. That's what you're sitting in."

She looked around at the rattling machine, and shouted over the noise, "It's so Rusty!"

"Yeah. Vintage stuff, a few pieces of it are almost two hundred years old. We copy the parts as they wear out."

"But why?"

"You can fly it anywhere, with or without a magnetic grid. And it's the perfect thing for spreading fires. The Rusties sure knew how to make a mess."

Tally shook her head. "And you spread fires because . . ."

He smiled and lifted one of her shoes, pulling a crushed but unburned flower from the sole. "Because of *phragmipedium panthera*," he said.

"Excuse me?"

"This flower used to be one of the rarest plants in the world. A white tiger orchid. In Rusty days, a single bulb was worth more than a house."

"A house? But there's zillions of them."

"You noticed?" He held up the flower, staring into its delicate mouth. "About three hundred years ago, some Rusty figured a way to engineer the species to adapt to wider conditions. She messed with the genes to make them propagate more easily."

"Why?"

"The usual. To trade them for lots of stuff. But she succeeded a little too well. Look down."

Tally peered out the window. The machine had gained altitude and left the firestorm behind. Below were endless fields of white, interrupted only by a few barren patches. "Looks like she did a good job. So what? They're nice."

"One of the most beautiful plants in the world. But too successful. They turned into the ultimate weed. What we call a monoculture. They crowd out every other species, choke trees and grass, and nothing eats them except one species of hummingbird, which feeds on their nectar. But the hummingbirds nest in trees."

"There aren't any trees down there," Tally said. "Just the orchids."

"Exactly. That's what monoculture means: Everything the same. After enough orchids build up in an area, there aren't enough hummingbirds to pollinate them. You know, to spread the seeds."

"Yeah," Tally said. "I know about the birds and the bees."

"Sure you do, kid. So the orchids eventually die out, victims of their own success, leaving a wasteland behind. Biological zero. We rangers try to keep them from spreading. We've tried poison, engineered diseases, predators to target the hummingbirds . . . but fire is the only thing that really works." He turned the orchid over in his hand and held up a firestarter, letting the flame lick into its mouth. "Have to be careful, you know?"

Tally noticed the other rangers were cleaning their boots and uniforms, searching for any trace of the flowers among the mud and foam. She looked down at the endless white. "And you've been doing this for . . ."

"Almost three hundred years. The Rusties started the job, after they figured out what they'd done. But we'll never win. All we can hope to do is contain the weed."

Tally sat back, shaking her head, coughing once more. The flowers were so beautiful, so delicate and unthreatening, but they choked everything around them.

The ranger leaned forward, handing her his canteen. She took it and drank gratefully.

"You're headed to the Smoke, aren't you?"

Tally swallowed some water the wrong way and sputtered. "Yeah. How'd you know?"

"Come on. An ugly waiting around in the flowers with a hoverboard and a survival kit?"

"Oh, yeah." Tally remembered the clue: "Look in the flowers for fire-bug eyes." They must have seen uglies before.

"We help the Smokies out, and they help us out," Tonk said. "They're crazy, if you ask me—living rough and staying ugly. But they know more about the wild than most city pretties. It's kind of admirable, really."

"Yeah," she said. "I guess so."

He frowned. "You guess so? But you're headed there. Aren't you sure?"

Tally realized that this was where the lies started. She could hardly tell the rangers the truth: that she was a spy, an infiltrator. "Of course I'm sure."

"Well, we'll be setting you down soon."

"In the Smoke?"

He frowned again. "Don't you know? The location's a big secret. Smokies don't trust pretties. Not even us rangers. We'll take you to the usual spot, and you know the rest, right?"

She nodded. "Sure. Just testing you."

The helicopter landed in a swirl of dust, the white flowers bending in a wide circle around the touchdown spot.

"Thanks for the ride," Tally said.

"Good luck," Tonk said. "Hope you like the Smoke."

"Me too."

"But if you change your mind, Tally, we're always looking for volunteers in the rangers."

Tally frowned. "What's a volunteer?"

The ranger smiled. "That's when you pick your own job."

"Oh, right." Tally had heard you could do that in some cities. "Maybe. In the meantime, keep up the good work. Speaking of which, you're not setting any fires around here, are you?"

The rangers laughed, and Tonk said, "We just work the edges of the infestation, to keep the flowers from spreading. This spot is right smack in the middle. No hope left."

Tally looked around. There wasn't a glimpse of any color but white as far as she could see. The sun had set an hour ago, but the orchids glowed like ghosts in the moonlight. Now that she knew what they were, the sight chilled Tally. What had he called it? Biological zero.

"Great."

She jumped out of the helicopter and yanked her hoverboard from the magnetic rack next to the door. She backed away, careful to crouch as the rangers had warned her to.

The machine whined back to life, and she peered upward into the shimmering disk. Tonk had explained that a pair of thin blades, spinning so quickly that you couldn't see them, carried the craft through the air. She wondered if he'd been kidding. It just looked like a typical force field to her.

The wind grew crazed again as the machine reared up, and she held on to her board tightly, waving until the aircraft disappeared into the dark sky. She sighed.

Alone again.

Looking around, she wondered how she could find the Smokies in this featureless desert of orchids.

"Then wait on the bald head until it's light," was the last line of Shay's note. Tally scanned the horizon, and a relieved smile broke onto her face.

A tall, round hill rose up not far away. It must have been one of the places where the engineered flowers had first taken root. The top half of the hill was dying, nothing left but bare soil, ruined by the orchids.

The cleared area looked just like a bald head.

She reached the bald hilltop in a few hours.

Her hoverboard was useless there, but the hiking was easy in the new shoes the rangers had given her, her own so burned that they had fallen apart in the helicopter. Tonk had also filled her purifier with water.

The ride in the helicopter had begun to dry out Tally's clothing, and the hike had done the rest. Her knapsack had survived the dunking, even the SpagBol remaining dry in its waterproof bag. The only thing lost to the river was Shay's note, reduced to a soggy wad of paper in her pocket.

But she had almost made it. As she looked out from the hilltop, Tally realized that, except for the burn blisters on her hands and feet, some bruises on her knees, and a few locks of hair that had gone up in smoke, she had pretty much survived. As long as the Smokies knew where to find her, and believed her story that she was an ugly coming to join them, and didn't figure out that she was actually a spy, then everything was just great.

She waited on the hill, exhausted but unable to sleep, wondering if she could really do what Dr. Cable wanted. The pendant around her neck had also survived the ordeal. Tally doubted a little water would have ruined the device, but she wouldn't know until she reached the Smoke and activated it.

She hoped for a moment that the pendant wouldn't work. Maybe one of the bumps along the way had broken its little eye-reader and it would never send its message back to Dr. Cable. But that was hardly worth hoping for. Without the pendant, Tally was stuck out here in the wild forever. Ugly for life.

Her only way home was to betray her friend.

LIES

A couple of hours after dawn, they came and got her.

Tally saw them hiking through the orchids, four figures carrying hoverboards and dressed all in white. Broad white hats in a dappled pattern hid their heads, and she realized that if they ducked down into the flowers, they would practically disappear.

These people went to a lot of trouble to stay hidden.

As the party drew close, she recognized Shay's pigtails

bobbing under one of the hats and waved frantically. Tally had planned to take the note literally and wait on the hill-top, but at the sight of her friend, she grabbed her board and dashed down to meet them.

Infiltrator or not, Tally couldn't wait to see Shay.

The tall, lanky form broke from the others and ran toward her, and the two embraced, laughing.

"It *is* you! I knew it was!"

"Of course it is, Shay. I couldn't stand missing you." Which was pretty much true.

Shay couldn't stop smiling. "When we spotted the helicopter last night, most people said it had to be another group. They said you'd taken too long, and that I should give up."

Tally tried to smile back, wondering if she hadn't made up enough time. She could hardly admit starting four days *after* her sixteenth birthday.

"I kind of got turned around. Could your note have been any more obscure?"

"Oh." Shay's face fell. "I thought you'd understand it."

Unable to bear Shay blaming herself, Tally shook her head. "Actually, the note was okay. I'm just a moron. And the biggest problem was when I got to the flowers. The rangers didn't see me at first, and I almost got roasted."

Shay's eyes widened as she took in Tally's scratched and sunburned face, the blisters on her hands, and her patchy, scorched hair. "Oh, Tally! You look like you went through a war zone."

"Just about."

The other three uglies walked up. They stood back a bit, one boy holding a device in the air. "She's carrying a bug," he said.

Tally's heart froze. "A what?"

Shay gently took Tally's board from her and handed it to the boy. He swept his device across it, nodded, and pulled one of the stabilizer fins off. "Here it is."

"They sometimes put trackers on the long-range boards," Shay said. "Trying to find the Smoke."

"Oh, I'm really . . . I didn't know. I swear!"

"Relax, Tally," the boy said. "It's not your fault. Shay's board had one too. That's why we meet you newbies down here." He held up the bug. "We'll take it away in some random direction and stick it on a migrating bird. See how the Specials like South America." The Smokies all laughed.

He stepped closer and swept the device up and down her body. Tally flinched when it passed close to the pendant. But he smiled. "It's okay. You're clean."

Tally sighed with relief. Of course, she hadn't activated the pendant yet, so his device couldn't detect it. The other bug was just Dr. Cable's way of misleading the Smokies, getting them to drop their guard. Tally herself was the real danger.

Shay stepped up next to the boy, taking his hand in hers. "Tally, this is David."

The boy smiled again. He was an ugly, but he had a nice smile. And his face held a kind of confidence that Tally had never seen in an ugly before. Maybe he was a few years older than she was. Tally had never watched anyone mature naturally past age sixteen. She wondered how much of being ugly was just an awkward age.

Of course, David was hardly a pretty. His smile was crooked, and his forehead too high. But, uglies or not, it was good to see Shay, David—all of them. Except for a couple of stunned hours with the rangers, she hadn't seen human faces in what seemed like years.

"So, what've you got?"

"Huh?"

Croy was one of the other uglies who'd come to meet her. He also looked older than sixteen, but it didn't suit him like it did David. Some people needed the operation more than others. He reached out a hand for her knapsack.

"Oh, thanks." Her shoulders were sore from being strapped to the thing for the last week.

He pulled it open as they hiked, looking inside. "Purifier. Position-finder." Croy pulled out the waterproof bag and opened it. "SpagBol! Yum!"

Tally groaned. "You can have it."

His eyes widened. "I can?"

Shay pulled the knapsack away from him. "No, you can't."

"Listen, I've eaten that stuff three times a day for the past . . . what seems like forever," Tally said.

"Yeah, but dehydrated food's hard to get in the Smoke," Shay explained. "You should save it to trade."

"Trade?" Tally frowned. "What do you mean?" In the city, uglies might trade chores or stuff they'd stolen, but trade *food*?

Shay laughed. "You'll get used to the idea. In the Smoke, things don't just come out of the wall. You've got to hang on to the stuff you brought with you. Don't go giving it away to anyone who asks." Shay glared at Croy, who looked down sheepishly.

"I was going to give her something for it," he insisted.

"Sure you were," David said.

Tally noticed his hand on Shay's shoulder, touching her

softly as they hiked. She remembered the way Shay had always talked about David, kind of dreamily. Maybe it wasn't just the promise of freedom that had brought her friend here.

They reached the edge of the flowers, a dense growth of trees and brush that started at the foot of a towering mountain.

"How do you keep the orchids from spreading?" Tally asked.

David's eyes lit up, as if this was his favorite subject. "This old-growth forest stops them. It's been around for centuries, probably even before the Rusties."

"It's got lots and lots of species," Shay said. "So it's strong enough to keep out the weed." She looked at David for approval.

"The rest of this land used to be farms or grazing pasture," he continued, gesturing back at the expanse of white behind them. "The Rusties had already broken its back before the weed arrived."

A few minutes into the forest, Tally realized why the orchids were no match for it. The tangled brush and thick trees were knotted together into an impassable wall on either side. Even on the narrow path, she was constantly shoving past branches and twigs, tripping over roots and rocks. She'd never seen any woodlands this raw and inhospitable. Vines dotted with cruel thorns ran through the semidarkness like barbed wire. "You guys *live* in here?"

Shay laughed. "Don't worry. We've got a ways to go. We're just making sure you weren't followed. The Smoke's much higher, where the trees aren't so intense. But the creek's coming up. We'll be on board soon."

"Good," Tally said. Her feet were already chafing in the

new shoes. But they were warmer than her destroyed grippies, she realized, and were better for hiking. She wondered what would have happened if the rangers hadn't given them to her. How did you get new shoes in the Smoke? Trade someone all your food? Make them yourself? She looked down at the feet ahead of her, David's, and saw that his shoes did look handmade, like a couple of pieces of leather crudely sewn together. Strangely, though, he moved gracefully through the undergrowth, silent and sure while the rest of them crashed along like elephants.

The very idea of making a pair of shoes by hand boggled her mind.

It didn't matter, Tally reminded herself, taking a deep breath. Once in the Smoke, she could activate the pendant and be home within a day, maybe within hours. All the food and clothes she would ever need, hers for the asking. Her face pretty at long last, and Peris and all their old friends around her.

Finally, this nightmare would be over.

Soon, the sound of running water filled the forest, and they reached a small clearing. David pulled his device out again, pointing it back toward the path. "Still nothing." He grinned at Tally. "Congratulations, you're one of us now."

Shay giggled and hugged Tally again as the others readied their boards. "I still can't believe you came. I thought I'd messed everything up, waiting so long to tell you about running away. And I was so stupid, getting into a fight instead of just telling you what I was going to do."

Tally shook her head. "You'd said everything already, I just wasn't listening. Once I realized you were serious, I needed a chance to think about it. It just took me a while . . . every minute, until the last night before my birthday." She took a deep breath, wondering why she was saying all this, lying to Shay when she didn't really have to. She should just shut up, get to the Smoke, and get it over with. But Tally found herself continuing. "Then I realized I'd never see you again if I didn't come. And I'd always wonder."

That last part was true, at least.

As they boarded higher up into the mountain the creek widened, cutting an archway of trees into the dense forest. The gnarled, smaller trees became taller pines, the undergrowth thinning, the brook breaking into occasional rapids. Shay cried out as she rode through the spray of churning white water.

"I've been dying to show you this! And the *really* good rapids are on the other side."

Eventually, they left the creek, following a vein of iron over a ridge. From the top, they looked down into a small valley that was mostly clear of forest.

Shay held Tally's hand. "There it is. Home."

The Smoke lay below them.

THE MODEL

The Smoke really was smoky.

Open fires dotted the valley, surrounded by small groups of people. The scents of wood smoke and cooking drifted up to Tally, smells that made her think of camping and outdoor parties. In addition to the smoke there was a morning mist in the air, a white finger creeping down into the valley from a bank of clouds nestled against the mountain higher up. A few solar panels glimmered feebly, gathering what sun was reflected from the mist. Garden plots were planted in random spots between the buildings, twenty or so one-story structures made from long planks of wood. There was wood everywhere: in fences; as cooking spits; laid down in walkways over muddy patches; and in big stacks by the fires. Tally wondered where they had found so much wood.

Then she saw the stumps at the edges of the settlement, and gasped. "Trees . . . ," she whispered in horror. "You cut down trees."

Shay squeezed her hand. "Only in this valley. It seems weird at first, but it's the way the pre-Rusties lived too, you know? And we're planting more on the other side of the mountain, pushing into the orchids."

"Okay," Tally said doubtfully. She saw a team of uglies moving a felled tree, pushing it along on a pair of hoverboards. "There's a grid?"

Shay nodded happily. "Just in places. We pulled up a bunch of metal from a railroad, like the track you came up the coast on. We've laid out a few hoverpaths through the Smoke, and eventually we'll do the whole valley. I've been working on that project. We bury a piece of junk every few paces. Like everything here, it's tougher than you'd think. You wouldn't *believe* how much a knapsack full of steel weighs."

David and the others were already headed down, gliding single file between two rows of rocks painted a glowing orange. "That's the hoverpath?" Tally asked.

"Yeah. Come on, I'll take you down to the library. You've got to meet the Boss."

The Boss wasn't really in charge here, Shay explained. He just acted like it, especially to newbies. But he was in command of the library, the largest of the buildings in the settlement's central square.

The familiar smell of dusty books overwhelmed Tally at the library door, and as she looked around, she realized that books were pretty much all the library had. No big airscreen, not even private workscreens. Just mismatched desks and chairs and rows and rows of bookshelves.

Shay led her to the center of it all, where a round kiosk was inhabited by a small figure talking on an old-fashioned handphone. As they drew closer, Tally felt her heart starting to pound. She'd been dreading what she was about to see.

The Boss was an *old* ugly. Tally had spotted a few from a distance on the way in, but had managed to turn her eyes away. But here was the wrinkled, veined, discolored, shuffling, horrific truth, right before her eyes. His milky eyes glared at them as he berated whoever was on the phone, in a rattling voice and waving one claw at them to go away.

Shay giggled and pulled her toward the shelves. "He'll get to us eventually. There's something I want to show you first."

"That poor man . . ."

"The Boss? Pretty wild, huh? He's, like, *forty*! Wait until you talk to him."

Tally swallowed, trying to erase the image of his sagging features from her mind. These people were insane to tolerate that, to *want* it. "But his face . . . ," Tally said.

"That's nothing. Check these out." Shay sat her down at

a table, turned to a shelf, and pulled out a handful of volumes in protective covers. She plonked them in front of Tally.

"Books on paper? What about them?"

"Not books. They're called 'magazines,'" Shay said. She opened one and pointed. Its strangely glossy pages were covered with pictures. Of people.

Uglies.

Tally's eyes widened as Shay turned the pages, pointing and giggling. She'd never seen so many wildly different faces before. Mouths and eyes and noses of every imaginable shape, all combined insanely on people of every age. And the *bodies*. Some were grotesquely fat, or weirdly overmuscled, or uncomfortably thin, and almost all of them had wrong, ugly proportions. But instead of being ashamed of their deformities, the people were laughing and kissing and posing, as if all the pictures had been taken at some huge party. "Who are these freaks?"

"They aren't freaks," Shay said. "The weird thing is, these are famous people."

"Famous for what? Being hideous?"

"No. They're sports stars, actors, artists. The men with stringy hair are musicians, I think. The really ugly ones are politicians, and someone told me the fatties are mostly comedians."

"That's funny, as in strange," Tally said. "So this is what people looked like before the first pretty? How could anyone stand to open their eyes?"

"Yeah. It's scary at first. But the weird thing is, if you keep looking at them, you kind of get used to it."

Shay turned to a full-page picture of a woman wearing only some kind of formfitting underwear, like a lacy swimsuit.

"What the . . . ," Tally said.

"Yeah."

The woman looked like she was starving, her ribs thrusting out from her sides, her legs so thin that Tally wondered how they didn't snap under her weight. Her elbows and pelvic bones looked sharp as needles. But there she was, smiling and proudly baring her body, as if she'd just had the operation and didn't realize they'd sucked out way too much fat. The funny thing was, her face was closer to being pretty than any of the rest. She had the big eyes, smooth skin, and small nose, but her cheekbones were too tight, the skull practically visible beneath her flesh. "What on earth is she?"

"A model."

"Which is what?"

"Kind of like a professional pretty. I guess when everyone else is ugly, being pretty is sort of, like, your job."

"And she's in her underwear because . . . ?" Tally began, and then a memory flashed into her mind. "She's got that disease! The one the teachers always told us about."

"Probably. I always thought they made that up to scare us."

Back in the days before the operation, Tally remembered, a lot of people, especially young girls, became so ashamed at being fat that they stopped eating. They'd lose weight too quickly, and some would get stuck and would keep losing weight until they wound up like this "model." Some even died, they said at school. That was one of the reasons they'd come up with the operation. No one got the disease anymore, since everyone knew at sixteen they'd turn beautiful. In fact, most people pigged out just before they turned, knowing it would all be sucked away.

Tally stared at the picture and shivered. Why go back to *this*?

"Spooky, huh?" Shay turned away. "I'll see if the Boss is ready yet."

Before she disappeared around a corner, Tally noticed how skinny Shay was. Not diseased skinny, just ugly skinny—she'd never eaten much. Tally wondered if, here in the Smoke, Shay's undereating would get worse and worse, until she wound up starving herself.

Tally fingered the pendant. This was her chance. Might as well get it over with now.

These people had forgotten what the old world was really like. Sure, they were having a great time camping out and playing hide-and-seek, and living out here was a great trick on the cities. But somehow they'd forgotten that the Rusties had been insane, almost destroying the world in a million different ways. This starving almost-pretty was only one of them. Why go back to that?

They were already cutting down *trees* here.

Tally popped open the heart pendant, looking down into the little glowing aperture where the laser waited to read her eye-print. She brought it closer, her hand shaking. It was foolish to wait. This would only get harder.

And what choice did she have?

"Tally? He's almost—"

Tally snapped closed the pendant and shoved it into her shirt.

Shay smiled slyly. "I noticed that before. What gives?"

"What do you mean?"

"Oh, come on. You never wore anything like that before. I leave you alone for two weeks and you get all romantic?"

Tally swallowed, looking down at the silver heart.

"I mean, it's a really nice necklace. Beautiful. But who gave it to you, Tally?"

Tally found she couldn't bring herself to lie. "Someone. Just someone."

Shay rolled her eyes. "Last-minute fling, huh? I always thought you were saving yourself for Peris."

"It's not like that. It's . . ."

Why not tell her? Tally asked herself. She'd figure it out when the Specials came roaring in, anyway. If she knew, Shay could at least prepare herself before this fantasy world came tumbling down. "I have to tell you something."

"Sure."

"My coming here is kind of . . . the thing is, when I went to get my—"

"What are you *doing*?"

Tally jumped at the craggy voice. It was like an old, broken version of Dr. Cable's, a rusty razor blade drawn across her nerves.

"Those magazines are over three centuries old, and you're not wearing gloves!" The Boss shuffled over to where Tally was sitting, producing white cotton gloves and pulling them on. He reached around her to close the one she was reading.

"Your fingers are covered with very nasty acids, young lady. You'll rot away these magazines if you're not careful. Before you go nosing around in the collection, you come to me!"

"Sorry, Boss," Shay said. "My fault."

"I don't doubt it," he snapped, reshelving the magazines with elegant, careful movements at odds with his harsh words. "Now, young lady, I suppose you're here for a work assignment."

"Work?" Tally said.

They both looked down at her puzzled expression, and Shay burst into laughter.

WORK

The Smokies all had lunch together, just like at an ugly dorm.

The long tables had clearly been cut from the hearts of trees. They showed knots and whorls, and wavy tracks of grain ran down their entire length. They were rough and beautiful, but Tally couldn't get over the thought that the trees had been taken alive.

She was glad when Shay and David took her outside to the cooking fire, where a group of younger uglies hung out. It was a relief to get away from the felled trees, and from the disturbing older uglies. Out here, at least, any of the Smokies could pass as a senior. Tally didn't have much experience in judging an ugly's age, but she turned out to be more or less right. Two had just arrived from another city, and weren't even sixteen yet. The other three—Croy, Ryde, and Astrix—were friends of Shay's, from the group that had run away together back before Tally and Shay had first met.

Here in the Smoke only five months, Shay's friends already had a hint of David's self-assurance. Somehow, they carried the authority of middle pretties without the firm jaw, the subtly lined eyes, or the elegant clothing. They spent lunch talking about projects they were up to. A canal to bring a branch of the creek closer to the Smoke; new patterns for the sheep wool their sweaters were made from; a new latrine. (Tally wondered what a "latrine" was.) They seemed so serious, as if their lives were a really complicated trick that had to be planned and replanned every day.

The food was serious too, and was piled on their plates in serious quantities. It was heavier than Tally was used to, the tastes too rich, like whenever her food history class tried to cook their own meals. But the strawberries were sweet without sugar, and although it seemed weird to eat it plain, the Smokies' bread had its own flavor without anything added. Of course, Tally would have happily devoured anything that wasn't SpagBol.

She didn't ask what was in the stew, though. The thought of dead trees was enough to deal with in one day.

As they emptied their plates, Shay's friends started pumping Tally for news from the city. Dorm sports results, soap opera story lines, city politics. Had she heard of anyone else running away? Tally answered their questions as best she could. No one tried to hide their homesickness. Their faces looked years younger as they remembered old friends and old tricks.

Then Astrix asked about her journey here to the Smoke.

"It was pretty easy, really. Once I got the hang of Shay's directions."

"Not that easy. Took you what, ten days?" David asked.

"You left the night before our birthday, right?" Shay said.

"Stroke of midnight," Tally said. "Nine days . . . and a half."

Croy frowned. "It took a while for the rangers to find you, didn't it?"

"I guess so. And they almost roasted me when they did.

They were doing a huge burn that got out of control."

"Really? Whoa." Shay's friends looked impressed.

"My board almost burned. I had to save it and jump in the river."

"Is that what happened to your face?" Ryde asked.

Tally touched the peeling skin on her nose. "Well, that's kind of . . ." *Sunburn,* she almost said. But the others' faces were rapt. She'd been alone so long, Tally found herself enjoying being the center of attention.

"The flames were all around me," she said. "My shoes melted crossing this big patch of burning flowers."

Shay whistled. "Incredible."

"That's weird. The rangers usually keep an eye out for us," David said.

"Well, I guess they missed me." Tally decided not to go into the fact that she'd intentionally hidden her hoverboard. "Anyway, I was in the river, and I'd never even seen a helicopter—except for the day before—and this thing came thundering out of the smoke, driving the fire toward me. And of course I had no idea the rangers were the good guys. I thought they were Rusty pyromaniacs risen from the grave!"

Everyone laughed, and Tally felt herself enjoying the warmth of the group's attention. It was like telling everyone at dorm about a really successful trick, but much better, because she really had survived a life-or-death situation. David and Shay were hanging on to every word. Tally was glad she hadn't activated the pendant yet. She could hardly sit here enjoying the Smokies' admiration if she'd just betrayed them all. She decided to wait until tonight, when she was alone, to do what she had to.

"That must have been creepy," David said, his voice

pulling her away from uncomfortable thoughts, "being alone in the orchids for all those days, just waiting."

She shrugged. "I thought they were kind of pretty. I didn't know about the whole superweed thing."

David frowned at Shay. "Didn't you tell her *anything* in your note?"

Shay flushed. "You told me not to write anything that would give the Smoke away, so I put it in code, sort of."

"It sounds like your code almost got her killed," David said, and Shay's face fell. He turned to Tally. "Hardly anyone ever makes the trip alone. Not their first time out of the city."

"I'd been out of the city before." Tally put her arm around Shay's shoulder comfortingly. "I was fine. It was just a bunch of pretty flowers to me, and I started with two weeks of food."

"Why did you steal all SpagBol?" Croy asked. "You must love the stuff." The others joined in his laughter.

Tally tried to smile. "I didn't even notice when I pinched it. Three SpagBols a day for nine days. I could hardly stomach the stuff after day two, but you get so hungry."

They nodded. They all knew about hard traveling, and hard work, too, apparently. Tally had already noticed how much everyone had consumed for lunch. Maybe Shay wasn't so likely to get the not-eating disease. She had cleaned her heaping plate.

"Well, I'm glad you made it," David said. He reached across and touched the scratches on Tally's face softly. "Looks like you had more adventures than you're telling us."

Tally swallowed and shrugged, hoping she looked modest.

Shay smiled and hugged David. "I knew you'd think Tally was awesome."

A bell rang across the grounds, and they hurried to finish their food.

"What's that?" she asked.

David grinned. "That's back to work."

"You're coming with us," Shay said. "Don't worry, it won't kill you."

On the way to work, Shay explained more about the long, flat roller coasters called railroads. Some stretched across the entire continent, one small part of the Rusty legacy still scarring the land. But unlike most ruins, the railroads were actually useful, and not just for hoverboarding. They were the main source of metal for the Smokies.

David had discovered a new railroad track a year or so earlier. It didn't run anywhere useful, so he had drawn up a plan to plunder it for metal and build more hoverpaths in and around the valley. Shay had been working on the project since she'd come to the Smoke ten days before.

Six of them took their boards up and out the other side of the valley, down a stream churning with white water, and along a razor-sharp ridge filled with iron ore. From there, Tally finally understood how far up the mountain she'd come since leaving the coast. The whole continent seemed to be spread out before them. A thin bank of clouds below the ridge mirrored the heavier layer overhead, but forests, grasslands, and the shimmering arcs of rivers were visible through the misty veil. The sea of white orchids could still be glimpsed from this side of the mountain, glowing like an encroaching desert in the sun.

"Everything's so big," Tally murmured.

"That's what you can never tell from inside," Shay said. "How small the city is. How small they have to make everyone to keep them trapped there."

Tally nodded, but she imagined all those people let loose

in the countryside below, cutting down trees and killing things for food, crashing across the landscape like some risen Rusty machine.

Still, she wouldn't have traded anything for this moment, standing there and looking down at the plains spread out below. Tally had spent the last four years staring at the skyline of New Pretty Town, thinking it was the most beautiful sight in the world, but she didn't think so anymore.

Lower down and halfway around the mountain, another river crossed David's railroad track. The route there from the Smoke twisted in all directions, taking advantage of veins of iron, rivers, and dry creek beds, but they'd never had to leave their boards. Walking wouldn't be an option, Shay explained, when they came back loaded with heavy metal.

The track was overgrown with vines and stunted trees, every wooden cross-tie in the grip of a dozen tentacles of vegetation. The forest had been hacked away in patches surrounding a few missing segments of rail, but it held the rest firmly in its grasp.

"How are we going to get any of this out?" Tally asked. She kicked at a gnarled root, feeling puny against the strength of the wild.

"Watch this," Shay said. She pulled a tool from her backpack, an arm-length pole that telescoped out almost to Tally's height. Shay twisted one end, and four short struts unfolded from the other like the ribs of an umbrella. "It's called a powerjack, and it can move just about anything."

Shay twisted the handle again, and the ribs retracted. Then she thrust one end of the jack under a cross-tie.

With another twist of her wrist, the pole began to shudder, and a groaning sound came from the wood. Shay's feet slipped backward, but she leaned her weight into the pole, keeping it wedged under the cross-tie. Slowly, the ancient wood began to rise, tearing free from plants and earth, bending the rail that lay across it. Tally saw the struts of the powerjack unfolding underneath the tie, gradually forcing it up, the rail above beginning to pull free of its moorings.

Shay grinned up at her. "I told you."

"Let me try," Tally said, holding out her hand, eyes wide.

Shay laughed and pulled another powerjack from her backpack. "Take that tie there, while I keep this one up."

The powerjack was heavier than it looked, but its controls were simple. Tally pulled it open and jammed it under the tie that Shay had indicated. She turned the handle slowly, until the jack started to shudder in her hands.

The wood began to shift, the stresses of metal and earth twisting in her hands. Vines tore from the ground, and Tally could feel their complaints through the soles of her shoes, like a distant earthquake rumbling. A metal shriek filled the air as the rail began to bend, pulling free of vegetation and the rusty spikes that had held it down for centuries. Finally, the jack had opened to its full extent, the rail still only half-free from its ancient bonds. She and Shay struggled to pull their jacks out.

"Having fun?" Shay asked, wiping sweat from her brow.

Tally nodded, grinning. "Don't just stand there, let's finish the job."

DAVID

A few hours later, a pile of scrap metal stood in one corner of the clearing. Each segment of rail took an hour to get free, and required all six of them to carry. The railroad ties sat in another pile; at least all the Smokies' wood didn't come from live trees. Tally couldn't believe how much they had salvaged, literally tearing the track from the forest's grasp.

She also couldn't believe her hands. They were red and raw, screaming with pain and covered with blisters.

"Looks pretty bad," David said, glancing over Tally's shoulder as she stared at them in amazement.

"*Feels* pretty bad," she said. "But I didn't notice until just now."

David laughed. "Hard work's a good distraction. But maybe you should take a break. I was just about to scout up the line for another spot to salvage. Want to come?"

"Sure," she said gratefully. The thought of picking up the powerjack again made her hands throb.

Leaving the others at the clearing, they hoverboarded up and over the gnarled trees, following the barely visible track below into dense forest. David rode low in the canopy, gracefully avoiding branches and vines as if this were a familiar slalom course. Tally noticed that, like his shoes, his clothes were *all* handmade. City clothing only used seams and stitching for decoration, but David's jacket seemed to be cut together from a dozen patches of leather, all different shades and shapes. Its patchwork appearance reminded her of Frankenstein's monster, which led to a terrible thought.

What if it were made of *real* leather, like in the olden days? Skins.

She shuddered. He couldn't be wearing a bunch of dead animals. They weren't savages here. And she had to admit that the coat fit him well, the leather following the line of his shoulders like an old friend. And it fended off the whips of branches better than her microfiber dorm jacket.

David slowed as they came into a clearing, and Tally saw that they had reached a wall of solid rock. "That's weird," she said. The railroad track seemed to plunge straight into the mountain, disappearing into a pile of boulders.

"The Rusties were serious about straight lines," David said. "When they built rails, they didn't like to go around stuff."

"So they just went *through*?"

David nodded. "Yeah. This used to be a tunnel, cut right into the mountain. It must have collapsed sometime after the Rusty panic."

"Do you think there was anyone . . . inside? When it happened, I mean."

"Probably not. But you never know. There could be a whole trainload of Rusty skeletons in there."

Tally swallowed, trying to imagine whatever was in there, flattened and buried for centuries in the dark.

"The forest's a lot clearer around here," David said. "Easier to work through. I'm just worried about these boulders collapsing if we start prying rails up."

"They look pretty solid."

"Oh, yeah? Check this out," David said. He stepped off his board onto a boulder, and deftly climbed to a spot that lay shadowed in the setting sun.

Tally angled her board closer and jumped onto a large

rock next to David. When her eyes adjusted to the darkness, she saw that a long space extended back between the boulders. David crawled inside, his feet disappearing into the darkness.

"Come on," his voice called.

"Um, there isn't really a trainload of dead Rusties in there, right?"

"Not that I've found. But today might be our lucky day."

Tally rolled her eyes and lowered herself onto her belly. She crawled inside, the cool weight of the rocks settling over her.

A light flicked on ahead. She could see David sitting up in a small space, a flashlight glowing in his hand. She pulled herself in and took a seat next to him on a flat bit of rock. Giant shapes were stacked above them. "So the tunnel didn't collapse completely."

"Not at all. The rock cracked into pieces, some big and some small." David pointed the flashlight down through a chink between where they sat. Tally squinted into the darkness and saw a much bigger open space below. A glint of metal revealed a segment of track.

"Just think. If we could get down there," David said, "we wouldn't have to pull up all those vines. All that track just waiting for us."

"Just a hundred tons of rock in the way, is all."

He nodded. "Yeah, but it would be worth it." He pointed the flashlight upward at his face, making himself hideous. "No one's been down there for hundreds of years."

"Great." Tally's skin tingled, her eyes picking out the dark fissures all around them. Maybe no human beings had been there for a long time, but lots of things liked to live in cool, dark caves.

"I keep thinking," David said, "the whole thing might tumble open if we could just move the exact right boulder. . . ."

"And not the exact wrong one, the one that makes the whole thing crush us?"

David laughed and pointed the flashlight so that it lit her face rather than his. "I thought you might say that."

Tally peered through the darkness, trying to make out his expression. "What do you mean?"

"I can see that you're struggling with this."

"Struggling? With what?"

"Being here in the Smoke. You're not sure about it all."

Tally's skin tingled again, but not from the thought of snakes or bats or long-dead Rusties. She wondered if David had somehow already figured out she was a spy. "No, I guess I'm not sure," she said evenly.

She caught a glimmer of reflected light from David's eyes as he nodded. "That's good. You take this seriously. A lot of kids come out here and think it's all fun and games."

"I don't think that for a minute," she said softly.

"I can tell. It's not just a trick to you, like it is to most runaways. Even Shay, who really believes the operation is wrong, doesn't get how deadly serious the Smoke is."

Tally didn't say anything.

After a long moment of silence in the dark, David continued. "It's dangerous out here. The cities are like these boulders. They may seem solid, but if you start messing with them, the whole pile could crumble."

"I think I know what you mean," Tally said. Since the day she'd gone to get her operation, she'd felt the massive weight of the city looming over her, and had learned first-hand how much places like the Smoke threatened people like Dr. Cable. "But I don't really understand why they care so much about you guys."

"It's a long story. But part of it is . . ."

She waited for a moment before saying, "Is what?"

"Well, this is a secret. I don't usually tell people until they've been here for a while. Years. But you seem . . . serious enough to handle it."

"You can trust me," Tally said, then immediately wondered why. She was a spy, an infiltrator. She was the last person David should trust.

"I hope I can, Tally," he said, reaching out to her. "Feel the palm of my hand."

She took it, running her fingers over the flesh. It was as rough as the wood grain of the table in the dining hall, the skin along his thumb as hard and dry as leather cracking with age. No wonder he could work all day and not complain. "Wow. How long does it take to get calluses like that?"

"About eighteen years."

"About . . . ?" She stopped in disbelief, then compared the horn of his palm with her own tender, blistered flesh. Tally could feel it there, the grueling afternoon of real work she'd put in today, but stretched across a lifetime. "But how?"

"I'm not a runaway, Tally."

"I don't understand."

"My parents were runaways, not me."

"Oh." She felt stupid now, but it had never once occurred to her. If you could live in the Smoke, you could raise children here too. But she hadn't seen any littlies. And the whole place seemed so tenuous, so temporary. It would be like having a child on a camping trip. "How did they manage? Without any doctors, I mean."

"They are doctors."

"Huh. But . . . hang on. Doctors? How old were they when they ran away?"

"Old enough. They weren't uglies anymore. I think it's called being a middle pretty?"

"Yeah, at least." New pretties worked or studied, if they wanted to, but few people got serious about a profession until their middle years. "Wait. What do you mean they *weren't* uglies?"

"They weren't. But they are now."

Tally tried to get her mind to process his words. "You mean, they never did the third operation? They still look middle, even though they're crumblies?"

"No, Tally. I told you: They're doctors."

A shock ran through her. This was more stunning than the felled trees or the cruel pretties; as overwhelming as anything she'd felt since Peris had gone away. *"They reversed the operation?"*

"Yes."

"They cut each other? Out here in the wild? To make themselves . . ." Her throat closed on the word, as if she was going to gag.

"No. They didn't use surgery."

Suddenly the dark cave seemed to be crushing her, squeezing the air from her chest. Tally forced herself to breathe.

David pulled his hand away, and with a corner of her panicked mind Tally realized she'd held on to it all that time.

"I shouldn't have told you all this."

"No, David, I'm sorry. I didn't mean to get all hyperventilated."

"It's my fault. You just got here, and I dumped all this on you."

"But I do want you to . . ."—she fought saying it, but lost—"to trust me. To tell me this stuff. I do take it seriously." That much was true.

"Sure, Tally. But maybe that's enough for now. We should get back." He turned and crawled toward the sunlight.

As she followed, Tally thought of what David had said about the boulders. However massive, they were ready to topple if you pushed them the wrong way. Ready to crush you.

She felt the pendant swinging from her neck, a tiny but insistent pull. Dr. Cable would be impatient by now, waiting for the signal. But David's revelation had suddenly made everything much more complicated. The Smoke wasn't just a hideout for assorted runaways, she realized now. It was a real town, a city in its own right. If Tally activated the tracker, it wouldn't just mean the end of Shay's big adventure. It would be David's home taken from him, his whole *life* stripped away.

Tally felt the weight of the mountain pressing down upon her, and found that she was still struggling to breathe as she pulled herself out into the sunlight.

HEARTTHROB

Around the fire at dinner that night, Tally told the story of how she'd hidden in the river when the rangers' helicopter first appeared. She had everyone wide-eyed again. Apparently, she'd had one of the more exciting journeys to the Smoke.

"Can you imagine? I'm naked and crouching down in the water, and this Rusty machine is destroying my camp!"

"Why didn't they land?" Astrix asked. "Didn't they see your stuff?"

"I thought they did."

"The rangers only pick up uglies in the white flowers," David explained. "That's the rendezvous spot we tell runaways to use. They can't just pick up anyone, or they might accidentally bring a spy here."

"I guess you wouldn't want that," Tally said softly.

"Still, they should be more careful with those helicopters," Shay said. "Someone's going to get chopped to pieces one day."

"Tell me about it. The wind almost took my hoverboard away," Tally said. "It lifted my sleeping bag right off the ground and up into the blades. It was totally shredded." She was pleased by the amazement on the faces of her audience.

"So where'd you sleep?" Croy asked.

"It wasn't that bad. It was only for—" Tally stopped herself just in time. She'd spent one night without the sleeping bag, but in her cover story she'd spent four days in the orchids. "It was warm enough."

"You'd better get a new one before bedtime," David said. "It's a lot colder up here than down in the weeds."

"I'll take her over to the trading post," Shay said. "It's like a requisition center, Tally. Only when you get something, you have to leave something else behind as payment."

Tally shifted uncomfortably in her seat. She still hadn't gotten used to the idea that you had to *pay* for things here. "All I've got is SpagBol."

Shay smiled. "That's perfect to trade with. We can't make dehydrated food here, except fruit, and traveling with regular food is a total pain. SpagBol's good as gold."

*

After dinner, Shay took her to a large hut near the center of town. The shelves were full of things made in the Smoke, along with a few objects that had come from the cities. The city-made stuff was mostly shabby and worn, repaired again and again, but the handmade things fascinated Tally. She ran her still-raw fingers across the clay pots and wooden tools, amazed at how each had its own texture and weight. Everything seemed so heavy and . . . serious.

An older ugly was running the place, but he wasn't as scary as the Boss. He brought out woolen gear and a few silvery sleeping bags. The blankets, scarves, and gloves were beautiful, in subdued colors and simple patterns, but Shay insisted that Tally get a city-made sleeping bag. "Much lighter, and it squishes up small. Much better for when we go exploring."

"Of course," Tally said, trying to smile. "That'll be great."

She wound up trading twelve packets of SpagBol for another sleeping bag, and six for a handmade sweater, which left her with eight. She couldn't believe that the sweater, brown with bands of pale red and green highlights, cost half as much as the sleeping bag, which was threadbare and patched.

"You're just lucky you didn't lose your water purifier," Shay said as they walked home. "Those things are impossible to trade for."

Tally's eyes widened. "What happens if they break?"

"Well, they say you can drink water from the streams without purifying it."

"You're kidding."

"Nope. A lot of the older Smokies do," Shay said. "Even if they've got a purifier, they don't bother."

"Yuck."

Shay giggled. "Yeah, no kidding. But hey, you can always use mine."

Tally put a hand on Shay's shoulder. "Same goes for mine."

Shay's pace slowed. "Tally?"

"Yeah?"

"You were going to say something to me, back in the library, before the Boss started yelling at you."

Tally's stomach sank. She pulled away, her fingers automatically going to the pendant at her neck.

"Yeah," Shay said. "About that necklace."

Tally nodded, but didn't know how to start. She still hadn't activated the pendant, and since her conversation with David, she wasn't sure she could. Maybe if she returned to the city in a month, starving and empty-handed, Dr. Cable would take mercy on her.

But what if the woman kept her promise, and Tally never got the operation? In twenty-something years, she would be lined and wrinkled, as ugly as the Boss, an outcast. And if she stayed here in the Smoke, she'd be sleeping in an old sleeping bag and dreading the day her water purifier broke down.

She was so tired of lying to everyone. "I haven't told you everything," she started.

"I know. But I think I've got it figured out."

Tally looked at her friend, afraid to speak.

"I mean, it's pretty obvious, right? You're all upset because you broke your promise to me. You didn't keep the Smoke a secret."

Tally's mouth fell open.

Shay smiled, taking her hand. "As you got closer to your birthday, you decided you wanted to run away. But in the meantime, you met someone. Someone important. The same someone who gave you that heart necklace. So you broke your promise to me. You told that someone where you were going."

"Um, kind of," Tally managed.

Shay giggled. "I *knew* it. That's why you've been all nervous. You want to be here, but you also wish you were somewhere else. With someone else. And before you ran away, you left directions, a copy of my note, in case your new heartthrob wants to join us. Am I right or am I right?"

Tally bit her lip. Shay's face glowed in the moonlight, obviously thrilled with herself for figuring out Tally's big secret. "Uh, you're partly right."

"Oh, Tally." Shay grabbed both her shoulders. "Don't you see that it's okay? I mean, I did the same thing."

Tally frowned. "What do you mean?"

"I wasn't supposed to tell anyone I was coming here. David made me promise I wouldn't even tell you."

"Why?"

Shay nodded. "He hadn't met you, and wasn't sure if he could trust you. Normally, runaways only recruit old friends, people they've tricked with for years. But I'd only known you since the beginning of summer. And I never once mentioned the Smoke to you until the day before I left. I was never brave enough, in case you said no."

"So you weren't supposed to tell me?"

"No way. So when you actually showed up, it made everyone nervous. They don't know whether they can trust you. Even David's been acting weird around me."

"Shay, I'm so sorry."

"It's not your fault!" Shay shook her head vigorously. "It's mine. I screwed everything up. But so what? Once they get to know you, they'll think you're really cool."

"Yeah," Tally said softly. "Everyone's been really nice." She wished she had activated the pendant the moment she'd gotten there. In only one day she'd begun to realize that it wasn't just Shay's dream she'd be betraying. Hundreds of people had made a life in the Smoke.

"And I'm sure your someone will be cool too," Shay said. "I can't wait till we're all together."

"I don't know if . . . that's going to happen." There had to be some other way out of this situation. Maybe if she went to another city . . . or found the rangers again and told them that she wanted to volunteer, they'd make her pretty. But she hardly knew anything about their city, except that she didn't know anyone there. . . .

Shay shrugged. "Maybe not. But I wasn't sure you'd come either." She squeezed Tally's hand. "I'm really glad you did, though."

Tally tried to smile. "Even though I got you into trouble?"

"It's not such a big deal. I think everyone's way too paranoid around here. They spend all this time disguising the place so satellites can't see it, and they mask the handphone transmissions so they won't be intercepted. And all the secrecy about runaways is way overdone. And dangerous. Just think—if you hadn't been smart enough to figure out my directions, you could be halfway to Alaska by now!"

"I don't know, Shay. Maybe they know what they're doing. The city authorities can be pretty tough."

Shay laughed. "Don't tell me you believe in Special Circumstances."

"I . . ." Tally closed her eyes. "I just think that the Smokies have to be careful."

"Okay, sure. I'm not saying we should advertise. But if people like you and me want to come out here and live differently, why shouldn't we? I mean, no one has the right to tell us we have to be pretty, right?"

"Maybe they're just worried because we're kids. You know?"

"That's the problem with the cities, Tally. Everyone's a kid, pampered and dependent and pretty. Just like they say in school: Big-eyed means vulnerable. Well, like you once told me, you have to grow up sometime."

Tally nodded. "I know what you mean, how the uglies here are more grown up. You can see it in their faces."

Shay pulled Tally to a stop and looked at her closely for a second. "You feel guilty, don't you?"

Tally looked back into Shay's eyes, speechless for a moment. She suddenly felt naked in the cold night air, as if Shay could see straight through her lies.

"What?" she managed.

"Guilty. Not just that you told your someone about the Smoke, but that they might actually come. Now that you've seen the Smoke, you're not sure if that was such a good idea." Shay sighed. "I know it seems weird at first, and it's a lot of hard work. But I think you'll eventually like it."

Tally looked down, feeling tears welling into her eyes. "It's not that. Well, maybe it is. I just don't know if I can . . ." Her throat felt too full to speak. If she said another word, she'd have to tell Shay the truth: that she was a spy, a traitor sent there to destroy everything around them.

And that Shay was the fool who had led her there.

"Hey, it's okay." Shay gathered Tally in her arms, rocking her gently as Tally began to cry. "I'm sorry. I didn't mean to unload everything on you at once. But I've felt kind of distant from you since you got here. It feels like you're not sure you want to look at me."

"I should tell you everything."

"Shhh." Tally felt Shay's fingers stroking her hair. "I'm just glad you're here."

Tally let herself cry, burying her face in the scratchy wool sleeve of her new sweater, feeling Shay's warmth against her, and feeling awful about every gesture of kindness from her friend.

With half her mind, Tally was actually glad she'd come and seen all this. She could have lived her whole life in the city and never seen this much of the world. With the other half, Tally still wished she had activated the pendant the moment she'd arrived in the Smoke. It would have been so much easier that way.

But there was no way back in time now. She had to decide whether to betray the Smoke or not, completely understanding what it would do to Shay, to David, to everyone here.

"It's okay, Tally," Shay murmured. "You'll be okay."

SUSPICION

As the days passed, Tally fell into the routines of the Smoke.

There was something comforting about the exhaustion of hard work. All her life, Tally had been troubled by insomnia, lying awake most nights thinking about arguments she'd had, or wanted to have, or things she should have done differently. But here in the Smoke her mind shut off the moment her head hit the pillow, which wasn't even a pillow, just her new sweater stuffed into a cotton bag.

Tally still didn't know how long she was going to stay there. She hadn't come to a decision about whether to activate the pendant, but she knew that thinking about it all the time would drive her crazy. So she decided to put it out of her mind. One day she might wake up and realize that she couldn't stand to live her entire life as an ugly, no matter who it hurt or what it cost . . . but for the moment, Dr. Cable could wait.

Forgetting her troubles was easy in the Smoke. Life was much more intense than in the city. She bathed in a river so cold that she had to jump in screaming, and she ate food pulled from the fire hot enough to burn her tongue, which city food never did. Of course, she missed shampoo that didn't sting her eyes, and flush toilets (she'd learned to her horror what "latrines" were), and mostly medspray. But however blistered her hands became, Tally felt stronger than ever before. She could work all day at the railroad site, then race David and Shay home on hoverboards, her backpack full of more scrap metal than she could have lifted a month before. She learned from David how to repair her clothes with a needle and thread, how to tell raptors from their prey, and even how to clean fish, which turned out to be not nearly as bad as cutting them up in bio class.

The physical beauty of the Smoke also cleared her mind of worries. Every day seemed to change the mountain, the sky, and the surrounding valleys, making them spectacular in a completely new way. Nature, at least, didn't need an operation to be beautiful. It just was.

One morning on the way to the railroad track, David pulled

his board up alongside Tally's. He rode silently for a while, taking the familiar turns with his usual grace. Over the last two weeks, she'd learned that his jacket was actually made of leather, real dead animals, but she'd gradually gotten used to the idea. The Smokies hunted, but they were like the rangers, killing only species that didn't belong in this part of the world or that had gotten out of control thanks to the Rusties' meddling. With its random patches, the jacket would probably look silly on anyone else. But it suited David, somehow, as if growing up here in the wild allowed him to fuse with the animals that had donated their skins to his clothes. And it probably didn't hurt that he had actually made the jacket himself.

He spoke up suddenly. "I've got a present for you."

"A present? Really?"

By now, Tally understood that nothing in the Smoke ever lost its value. Nothing was discarded or given away just because it was old or broken. Everything was repaired, refitted, and recycled, and if one Smokey couldn't put it to use, it was traded to another. Few things were given away lightly.

"Yeah, really." David angled closer and handed her a small bundle.

She unwrapped it, following the familiar route down the stream almost without looking. It was a pair of gloves, handmade in light brown leather.

She shoved the bright, city-made wrapping paper into her pocket, then pulled the gloves onto her blistered hands. "Thanks! They fit perfectly."

He nodded. "I made them when I was about your age. They're a little small for me these days."

Tally smiled, wishing she could hug him. When they

spread their arms to take a hard turn, she held his hand for a second.

Flexing her fingers, Tally found that the gloves were soft and pliant, the palms worn pale from years of use. White lines across the finger joints revealed how they had fitted David's hands. "They're wonderful."

"Come on," David said. "It's not like they're magic or anything."

"No, but they've got . . . something." History, Tally realized. In the city, she'd owned lots of things—practically anything she wanted came out of the wall. But city things were disposable and replaceable, as interchangeable as the T-shirt, jacket, and skirt combinations of dorm uniforms. Here, in the Smoke, objects grew old, carrying their histories with them in dings and scratches and tatters.

David chuckled at her and sped up, joining Shay at the front of the pack.

When they got to the railroad site, David announced that they had to clear more track, using vibrasaws to cut through the vegetation that had grown up around the metal rails.

"What about the trees?" Croy asked.

"What about them?"

"Do we have to chop them down?" Tally asked.

David shrugged. "Scrub trees like this aren't good for much. But we won't waste them. We'll take them back to the Smoke for burning."

"Burning?" Tally said. The Smokies usually only cut down trees from the valley, not the rest of the mountain. These trees had been growing there for decades, and David wanted to use them just to cook a meal? She looked at Shay for support, but her friend's expression was carefully neutral. She probably agreed, but didn't want to argue with David in front of everyone about how to run his project.

"Yes, burning," he said. "And after we've salvaged the track, we'll replant. Put a row of useful trees where the railroad used to be."

The five others looked at him silently. He spun a saw in his hand, anxious to get started, but aware he didn't have their full support yet.

"You know, David," Croy said. "These trees aren't useless. They protect the underbrush from sunlight, which keeps the soil from eroding."

"Okay, you win. Instead of planting some other kind of tree, we'll let the forest take back the land. All the crappy scrub and underbrush you want."

"But do we have to clear-cut them?" Astrix asked.

David took a slow breath. "Clear-cutting" was the word for what the Rusties had done to the old forests: felling every tree, killing every living thing, turning entire countries into grazing land. Whole rain forests had been consumed, reduced from millions of interlocking species to a bunch of cows eating grass, a vast web of life traded for cheap hamburgers.

"Look, we're not clear-cutting. All we're doing is pulling out the garbage that the Rusties left behind," David said. "It just takes a little surgery to do it."

"We could chop around the trees," Tally said. "Only cut into them where we need to. Like you said: surgery."

"Okay, fine." He chuckled. "Let's see what you think of these trees after you've had to hack a few out of the ground."

He was right.

The vibrasaw purred through heavy vines, parted tangled underbrush like a comb through wet hair, and sliced cleanly through metal when the odd misstroke brought the cutting edge down onto the track. But when its teeth met the gnarled roots and twisted branches of the scrub trees, it was a different story.

Tally grimaced as her saw bounced across the hard wood again, spitting bits of bark at her face, its low hum transformed into a protesting howl. She struggled to force the edge down into the tough old branch. One more cut and this section of track would be clear.

"Going good. You almost got it, Tally."

She noticed that Croy stood well back, poised to jump if the saw somehow slipped from her hands. She could see now why David had wanted to chop the scrub trees into pieces. It would have been a lot easier than reaching through the tangle of roots and branches, trying to bring the vibrasaw to bear against a precise spot.

"Stupid trees," Tally muttered, gritting her teeth as she plunged the blade down again.

Finally, the saw found purchase in the wood, letting out a high-pitched scream as it bit into the branch. Then it slipped through, free for a second before it thrust, spitting and screeching, into the dirt below.

"Yeah!" Tally stepped back, lifting her goggles, the saw powering down in her hands.

Croy stepped forward and kicked the section of branch away from the track. "Perfect surgical slice, Doctor," he said.

"I think I'm getting the hang of this," Tally said, wiping her brow.

It was almost noon, and the sun was beating down into the clearing mercilessly. She pulled off her sweater, realizing that the morning chill was long gone. "You were right about the trees giving shade."

"You said it," Croy said. "Nice sweater, by the way."

She smiled. Along with her new gloves, it was her prized possession. "Thanks."

"What did it cost you?"

"Six SpagBols."

"A little pricey. Pretty, though." Croy caught her eye. "Tally, remember that first day you got here? When I kind of grabbed your knapsack? I really wouldn't have taken your stuff. Not without giving you something for it. You just surprised me when you said I could have everything."

"Sure, no problem," she said. Now that she'd worked with Croy, he seemed like a nice enough guy. She'd rather have been teamed up with David or Shay, but those two were cutting together today. And it was probably time she got to know some of the other Smokies better.

"And you got a new sleeping bag, too, I hope."

"Yeah. Twelve SpagBols."

"Must be almost out of trade."

She nodded. "Only eight left."

"Not bad. Still, I bet you didn't realize on your way here that you were eating your future wealth."

Tally laughed. They crouched under the partly cut tree, pulling handfuls of cut vines from around the track.

"If I'd known how valuable food packets were, I probably wouldn't have eaten so many, starving or not. I don't even like it anymore. The worst was SpagBol for breakfast."

"Sounds good to me." Croy chuckled. "This section look clear to you?"

"Sure. Let's start on the next one." She handed him the saw.

Croy did the easy part first, attacking the underbrush with the humming saw. "So, Tally, there's one thing that's kind of confusing."

"What's that?"

The saw glanced off metal, sending up a smattering of sparks.

"The first day you were here, you said you left the city with two weeks of food."

"Yeah."

"If it took you nine days to get here, you should only have had five days of food left. Maybe fifteen packets altogether. But I remember on that first day, when I looked into your bag, I was, like, 'She's got tons!'"

Tally swallowed, trying not to show any expression.

"And it turns out I was right. Twelve plus six plus eight is . . . twenty-six?"

"Yeah, I guess."

He nodded, working the saw carefully beneath a low branch. "I thought so. But you left the city *before* your birthday, right?"

Tally thought fast. "Sure. But I guess I didn't really eat three meals every day, Croy. Like I said, I was pretty sick of SpagBol after a while."

"Seems like you didn't eat much at all, for such a long trip."

Tally struggled to do the math in her head, to figure out what sort of numbers would add up. She remembered what Shay had said that first night: Some Smokies were suspicious of her, worried that she might be a spy. Tally had thought they all accepted her by now. Apparently not.

She took a deep breath, trying to keep the fear out of her voice. "Look, Croy, let me tell you something. A secret."

"What's that?"

"I probably left the city with more than just two weeks' worth of food. I never really counted."

"But you kept saying—"

"Yeah, I might have exaggerated a little, just to make the trip sound more interesting, you know? Like I could have run out of food when the rangers didn't turn up. But you're right, I always had plenty."

"Sure." He looked up at her, smiling gently. "I thought maybe so. Your trip did sound a little bit too . . . interesting to be true."

"But most of what I said was—"

"Of course." The saw whined to a stop in his hand. "I'm sure most of it was. Question is, how much?"

Tally met his piercing eyes, struggling to think of what to say. It was nothing but a few extra food packets, hardly proof that she was a spy. She should just laugh it off. But the fact that he was dead right silenced her.

"You want the saw for a while?" he said mildly. "Clearing this up is hard work."

Since they were clearing brush, there was no load of metal to take back at midday, so the railroad crew had brought their lunch out with them: potato soup, and bread with salty olives dotted through it. Tally was glad when Shay took her lunch away from the rest of the group, to the edge of the dense forest. She followed, settling next to her friend in the dappled light. "I need to talk to you, Shay."

Shay, not looking at her, sighed softly as she tore her bread into pieces. "Yeah, I guess you do."

"Oh. Did he talk to you, too?"

Shay shook her head. "He didn't have to say anything."

Tally frowned. "What do you mean?"

"I mean it's obvious. Ever since you got here. I should have seen it right away."

"I never—" Tally started, but her voice betrayed her. "What are you saying? You think Croy's right?"

Shay sighed. "I'm just saying that—" She stopped and turned to face Tally. "Croy? What about Croy?"

"He was talking to me before lunch, and he noticed my sweater and asked if I got a sleeping bag. And he figured that after nine days getting here I had too much SpagBol left."

"You had too much *what*?" Shay's expression was one of total confusion. "What on earth are you talking about?"

"Remember when I got here? I told everyone that . . ." Tally trailed off, for the first time noticing Shay's eyes. They were lined with red, as if she hadn't slept. "Wait a second, what did you think I was talking about?"

Shay held out a hand, fingers splayed. "This."

"What?"

"Hold out yours."

Tally opened one hand, making a mirror image of Shay's.

"Same size," Shay said. She turned both her palms up. "Same blisters, too."

Tally looked down and blinked. If anything, Shay's hands were in worse shape, red and dry and cracked with the ragged edges of burst blisters. Shay always worked so hard, diving in first, always taking the hardest jobs.

Tally's fingers went to the gloves tucked into her belt. "Shay, I'm sure David didn't mean to—"

"I'm sure he did. People always think long and hard about gifts in the Smoke."

Tally bit her lip. It was true. She pulled the gloves from her belt. "You should take them."

"I. Don't. Want. Them."

Tally sat back, stunned. First Croy, now this.

"No, I guess you don't." She dropped the gloves. "But Shay, shouldn't you talk to David before you go nuts about this?"

Shay chewed at a fingernail, shaking her head. "He doesn't talk to me that much anymore. Not since you showed up. Not about anything important. He's got stuff on his mind, he says."

"Oh." Tally gritted her teeth. "I never . . . I mean, I like David, but . . ."

"It's not your fault, okay? I know that." Shay reached out and gave Tally's heart-shaped pendant a little flick. "And besides, maybe your mysterious someone will show up, and it won't matter anyway."

Tally nodded. True enough, once the Specials got here, Shay's romantic life would be the least of anyone's worries.

"Have you even mentioned that to David? It seems like it might be an issue."

"No. I haven't."

"Why not?"

"It just never came up."

Shay's mouth tightened. "That's convenient."

Tally let out a groan. "But Shay, you said it yourself: I wasn't supposed to be giving out directions to the Smoke. I feel really bad about the whole thing. I'm not going to go advertising it."

"Except by wearing that thing around your neck. Which didn't do much good, though, since apparently David didn't notice it."

Tally sighed. "Or maybe he doesn't care, because this is

all just in your . . ." She couldn't finish. It wasn't just in Shay's head; she could see it now, and feel it too. When David showed her the railway cave, and told her his secret about his parents, he had trusted her, even when he shouldn't have. And now this present. Could it really be just Shay overreacting?

In a quiet part of her mind, Tally realized that she hoped it wasn't.

She took a deep breath, expelling the thought. "Shay, what do you want me to do?"

"Just tell him."

"Tell him what?"

"About why you wear that heart. About your mysterious someone."

Too late, Tally felt the expression on her face.

Shay nodded. "You don't want to, do you? That's pretty clear."

"No, I will. Really."

"Sure you will." Shay turned away, pulling a hunk of bread from her soup and taking a vicious bite.

"I *will*." Tally touched her friend's shoulder, and instead of pulling away, Shay turned back to her, her expression almost hopeful.

Tally swallowed. "I'll tell him everything, I promise."

BRAVERY

That night at dinner, she ate alone.

Now that she'd spent a day cutting trees herself, the

wooden table in the dining hall no longer horrified her. The grain of the wood felt reassuringly solid, and tracing its whorls with her eyes was easier than thinking.

For the first time, Tally noticed the sameness of the food. Bread again, stew again. A couple of days ago, Shay had explained that the plump meat in the stew was rabbit. Not soy-based, like the dehydrated meat in her SpagBol, but real animals from the overcrowded pen on the edge of the Smoke. The thought of rabbits being killed, skinned, and cooked suited her mood. Like the rest of her day, this meal tasted brutal and serious.

Shay hadn't talked to her after lunch, and Tally had no idea what to say to Croy, so she'd worked the rest of the day in silence. Dr. Cable's pendant seemed to grow heavier and heavier, wound around her neck as tightly as the vines, brush, and roots grasping the railroad tracks. It felt as if everyone in the Smoke could see what the necklace really was: a symbol of her treachery.

Tally wondered if she could ever stay there now. Croy suspected what she was, and it seemed like it would be only a matter of time before everyone else knew. All day long a terrible thought had kept crossing her mind: Maybe the Smoke was where she really belonged, but she'd lost her chance by going there as a spy.

And now Tally had come between David and Shay. Without even trying, she'd shafted her best friend. Like walking poison, she killed everything.

She thought of the orchids spreading across the plains below, choking the life out of other plants, out of the soil itself, selfish and unstoppable. Tally Youngblood was a weed. And, unlike the orchids, she wasn't even a pretty one.

Just as she finished eating, David sat down across from her. "Hey."

"Hi." She managed to smile. Despite everything, it was a relief to see him. Eating alone had reminded her of the days after her birthday, trapped as an ugly when everyone knew she should be pretty. Today was the first time she'd felt like an ugly since coming to the Smoke.

David reached across and took her hand. "Tally, I'm sorry."

"You're sorry?"

He turned her palm up to reveal her freshly blistered fingers.

"I noticed you didn't wear the gloves. Not after you had lunch with Shay. It wasn't hard to guess why."

"Oh, yeah. It's not that I didn't like them. I just couldn't."

"Sure, I know. This is all my fault." He looked around the crowded hall. "Can we get out of here? I've got something to tell you."

Tally nodded, feeling the cold pendant against her neck and remembering her promise to Shay. "Yeah. I've got something to tell you, too."

They walked through the Smoke, past cook fires being extinguished with shovelfuls of dirt; windows coming alight with candles and electric bulbs; and a handful of young uglies pursuing an escaped chicken. They climbed the ridge from which Tally had first looked down on the settlement, and David led her along it to a cool, flat outcrop of stone where a view opened up between the trees. As always, Tally noticed how graceful David was, how he seemed to know every step of the path intimately. Not even pretties, whose bodies were perfectly balanced, designed for elegance in every kind of clothing, moved with such effortless control.

Tally deliberately turned her eyes away from him. In the valley below, the orchids glowed with pale malevolence in the moonlight, a frozen sea against the dark shore of the forest.

David started talking first. "Did you know you're the first runaway to come here all alone?"

"Really?"

He nodded, still staring down at the white expanse of flowers. "Most of the time, I bring them in."

Tally remembered Shay, the last night they'd seen each other in the city, saying that the mysterious David would take her to the Smoke. Back then Tally had hardly believed there was such a person. Now, sitting next to her, David seemed very real. He took the world more seriously than any other ugly she'd ever met—more seriously, in fact, than middle pretties like her parents. In a funny way, his eyes held the same intensity that the cruel pretties' had, though without their coldness.

"My mother used to in the old days," he said. "But now she's too old."

Tally swallowed. They always explained in school about how uglies who didn't have the operations eventually became infirm. "Oh, I'm so sorry. How old is she, anyway?"

He laughed. "She's plenty fit, but uglies have an easier time trusting someone like me, someone their own age."

"Oh, of course." Tally remembered her reaction to the Boss that first day. Only a couple of weeks later she was much more used to all the different kinds of faces that age created.

"Sometimes, a few uglies will make it on their own, following coded directions like you did. But it's always been three or four in a group. No one's ever come all alone."

"You must think I'm an idiot."

"Not at all." He took her hand. "I think it was really brave."

She shrugged. "It wasn't that bad a trip, really."

"It's not the traveling that takes courage, Tally. I've done much longer trips on my own. It's leaving home." He traced a line on her sore hand with a finger. "I can't imagine having to walk away from the Smoke, away from everything I've ever known, realizing I'd probably never come back."

Tally swallowed. It hadn't been easy. Of course, she hadn't really had a choice.

"But you left your city, the only place you'd ever lived, all alone," David continued. "You hadn't even met a Smokey, someone to convince you firsthand that it was a real place. You did it all on trust, because your friend asked you. I guess that's why I feel I can trust you."

Tally looked out at the weeds, feeling worse with every word David said. If he only knew the real reason she was there.

"When Shay first told me you were coming, I was really angry at her."

"Because I might have given the Smoke away?"

"Partly. And partly because it's really dangerous for a city-bred sixteen-year-old to cross hundreds of miles alone. But mostly I thought it was a wasted risk, because you probably wouldn't even make it out of your dorm window."

He looked up at her, squeezing her hand softly. "I was amazed when I saw you running down that hill."

Tally smiled. "I was a pretty sorry sight that day."

"You were so scratched up, your hair and clothes all singed from that fire, but you had the biggest smile on your face." David's face seemed to glow in the soft moonlight.

Tally closed her eyes and shook her head. Great. She was going to get an award for bravery when she should really be kicked out of the Smoke for treachery.

"You don't look quite so happy now, though," he said softly.

"Not everyone thinks it's great that I came here."

He laughed. "Yeah, Croy told me about his big revelation."

"He did?" She opened her eyes.

"Don't listen to him. From the moment you got here, he was suspicious about your coming alone. He thought you must have had help along the way. City help. But I told him he was crazy."

"Thanks."

He shrugged. "When you and Shay saw each other, you were so happy. I could tell that you'd really missed her."

"Yeah. I was worried about her."

"Of course you were. And you were brave enough to come looking yourself, even if it meant walking away from everything you'd ever known, alone. You didn't really come because you wanted to live in the Smoke, did you?"

"Um . . . what do you mean?"

"You came to see if Shay was all right."

Tally looked into David's eyes. Even if he was completely wrong about her, it felt good to bask in his words. Up until now, the whole day had been tainted by suspicion and doubt, but David's face shone with admiration for what she had done. A feeling spread through her, a warmth that pushed away the cold wind cutting across the ridge.

Then Tally trembled inside, realizing what the feeling was. It was that same warmth she'd felt talking to Peris after his operation, or when teachers looked at her with approval. It was not a feeling she'd ever gotten from an ugly before. Without large, perfectly shaped eyes, their faces couldn't make you feel that way. But the moonlight and the setting, or maybe just the words he was saying, had somehow turned David into a pretty. Just for a moment.

But the magic was all based on lies. She didn't deserve the look in David's eyes.

She turned to face the ocean of weeds again. "I bet Shay wishes she'd never told me about the Smoke."

"Maybe right now. Maybe for a while," David said. "But not forever."

"But you and she . . ."

"She and I." He sighed. "Shay changes her mind pretty quickly, you know."

"What do you mean?"

"The first time she wanted to come to the Smoke was back in spring. When Croy and the others came."

"She told me. She chickened out, right?"

David nodded. "I always figured she would. She just wanted to run away because her friends were. If she stayed in the city, she'd be left all alone."

Tally thought of her friendless days after Peris's operation. "Yeah. I know that feeling."

"But she never showed up that night. Which happens. I was really surprised to see her in the ruins a few weeks ago, suddenly convinced she wanted to leave the city forever. And she was already talking about bringing a friend, even though she hadn't said a word to you yet." He shook his head. "I almost told her to just forget about it, to stay in the city and become pretty."

She took a deep breath. Everything would have been so much easier if David had done exactly that. Tally would be pretty right now, high up in a party tower with Peris and Shay and a bunch of new friends at this very moment. But the image in her mind didn't give Tally the thrill it usually did; it just fell flat, like a song she'd heard too many times.

David squeezed her hand. "I'm glad I didn't."

Something made Tally say, "Me too." The words amazed her, because somehow they felt true. She looked at David closely, and the feeling was still there. She could see that his forehead was too high, that a small scar cut a white stroke through his eyebrow. And his smile was pretty crooked, really. But it was as if something had changed inside Tally's head, something that had turned his face pretty to her. The warmth of his body cut the autumn chill, and she moved closer.

"Shay's tried hard to make up for chickening out that first time, and for giving you directions when she promised me she wouldn't," he said. "Now she's decided the Smoke is the greatest place in the world. And that I'm the best person in the world for bringing her here."

"She really likes you, David."

"And I really like her. But she's just not . . ."

"Not what?"

"Not serious. Not you."

Tally turned away, her head swimming. She knew she had to keep her promise now, or she never would. Her fingers went to the pendant. "David . . ."

"Yeah, I noticed that necklace. After your smile, it was the second thing I noticed about you."

"You know someone gave it to me."

"That's what I figured."

"And I . . . I told them about the Smoke."

He nodded. "I figured that, too."

"You're not mad at me?"

He shrugged. "You never promised me anything. I hadn't even met you."

"But you still . . ." David was gazing into her eyes, his face glowing again. Tally looked away, trying to drown her uncanny pretty feelings in the sea of white weeds.

David sighed softly. "You left a lot of things behind when you came here—your parents, your city, your whole life. And you are starting to like the Smoke, I can tell. You get what we're doing here in a way that most runaways don't."

"I like the way it feels here. But I might not . . . stay."

He smiled. "I know. Listen, I'm not rushing you. Maybe whoever gave you that heart is coming, maybe not. Maybe you'll go back to them. But in the meantime, could you do something for me?"

"Sure. I mean, what?"

He stood, offering her his hand. "I'd like you to meet my parents."

THE SECRET

They descended the ridge on the far side, down a steep, narrow path. David led her quickly in the darkness, finding footing on the almost invisible trail without hesitation. It was all Tally could do to keep up.

The whole day had been one shock after another, and now to top it all off she was going to meet David's parents. That was the last thing she'd expected after showing him her pendant and telling him she hadn't kept the Smoke a secret. His reactions were different from those of anyone she'd ever met before. Maybe it was because he'd grown up out here, away from the customs of the city. Or maybe he was just . . . different.

They left the familiar ridge line far behind, and the mountain rose steeply to one side.

"Your parents don't live in the Smoke?"

"No. It's too dangerous."

"Dangerous how?"

"It's part of what I was telling you your first day here, in the railroad cave."

"About your secret? How you were raised in the wild?"

David stopped for a moment, turning back to face her in the darkness. "There's more to it than that."

"What?"

"I'll let them tell you. Come on."

A few minutes later, a small square filled with faint light appeared, hovering in the darkness of the mountainside. Tally saw that it was a window, a light inside glowing deep red through a closed curtain. The house seemed half buried, as if it had been wedged into the mountain.

When they were still a stone's throw away, David stopped. "Don't want to surprise them. They can be jumpy," he said, then shouted, "Hello!"

A moment later a doorway opened, letting out a shaft of light.

"David?" a woman's voice called. The door opened wider until the light spilled across them. "Az, it's David."

As they drew closer, Tally saw that she was an old ugly. Tally couldn't tell if she was younger or older than the Boss, but she certainly wasn't as terrifying to look at. Her eyes flashed liked a pretty's, and the lines of her face disappeared into a welcoming smile as she gathered her son into a hug.

"Hi, Mom."

"And you must be Tally."

"Nice to meet you." She wondered if she should shake hands or something. In the city, you never spent much time with other uglies' parents, except when you hung out at friends' houses during school breaks.

The house was much warmer than the bunkhouse, and the timber floors weren't nearly as rough, as if David's parents had lived there so long, their feet had worn them smooth. The house somehow felt more solid than any building in the Smoke. It was really cut into the mountain, she saw now. One of the walls was exposed stone, glistening with some kind of transparent sealant.

"Nice to meet you, too, Tally," David's mother said. Tally wondered what her name was. David always referred to them as "Mom" and "Dad," words Tally hadn't used for Sol and Ellie since she was a littlie.

A man appeared, shaking David's hand before turning to her. "Good to meet you, Tally."

She blinked, her breath catching, for a moment unable to speak. David and his father somehow looked . . . alike.

It didn't make any sense. There had to be more than thirty years between them, if his father really had been a doctor when David was born. But their jaws, foreheads, even their slightly lopsided smiles were all so similar.

"Tally?" David said.

"Sorry. You just . . . you look the same!"

David's parents burst into laughter, and Tally felt her face turning red.

"We get that a lot," his father said. "You city kids always find it a shock. But you know about genetics, don't you?"

"Sure. I know all about genes. I knew two sisters, uglies, who looked almost the same. But parents and children? That's just weird."

David's mother forced a serious expression onto her face, but the smile stayed in her eyes. "The features that we take from our parents are the things that make us different. A big nose, thin lips, high forehead—all the things that the operation takes away."

"The preference toward the mean," his dad said.

Tally nodded, remembering school lessons. The overall average of human facial characteristics was the primary template for the operation. "Sure. Average-looking features are one of the things people look for in a face."

"But families pass on nonaverage looks. Like our big noses." The man tweaked his son's nose, and David rolled his eyes. Tally realized that David's nose was much bigger than any pretty's. Why hadn't she noticed that before now?

"That's one of the things you give up, when you become pretty. The family nose," his mother said. "Az? Why don't you turn up the heat."

Tally realized that she was still shivering, but not from the cold outside. This was all so weird. She couldn't get over the similarity between David and his father. "That's okay. It's lovely in here, uh . . ."

"Maddy," the woman said. "Shall we all sit down?"

Az and Maddy apparently had been expecting them. In the front room of the house, four antique cups were set out on little saucers. Soon a kettle began to whistle softly on an electric heater, and Az poured the boiling water into an antique pot, releasing a floral scent into the room.

Tally looked around her. The house was unlike any other in the Smoke. It was like a standard crumbly home, filled with impractical objects. A marble statuette stood in one corner, and rich rugs had been hung on the walls, lending their colors to the light in the room, softening the edges of everything. Maddy and Az must have brought a lot of things from the city when they ran away. And, unlike uglies, who had only their dorm uniforms and other disposable possessions, the two had actually spent half a lifetime collecting things before escaping the city.

Tally remembered growing up surrounded by Sol's woodwork, abstract shapes fashioned from fallen branches she would collect from parks as a littlie. Maybe David's childhood hadn't been completely different from her own. "This all looks so familiar," she said.

"David hasn't told you?" Maddy said. "Az and I come from the same city as you. If we'd stayed, we might have been the ones to turn you pretty."

"Oh, I guess so," Tally murmured. If they'd stayed in the city, there would have been no Smoke, and Shay never would have run away.

"David says that you made it all the way here on your own," Maddy said.

She nodded. "I was following a friend of mine. She left me directions."

"And you decided to come alone? Couldn't you wait for David to come around again?"

"There wasn't time to wait," David explained. "She left the night before her sixteenth birthday."

"That's leaving things until the last minute," Az said.

"But very dramatic," Maddy said approvingly.

"Actually, I didn't have much choice. I hadn't even heard of the Smoke until Shay, my friend, told me she was leaving. That was about a week before my birthday."

"Shay? I don't believe we've met her," Az said.

Tally looked at David, who shrugged. He had never brought Shay here? She wondered for a moment what had really gone on between David and Shay.

"You certainly made up your mind quickly, then," Maddy said.

Tally brought her mind back to the present. "I had to. I only had one chance."

"Spoken like a true Smokey," Az said, pouring a dark liquid from the kettle into the cups. "Tea?"

"Uh, please." Tally accepted a saucer and felt the scalding heat through the thin, white material of the cup. Realizing that this was one of those Smokey concoctions that burned your tongue, she sipped carefully. Her face twisted at the bitter taste. "Ah. I mean . . . sorry. I've never had tea before, actually."

Az's eyes widened. "Really? But it was very popular back when we lived there."

"I've heard of it. But it's more of a crumbly drink. Um, I mean, mostly only late pretties drink it." Tally willed herself not to blush.

Maddy laughed. "Well, we're pretty crumbly, so I guess it's okay for us."

"Speak for yourself, my dear."

"Try this," David said. He dropped a white cube into Tally's tea. The next time she drank, a sweetness had spread through it, cutting the bitterness. It was possible to sip the stuff now without grimacing.

"David's told you a little about us, I suppose," Maddy said.

"Well, he said you ran away a long time ago. Before he was born."

"Oh, did he?" Az said. The expression on his face was exactly like David's when a member of the railroad crew did something thoughtless and dangerous with a vibrasaw.

"I didn't tell her everything, Dad," David said. "Just that I grew up in the wild."

"You left the rest to us?" Az said a bit stiffly. "Very good of you."

David held his father's gaze. "Tally came here to make sure her friend was okay. All the way here alone. But she might not want to stay."

"We don't force anyone to live here," Maddy said.

"That's not what I mean," David said. "I think she should know, before she decides about going back to the city."

Tally looked from David to his parents, quietly amazed. The way they communicated was so strange, not like uglies and crumblies at all. It was more like uglies arguing. Like equals.

"I should know what?" she asked softly.

They all looked at her, Maddy and Az measuring her with their eyes.

"The big secret," Az said, "the one that made us run away almost twenty years ago."

"One we usually keep to ourselves," Maddy said evenly, her eyes on David.

"Tally deserves to know," David said, his eyes locked with his mother's. "She'll understand how important it is."

"She's a kid. A city kid."

"She made it here alone, with only a bunch of gibberish directions to guide her."

Maddy scowled. "You've never even been to a city, David. You have no idea how coddled they are. They spend their whole lives in a bubble."

"She survived alone for nine days, Mom. Made it through a brush fire."

"Please, you two," Az interjected. "*She* is sitting right here. Aren't you, Tally?"

"Yeah, I am," Tally said quietly. "And I wish you'd tell me what you're talking about."

"I'm sorry, Tally," Maddy said. "But this secret is very important. And very dangerous."

Tally nodded her head, looking down at the floor. "Everything out here is dangerous."

They were all silent for a moment. All Tally heard was the tinkle of Az stirring his tea.

"See?" David said finally. "She understands. You can trust her. She deserves to know the truth."

"Everyone does," Maddy said quietly. "Eventually."

"Well," Az said, then paused to sip his tea. "I suppose we'll have to tell you, Tally."

"Tell me *what*?"

David took a deep breath. "The truth about being pretty."

PRETTY MINDS

"We were doctors," Az began.

"Cosmetic surgeons, to be precise," Maddy said. "We've both performed the operation hundreds of times. And when we met, I had just been named to the Committee for Morphological Standards."

Tally's eyes widened. "The Pretty Committee?"

Maddy smiled at the nickname. "We were preparing for a Morphological Congress. That's when all the cities share data on the operation."

Tally nodded. Cities worked very hard to stay independent of one another, but the Pretty Committee was a global institution that made sure pretties were all more or less the same. It would ruin the whole point of the operation if the people from one city wound up prettier than everyone else.

Like most uglies, Tally had often indulged the fantasy that one day she might be on the Committee, and help decide what the next generation would look like. In school, of course, they always managed to make it sound really boring, all graphs and averages and measuring people's pupils when they looked at different faces.

"At the same time, I was doing some independent research on anesthesia," Az said. "Trying to make the operation safer."

"Safer?" Tally asked.

"A few people still die each year, as with any surgery," he said. "From being unconscious so long, more than anything else."

Tally bit her lip. She'd never heard that. "Oh."

"I found that there were complications from the anesthetic used in the operation. Tiny lesions in the brain. Barely visible, even with the best machines."

Tally decided to risk sounding stupid. "What's a lesion?"

"Basically it's a bunch of cells that don't look right," Az

said. "Like a wound, or a cancer, or just something that doesn't belong there."

"But you couldn't just *say* that," David said. He rolled his eyes toward Tally. "Doctors."

Maddy ignored her son. "When Az showed me his results, I started investigating. The local committee had millions of scans in its database. Not the stuff they put in medical textbooks, but raw data from pretties all over the world. The lesions turned up everywhere."

Tally frowned. "You mean, people were sick?"

"They didn't seem to be. And the lesions weren't cancerous, because they didn't spread. Almost everyone had them, and they were always in exactly the same place." She pointed to a spot on the top of her head.

"A bit to the left, dear," Az said, dropping a white cube into his tea.

Maddy obliged him, then continued. "Most importantly, almost everyone all over the world had these lesions. If they were a health hazard, ninety-nine percent of the population would show some kind of symptoms."

"But they weren't natural?" Tally asked.

"No. Only post-ops—pretties, I mean—had them," Az said. "No uglies did. They were definitely a result of the operation."

Tally shifted in her chair. The thought of a weird little mystery in everyone's brain made her queasy. "Did you find out what caused them?"

Maddy sighed. "In one sense, we did. Az and I looked very closely at all the negatives—that is, the few pretties who didn't have the lesions—and tried to figure out why they were different. What made them immune to the lesions? We ruled out blood type, gender, physical size, intelligence factors, genetic markers—nothing seemed to account for the negatives. They weren't any different from everyone else."

"Until we discovered an odd coincidence," Az said.

"Their jobs," Maddy said.

"Jobs?"

"Every negative worked in the same sort of profession," Az said. "Firefighters, wardens, doctors, politicians, and anyone who worked for Special Circumstances. Everyone with those jobs didn't have the lesions; all the other pretties did."

"So you guys were okay?"

Az nodded. "We tested ourselves, and we were negative."

"Otherwise, we wouldn't be sitting here," Maddy said quietly.

"What do you mean?"

David spoke up. "The lesions aren't an accident, Tally. They're part of the operation, just like all the bone sculpting and skin scraping. It's part of the way being pretty changes you."

"But you said not everyone has them."

Maddy nodded. "In some pretties, they disappear, or are intentionally cured—in those whose professions require them to react quickly, like working in an emergency room, or putting out a fire. Those who deal with conflict and danger."

"People who face challenges," David said.

Tally let out a slow breath, remembering her trip to the Smoke. "What about rangers?"

Az nodded. "I believe I had a few rangers in my database. All negatives."

Tally remembered the look on the faces of the rangers

who had saved her. They had an unfamiliar confidence and surety, like David's, completely different from the new pretties she and Peris had always made fun of.

Peris . . .

Tally swallowed, tasting something more bitter than tea in the back of her throat. She tried to remember how Peris had acted when she'd crashed the Garbo Mansion party. She'd been so ashamed of her own face, it was hard to remember anything specific about Peris. He'd looked so different and, if anything, he seemed older, more mature.

But in some way, they hadn't connected . . . it was as if he'd become a different person. Was it only because since his operation they had lived in different worlds? Or had it been something more? She tried to imagine Peris coping out here in the Smoke, working with his hands and making his own clothes. The old, ugly Peris would have enjoyed the challenge. But what about pretty Peris?

Her head felt light, as if the house were in an elevator heading swiftly downward.

"What do the lesions do?" she asked.

"We don't know exactly," Az said.

"But we've got some pretty good ideas," David said.

"Just suspicions," Maddy said. Az looked uncomfortably down into his tea.

"You were suspicious enough to run away," Tally said.

"We had no choice," Maddy said. "Not long after our discovery, Special Circumstances paid a visit. They took our data and told us not to look any further or we'd lose our licenses. It was either run away, or forget everything we'd found."

"And it wasn't something we could forget," Az said.

Tally turned to David. He sat beside his mother, grim-faced, his cup of tea untouched before him. His parents were still reluctant to say everything they suspected. But she could tell that David saw no need for caution. "What do you think?" she asked him.

"Well, you know all about how the Rusties lived, right?" he said. "War and crime and all that?"

"Of course. They were crazy. They almost destroyed the world."

"And that convinced people to pull the cities back from the wild, to leave nature alone," David recited. "And now everybody is happy, because everyone looks the same: They're all pretty. No more Rusties, no more war. Right?"

"Yeah. In school, they say it's all really complicated, but that's basically the story."

He smiled grimly. "Maybe it's not so complicated. Maybe the reason war and all that other stuff went away is that there are no more controversies, no disagreements, no people demanding change. Just masses of smiling pretties, and a few people left to run things."

Tally remembered crossing the river to New Pretty Town, watching them have their endless fun. She and Peris used to boast they'd never wind up so idiotic, so shallow. But when she'd seen him . . . "Becoming pretty doesn't just change the way you look," she said.

"No," David said. "It changes the way you think."

BURNING BRIDGES

They stayed up late into the night, talking with Az and Maddy about their discoveries, their escape into the wild, and the founding of the Smoke. Finally, Tally had to ask the question that had been on her mind since she'd first seen them.

"So how did you two change yourselves back? I mean, you were pretty, and now you're . . ."

"Ugly?" Az smiled. "That part was simple. We're experts in the physical part of the operation. When surgeons sculpt a pretty face, we use a special kind of smart plastic to shape the bones. When we change new pretties to middle or late, we add a trigger chemical to that plastic, and it becomes softer, like clay."

"Eww," Tally said, imagining her face suddenly softening so she could squish it around to a different shape.

"With daily doses of this trigger chemical, the plastic will gradually melt away and be absorbed into the body. Your face goes back to where it started. More or less."

Tally's eyebrows rose. "More or less?"

"We can only approximate the places where bone was shaved away. And we can't make big changes, like someone's height, without surgery. Maddy and I have all the non-cosmetic benefits of the operation: impervious teeth, perfect vision, disease resistance. But we look pretty close to the way we would have without the operation. As far as the fat that was sucked out"—he patted his stomach—"that proves very easy to replace."

"But *why*? Why would you want to be ugly? You were doctors, so there was nothing wrong with your brains, right?"

"Our minds are fine," Maddy answered. "But we wanted to start a community of people who didn't have the lesions, people who were free of pretty thinking. It was the only way to see what difference the lesions really made. That meant we had to gather a group of uglies. Young people, recruited from the cities."

Tally nodded. "So you had to become ugly too. Otherwise, who'd trust you?"

"We refined the trigger chemical, created a once-a-day pill. Over a few months, our old faces came back." Maddy looked at her husband with a twinkle in her eye. "It was a fascinating process, actually."

"It must have been," Tally said. "What about the lesions? Can you create a pill that cures them?"

They were both silent for a moment, then Maddy shook her head. "We didn't find any answers before Special Circumstances showed up. Az and I are not brain specialists. We've worked on the question for twenty years without success. But here in the Smoke we've *seen* the difference that staying ugly makes."

"I've seen that myself," Tally said, thinking of the differences between Peris and David.

Az raised an eyebrow. "You catch on pretty fast, then."

"But we know there's a cure," David said.

"How?"

"There has to be," Maddy said. "Our data showed that everyone has the lesions after their first operation. So when someone winds up in a challenging line of work, the authorities somehow cure them. The lesions are removed secretly, maybe even fixed with a pill like the bone plastic, and the brain returns to normal. There must be a simple cure."

"You'll find it one day," David said quietly.

"We don't have the right equipment," Maddy said, sighing. "We don't even have a pretty human subject to study."

"But hang on," Tally said. "You used to live in a city full of pretties. When you became doctors, your lesions went away. Didn't you notice that you were changing?"

Maddy shrugged. "Of course we did. We were learning how the human body worked, and how to face the huge responsibility of saving lives. But it didn't feel as if our brains were changing. It felt like growing up."

"Oh. But when you looked around at everyone else, how come you didn't notice they were . . . brain damaged?"

Az smiled. "We didn't have much to compare our fellow citizens with, only a few colleagues who seemed different from most people. More engaged. But that was hardly a surprise. History would indicate that the majority of people have always been sheep. Before the operation, there were wars and mass hatred and clear-cutting. Whatever these lesions make us, it isn't a far cry from the way humanity was in the Rusty era. These days we're just a bit . . . easier to manage."

"Having the lesions is normal now," Maddy said. "We're all used to the effects."

Tally took a deep breath, remembering Sol and Ellie's visit. Her parents had been so sure of themselves, and yet in a way so clueless. But they'd *always* seemed that way: wise and confident, and at the same time disconnected from whatever ugly, real-life problems Tally was having. Was that pretty brain damage? Tally had always thought that was just how parents were *supposed* to be.

For that matter, shallow and self-centered was how brand-new pretties were supposed to be. As an ugly Peris had made fun of them—but he hadn't waited a moment to join in the fun. No one ever did. So how could you tell how much was the operation and how much was just people going along with the way things had always been?

Only by making a whole new world, which is just what Maddy and Az had begun to do.

Tally wondered which had come first: the operation or the lesions? Was becoming pretty just the bait to get everyone under the knife? Or were the lesions merely a finishing touch on being pretty? Perhaps the logical conclusion of everyone looking the same was everyone thinking the same.

She leaned back in her chair. Her eyes were blurry, and her stomach clenched whenever she thought about Peris, her parents, and every other pretty she'd ever met. How different were they? she wondered. How did it feel to be pretty? What was it really like behind those big eyes and exquisite features?

"You look tired," David said.

She laughed softly. It seemed like weeks since she and David had arrived there. A few hours of conversation had changed her world. "Maybe a little."

"I guess we'd better go, Mom."

"Of course, David. It's late, and Tally has a lot to digest."

Maddy and Az stood, and David helped Tally up from the chair. She said good-bye to them in a daze, flinching inside when she recognized the expression in their old and ugly faces: They felt *sorry* for her. Sad that she'd had to learn the truth, sad that they'd been the ones to tell her. After twenty years, maybe they'd gotten used to the idea, but they still understood that it was a horrible fact to learn.

Ninety-nine percent of humanity had had something

done to their brains, and only a few people in the world knew exactly what.

"You see why I wanted you to meet my parents?"

"Yeah, I guess I do."

Tally and David were in the darkness, climbing the ridge back toward the Smoke, the sky full of stars now that the moon had set.

"You might have gone back to the city not knowing."

Tally shivered, realizing how close she had come so many times. In the library, she'd actually opened the pendant, almost holding it to her eye. And if she had, the Specials would have arrived within hours.

"I couldn't stand that," David said.

"But some uglies must go back, right?"

"Sure. They get bored with camping out, and we can't make them stay."

"You let them go? When they don't even know what the operation really means?"

David stopped and took hold of Tally's shoulder, anguish on his face. "Neither do we. And what if we told everyone what we suspect? Most of them wouldn't believe us, but others would go charging back to the city to rescue their friends. And eventually, the cities would find out what we were saying, and would do everything in their power to hunt us down."

They already are, Tally said to herself. She wondered how many other spies the Specials had blackmailed into looking for the Smoke, how many times they'd come close to finding it. She wanted to tell David what they were up to, but how? She couldn't explain that she had come here as a spy, or David would never trust her again.

She sighed. That would be the perfect way to stop herself from coming between him and Shay.

"You don't look very happy."

Tally tried to smile. David had shared his biggest secret with her; she should tell him hers. But she wasn't brave enough to say the words. "It's been a long night. That's all."

He smiled back. "Don't worry, it won't last forever."

Tally wondered how long it was until dawn. In a few hours she'd be eating breakfast alongside Shay and Croy, and everyone else she had almost betrayed, almost condemned to the operation. She flinched at the thought.

"Hey," David said, lifting her chin with his palm. "You did great tonight. I think my parents were impressed."

"Huh? With me?"

"Of course, Tally. You understood immediately what this all means. Most people can't believe it at first. They say the authorities would never be so cruel."

She smiled grimly. "Don't worry, I believe it."

"Exactly. I've seen a lot of city kids come through here. You're different from the rest of them. You can see the world clearly, even if you did grow up spoiled. That's why I had to tell you. That's why . . ."

Tally looked into his eyes and saw that his face was glowing again—touching her in that pretty way she'd felt before.

"That's why you're beautiful, Tally."

The words made her dizzy for a moment, like the falling feeling of looking into a new pretty's eyes. "Me?"

"Yes."

She laughed, shaking her head clear. "What, with my thin lips and my eyes too close together?"

"Tally . . ."

"And my frizzy hair and squashed-down nose?"

"Don't say that." His fingers brushed her cheeks where the scratches were almost healed, and ran fleetingly across her lips. She knew how callused his fingertips were, as hard and rough as wood. But somehow their caress felt soft and tentative.

"That's the worst thing they do to you, to any of you. Whatever those brain lesions are all about, the worst damage is done before they even pick up the knife: You're all brainwashed into believing you're ugly."

"We are. Everyone is."

"So you think I'm ugly?"

She looked away. "It's a pointless question. It's not about individuals."

"Yes it is, Tally. Absolutely."

"I mean, no one can really be . . . you see, biologically, there're certain things we all—" The words choked off. "You really think I'm beautiful?"

"Yes."

"More beautiful than Shay?"

They both stood silent, their mouths gaping. The question had popped out of Tally before she could think. How had she uttered something so horrible?

"I'm sorry."

David shrugged, turned away. "It's a fair question. Yes, I do."

"Do what?"

"I think you're more beautiful than Shay." He said it so matter-of-factly, as if talking about the weather.

Tally's eyes closed, every bit of exhaustion from the long day crashing into her at once. She saw Shay's face—too thin, eyes too far apart—and an awful feeling welled up inside her. The warmth she'd felt from David was crushed by it.

Every day of her life she'd insulted other uglies and

had been insulted in return. Fattie, Pig-Eyes, Boney, Zits, Freak—all the names uglies called one another, eagerly and without reserve. But equally, without exception, so that no one felt shut out by some irrelevant mischance of birth. And no one was considered to be even remotely beautiful, privileged because of a random twist in their genes. That was why they'd made everyone pretty in the first place.

This was not fair.

"Don't say that. Please."

"You asked me."

She opened her eyes. "But it's horrible! It's wrong."

"Listen, Tally. That's not what's important to me. What's inside you matters a lot more."

"But *first* you see my face. You react to symmetry, skin tone, the shape of my eyes. And you decide what's inside me, based on all your reactions. You're programmed to!"

"*I'm* not programmed. I didn't grow up in a city."

"It's not just culture, it's evolution!"

He shrugged in defeat, the anger draining from his voice. "Maybe some of it is." He chuckled tiredly. "But you know what first got me interested in you?"

Tally took a deep breath, trying to calm herself. "What?"

"The scratches on your face."

She blinked. "The *what*?"

"These scratches." He softly touched her cheek again.

She shook away the electric feeling his fingers left behind. "That's nuts. Imperfect skin is a sign of a poor immune system."

David laughed. "It was a sign that you'd been in an adventure, Tally, that you'd bashed your way across the wild to get here. To me, it was a sign that you had a good story to tell."

Her outrage faded. "A good story?" Tally shook her head, a laugh building inside her. "Actually, my face got scratched up back in the city, hoverboarding through some trees. At high speed. Some adventure, huh?"

"It does tell a story, though. As I thought the first time I saw you—you take risks." His fingers wound into a lock of her singed hair. "You're still taking risks."

"I guess so." Standing here in the darkness with David felt like a risk, like everything was about to change again. He still had the look in his eye, the pretty look.

Maybe he really could see past her ugly face. Maybe what was inside her did matter to him more than anything else.

Tally stepped onto a fist-size stone on the path and found an uneasy balance on it. They were eye to eye now.

She swallowed. "You really think I'm beautiful."

"Yes. What you do, the way you think, makes you beautiful."

A strange thought crossed her mind, and Tally said, "I'd hate it if you got the operation." She couldn't believe she was saying it. "Even if they didn't do your brain, I mean."

"Gee, thanks." His smile shone in the darkness.

"I don't want you to look like everyone else."

"I thought that was the point of being pretty."

"I did too." She touched his eyebrow where the line of white cut through it. "So how'd you get that scar?"

"An adventure. A good story. I'll tell you sometime."

"You promise?"

"I promise."

"Good." She leaned forward, her weight pressing into him, and as her feet gradually slipped down the stone, their lips met. His arms wrapped around her and pulled her closer. His body was warm in the predawn cold, and formed something solid and certain in Tally's shaken reality. She held on tightly, amazed at how intense the kiss became.

A moment later, she pulled away to take a breath, thinking for just a second how odd this was. Uglies did kiss each other, and a lot more, but it always felt as if nothing counted until you were a pretty.

But this counted.

She pulled David toward her again, her fingers digging into the leather of his jacket. The cold, her aching muscles, the awful thing she had just learned, all of it just made this feeling stronger.

Then one of his hands touched the back of her neck, traced the slender chain there, down to the cold, hard metal of the pendant.

She stiffened, and their lips parted.

"What about this?" he said.

She enclosed the metal heart in her fist, her other arm still wrapped around him. There was no way she could tell David about Dr. Cable now. He would pull away, maybe forever. The pendant was still between them.

Suddenly, Tally knew what to do. It was perfect. "Come with me."

"Where?"

"To the Smoke. I have to show you something."

She pulled him up the slope, scrambling until they reached the top of ridge.

"Are you okay?" he asked, panting. "I didn't mean to—"

"I'm great." She smiled broadly at him, then peered down on the Smoke. A single campfire burned near the center of town, where the night-watch gathered to warm up every hour or so. "Come on."

Suddenly, it seemed important to get there fast, before her certainty faded, before the warm feeling inside her could give way to doubt. She scrambled down between the painted stones of the hoverboard path, David struggling to keep up. When her feet reached level ground, she ran, heedless of the dark and silent huts on either side, seeing only the firelight ahead. Her speed was effortless, like hoverboarding on an open straightaway.

Tally ran until she reached the fire, skidding to a halt against its cushion of heat and smoke. She reached up to unclasp the pendant's chain.

"Tally?" David ran up panting, confusion on his face. He tried breathlessly to say more.

"No," she said. "Just watch."

The pendant swung by its chain in her fist, sparkling red in the firelight. Tally focused all her doubts on it, all her fear of discovery, her terror at Dr. Cable's threats. She clutched the pendant, squeezing the unyielding metal until her muscles ached, as if forcing into her own mind the almost unthinkable fact that she might really remain an ugly for life. But somehow not ugly at all.

She opened her hand and threw the necklace into the center of the fire.

It landed on a crackling log, the metal heart burning black for a moment, then gradually turning yellow and white in the heat. Finally, a small *pop* came from it, as if something trapped inside had exploded, and it slid from the log and disappeared among the flames.

She turned to David, her vision spotted with sinuous shapes from staring into the fire. He coughed at the smoke. "Wow. That was dramatic."

Tally suddenly felt foolish. "Yeah, I guess so."

He moved closer. "You really meant that. Whoever gave it to you—"

"Doesn't matter anymore."

"What if they come?"

"No one's coming. I'm sure of it."

David smiled and gathered Tally into a hug, pulling her away from the edge of the fire. "Well, Tally Youngblood, you certainly know how to make a point. You know, I would have believed you if you just told me—"

"No, I had to do it like this. I had to burn it. To know for sure."

He kissed her forehead and laughed. "You're beautiful."

"When you say that, I almost . . . ," she whispered.

Suddenly, a wave of exhaustion struck Tally, as if her last bit of energy had gone into the fire with the pendant. She was tired from the wild run here, from the long night with Maddy and Az, from a hard day's work. And tomorrow she would have to face Shay again, and explain what had happened between her and David. Of course, the moment Shay saw that the pendant was gone from around Tally's neck, she would know.

But at least she'd never know the real truth. The pendant was charred beyond recognition, its true purpose hidden forever. Tally slumped into David's arms, closing her eyes. The image of the glowing heart was burned into her vision.

She was free. Dr. Cable would never come here now, and no one could ever take her away from David or the Smoke, or do to Tally's brain whatever the operation did to pretties'. She was no longer an infiltrator. She finally belonged here.

Tally found herself crying.

David silently walked her to the bunkhouse. At the

door, he leaned forward to kiss her, but she pulled away and shook her head. Shay was just inside. Tally would have to talk to her tomorrow. It wouldn't be easy, but Tally knew she could face anything now.

David nodded, kissed his finger, and traced one of the remaining scratches on her cheek. "See you tomorrow," he whispered.

"Where are you going?"

"For a walk. I need to think."

"Don't you ever sleep?"

"Not tonight." He smiled.

Tally kissed his hand and slipped inside, where she kicked off her shoes and crawled into bed with her clothes on, falling asleep in seconds, as if the weight of the world had lifted from her shoulders.

The next morning she awoke to chaos, the sounds of running, shouting, and the scream of machines invading her dreams. Out the bunkhouse window, the sky was full of hovercars.

Special Circumstances had arrived.

Part III

INTO THE FIRE

Beauty is that Medusa's head
Which men go armed to seek and sever.
It is most deadly when most dead,
And dead will stare and sting forever.
—Archibald MacLeish, "Beauty"

INVASION

Tally turned from the window and saw nothing but empty beds. She was alone in the bunkhouse.

She shook her head, foggy from sleep and disbelief. The ground rumbled beneath her bare feet, and the bunkhouse shuddered around her. Suddenly, the plastic in one of the windows shattered, and the muffled cacophony from outside rushed in to batter her ears. The entire building shook as if it would collapse.

Where was everyone? Had they already fled the Smoke, leaving her there to face this invasion alone?

Tally ran for the door and threw it open. Before her, a hovercar was landing, blinding her for a moment with a face full of dust. She recognized the machine's cruel lines from the Special Circumstances car that had first taken her to see Dr. Cable. But this one was equipped with four shimmering blades—one each where the wheels of a groundcar would be—a cross between a normal hovercar and the rangers' helicopter.

It could travel anywhere, Tally realized, inside a city or out in the wild. She remembered Dr. Cable's words: *We'll be there in a few hours.* Tally forced the thought from her head. This attack couldn't have anything to do with her.

The hovercar struck the dusty ground with a thud. This was no time to stand there wondering. She turned and ran.

The camp was a chaos of smoke and running figures. Cooking fires had been blown from their pits, and scattered embers burned everywhere. Two of the encampment's big buildings were ablaze. Chickens and rabbits scampered underfoot, dust and ashes coiled in rampant whirlwinds. Dozens of Smokies ran about, some trying to put out the fires, some trying to escape, some simply panicking.

Through everything else, the forms of cruel pretties moved. Their gray uniforms passed like fleeting shadows through the confusion. Graceful and unhurried, as if unaware of the chaos around them, they set about subduing the panicking Smokies. They moved in a blur, without any weapons that Tally could see, leaving everyone in their wake lying on the ground, bound and dazed.

They were superhumanly fast and strong. The Special operation had given them more than just terrible faces.

Near the mess hall, about two dozen Smokies were making a stand, holding off a handful of Specials with axes and makeshift clubs. Tally made her way toward the fight, and the incongruous smells of breakfast reached her through the choking haze of smoke. Her stomach growled.

Tally realized that she had slept through the breakfast call, too exhausted to wake up with everyone else. The Specials must have waited until most of the Smokies were gathered in the mess hall before launching their invasion.

Of course. They wanted to capture as many Smokies as possible in a single stroke.

The Specials weren't attacking the large group at the

mess hall. They waited patiently in a ring around the building while their numbers increased, more hovercars landing every minute. If anyone tried to get past the cordon, they reacted swiftly, disarming and incapacitating whoever dared to run. But most of the Smokies were too shocked to resist, paralyzed by the terrible faces of their opponents. Even here, most people had never seen a cruel pretty.

Tally pinned herself against a building, trying to disappear next to a stack of firewood. She shielded her eyes from the dust storm, searching for an escape route. There was no way to get into the center of the Smoke, where her hoverboard lay on the broad roof of the trading post, charging in the sun. The forest was the only way out.

A stretch of uncleared trees lay at the closest edge of town, only a twenty-second dash away. But a Special stood between her and the border of dense trees and brush, waiting to intercept any stray Smokies. The woman's eyes scanned the approach to the forest, her head moving from side to side in a weirdly regular motion, like someone watching a slow-motion tennis match without much interest.

Tally crept closer, staying pressed against the building. A hovercar passed overhead, blowing a maelstrom of dust and loose wood chips into her eyes.

When she could see again, Tally found an aging ugly crouching next to her, against the wall.

"Hey!" he hissed.

She recognized the sagging features, the bitter expression.

It was the Boss.

"Young lady, we have a problem." His harsh voice cut through the cacophony of the attack.

She glanced in the direction of the waiting Special. "Yeah, I know."

Another hovercar roared over them, and he pulled her around the corner of the building and down behind a drum that collected rainwater from the gutters.

"You noticed her too?" He grinned, showing a missing tooth. "Maybe if we both run at once, one of us might make it. If the other puts up a fight."

Tally swallowed. "I guess." She peered out at the Special, who stood as calmly as a crumbly waiting for a pleasure ferry. "But they're pretty fast."

"That depends." He dropped the duffel bag from his shoulder. "There're two things I keep ready for emergencies."

The Boss unzipped the bag and pulled out a plastic container big enough for a sandwich. "This is one." He popped open one corner of the top, and a puff of dust rose up. A second later, a wave of fire rushed into Tally's head. She covered her face, eyes watering, and tried to cough up the finger of flame that had crawled down her throat.

"Not bad, eh?" the Boss chuckled. "That's pure habanero pepper, dried and ground down to dust. Not too bad in beans, but hell in your eyes."

Tally blinked away her tears and managed to speak. "Are you nuts?"

"The other thing is this bag, which contains a representative sample of two hundred years of Rusty-era visual culture. Priceless and irreplaceable artifacts. So which do you want?"

"Huh?"

"Do you want the habanero pepper or the bag of magazines? Do you want to get caught while taking out our

Special friend? Or save a precious piece of human heritage from these barbarians?"

Tally coughed once more. "I guess . . . I want to escape."

The Boss smiled. "Good. I'm sick of running. Sick of losing my hair too, and being short-sighted. I've done my bit, and you look pretty fast."

He handed her the duffel bag. It was heavy, but Tally had grown stronger since she'd come to the Smoke. Magazines were nothing compared with scrap metal.

She thought of the first day she had arrived there, seeing a magazine for the first time in the library, realizing with horror what humanity had once looked like. The pictures had made her sick that first day, and now here she was ready to save them.

"Here's the plan," the Boss said. "I'll go first, and when that Special grabs me, I'll give her a face full of pepper. You run straight and fast and don't look back. Got that?"

"Yeah."

"With any luck, we both might make it. Though I wouldn't mind a face-lift. Ready?"

Tally pulled the bag farther up on her shoulder. "Let's go."

"One . . . two . . ." The Boss paused. "Oh, dear. There's a problem, young lady."

"What?"

"You haven't got any shoes."

Tally looked down. In her confusion, she had stumbled barefoot out of the bunkhouse. The packed dirt of the Smoke compound was easy enough to walk on, but in the forest . . .

"You won't make it ten meters, kid."

The Boss pulled the duffel bag away from her and handed her the plastic container. "Now get going."

"But I . . . ," Tally said. "I don't want to go back to the city."

"Yes, young lady, and I wouldn't mind getting some decent dental work. But we all have to make sacrifices. Starting *now*!" On the last word, he shoved her out from behind the drum.

Tally stumbled forward, utterly exposed in the middle of the street. The roar of a hovercar seemed to pass right over her head, and she instinctively ducked, dashing toward the cover of the forest.

The Special cocked her head toward Tally, calmly folded her arms, and frowned like a teacher spotting littlies playing where they shouldn't.

Tally wondered if the pepper would do anything to the woman. If it affected the Special like it had Tally, she might still make it into the forest. Even if she was supposed to be the bait. Even if she had no shoes.

Even if it turned out David had already been caught and she'd never see him again . . .

The thought unleashed a sudden torrent of anger inside her, and she ran straight at the woman, the container clenched in both hands.

A smile broke out on the Special's cruel features.

A split second before they collided, the Special seemed to disappear, slipping out of sight like a coin in a magician's hand. In her next stride Tally felt something hard connect with her shin, and pain shot up her leg. Her body tumbled forward, hands reaching out to break her fall, the container slipping from her grasp.

She hit the ground hard, skidding on her palms. As

she rolled through the dirt, Tally glimpsed the Special crouching behind her. The woman had simply ducked, invisibly fast, and Tally had tripped over her like some awkward littlie in a brawl.

Shaking her head and spitting the dirt out of her mouth, Tally spotted the container just out of reach. She scrambled toward it, but a staggering weight crashed down on her, driving her face-first into the ground. She felt her wrists pulled back and bound, hard plastic cuffs cutting into her flesh.

She struggled, but couldn't move.

Then the awful weight lifted, and a nudge from a boot flipped her over effortlessly. The Special stood over her, smiling coldly, holding the container. "Now, now, ugly," the cruel pretty said. "You just calm down. We don't want to hurt you. But we will if we have to."

Tally started to speak, but her jaw clenched with pain. It had plowed into the ground when she'd fallen.

"What's so important about this?" the Special asked, shaking the container and trying to peer through its translucent plastic.

Out of the corner of her eye, Tally saw the Boss making his way toward the forest. His run was slow and tortured, the duffel bag too heavy for him.

"Open it and see," Tally spat painfully.

"I will," she said, still smiling. "But first things first." She turned her attention toward the Boss, and her posture suddenly transformed into something animal, crouched and coiled like a cat ready to spring.

Tally rolled back onto her shoulders, thrashing out wildly with both feet. Her kick connected with the container, and it popped open, a puff of brownish-green dust spraying out over the Special.

For a second, a disbelieving expression spread over the woman's face. She made a gagging noise, her whole body shuddering. Then her eyes and fists clamped shut, and she screamed.

The sound wasn't human. It cut into Tally's ears like a vibrasaw striking metal, and every muscle in her body fought to get free of the handcuffs, her instincts demanding that she cover her ears. With another wild kick, she rolled herself over and stumbled to her feet, staggering in the direction of the forest.

A tickle grew in Tally's throat as the pepper dust dispersed on the wind. She coughed as she ran, eyes watering and stinging until she was half-blind. With her hands tied behind her, Tally lurched into the brush off-balance, tumbling to the ground as her bare feet caught on something in the dense vegetation.

She struggled forward, trying to drag herself out of sight.

Blinking away tears, she saw that the Special's inhuman scream had been some kind of alarm. Three more of the cruel pretties had responded. One led the pepper-covered Special away at arm's length, and the others approached the forest.

Tally froze, the brush barely concealing her.

Then she felt a tickle in her throat, a slowly growing irritation. Tally held her breath, closing her eyes. But her chest began to shudder, her body twitching, demanding to expel traces of the pepper from her lungs.

She *had* to cough.

Tally swallowed again and again, hoping spit could put out the fire in her throat. Her lungs demanded oxygen, but she didn't dare breathe. One of the Specials was only a stone's throw away, scanning the forest with slow back-and-forth sweeps of his head, his eyes searching the dense trees relentlessly.

Gradually, painfully, the flames seemed to expire in Tally's chest, the cough dying a quiet death inside her. She relaxed, finally letting out her breath.

Over the thunder of hovercars and crackle of burning buildings and sounds of battle, the Special somehow heard her soft exhalation. His head turned swiftly, eyes narrowing, and in what seemed like a single motion he was by her side, a hand on the back of her neck. "You're a tricky one," he said.

She tried to answer, but wound up coughing savagely instead, and he forced her face down in the dirt before she could manage another breath.

THE RABBIT PEN

They marched her to the rabbit pen, where about forty handcuffed Smokies sat inside the wire fence. A dozen or so Specials stood in a cordon around them, watching their captives with empty expressions. By the entrance to the compound a few rabbits hopped aimlessly, too addled by their sudden freedom to make a break for it.

The Special who had captured Tally took her to the end farthest from the gate, where a handful of Smokies with bloody noses and black eyes were clustered.

"Armed resistor," he said to the two cruel pretties who guarded this end of the pen, and shoved her down to the ground among the others.

She stumbled and fell onto her back, where her weight stretched the cuffs painfully across her wrists. When she struggled to turn over, a foot planted itself into her back and pushed her up. For a moment, she thought the shoe belonged to a Special, but it was one of the other Smokies, helping her up the only way he could. She managed to sit up cross-legged.

The wounded Smokies around her smiled grimly, nodding encouragement.

"Tally," someone hissed.

She struggled to turn toward the voice. It was Croy, a cut over his eye bleeding down onto his cheek, one side of his face covered with dirt. He scooted himself a bit closer. "You resisted?" he said. "Huh. Guess I was wrong about you."

Tally could only cough. Traces of the burning pepper seemed stuck in her lungs, like the embers of a fire that wouldn't go out. Tears still streamed from her eyes.

"I noticed you slept through breakfast call this morning," he said. "Then when the Specials came, I figured you'd picked an awfully convenient time to disappear."

She shook her head, forced words through the cinders in her throat. "I was out late with David. That's all." Speaking made her sore jaw ache.

Croy frowned. "I haven't seen him all morning."

"Really?" She blinked away tears. "Maybe he got away."

"I doubt anyone did." Croy jutted his chin toward the gate of the pen. A large group of Smokies was on its way, guarded by a squad of Specials. Among them, Tally recognized faces from those who'd made a stand at the mess hall.

"They're just mopping up now," he said.

"Have you seen Shay?"

Croy shrugged. "She was at breakfast when they attacked, but I lost track of her."

"What about the Boss?"

Croy looked around. "No."

"I think he got away. He and I made a run together."

A dark smile crossed Croy's face. "That's funny. He always said he wouldn't mind getting captured. Something about a face-lift."

Tally managed to smile. But then she thought about the brain lesions that went along with becoming pretty, and a shiver passed through her body. She wondered how many of these captives knew what was really going to happen to them.

"Yeah, the Boss was going to give himself up, to help me get away, but I couldn't have made it through the forest."

"Why not?"

She wriggled her toes. "No shoes."

Croy raised an eyebrow. "You picked the wrong day to sleep late."

"I guess so."

Outside the overcrowded rabbit pen, the new arrivals were being organized into groups. A pair of Specials moved through the pen, flashing a reader into the bound Smokies' eyes, taking them outside one by one.

"They must be separating everyone by city," Croy said.

"Why?"

"To take us home," he said coldly.

"Home," she repeated. Just last night, that word had changed its meaning in her mind. And now *home* was destroyed. It lay around her in ruins, burning and captured.

She scanned the captives, looking for Shay and David.

The familiar faces in the crowd were haggard, dirty, crumpled by shock and defeat, but Tally realized that she no longer thought of them as ugly. It was the cold expressions of the Specials, beautiful though they were, that seemed horrific to her now.

A disturbance caught her eye. Three of the invaders were carrying a struggling figure, bound hand and foot, through the pen. They marched straight to the resistors' corner and dumped her onto the ground.

It was Shay.

"Watch this one."

The two Specials guarding them glanced at the still writhing figure. "Armed resistor?" one asked.

There was a pause. Tally saw that one of the Specials had a bruise marring his pretty face.

"Unarmed. But dangerous."

The three left their captive behind, their cruel grace marked with a touch of hurry.

"Shay!" Croy hissed.

Shay rolled herself over. Her face was red, her lips puffy and bleeding. She spat, saliva trailing from her mouth to a bloodred glob on the dusty ground.

"Croy," she managed with a thick tongue.

Then her eyes fell on Tally.

"You!"

"Uh, Shay . . . ," Croy began.

"You did this!" Her whole body writhed like a snake in its death throes. "Stealing my boyfriend wasn't enough? You had to betray the whole Smoke!"

Tally closed her eyes and shook her head. It couldn't be true. She had destroyed the pendant. The fire had consumed it.

"Shay!" Croy said. "Calm down. Look at her. She fought them."

"Are you blind, Croy? Look around you! *She* did this!"

Tally took a deep breath and forced herself to look at Shay. Her friend's eyes burned with hatred.

"Shay, I swear to you, I didn't. I never . . ." Her voice faltered.

"Who else could have led them here?"

"I don't know."

"We can't blame each other, Shay," Croy said. "It could've been anything. A satellite image. A scouting mission."

"A spy."

"Will you *look at her,* Shay?" Croy cried. "She's tied up, like us. She resisted!"

Shay slammed her eyes shut and shook her head.

The two Specials with the eye-reader had reached the resistors' corner of the pen. One stood back while the other stepped forward warily. "We don't want to hurt you," she announced. "But we will if we have to."

The cruel pretty grabbed Croy's chin and flashed the reader in his eye. She looked at its readout.

"Another one of ours," she said.

The other Special raised an eyebrow. "Didn't know we had so many runaways."

The two hauled Croy to his feet and marched him toward the largest group of Smokies outside. Tally bit her lip. Croy was one of Shay's old friends, so these two Specials were from her own city. Maybe all the invaders were.

It had to be a coincidence. This couldn't be her fault. She'd seen the pendant burn!

"So you've got Croy on your side too now, I see," Shay hissed.

Tears began to fill Tally's eyes, but not from the pepper this time. "Look at me, Shay!"

"He suspected you from the beginning. But I told him every time, 'No, Tally's my friend. She'd never do anything to hurt me.'"

"Shay, I'm not lying."

"How did you change Croy's mind, Tally? The same way you changed David's?"

"Shay, I never meant for that to happen."

"So where were you two last night?"

Tally swallowed, trying to hold her voice steady. "Just talking. I told him about my necklace."

"That took all night? Or did you just decide to make your move before the Specials came? One last game with him. With me."

Tally lowered her head. "Shay . . ."

A hand grabbed her chin and forced it up. She blinked, and a dazzling red light flashed.

The Special looked at the device closely. "Hey, it's her."

Tally shook her head. "No."

The other Special looked at the readout, nodding confirmation. "Tally Youngblood?"

She didn't answer. They lifted her to her feet and dusted her off.

"Come with us. Dr. Cable wants to see you immediately."

"I knew it," Shay hissed.

"No!"

They pulled Tally toward the gate of the pen. She twisted her head around to look back, trying to think of words that would explain.

Shay glared up at her from the ground, bloody teeth gritted, her eyes falling to Tally's bound wrists. A second later, Tally felt the pressure release, and her hands popped apart. The Specials had cut her handcuffs.

"No," she said softly.

One of the Specials squeezed her shoulder. "Don't worry, Tally, we'll have you home in no time."

The other chimed in. "We've been looking for this bunch for years."

"Yeah, good work."

IN CASE OF DAMAGE

They took her to the library. It had been transformed into a headquarters for the invasion, the long tables filled with portable workscreens manned by Specials, its usual quiet replaced by a buzz of clipped exchanges and commands. The razor voices of the cruel pretties set Tally's teeth on edge.

Dr. Cable waited at one of the long tables. Reading an old magazine, she seemed almost relaxed, at a remove from the activity around her.

"Ah, Tally." She bared her teeth in an attempt at a smile. "Nice to see you. Sit down."

Tally wondered what was behind the doctor's greeting. The Specials had treated Tally like an accomplice. Had some signal from the pendant reached them before she had destroyed it?

In any case, her only chance of escape was to play along. She pulled out a chair and sat down.

"Goodness. Look at you," Dr. Cable said. "For someone who wants to be a pretty, you're always such a sight."

"I've had a rough morning."

"You seem to have been in a scrape."

Tally shrugged. "I was just trying to get out of the way."

"Indeed." Dr. Cable placed the magazine facedown on the table. "That's something you don't seem to be very good at."

Tally coughed twice, the last bit of pepper leaving her lungs. "I guess not."

Dr. Cable glanced at her workscreen. "I see we had you among the resistors?"

"Some of the Smokies already suspected me. So when I heard you guys coming, I tried to get out of town. I didn't want to be around when everyone realized what was happening. In case they got mad at me."

"Self-preservation. Well, at least you're good at something."

"I didn't ask to come here."

"No, and you took your time, too." Dr. Cable leaned back, making a steeple of her long, thin fingers. "How long have you been here exactly?"

Tally forced herself to cough again, wondering if she dared lie. Her voice, still harsh and uneven from inhaling the pepper, wasn't likely to give her away. And although Dr. Cable's office back in the city might be one big lie detector, this table and chair were solid wood, without any tricks inside.

But Tally hedged. "Not that long."

"You didn't get here as quickly as I'd hoped."

"I almost didn't make it at all. And when I did, it was ages after my birthday. That's why they suspected me."

Dr. Cable shook her head. "I suppose I should have

been worried about you, out in the wild all alone. Poor Tally."

"Thanks for your concern."

"I'm sure you would have used the pendant if you'd gotten into any real trouble. Self-preservation being your one skill."

Tally sneered. "Unless I'd fallen off a cliff. Which almost happened."

"We still would have come for you. If the pendant had been damaged, it would have sent a signal automatically."

The words sunk in slowly: *If the pendant had been damaged* . . . Tally gripped the edge of the table, trying not to show any emotion.

Dr. Cable narrowed her eyes. She might not have machines to read Tally's voice and heartbeat and sweat, but her own perceptions were alert. She'd chosen those words to provoke a reaction. "Speaking of which, where is it?"

Tally's fingers went to her neck. Of course, Dr. Cable had noticed the pendant's absence immediately. Her questions had been leading to this moment. Tally's brain raced for an answer. The handcuffs were off. She had to get out of there, to the trading post. Hopefully, her hoverboard still lay on the roof, unfolded and charging in the morning sun. "I hid it," she said. "I was scared."

"Scared of what?"

"Last night, after I was sure this really was the Smoke, I activated the pendant. But they have this thing that detects bugs. They found the one on my board—the one you put there without telling me."

Dr. Cable smiled, spreading her hands helplessly.

"That almost blew the whole thing," Tally continued.

"So after I activated the pendant, I got scared they'd know a transmission had been sent. I hid it, in case they came looking."

"I see. A certain amount of intelligence sometimes accompanies a strong sense of self-preservation. I'm glad you decided to help us."

"Like I had a choice?"

"You always had a choice, Tally. But you made the right choice. You decided to come here and find your friend, to save her from a life of being ugly. You should be happy about that."

"I'm thrilled."

"So pugnacious, you uglies. Well, you'll be growing up soon."

A chill went down Tally's spine at the words. To Dr. Cable, "growing up" meant having your brain changed.

"There's just one more thing you have to do for me, Tally. Do you mind getting the pendant from where you've hidden it? I don't like to leave loose ends lying around."

Tally smiled. "I'd be happy to."

"This officer will accompany you." Dr. Cable lifted a finger, and a Special appeared at her side. "And just to keep you safe from your Smokey friends, we'll make it look like you've been a brave resistor."

The Special pulled Tally's hands together behind her back, and she felt plastic bite into her wrists again.

She took a breath, her pulse pounding in her head, then forced herself to say, "Whatever."

"This way."

Tally led the Special toward the trading post, taking in the situation. The Smoke had been beaten into silence.

Fires were left to burn freely. Some were already exhausted, clouds of smoke still rising from the blackened wood and swirling through the camp.

A few faces turned to look up with suspicion at Tally. She was the only Smokey still walking around. Everyone else was on the ground, handcuffed and under guard, most of them gathered near the rabbit pen.

She tried to give those who saw her a grim smile, hoping they noticed that she was handcuffed just like they were.

When they reached the trading post, Tally looked up. "I hid it on the roof."

The Special eyed the building suspiciously. "All right, then," he said. "You wait here. Sit down and don't stand up."

She shrugged, kneeling carefully.

The Special swung himself onto the roof with an ease that made Tally shiver. How was she going to overcome this cruel pretty? Even if her hands weren't tied, he was bigger, stronger, faster.

A moment later, his head stuck out over the edge. "Where is it?"

"Under the rapchuck."

"The what?"

"The *rapchuck*. You know, the old-fashioned thingie where the roofline connects with the abbersnatch."

"What the hell are you talking about?"

"It's Smokey slang, I guess. Let me show you."

A fleeting expression crossed the Special's impassive face—annoyance mixed with suspicion. But he leaped down again and stacked a couple of crates. He jumped onto them and pulled Tally up, sitting her on the edge of the roof as if she weighed nothing. "You touch one of those hoverboards, I'll put you on your face," he threatened casually.

"There're hoverboards up here?"

He leaped past her and hauled her onto the roof. "Find it."

"No problem." She walked gingerly up the slanted roof, exaggerating the difficulty of balancing without her hands. The solar cells of the recharging hoverboards were blindingly bright in the sun. Tally's board lay too far away, on the other side of the roof, and it was unfolded into eight sections. Folding it back up would take a solid minute. But Tally saw one nearby, Croy's maybe, that had only been unfolded once. Its light was green. One kick to close it and the board would be ready to fly.

But Tally couldn't fly with her hands bound. She'd fall off on the first turn.

She took a deep breath, ignoring the part of her brain that saw only the distance to the ground. As long as the Special was as fast and strong as he seemed . . .

"I'm wearing a bungee jacket," she lied to herself. "Nothing can possibly happen."

Tally let her bare feet trip, and tumbled down the slope.

The rough shingles battered Tally's knees and elbows as she rolled, letting out a cry of pain. She fought to stay on the roof, her feet scrambling against the wood to slow herself down.

Just as she reached the edge, an iron grip fastened onto her shoulder. She rolled off into space, the ground looming below. But Tally jerked to a halt, her arm wrenching in its socket, and she heard the Special's razor voice curse.

She swung for a moment, her fall arrested, then they both started to slip.

She could hear the Special's fingers and feet scrabbling

for purchase. However strong he might be, there was nothing for him to hold on to. Tally was going to fall.

But at least she was going to take him with her.

Then a grunt came from the Special, and Tally felt herself being pulled up in a mighty heave. She was thrown back onto the roof, and a shadow passed over her. Something hit the ground below. The Special had thrown himself off the roof to save her!

She rolled up into a crouch, stood, and lifted half of Croy's hoverboard with one foot, flipping it closed. A noise came from the edge of the roof, and Tally stepped away from Croy's board.

The Special's fingers appeared, then his body swung into view. He was completely unhurt.

"Are you okay?" she asked. "Wow. You guys are strong. Thanks for saving me."

He looked at her coolly. "Just get what we came for. And try not to kill yourself."

"Okay." Tally turned, managed to get a foot tangled on a shingle, and teetered again. The Special had her in his arms in a second. Finally, she heard real anger in his voice. "You uglies are so . . . incompetent!"

"Well, maybe if you could—"

Even before it was out of her mouth, she felt the pressure on her wrists disappear. She brought her hands around in front, rubbing her shoulders. "Ow. Thanks."

"Listen," he said, the razors in his cruel voice sharper than ever, "I don't want to hurt you, but—"

"You will if you have to." Tally smiled. He was standing in exactly the right place.

"Just get whatever Dr. Cable wants. And don't you dare touch one of those hoverboards."

"Don't worry, I don't have to," she said, and snapped the fingers of both hands as loudly as she could.

Croy's hoverboard jumped into the air, knocking the Special's feet out from under him. The man rolled off the roof again, and Tally leaped onto the board.

RUN

Tally had never ridden a hoverboard barefoot before. Young Smokies had all kinds of competitions, carrying weights or riding double, but no one was ever *that* stupid.

She almost fell off on the first turn, zooming down a new path they'd spiked with scrap metal only a few days before. The moment the board banked, her dirty feet skidded across the surface, spinning her halfway around. Her arms flailed wildly, but somehow Tally kept her footing, shooting across the compound and over the rabbit pen.

A ragged cheer rose up below as the captives below saw her fly past and realized that someone was making an escape. Tally was too busy staying on board to glance down.

Regaining her balance, Tally realized she wasn't wearing crash bracelets. Any fall would be for real. Her toes gripped the board, and she vowed to take the next turn more slowly. If the sky had been cloudy this morning, the sun wouldn't have burned the dew off Croy's board yet. She'd be lying in a crumpled heap in the pen, probably with a broken neck. It was lucky she, like most young Smokies, slept with her belly sensor on.

Already, the whine of hovercars taking off came from behind.

Tally knew only two ways out of the Smoke by hoverboard. Instinctively, she headed for the railroad tracks where she worked every day. The valley dropped behind her, and she managed to make the tight turn onto the white-water stream without falling off. With no knapsack and her heavy crash bracelets missing, Tally felt practically naked.

Croy's board wasn't as fast as hers, and it didn't know her style. Riding it was like breaking in new shoes—while running for your life.

Over the water, spray struck her face, hands, and feet. Tally knelt, grasping the edge of the board with wet hands, flying as low as she dared. Down here, the spray might make it even harder to ride, but the barrier of the trees kept her invisible. She dared a glance backward. No hovercars had appeared yet.

As she shot down the winding stream, swerving through the familiar hard turns, Tally thought of all the times she and David and Shay had raced each other to the work site. She wondered where David was. Back in camp, bound and ready to be taken to a city he'd never seen before? Would he have his face filed down and replaced by a pretty mask, his brain turned into whatever mush the authorities decided would be acceptable for a former renegade raised in the wild?

She shook her head, forcing the image from her mind. David hadn't been among the captured resistors. If he'd been caught, he definitely would have put up a fight. He must have escaped.

The roar of a hovercar passed overhead, the shock wave of its passage almost throwing Tally from the board. A few seconds later, she knew it had spotted her, its screaming turn echoing through the forest as it cut back to the river.

Shadows passed over Tally, and she glanced up to see two hovercars following her, their blades shimmering as bright as knives in the midmorning sun. The hovercars could go anywhere, but Tally was limited by her magnetic lifters. She was trapped on the route to the railroad.

Tally remembered her first ride out to Dr. Cable's office, the violent agility of the hovercar with its cruel pretty driver. In a straight line, they were much faster than any board. Her only advantage was that she knew this path backward and forward.

Fortunately, it was hardly a straight line.

Tally gripped the board with both hands and jumped from the river to the ridge line. The cars disappeared into the distance, overshooting as she skimmed the iron vein. But Tally was out in the open now, the plains spreading out below her as huge as ever.

She noticed fleetingly that it was a perfect day, not a cloud in the sky.

Tally lay almost flat to cut down wind resistance, coaxing every ounce of speed from Croy's board. It didn't look like she'd make it to the next cover before the two cars had swung around.

She wondered how they planned to capture her. Use a stunner? Throw a net? Simply bowl her over with their shock waves? At this speed and without crash bracelets, anything that knocked Tally off the board would kill her.

Maybe that was just fine with them.

The scream of their blades came from her right, louder and louder.

Just before the sound reached her, Tally dragged herself

into a full hoverskid, her momentum crushing her down into the board. The two hovercars shot past ahead, missing by a mile, but the wind of their passage spun her around in circles. The board flipped over and then back upright, Tally hanging on with both arms as the world spun wildly around her.

She regained control and urged it forward again, bringing it back to full speed before the hovercars could turn back around. The Specials might be faster, but her hoverboard was more maneuverable.

As the next turn drew near, the hovercars were headed straight for her, moving slower now, their pilots realizing that at top speed they would overshoot her every time.

Let them try to fly below tree level, though.

Now riding on her knees, gripping the board with both hands, Tally twisted into the next turn, dropping to skim just above the cracked dirt of the dry creek bed. She heard the whine of the hovercars steadily build.

They were tracking her too easily, probably using her body heat to pick her out among the trees, like the minders back home. Tally remembered the little portable heater she'd used to sneak out of the dorm so many times. If only she had it now.

Then Tally remembered the caves that David had shown her on her first day in the Smoke. Under the cold stones of the mountain, her body heat would disappear.

She ignored the sound of her pursuers, shooting down the creek bed and across a spur of ore, then onto the river that led to the railroad. She careened along above the water, and the hovercars stayed above tree height, patiently waiting for her to run out of cover.

As the turnoff to the railroad approached, Tally

increased her speed, skimming the water as fast as she dared. She took the turn at full skid and hurtled down the track.

The cars swept away down the river. The Specials might have expected her to turn off on another river, but the sudden appearance of an old railroad track had surprised them. If she could make it to the mountain before the hover-cars completed their slow turns, she would be safe.

Just in time, Tally remembered the spot where they had pulled up the track for scrap metal, and angled her board for a stomach-wrenching moment of freefall, soaring over the gap in a high arc. The lifters found metal again, and thirty seconds later she came to a skidding halt at the end of the line.

Tally jumped from the hoverboard, turned it around, and gave it a shove back toward the river. Without her crash bracelets to pull it back, the board would drift along the straight line of the railroad until it reached the break, where it would drop to the ground.

Hopefully, the Specials would think she'd fallen off, and start their search back there.

Tally crawled up the boulders and into the cave, scrambling back into the darkness. She pulled herself as far as she could go, hoping that the tons of stone overhead would be enough to hide her from the Specials. When the tiny aperture of light at the mouth of the cave had shrunk to the size of an eye, Tally dropped to the stone, panting, her hands still shaking from the flight, telling herself again and again that she'd made it.

But what had she made it to? She had no shoes, no hoverboard, no friends, not even a water purifier or a packet of SpagBol. No home to go back to.

Tally was completely alone. "I'm so dead," she said aloud.

A voice came out of the dark.

"Tally? Is that *you*?"

AMAZING

Hands grasped Tally's shoulders in the darkness.

"You made it!" It was David's voice.

In her surprise, Tally couldn't speak, but pulled him close, burying her face in his chest.

"Who else is with you?"

She shook her head.

"Oh," David whispered. Then his grip tightened as the cave shuddered around them. The roar of a hovercar passed slowly overhead, and Tally imagined the Specials' machines searching every crevice in the rock for signs of their prey.

Had she led them to David? That would be perfect, her final betrayal.

The low rumble of pursuit passed over them again, and David pulled her deeper into the blackness, down a long, twisting path that grew colder and darker. A stillness settled around her, damp and chill, and Tally imagined again the trainload of dead Rusties buried among the stones.

They waited in silence for what seemed like hours, holding each other, not daring to speak until long after the sounds of the cars had faded.

Finally David whispered, "What's happening back at the Smoke?

"The Specials came this morning."

"I know. I saw." He held her tighter. "I couldn't sleep, so I took my board up the mountain to watch the sunrise. They went right over me, twenty hovercars at once coming across the ridge. But what's happening now?"

"They put everyone in the rabbit pen, separating us into groups. Croy said they're going to take us all back to our cities."

"Croy? Who else did you see?"

"Shay, a couple of her friends. The Boss might have made it out. He and I made a break together."

"What about my parents?"

"I don't know." She was glad for the darkness. The fear in David's voice was painful enough. His parents had founded the Smoke, and they knew the secret of the operation. Whatever punishment awaited the other Smokies, it would be a hundred times worse for them.

"I can't believe it finally happened," he said softly.

Tally tried to think of something comforting to say. All she could see in the darkness was Dr. Cable's mocking smile.

"How did you get away?" he asked.

She pulled his hands to feel her wrists, where the plastic bracelets of the handcuffs remained. "I cut through these, got up onto the roof of the trading post, and stole Croy's hoverboard."

"With Specials guarding you?"

She bit her lip, saying nothing.

"That's amazing. My mother says they're superhuman. Their second operation augments all their muscles and rewires their nervous system. And they're so scary-looking, a lot of people just panic the first time they see one." He held her tighter. "But I should have known you would escape."

Tally closed her eyes, which made no difference in the utter darkness. She wished they could stay in there forever, never having to face what was outside. "It was just good luck."

Tally was amazed that she was lying again, already. If she had only told the truth about herself in the first place, the Smokies would have known what to do with the pendant. They could have attached it to some migratory bird, and Dr. Cable would be on her way to South America instead of in the library overseeing the destruction of the Smoke.

But Tally knew she couldn't tell the truth, not now. David would never trust her again, not after she'd destroyed his home, his family. She'd already lost Peris, Shay, and her new home. She couldn't bear to lose David as well.

And what good would a confession do now? David would be left alone, and so would she, when they most needed each other.

His hands ran across her face. "You still amaze me, Tally."

She felt herself shudder, the words twisting in her like a knife.

In that moment, Tally made a deal with herself. Eventually she would have to tell David what she had unwittingly done. Not now, but someday. When she'd made things better, fixed part of what she had destroyed, maybe then he would understand. "We'll go after them," she said. "Rescue them."

"Who? My parents?"

"They came from my city, right? So that's where they'll take them. And Shay and Croy, too. We'll rescue them all."

David laughed bitterly. "Us two? Against a bunch of Specials?"

"They won't expect us."

"But how will we find them? I've never been inside a city, but I hear they're pretty big. More than a million people."

Tally took a slow breath, once again remembering her first trip out to Dr. Cable's office. The low, dirt-colored buildings at the edge of the city, past the greenbelt and among the factories. The huge, misshapen hill nearby. "I know where they'll be."

"You what?" David pulled away from their embrace.

"I've been there. Special Circumstances headquarters."

There was a moment of silence. "I thought they were secret. Most of the kids who come out here don't even believe in them."

She went on, quietly horrified that another lie was coming into her head with such ease. "A while ago I pulled a really bad trick, the kind that gets you special attention." She rested her head against David again, glad that she couldn't see his trusting expression. "I snuck into New Pretty Town. That's where you live right after the operation, having fun all the time."

"I've heard of it. And uglies aren't allowed in, right?"

"Yeah. It's a pretty serious trick. Anyway, I wore this mask and crashed a party. They almost caught me, so I grabbed a bungee jacket."

"Which is?"

"Like a hoverboard, but you wear it. It was invented for escaping tall buildings in a fire, but new pretties use it mostly for goofing around. So I grabbed one, pulled a fire alarm, and jumped off the roof. It freaked a lot of people out."

"Right. Shay told me the whole story on our way to the Smoke, saying you were the coolest ugly in the world," he said. "But all I was thinking was that things must be *really* boring in the city."

"Yeah, I guess so."

"But you got caught? Shay didn't mention that."

The lie took form as she spoke, pulling on as many strands of truth as it could reach. "Yeah, I thought I'd gotten away, but they found my DNA or something. A few days later they took me to Special Circumstances, introduced me to this scary woman. I think she was in charge there. It was the first time I'd ever seen Specials."

"Are they really that bad up close?"

She nodded in the dark. "They're beautiful, absolutely. But in a cruel, horrible way. The first time's the worst. They only wanted to scare me, though. They warned me I'd be in big trouble if I ever got caught again. Or if I ever told anyone. That's why I never mentioned it to Shay."

"That explains a lot."

"About what?"

"About you. You always seemed to know how dangerous it was here in the Smoke. Somehow, you understood what the cities were really like, even before my parents told you the truth about the operation. You were the only runaway I ever met who really got it."

Tally nodded. That much was true. "I get it."

"And you still want to go back there for my parents and Shay? To risk getting caught? To risk your mind?"

A sob broke in her voice. "I have to." *To make it up to you.*

David held her tighter, tried to kiss her. She had to turn her face away, tears finally coming.

"Tally, you are amazing."

RUIN

They didn't leave the cave until the next morning.

Tally squinted in the dawn light, eyes scanning the sky for a fleet of hovercars suddenly rising above the trees. But they hadn't heard any sound of a search all night. Maybe now that the Smoke was destroyed, catching the last few runaways wasn't worth the trouble.

David's hoverboard had spent the night hidden in the cave, and hadn't had any sunlight for a whole day now, but it had just enough charge to get them back up the mountain. They rode to the river. Tally's stomach rumbled after a whole day without food, but the first thing she needed was water. Her mouth was so dry, she could hardly talk.

David knelt at the bank and dipped his head under the icy water. Tally shivered at the sight. Without a blanket or shoes, she'd frozen in the cave all night long, even huddled in David's arms. She needed warm food in her before she could face anything colder than the morning breeze.

"What if the Smoke's still occupied?" she asked. "Where will we get food?"

"You said they put prisoners in the rabbit pen? Where'd the rabbits go?"

"All over."

"Exactly. They should be everywhere by now. And they aren't hard to catch."

She grimaced. "Well, okay. As long as we cook them."

David laughed. "Of course."

"I've never actually started a fire," she admitted.

"Don't worry. You're a natural." He stepped onto his board and held out his hand.

Riding double was something Tally had never done before, and she found herself glad she was with David and not just anyone. She stood in front of him, bodies touching, her arms out, his hands around her waist. They negotiated the turns without words, Tally shifting her weight gradually, waiting for David to follow her lead. As they slowly got the hang of it, their bodies began to move together, threading the board down the familiar path as one.

It worked, as long as they went slowly, but Tally kept her ears open for sounds of pursuit. If a hovercar appeared, a full-speed escape was going to be tricky.

They smelled the Smoke long before they saw it.

From high up the mountain, the buildings had the look of a burned-out campfire, smoking, crumbling, blackened through and through. Nothing moved in the compound, except a few pieces of paper stirred by the wind.

"Looks like it burned all night," Tally said.

David nodded, speechless. Tally grasped his hand, wondering what it was like to see your childhood home reduced to a smoking ruin.

"I'm so sorry, David," she said.

"We have to go down. I need to see if my parents . . ." He swallowed the words.

Tally searched for signs of anyone remaining in the

Smoke. It seemed entirely deserted, but there might be a few Specials in hiding, waiting for stragglers to reappear. "We should wait."

"I can't. My parents' house is on the other side of the ridge. Maybe the Specials didn't see it."

"If they missed it, Maddy and Az will still be there."

"But what if they ran?"

"Then we'll find them. In the meantime, let's not get caught ourselves."

David sighed. "All right."

Tally held his hand tight. They unfolded the hoverboard and waited as the sun climbed, watching for any sign of a human being below. Occasionally, the embers of the fires flared to life in the breeze, the last standing columns of wood collapsing one by one, crumbling into ash.

A few animals rummaged for food, and Tally watched in silent horror as a stray rabbit was taken by a wolf, the short struggle leaving only a patch of blood and fur. This was what was left of nature, raw and wild, only hours after the Smoke had fallen.

"Ready to go down?" David asked after an hour.

"No," Tally said. "But I never will be."

They approached slowly, ready to turn and fly if any Specials appeared. But when they reached the edge of town, Tally felt her anxiety turn to something worse: a horrible certainty that no one remained there.

Her home was gone, replaced by nothing but charred wreckage.

At the rabbit pen, footprints showed where groups of Smokies had been moved in and out through the gates, a whole community turned into cattle. A few rabbits still hopped around on the dirt.

"Well, at least we won't starve," David said.

"I guess not," Tally said, although the sight of the Smoke had stilled her hunger. She wondered how David always managed to think practical thoughts, no matter what horrors were in front of him. "Hey, what's that?"

At one corner of the pen, just outside the fence, clusters of little shapes lay on the ground.

They edged the board closer, David squinting through a drifting wall of smoke. "It looks like . . . shoes."

Tally blinked. He was right. She lowered the board and jumped off, running to the spot.

Tally looked around in amazement. Around her were scattered twenty or so pairs of shoes, in all sizes. She fell to her knees to look closer. The laces were still tied, as if the shoes had been kicked off by people whose hands were bound behind them. . . .

"Croy recognized me," she murmured.

"What?"

Tally turned to David. "When I escaped, I flew right over the pen. Croy must have seen it was me. He knew I didn't have shoes. We joked about it."

She imagined the Smokies, helplessly awaiting their fate, making one last gesture of defiance. Croy would have kicked his own shoes off, then whispered to whomever he could: "Tally's free, and barefoot." They'd left her with a score of pairs to pick from, the only way they could help the one Smokey they'd seen escape.

"They knew I'd come back here." Her voice faltered. What they didn't know was who had betrayed them.

She picked a pair that looked about the right size,

with grippy soles for hoverboarding, and pulled them on. They fit, even better than the ones the rangers had given her.

Jumping back on the board, Tally had to hide the pained expression on her face. This is what it would be like from now on. Every gesture of kindness from her victims would only make her feel worse. "Okay, let's go."

The hoverpath wound through the smoking camp, over what streets remained between the charred ruins. Beside a long building, now little more than a ridge of blackened rubble, David pulled the board to a halt.

"I was afraid of this."

Tally tried to picture what had stood there. Her knowledge of the Smoke had evaporated, the familiar streets reduced to an unrecognizable sprawl of ash and embers.

Then she saw a few blackened pages fluttering in the wind. The library.

"They didn't take the books out before they . . . ," she cried. "But why?"

"They don't want people to know what it was like before the operation. They want to keep you hating yourselves. Otherwise, it's too easy to get used to ugly faces, *normal* faces."

Tally turned around to look into David's eyes. "Some of them, anyway."

He smiled sadly.

Then a thought crossed her mind. "The Boss was running away with some old magazines. Maybe he escaped."

"On foot?" David sounded dubious.

"I hope so." She leaned, and the board slid toward the edge of town.

A blotch of pepper still marked the ground where

she had fought the Special. Tally jumped off, trying to remember exactly where the Boss had escaped into the forest.

"If he got away, he must be long gone," David said.

Tally pushed her way into the brush, looking for signs of a struggle. The morning sun was streaming through the leaves, and a trail of broken bushes cut into the forest. The Boss had been none too graceful, leaving a path like a charging elephant.

She found the duffel bag half-hidden, shoved under a moss-covered fallen tree. Zipping it open, Tally saw that the magazines were still there, each one lovingly wrapped in its own plastic cover. She slung the bag over her shoulder, glad to have salvaged something from the library, a small victory over Dr. Cable.

A moment later, she found the Boss.

He lay on his back, his head turned at an angle that Tally instantly knew was utterly wrong. His fingers were clenched, the nails bloody from clawing at someone. He must have fought to distract them, maybe to keep them from finding the duffel bag. Or maybe for Tally's sake, having seen that she'd reached the forest too.

She remembered what the Specials had said to her more than once: *We don't want to hurt you, but we will if we have to.*

They'd been serious. They always were.

She stumbled back out of the forest, stunned, the bag still hanging from her shoulder.

"You found something?" David asked.

She didn't answer.

He saw the expression on her face and jumped down from the board. "What happened?"

"They caught him. They killed him."

David looked at her, his mouth open. He took a slow breath. "Come on, Tally. We have to go."

She blinked. The sunlight seemed wrong, twisted out of shape, like the Boss's neck. As if the world had become horribly distorted while she was among the trees. "Where?" she murmured.

"We have to go to my parents' house."

MADDY AND AZ

David took the board over the ridge so fast that Tally thought she would tumble off. She sank her fingertips into David's jacket to steady herself, thankful for the new shoes' grippy soles. "Listen, David. The Boss fought them, that's why they killed him."

"My parents would fight too."

She bit her lip and focused her whole mind on staying on board. When they reached the closest approach of the hoverpath to his parents' house, David jumped off and dashed down the slope.

Tally realized that the board still wasn't fully charged, and took a moment to unfold it before following, in no hurry to discover what the Specials had done to Maddy and Az. But when she thought of David finding his parents on his own, Tally ran after him.

It took her long minutes to find the path in the dense brush. Two nights ago they had come in the dark, and from a different direction. She listened for David, but couldn't hear anything. But then the wind shifted, and the smell of smoke came through the trees.

Burning the house hadn't been easy.

Set into the mountain, the stone walls and roof had provided no fuel for the fire. But the attackers had evidently thrown something inside that had contained its own fuel. The windows were blown outward, glass littering the grass in front of the house, nothing left of the door but a few charred scraps swinging on their hinges in the breeze.

David stood in front, unable to cross the threshold.

"Stay here," Tally said.

She stepped through the doorway, but the air overpowered her for the first moments. Morning light slanted in, picking out floating particles of ash. They swirled around Tally, little spiral galaxies set in motion by her passage.

The blackened floorboards crumbled under her feet, burned away to bare stone in some places. But some things had survived the fire. She remembered the marble statuette from her visit, and one of the rugs hanging on the wall remained mysteriously untouched. In the parlor, a few teacups stood out white against the charred furniture. Tally picked one up, realizing that if these cups had survived, a human body would leave more than traces.

She swallowed. If David's parents had been here, whatever was left of them would be easy to find.

Deeper into the house, in a small kitchen, city-made pots and pans hung from the ceiling, their warped, blackened metal still shining through in a few spots. Tally noted a bag of flour, and a few pieces of dried fruit somehow made her empty stomach growl.

The bedroom was last.

The stone ceiling was low and angled, the paint cracked

and blackened from the heat of a raging fire. Tally felt the heat still rising from the bed, the straw mattress and thick quilts fuel for the conflagration.

But Az and Maddy had not been there. There was nothing in the room that could have been human remains. Tally sighed with relief and made her way back outside, rechecking every room.

She shook her head as she stepped through the door. "Either the Specials took them, or they got away."

David nodded and pushed past her. Tally collapsed on the ground and coughed, her lungs finally protesting against the smoke and dust particles she had inhaled. Her hands and arms were black with soot, she realized.

When David came out, he held a long knife. "Hold out your hands."

"What?"

"The handcuffs. I can't stand them."

She nodded and held out her hands. He carefully threaded the blade between flesh and plastic, working it back and forth to saw the cuffs.

A solid minute later, he pulled the knife away in frustration. "It's not working."

Tally looked closer. The plastic had hardly been marked. She hadn't seen how the Special had snipped her handcuffs in two behind her, but it had only taken a moment. Perhaps they'd used a chemical trigger.

"Maybe it's some kind of aircraft plastic," she said. "Some of that stuff is stronger than steel."

David frowned. "So how did you get them apart?"

Tally opened her mouth, but nothing came out. She could hardly tell him that the Specials had released her themselves.

"And why do you have two cuffs on each wrist, anyway?"

She looked down dumbly, remembering that they'd handcuffed her first when she was captured, then again in front of Dr. Cable, before taking her to look for the pendant.

"I don't know," Tally managed. "I guess they double-cuffed us. But breaking out was easy. I cut them on a sharp rock."

"That doesn't make sense." David looked at the knife. "Dad always said this was the most useful thing he'd ever brought from the city. It's all high-tech alloys and monofilaments."

She shrugged. "Maybe the part that joined the cuffs was made out of different stuff."

He shook his head, not quite accepting her story. Finally, he shrugged. "Oh well, we'll just have to live with them. But one thing's for sure: My parents didn't get away."

"How do you know?"

He held up the knife. "If he'd had any warning, my dad never would have left without this. The Specials must have surprised them completely."

"Oh. I'm sorry, David."

"At least they're alive."

He looked into her eyes, and Tally saw that his panic had faded. "So, Tally, do you still want to go after them?"

"Yes, of course."

David smiled. "Good." He sat next to her, looking back at the house and shaking his head. "It's funny, Mom always warned me that this would happen. They tried to prepare me the whole time I was growing up. And for a long while I believed them. But after all those years, I started to wonder. Maybe my parents were just being paranoid. Maybe, like runaways always said, Special Circumstances wasn't real."

Tally nodded silently, not trusting herself to speak.

"And now that it's happened, it seems even less real."

"I'm sorry, David." But he could never know how sorry. Not until she'd helped save his parents, at least. "Don't worry, we'll find them."

"One stop to make first."

"Where?"

"As I said, my parents were ready for this, ever since they founded the Smoke. They made preparations."

"Like making sure you could take care of yourself," she said, touching the soft leather of his handmade jacket.

He smiled at her, rubbing soot from her cheek with one finger. "They did a lot more than that. Come with me."

In a cave near the house, the opening so small that Tally had to crawl inside on her belly, David showed her the cache of gear his parents had tended for twenty years.

There were water purifiers, direction finders, lightweight clothes, and sleeping bags—by Smokey standards, an absolute fortune in survival equipment. The four hoverboards had old-fashioned styling, but they were fitted with the same features as the one Dr. Cable had supplied Tally with for the trip to the Smoke, and there was a package of spare belly sensors, sealed against moisture. Everything was of the highest quality.

"Wow, they did plan ahead."

"Always," he said. He picked up a flashlight and tested its beam against the stone. "Every time I came here to check on all this stuff, I would imagine this moment. A million times I planned exactly what I would need. It's almost like I imagined it so much that it *had* to happen."

"It's not your fault, David."

"If I'd been here—"

"You'd be in a Special Circumstances hovercar right now, handcuffed, not likely to rescue anyone."

"Yeah, and instead, I'm here." He looked at her. "But at least you are too. You're the one thing I never imagined, all those times. An unexpected ally."

She managed to smile.

He pulled out a big waterproof bag. "I'm starving."

Tally nodded, and her head swam for a moment. She hadn't eaten since dinner two nights before.

David rummaged through the bag. "Plenty of instant food. Let's see: VegiRice, CurryNoods, SwedeBalls, Pad-Thai . . . any favorites?"

Tally took a deep breath. Back to the wild.

"Anything but SpagBol."

THE OIL PLAGUE

Tally and David left at sunset.

Each of them rode two hoverboards. Pressed together like a sandwich, the paired boards could carry twice as much weight, most of it in saddlebags slung on the underside. They packed everything useful they could find, along with the magazines the Boss had saved. Whatever happened, there would be no point in returning to the Smoke.

Tally took the river down the mountain carefully, the extra weight swaying below her like a ball and chain around both ankles. At least she was wearing crash bracelets again.

Their journey would follow a path very different from the one Tally had taken there. That route had been designed to be easy to follow, and had included a helicopter ride with the rangers. This one wouldn't be as direct. Overloaded as they were, Tally and David couldn't manage even short distances on foot. Every inch of the journey had to be over hoverable land and water, no matter how far it took them out of their way. And after the invasion, they would be giving any cities a wide berth.

Fortunately, David had made the journey to and from Tally's city dozens of times, alone and with inexperienced uglies in tow. He knew the rivers and rails, the ruins and natural veins of ore, and dozens of escape routes he'd devised in case he was ever pursued by city authorities.

"Ten days," he announced when they started. "If we ride all night and stay low during the day."

"Sounds good," Tally said, but she wondered if that would be soon enough to save anyone from the operation.

Around midnight the first night of travel, they left the brook that led down to the bald-headed hill, and followed a dry creek bed through the white flowers. It took them to the edge of a vast desert.

"How do we get through that?"

David pointed at dark shapes rising up from the sand, a row of them receding into the distance. "Those used to be towers, connected by steel cables."

"What for?"

"They carried electricity from a wind farm to one of the old cities."

Tally frowned. "I didn't know the Rusties used wind power."

"They weren't all crazy. Just most of them." He shrugged. "You've got to remember, we're mostly descended from Rusties, and we're still using their basic technology. *Some* of them must have had the right idea."

The cables still lay buried in the desert, protected by the shifting sands and a near-total absence of rainfall. In spots, they had broken or rusted through, so Tally and David had to ride carefully, eyes glued to the boards' metal detectors. When they reached a gap they couldn't jump, they would unroll a long piece of cable David carried, then walk the boards along it, guiding them like reluctant donkeys across some narrow footbridge before rolling it up again.

Tally had never seen a real desert before. She'd been taught in school that they were full of life, but this one was like the deserts she'd imagined as a littlie—featureless humps stretching into the distance, one after another. Nothing moved but slow snakes of sand borne by the wind.

She only knew the name of one big desert on the continent. "Is this the Mojave?"

David shook his head. "This isn't nearly that big, and it isn't natural. We're standing where the white weed started."

Tally whistled. The sand seemed to go forever. "What a disaster."

"Once the undergrowth was gone, replaced by the orchids, there was nothing to hold the good soil down. It blew away, and all that's left is sand."

"Will it ever be anything but desert?"

"Sure, in a thousand years or so. Maybe by then someone will have found a way to stop the weed from coming back. If we haven't, the process will just start all over again."

*

They reached a Rusty city around daybreak, a cluster of unremarkable buildings stranded on the sea of sand.

The desert had invaded over the centuries, dunes flowing through the streets like water, but the buildings were in better shape than other ruins Tally had seen. Sand wore away the edges of things, but it didn't tear them down as hungrily as rain and vegetation.

Neither of them was tired yet, but they couldn't travel during the day; the desert offered no protection from the sun, nor any concealment from the air. They camped in the second floor of a low factory building that still had most of its roof. Ancient machines, each as big as a hovercar, stood silent around them.

"What was this place?" Tally asked.

"I think they made newspapers here," David said. "Like books, but you threw them away and got a new one every day."

"You're kidding."

"Not at all. And you thought we wasted trees in the Smoke!"

Tally found a patch of sun shining through where the roof had collapsed, and unfolded the hoverboards to recharge. David pulled out two packets of EggSal.

"Will we make it out of the desert tonight?" she asked, watching David coax their last few drops of bottled water into the purifiers.

"No problem. We'll hit the next river before midnight."

She remembered something that Shay had said a long time ago, the first time she'd shown Tally her survival gear. "Can you really pee in a purifier? And then drink it, I mean?"

"Yeah. I've done it."

Tally grimaced and looked out the window. "Okay, I shouldn't have asked."

He came up behind her, laughing softly, placing his hands on her shoulders. "It's amazing what people will do to survive," he said.

She sighed. "I know."

The window overlooked a side street, partly protected from the encroaching desert. A few burned-out groundcars stood half-buried, their blackened frames stark against the white sand.

She rubbed the handcuff bracelets still encircling her wrists. "The Rusties sure wanted to survive. Every ruin I've seen, those cars are always all over, trying to get out. But they never seem to make it."

"A few of them did. But not in cars."

Tally leaned back into his reassuring warmth. The morning sun was hours away from burning off the chill of the desert.

"It's funny. At school, they never talk much about how it happened—the last panic, when the Rusty world fell apart. They shrug and say that all their mistakes just kept adding up, until it all collapsed like a house of cards."

"That's only partly true. The Boss had some old books about it."

"What did they say?"

"Well, the Rusties did live in a house of cards, but someone gave it a pretty big shove. No one ever found out who. Maybe it was a Rusty weapon that got out of control. Maybe it was people in some poor country who didn't like the way the Rusties ran things. Maybe it was just an accident, like the flowers, or some lone scientist who wanted to mess things up."

"But what happened?"

"A bug got loose, but it didn't infect people. It infected petroleum."

"Oil got infected?"

He nodded. "Oil is organic, made from old plants and dinosaurs and stuff. Somebody made a bacterium that ate it. The spores spread through the air, and when they landed in petroleum, processed or crude, they sprouted. Like a mold or something. It changed the chemical composition of the oil. Have you ever seen phosphorus?"

"It's an element, right?"

"Yeah. And it catches fire on contact with air."

Tally nodded. She remembered playing with the stuff in chem class, wearing goggles and talking about all the tricks you could do with it. But no one ever thought of a trick that wouldn't kill someone.

"Oil infected by this bacterium was just as unstable as phosphorus. It exploded on contact with oxygen. And as it burned, the spores were released in the smoke, and spread on the wind. Until the spores got to the next car, or airplane, or oil well, and started growing again."

"Wow. And they used oil for everything, right?"

David nodded. "Like those cars down there. They must have been infected as they tried to get out of town."

"Why didn't they just *walk*?"

"Stupid, I guess."

Tally shivered again, but not from the cold. It was hard to think of the Rusties as actual people, rather than as just an idiotic, dangerous, and sometimes comic force of history. But there were human beings down there, whatever was left of them after a couple of hundred years, still sitting in their blackened cars, as if still trying to escape their fate.

"I wonder why they don't tell us that in history class. They usually love any story that makes the Rusties sound pathetic."

David lowered his voice. "Maybe they didn't want you to realize that every civilization has its weakness. There's always one thing we depend on. And if someone takes it away, all that's left is some story in a history class."

"Not us," she said. "Renewable energy, sustainable resources, a fixed population."

The two purifiers *pinged*, and David left her to get them. "It doesn't have to be about economics," he said, bringing the food over. "The weakness could be an idea."

She turned to take her EggSal, cupping its warmth in her hands, and saw how serious he looked. "So, David, is that one of the things you thought about all those years, when you imagined the Smoke being invaded? Did you ever wonder what would turn the cities into history?"

He smiled and took a big bite.

"It gets clearer every day."

FAMILIAR SIGHTS

They reached the edge of the desert the next night, on schedule, then followed a river for three days, all the way to the sea. It took them still farther north, and the October chill turned as cold as any winter Tally had ever felt. David unpacked city-made arctic gear of shiny silver Mylar, which Tally wore over her handmade sweater, her only possession left from the Smoke. She was glad she'd dropped off to sleep in it the night before the Specials had invaded, so it hadn't been lost that day like everything else.

The nights spent on board seemed to pass quickly. On this journey, there were none of Shay's cryptic clues to puzzle through, no brush fires to escape, and no antique Rusty machines descending to scare her to death. The world seemed to be empty except for the occasional ruins, as if Tally and David were the last people alive.

They augmented their diet with fish caught from the river, and Tally roasted a rabbit on a fire she'd built herself. She watched David repair his leather clothes and decided she would never be able to manage a needle and thread well. He taught her how to tell time and direction from the stars, and she showed him how to open the expert software in the boards to optimize them for night travel.

At the sea they turned south, heading down the northern reaches of the same coastal railway that Tally had followed on her way to the Smoke. David said it had once stretched unbroken all the way back to Tally's home city and beyond. But now there were large gaps in the track, and new cities built on the sea, so they had to travel inland more than once. But David knew the rivers, the spurs of the railroad, and the other metal paths the Rusties had left behind, so they made good time toward their goal.

Only the weather stopped them. After a few days' travel down the coast, a dark and threatening mountain of clouds appeared over the ocean. At first, the storm seemed reluctant to come ashore, building up its nerve over a slow twenty-four hours, the air pressure changing in a way that made the hoverboards jittery to ride. The storm gave plenty of warning, but when it finally arrived, it was much worse than Tally had imagined weather could be.

She'd never faced the full force of a hurricane, except from within the solid structures of her inland city. It was another lesson in nature's savage power.

For three days Tally and David huddled in a plastic tent in the shelter of a rock outcrop, burning chemical glow-sticks for heat and light, hoping the magnets in the hover-boards wouldn't bring down a lightning strike. For the first hours, the drama of the storm kept them fascinated, amazed at its power, wondering when the next peal of thunder would shake the cliffs. Then the driving rain became simply monotonous, and they spent a whole day talking to each other about anything and everything, but especially their childhoods, until Tally was sure that she understood David better than anyone she'd ever known. On their third day trapped in the tent they had a terrible fight—Tally could never remember about what—that ended when David stormed out and stood alone in the icy wind for a solid hour. When he finally returned, it took him hours to stop shivering, even wrapped in her arms. "We're taking too long," he finally said.

Tally squeezed tighter. It took time to prepare subjects for the operation, especially if they were older than sixteen. But Dr. Cable wouldn't wait forever to turn David's parents. Every day the storm delayed them, there was a greater chance that Maddy and Az had already gone under the knife. For Shay, the perfect age for turning, the odds were even worse.

"We'll get there, don't worry. They measured me every week for a year before I was supposed to turn. It takes time to do it right."

A shudder passed through his body.

"Tally, what if they don't bother to do it right?"

*

The storm ended the next morning, and they emerged to find that the world's colors had been transformed. The clouds were bright pink, the grass an unearthly green, and the ocean darker than Tally had ever seen it, marked only by the foam crests of waves and a peppering of driftwood driven into the sea by the wind. They rode all day to make up for lost time, in a state of shock, amazed that the world could still exist after the storm.

Then the railway turned inland, and a few nights later they reached the Rusty Ruins.

The ruins looked smaller, as if the spires had shrunk since Tally had left them behind more than a month before, headed to the Smoke with nothing but Shay's note and a knapsack full of SpagBol. As she and David passed through the dark streets, the ghosts of the Rusties no longer seemed to threaten from the windows.

"The first time I came here at night, this place really scared me," she said.

David nodded. "It's kind of creepy how well preserved it is. Of all the ruins I've seen, it looks the most recent."

"They sprayed it with something to keep it up for school trips." And that was her city in a nutshell, Tally realized. Nothing left to itself. Everything turned into a bribe, a warning, or a lesson.

They stowed most of their gear in a collapsed building far from the center, a crumbling place that even truant uglies would probably avoid, packing only water purifiers, a flashlight, and a few food packets. David had never been any closer to the city than the ruins, so Tally took the lead for once, following the vein of iron that Shay had shown her months before.

"Do you think we'll ever be friends again?" she asked as they hiked toward the river, lugging their boards for the first time the entire trip.

"You and Shay? Of course."

"Even after . . . you and me?"

"Once we've rescued her from the Specials, I figure she'll forgive you for just about anything."

Tally was silent. Shay had already guessed that Tally had betrayed the Smoke. She doubted anything would ever make up for that.

Once they reached the river, they shot down the white water at top speed, glad to be finally free of the heavy saddlebags. With the spray hitting her face, the roar of water all around her, Tally could almost imagine this was one of her expeditions, back when she was a carefree city kid and not a . . .

What was she now? No longer a spy, and she couldn't call herself a Smokey anymore. Hardly a pretty, but she didn't feel like an ugly, either. She was nothing in particular. But at least she had a purpose.

The city came into view.

"There it is," she called to David over the churning water. "But you've seen cities before, right?"

"I've been this close to a few. But not much closer."

Tally gazed down at the familiar skyline, the slender trails of fireworks silhouetting the party towers and mansions. She felt a pang of something like homesickness, but much worse. The sight of New Pretty Town had once filled her with longing. Now the skyline was like a vacant shell, all its promises gone. Like David, she had lost her home. But unlike the Smoke, her city still existed, right in front of her eyes—but emptied of everything it had once meant.

“We’ve got a few hours before sunrise,” she said. “Want to take a look at Special Circumstances?”

“The sooner the better,” David said.

Tally nodded, her eyes tracing the familiar patterns of light and darkness surrounding the city. There was time to make it there and back before daybreak.

“Let’s go.”

They followed the river as far as the ring of trees and brush that separated Uglyville from the suburbs. The greenbelt was the best place to travel without being seen, and a good ride as well.

“Don’t go so fast!” David hissed from behind as she whipped through the trees.

She slowed down. “You don’t have to whisper. No one comes here at night. It’s ugly territory, and they’re all in bed, unless they’re tricking.”

“Okay,” he said. “But shouldn’t we be more careful about hoverpaths?”

“Hoverpaths? David, hoverboards work *everywhere* in the city. There’s a metal grid under the whole thing.”

“Oh, right.”

Tally smiled. She had been so used to living in David’s world, it was good to be explaining things to him for once. “What’s the matter,” she taunted, “can’t keep up?”

David grinned. “Try me.”

Tally turned and shot ahead, cutting a zigzag path between the tall poplars, letting her reflexes guide her.

She remembered her two hovercar rides to Special Circumstances. They’d flown across the greenbelt on the far side of town, then out to the transport ring, the industrial zone between the middle-pretty suburbs and outer

Crumblyville. The hard part would be getting across the burbs, a risky place to have an ugly face. Luckily, middle pretties went to bed early. Most of them, anyway.

She raced David halfway around the greenbelt, until the lights of the big hospital sat directly across the river from them. Tally remembered that first terrible morning, yanked away from the promised operation, flown out to be interrogated, her future pulled out from under her. She made a grim face, realizing that this time she was actually going out *looking* for Special Circumstances.

A tingle passed through her as they left the greenbelt. A minuscule part of Tally still expected her interface ring to warn her that she was leaving Uglyville. How had she worn that stupid thing for sixteen years? It had seemed such a part of her back then, but now the idea of being tracked and monitored and advised every minute of the day repelled Tally.

"Stick close," she said to David. "This is the part where you should whisper."

As a littlie, Tally had lived in the middle-pretty burbs with Sol and Ellie. But back then her world had been pathetically tiny: a few parks, the path to littlie school, one corner of the greenbelt where she would sneak in to spy on uglies. Like the Rusty Ruins, the neat row houses and gardens seemed much smaller to her now, an endless village of dollhouses.

They skimmed the rooftops, crouching low. If anybody was awake, going for a late-night run or walking a dog, they wouldn't be looking up, hopefully. Their boards barely a hand's breadth above the housetops, the patterns of shingles passed underneath hypnotically. All they encountered were nesting birds and a few cats, who flew or scrambled out of their way in surprise.

The burbs ended suddenly, a last band of parks fading into the transport ring, where underground factories stuck their heads aboveground and cargo trucks drove concrete roads all day and night. Tally lofted her board and gained speed.

"Tally!" David hissed. "They'll see us!"

"Relax. Those trucks are automatic. Nobody comes out here, especially at night."

He stared down at the lumbering vehicles nervously.

"Look, they don't even have headlights." She pointed down at a giant road-train passing below, the only light coming from it a dim red flicker from underneath, the navigation laser reading the bar codes painted onto the road.

They rode on, David still anxious at the sight of moving vehicles below.

Soon, a familiar landmark rose above the industrial wasteland.

"See that hill? Special Circumstances is just below it. We'll climb up top and take a look."

The hill was too steep to put a factory on, and apparently too big and solid to flatten with explosives and bulldozers, so it stood out on the flat plain like a lopsided pyramid, steep on one side and sloping on the other, covered with scrub and brown grass. They skimmed up the sloping side, dodging a few boulders and hardscrabble trees, until they reached the top.

From this height, Tally could see all the way back to New Pretty Town, the glowing disk of the island about as big as a dinner plate. The outer city was in darkness, and below her, the low, brown buildings of Special Circumstances were lit only with the harsh glare of security lights.

"Down there," she said, her voice falling to a whisper.

"Doesn't look like much."

"Most of it's underground. I don't know how far down it goes."

They stared at the cluster of buildings in silence. From up here, Tally could see the perimeter wire clearly, stretching around the buildings in an almost perfect square. That meant serious security. There weren't many barriers in the city—not that you could see, anyway. If you weren't supposed to be someplace, your interface ring just politely warned you to move along.

"That fence looks low enough to fly over."

Tally shook her head. "It's not a fence, it's a sensor wire. You get within twenty meters of it and the Specials will know you're there. Same goes if you touch the ground inside it."

"Twenty meters? Too high to clear on boards. So what do we do, knock on the gate?"

"There's no gate that I can see. I went in and out by hovercar."

David drummed his fingers on his board. "What about stealing one?"

"A hovercar?" Tally whistled. "That'd be a pretty good trick. I knew uglies who used to go joyriding, but not in Special Circumstances hovercars."

"It's too bad we can't just jump down."

Tally narrowed her eyes. "Jump?"

"From here. Get on our hoverboards back at the bottom of the hill, zoom up at maximum speed, then jump off from about this spot. We'd probably hit that big building dead center."

"Dead is right. We'd splat."

"Yeah, I guess. Even with crash bracelets, our arms would probably yank out of their sockets after a fall like that. We'd need parachutes."

Tally looked down, plotting trajectories from the hilltop, shushing David when he started to speak again, the wheels of her brain spinning. She remembered the party at Garbo Mansion, which seemed like years ago.

Finally, she allowed herself to smile.

"Not parachutes, David. Bungee jackets."

ACCOMPLICES

"There's enough time, if we hurry."

"Enough time to what?"

"To drop by the Uglyville art school. They have bungee jackets in the basement. A whole rack of spares."

David took a deep breath. "Okay."

"You're not scared, are you?"

"I'm not . . ." He grimaced. "It's just that I've never seen this many people before."

"People? We haven't seen anyone."

"Yeah, but all those houses on the way here. I keep thinking of people living in every single one, all crowded together like that."

Tally laughed. "You think the burbs are crowded? Wait until we get to Uglyville."

They headed back, taking the rooftops at top speed. The sky was pitch-black, but by now Tally could read the stars well enough to know that the first notes of dawn were only a couple of hours away.

Reaching the greenbelt, they turned back the way they'd come, neither of them speaking, concentrating instead on navigating through the trees. This arc of the belt brought them through Cleopatra Park, where Tally threaded the slalom poles for old times' sake. Her instincts twitched as they passed the path down to her old dorm. For a split second, it felt as if she could make the turnoff, climb in through her window, and go to bed.

Soon, the jumbled spires of the Uglyville art school rose up, and Tally brought the two of them to a halt.

This part was easy. It seemed like a million years ago that Tally and Shay had borrowed one of the school's bungee jackets for their final trick, Shay's leap onto the new uglies in the dorm library. Tally retraced her steps to the exact window they'd jimmied, a dirty, forgotten pane of glass concealed behind decorative bushes, and found that it was still unlocked.

Tally shook her head. This sort of burglary had seemed so daring two months before. Back then, the library stunt was the wildest prank she and Shay could dream up. Now she saw tricks for what they were: a way for uglies to blow off steam until they reached sixteen, nothing but a meaningless distraction until their mutinous natures were erased by adulthood, and the operation.

"Give me the flashlight. And wait here."

She slipped in, found the rack of spares, grabbed two bungee jackets, and was out in less than a minute. When she pulled herself out of the window, she found David staring at her with wide eyes. "What?" she asked.

"You're just so . . . good at all this. So confident. It

makes me nervous just being inside city limits."

She grinned. "This is no big deal. Everyone does it."

Still, Tally was happy to impress David with her burglary skills. In the last few weeks he'd taught her how to build a fire, scale a fish, pitch a tent, and read a contour map. It was nice to be the competent one for a change.

They crept back to the greenbelt and reached the river before the sky had even shown a sliver of pink. Zooming past the white water and onto the vein of ore, they sighted the ruins just as the sky was beginning to change.

On the hike down, Tally asked, "Tomorrow night, then?"

"No point in waiting."

"No." And there was every reason to attempt the rescue soon. It had been more than two weeks since the invasion of the Smoke.

David cleared his throat. "So, how many Specials do you think will be in there?"

"When I was there, a lot. But that was during the day. I assume they have to sleep sometime."

"So it'll be empty at night."

"I doubt that. But maybe just a few guards." She didn't say more. Even one Special would be more than a match for a pair of uglies. No amount of surprise would make up for the cruel pretties' superior strength and reflexes. "We'll just have to make sure they don't see us."

"Sure. Or hope they've got something else to do that night."

Tally trudged ahead, exhaustion taking over now that they were safely out of the city, her confidence ebbing with every step. They'd traveled all this way without thinking very hard about the task ahead of them. Rescuing people from Special Circumstances wasn't just another ugly-trick, like stealing a bungee jacket or sneaking up the river. It was serious business.

And although Croy, Shay, Maddy, and Az were probably all prisoners in those horrible underground buildings, there was always the possibility that the Smokies had been taken somewhere else. And even if they hadn't, Tally had no idea exactly where they'd be inside the warren of puke-brown hallways.

"I just wish we had some help," she said softly.

David's hand settled on her shoulder, bringing her to a halt. "Maybe we do."

She looked at him questioningly, then followed his gaze down toward the ruins. At the top of the highest spire, the last few flickers of a safety sparkler were sputtering out.

There were uglies down there.

"They're looking for me," he said.

"So what do we do?"

"Is there any other way back to the city?" David asked.

"No. They'll come hiking right up this path."

"Then we wait."

Tally squinted, peering at the ruins. The sparkler had faded, and nothing was visible in the dawn light just starting to spill across the sky. Whoever was down there had waited until the last possible minute to head for home.

Of course, if they were looking for David, these uglies were potential runaways. Rebellious seniors, not that worried about missing breakfast.

She turned to David. "So, I guess uglies are still looking for you. And not just here."

"Of course," he said. "The rumors will go on for generations, in cities all over, whether I'm around or not. Lighting a sparkler doesn't usually get an answer, so it'll be a long time before even the uglies I've met figure out I'm not showing up. And most of them already don't even think the Smoke—"

His voice caught, and Tally took his hand. For a moment he'd forgotten that the Smoke didn't, in fact, exist anymore.

They waited in silence, until the sound of scrambling feet came across the rocks. It sounded like three or so uglies, talking in low tones as if still wary of the ghosts of the Rusty ruins.

"Watch this," David whispered, pulling a flashlight from his pocket. He stood and pointed the light up at his own face, switching it on.

"Looking for me?" he said in a loud, commanding voice.

The three uglies froze, wide-eyed and open-mouthed. Then the boy dropped his board, and it crashed onto the stones beside him, breaking their paralysis.

"Who are you?" one of the girls managed.

"I'm David."

"Oh. You mean you're . . ."

"Real?" He switched off the light and grinned. "Yeah, I get that question a lot."

Their names were Sussy, An, and Dex, and they had been coming to the ruins for a month now. They'd heard rumors about the Smoke for years, since an ugly in their dorm had run away.

"I'd just moved to Uglyville," Sussy said, "and Ho was a senior. When he disappeared, everyone had these crazy theories about where he'd gone."

"Ho?" David nodded. "I remember him. He stayed for a few months, then changed his mind and came back. By now, he's a pretty."

"But he really made it? To the Smoke?" An asked.

"Yeah. I took him there."

"Wow. So it's real." An shared an excited look with her two friends. "We want to see it too."

David opened his mouth, then closed it. His eyes drifted away to one side.

"You can't," Tally spoke up. "Not right now."

"Why not?" Dex asked.

Tally paused. The truth, that the Smoke had been destroyed by an armed invasion, seemed too far-fetched. A few months ago, she wouldn't have believed what her own city was capable of. And if she admitted that the Smoke was gone, the rumor would make its way down through generations of uglies. Dr. Cable's work would be complete, even if a few rescued Smokies somehow managed to create another community in the wild. "Well," she started, "every so often the Smoke has to move, to stay secret. Right now, it doesn't really exist. Everyone's scattered, so we're not recruiting."

"The whole place moves?" Dex said. "Whoa."

An frowned. "Hang on. If you're not recruiting, then why are you here?"

"To do a trick," Tally said. "A really big one. Maybe you could help us. And then when the Smoke is back on its feet, you'll be the first to know."

"You want us to help? Like an initiation?" Dex asked.

"No," David said firmly. "We don't make anyone do anything to get into the Smoke. But if you do want to help, Tally and I would appreciate it."

"We just need a diversion," Tally said.

"Sounds like fun," An said. She looked at the others, and they waggled their heads.

Up for anything, Tally thought, just like she used to be herself. They were definitely seniors, less than a year behind her, but she was amazed at how young they seemed.

David stared at Tally along with the others, waiting for the rest of her idea. She had to come up with a diversion right away. A good one. Something that would intrigue the Specials enough to investigate.

Something that would make Dr. Cable herself take notice.

"Well, you'll need a lot of sparklers."

"No problem."

"And you know how to get into New Pretty Town, right?"

"New Pretty Town?" An looked at her friends. "But don't the bridges report everyone who crosses the river?"

Tally smiled, always happy to teach someone a new trick.

OVER THE EDGE

The two waited all day in the Rusty Ruins, patches of sunlight crawling across the floor through the crumbling roof, like slow searchlights marking the hours. It took Tally ages to get to sleep, imagining the leap from the hilltop down into uncertainty. Finally she passed out, too tired to dream.

Awakening at dusk, she found that David had already packed two knapsacks with everything they might need during the rescue. They hoverboarded to the edge of the ruins, riding two sandwiched hoverboards each. Hopefully, they would need the extra boards when they emerged from Special Circumstances, escapees in tow.

Eating breakfast by the river, Tally took time to appreciate her SwedeBalls. If they got caught tonight, at least she would never have dehydrated food again. Sometimes Tally felt she could almost accept brain damage if it meant a life without reconstituted noodles.

As darkness fell, Tally and David reached the white water, and they passed through the greenbelt at the very moment the lights winked off in Uglyville. By midnight, they were atop the hill overlooking Special Circumstances.

Tally pulled out her binoculars and trained them inward, toward New Pretty Town, where the party towers were just coming alight.

David blew into his hands, his breath visible in the October chill. "You really think they'll do it?"

"Why not?" she said, watching the dark spaces of the city's largest pleasure garden. "They seemed into it."

"Yeah, but aren't they taking a big risk? I mean, they just met us."

She shrugged. "An ugly lives for tricks. Haven't you ever done something just because a mysterious stranger intrigued you?"

"I gave my gloves to one once. But it got me into all kinds of trouble."

She lowered the binoculars and saw that David was smiling. "You don't look as nervous tonight," she said.

"I'm glad we're finally here, finally ready to *do* something. And after those three kids agreed to help us, I feel like . . ."

"Like this might actually work?"

"No, something better." He looked down at the Special Circumstances compound. "They were so ready to help, just to make trouble, just to play a trick. At first, it killed me to hear you act like the Smoke still existed. But if there are enough uglies like them, maybe it will again."

"Of course it will," she said softly.

David shrugged. "Maybe, maybe not. But even if we blow it tonight, and both wind up under the knife, at least someone will still keep fighting. Making trouble, you know?"

"I hope it's us, making trouble," Tally said.

"Me too." He drew Tally closer, and kissed her. When he released her, Tally took a deep breath and closed her eyes. It felt better to kiss him, more real, now that she was about to begin undoing the damage she had done.

"Look," David said.

In the dark spaces of New Pretty Town, something was happening.

She raised her binoculars.

A shimmering line cut its way across the black expanse of the pleasure garden, like a bright fissure opening in the earth. Then more lines appeared, one by one, tremulous arcs and circles sweeping through the darkness. The various segments seemed to sparkle into existence in random order, but they eventually formed letters, and words.

Finally, the whole glittering thing was finished, some parts of it newly sprung to life, the first few lines already starting to fade as the sparklers exhausted themselves. But for a few moments, Tally could read the whole thing, even without her binoculars. From Uglyville, it must have been huge, visible to anyone staring longingly out their window. It said: THE SMOKE LIVES.

As Tally watched it fade, breaking down into random lines and arcs again as the sparklers extinguished, she wondered if the words were really true.

"There they go," David said.

Below them, a large circular opening had appeared in the

largest building's roof, and three hovercars rose up through the gap in quick succession, screaming toward the city. Tally hoped that An, Dex, and Sussy had followed her advice and were long gone from New Pretty Town. "Ready?" she said.

In answer, David tightened the straps of his bungee jacket and jumped onto his boards.

They rode down the hill, turned around, and started back up.

For the tenth time, Tally checked the light on the collar of her jacket. It was still green, and she could see David's light bobbing along beside her. No excuses now.

They gained speed as they climbed toward the dark sky, the entire hill like a giant ramp before them. The wind pushed Tally's hair back, and she blinked as bugs *pinged* against her face. She slid carefully toward the front of the paired boards, the toes of one grippy shoe sticking out past the riding surface.

Then the horizon seemed to slip away in front of her, and Tally crouched, ready to jump.

The ground disappeared.

Tally pushed off with all her strength, forcing her hoverboards down the steep side of the hill, where they would bring themselves to a halt. She and David had switched off their crash bracelets—they didn't want the boards following them over the wire. Not yet.

Tally soared into midair, still climbing for a few more seconds. The outer city lay below her, a vast patchwork of light and dark. She spread her arms and legs.

At the peak of her arc, the silence seemed to overwhelm everything—her stomach-churning weightlessness, the mix of excitement and fear rushing through her, the wind against her face. Tally tore her eyes from the silently waiting earth and dared a glance at David. Hardly an arm's length away, he was looking back at her, his face alight.

She grinned at him and turned back to see that the ground was approaching now, the speed of her fall building slowly. As she'd calculated, they were coming down right in the middle of the wire. Tally began to anticipate the sickening jolt of her bungee jacket pulling her up.

For long moments nothing happened, except the ground getting closer, and Tally wondered again if bungee jackets could handle a fall from this distance. A hundred versions of what a hard landing would feel like managed to squeeze into her head. Of course, it probably wouldn't feel like anything.

Ever again.

The ground grew closer and closer, until Tally was certain something had gone wrong. Then, with sudden violence, the straps of the jacket came alive, cutting cruelly into her thighs and shoulders, crushing the air from her lungs, the pressure building as if a huge rubber band were wrapped around her, trying to bring her to a halt. The bare dirt of the compound rushed up toward her, looking flat and packed and *hard*, the jacket fighting her momentum desperately now, crushing her like a fist in its grasp.

Finally, the invisible rubber band stretching toward its breaking point, she slowed to a shuddering halt within reach of the ground, pulling her hands back to keep from touching it, her eyeballs straining forward as if they wanted to pop out of her skull.

Then her fall reversed, and she pulled back upward, hover-bouncing head over heels, sky and horizon spinning around her like a playground ride. Tally had no idea where David was—or where up and down were, for that matter.

This jump was ten times her plunge off Garbo Mansion. How many bounces would it take to come to a stop?

Now she was falling again, the dirt of the compound replaced by a building below her. One foot almost touched down onto the roof, but Tally was pulled up again, still barreling forward with the momentum of her leap off the hill.

She managed to orient herself, sorting out up and down just in time to see the edge of the roof coming toward her. She was overshooting the building. . . .

Flailing in the grasp of the jacket, flying helplessly upward and then down again, she passed the roof's edge. But her outstretched hand caught a rain gutter, bringing Tally to a sudden halt. "Phew," she said, looking down.

The building wasn't very tall, and Tally would bounce in her jacket if she fell, but the moment her feet touched the ground, the wire would sound an alarm. She gripped the rain gutter with both hands.

But the bungee jacket, satisfied that her fall had stopped, was shutting itself down, gradually returning her to normal weight. She struggled to pull herself up onto the roof, but the heavy knapsack full of rescue equipment dragged her downward. It was like trying to do a pull-up wearing lead shoes.

She hung there, out of ideas, waiting to fall.

Footsteps came toward her along the roof, and a face appeared. David.

"Having trouble?"

She grunted an answer, and he reached over, grabbing a strap of the knapsack. The weight mercifully lifted from her shoulders, and Tally pulled herself over the edge.

David sat back onto the roof, shaking his head. "So, Tally, you used to do that for *fun*?"

"Not every day."

"Didn't think so. Can we rest for a minute?"

She scanned the rooftop. No one coming, no alarms ringing. Apparently, the wire wasn't built to sense them up there. Tally smiled.

"Sure. Take two minutes, if you want. It looks like the Specials weren't expecting anyone to jump out of the sky."

INSIDE

The roof of Special Circumstances had looked flat and featureless from way up on top of the hill. But standing on it, Tally could see air vents, antennae, maintenance hatchways, and of course the big circular door that the hovercars had come through, now closed. It was a wonder neither she nor David had cracked their heads hover-bouncing across it.

"So how do we get in?" David asked.

"We should start with this." She pointed toward the hovercar door.

"Don't you think they'll notice if we come through there and we're not a hovercar?"

"Agreed. But what if we jam the door? If any more Specials show up, we don't want to make it easy for them to come in after us."

"Good idea." David searched through his knapsack, bringing out what looked like a tube of hair gel. He squeezed out white goo along the edges of the door, careful not to let any touch his fingers.

"What's that?"

"Glue. The nano kind. You can stick your shoes to the ceiling with this stuff and hang upside down."

Tally's eyes widened. She'd heard rumors of tricks you could play with nanotech glue, but uglies weren't allowed to requisition it. "Tell me you haven't done that."

He smiled. "I had to leave them up there. Waste of good shoes. So how do we get down?"

Tally pulled a powerjack from her pack and pointed. "We take the elevator."

The big metal box sticking up from the roof looked like a storage shed, but the double doors and eye-reader gave it away. Tally squinted, making sure the reader didn't flash her, and worked her powerjack between the doors. They crumpled like foil.

Through the doors, a dark shaft dropped away to nothingness. Tally clicked her tongue, and the echoes indicated that it was a long way down. She glanced at her collar light. Still green.

Tally turned to David. "Wait for me to whistle."

She stepped off into thin air.

Falling down the shaft was much scarier than leaping off Garbo Mansion, or even flying into space from the hilltop. The darkness offered no clue how deep the shaft was, and it felt to Tally as if she might fall forever.

She sensed the walls rushing past, and wondered if she was drifting toward one side as she fell, about to crash against it. She imagined herself bouncing from one wall to another all the way down, coming to a soft landing already broken and bleeding.

Tally kept her arms close to her sides.

At least she was sure the jacket would work in here.

Elevators used the same magnetic lifters as any other hovercraft, so there was always a solid metal plate at the bottom.

After a long count of five, the jacket gripped Tally. She bounced twice, straight up and down, then settled onto a hard surface and found herself in silence and absolute blackness. Stretching out her hands, she felt the four walls around her. Nothing suggested the inside of closed doors. Her fingers came away greasy.

Tally peered upward. A tiny shaft of light shone above, and she could just make out David's face peering down. She pursed her lips to whistle, but stopped.

A muffled sound came from below her feet. Someone talking.

She crouched, trying to grasp the words. But all Tally could hear was the razor sound of a cruel pretty's voice. The mocking tone reminded her of Dr. Cable.

Without warning, the floor dropped out from under her. Tally struggled to keep her footing. When the elevator stopped again, one of her ankles twisted painfully under her weight, but she managed not to fall.

The sound below her faded. One thing was certain now: The complex wasn't empty.

Tally lifted her head and whistled, then huddled in one corner of the shaft, hands covering her head, counting.

Five seconds later, a pair of feet dangled next to her, then jerked back up, the beam of David's flashlight swinging around drunkenly. Gradually, he settled beside her. "Wow. It's dark down here."

"Shhh," she hissed.

He nodded, sweeping the flashlight around the shaft. Just above them, it fell on the inside of closed doors. Of course. Standing on the elevator's roof, they were midway between floors.

Tally interlaced her fingers, locking her hands together to give David a boost up to where he could wedge the powerjack between the doors. They crumpled open with a metal screech that set her hair on end. He pulled himself through, then extended his hand back down to her. Tally grabbed it and pulled, her grippy shoes squeaking on the walls of the elevator shaft like a herd of panicked mice.

Everything was making too much noise.

The hallway was dark. Tally tried to convince herself that no one had heard them yet. Maybe this whole floor was empty at night.

She pulled out her own flashlight, pointing it at the doors as they walked down the hall. Small brown labels marked each of them.

"Radiology. Neurology. Magnetic Imaging," she read softly. "Operating Theater Two."

She looked at David. He shrugged and gave the door a push. It opened.

"I guess when you're in an underground bunker, there's no point in locking up," he said softly. "After you."

Tally crept inside. The room was big, the walls lined with dark and silent machines. An operating tank stood in the middle, the liquid drained out of it, tubes and electrodes hanging loosely in a puddle at the bottom. A metal table glistened with the cruel shapes of knives and vibrasaws.

"This looks like photos Mom showed me," David said. "They do the operation here."

Tally nodded. Doctors only put you in a tank if they were doing major surgery.

"Maybe this is where they make Specials special," she said. The thought didn't cheer her up.

They returned to the hall. A few doors later, they found a room labeled MORGUE.

"Do you . . . ," she started to ask.

David shook his head. "No."

They searched the rest of the floor. Basically, it was a small, well-equipped hospital. There were no torture chambers or prison cells. And no Smokies.

"Where to now?"

"Well," Tally said. "If you were the evil Dr. Cable, where would you put your prisoners."

"The evil who?"

"Oh. That's her name, the woman who runs this place. I remember from when I got busted."

David frowned, and Tally wondered if she'd said too much.

Then he shrugged. "I guess I'd put them in the dungeon."

"Okay. Down, then."

They found a set of fire stairs that led down, but they ended after only one flight. Apparently, they had reached the bottom floor of Special Circumstances.

"Careful," Tally whispered. "Before, I heard people getting out of the elevator below me. They must be somewhere down here."

This floor was lit by a soft glowstrip running down the middle of the hallway. A cold finger crept down Tally's spine as she read the labels on the doors.

"Interrogation Room One. Interrogation Room Two. Isolation Room One," she whispered, her flashlight flickering across the words like an anxious firefly. "Disorientation Room One. Oh, David, they must be down here somewhere."

He nodded, and pushed one of the doors softly, but it didn't budge. He ran his fingers around the edge, searching for a place where the powerjack could get purchase.

"Don't let the eye-reader flash you," Tally warned softly. She pointed at the little camera by the door. "If it thinks it sees an eye, it'll read your iris and check with the big computer."

"It won't have any record of me."

"And that will freak it out totally. Just don't get too close. It's automatic."

"Okay," David said, nodding. "These doors are too smooth, anyway. No place to fit a jack in. Let's keep looking."

Farther down the hall, a label caught Tally's eye. "Long-Term Detention," she whispered. The door had a long expanse of blank wall on either side, as if the room behind it was bigger than the others. She put her ear to it, listening for any hint of sound.

She heard a familiar voice. It was coming closer. "David!" she hissed, pulling away from the door and throwing herself against the wall. David looked around frantically for a place to hide. Both of them were in plain view.

The door slid open, and Dr. Cable's malevolent voice poured out.

"You're simply not trying hard enough. You just have to convince her that—"

"Dr. Cable," Tally said.

The woman spun to face Tally, her hawklike features twisted in surprise.

"I'd like to give myself up."

"Tally Youngblood? How—"

From behind, David's powerjack thudded against the side of Dr. Cable's head, and she slumped to the floor.

"Is she . . . ," David stammered. His face was white.

Tally knelt and turned Dr. Cable's head to inspect the wound. No blood, but she was out cold. No matter how formidable cruel pretties were, surprise still had its advantages. "She'll be okay."

"Dr. Cable? What's going—"

Tally turned toward the voice, her eyes taking in the young woman before her.

She was tall and elegant, every feature perfection. Her eyes—deep and soulful, flecked with copper and gold—widened with a troubled look. Her generous lips parted wordlessly, and she raised one graceful hand. Tally's heart almost stopped at the beauty of her confusion.

Then recognition filled the woman's face, her broad smile illuminating the darkness, and Tally felt herself smiling in return. It felt good to make this woman happy.

"Tally! It *is* you."

It was Shay. She was pretty.

RESCUE

"Shay . . ."

"You made it!" Shay's stunning smile faded as she looked down at the crumpled form of Dr. Cable. "What's with her?"

Tally blinked, awed by the transformation of her friend. Shay's beauty seemed to snuff out everything inside Tally;

her fear, surprise, and excitement fled, leaving nothing but amazement. "You . . . turned."

"Duh," she said. "David! You're both okay!"

"Uh, hi." His voice was dry, his hands shaking as they gripped the powerjack. "We need your help, Shay."

"Yeah, I guess you do." She looked down at Dr. Cable again and sighed. "You guys still know how to make trouble, I see."

Tally averted her eyes from Shay's beauty, trying to focus her thoughts. "Where's everyone else? David's parents? Croy?"

"Right in here." Shay gestured over one shoulder. "All locked up. Dr. C has been totally bogus to us."

"Keep her here," David said. He pushed past Shay and through the door. Tally saw a row of small doors inside the long room, each with a tiny window set in it.

Shay beamed at her. "I'm so glad you're all right, Tally. The thought of you all alone in the wild . . . of course, you weren't alone, were you?"

Meeting Shay's eyes, Tally was overwhelmed all over again. "What did they do to you?"

Shay smiled. "Besides the obvious?"

"Yeah. I mean, no." Tally shook her head, not knowing how to ask Shay if she was brain damaged. "Are any of the rest of them . . ."

"Pretty? No. I got to be first, because I made the most trouble. You should have seen me kicking and biting." Shay chuckled.

"They forced you."

"Yeah, Dr. C can be a major pain. It's kind of a relief, though."

Tally swallowed. "A relief . . ."

"Yeah, I hated this place. The only reason I'm here is that Dr. C wanted me to come by and talk to the Smokies."

"You live in New Pretty Town," Tally said softly. She tried to see past the beauty, to find whatever was behind Shay's wide, perfect eyes.

"Yeah. I just came from the *best* party."

Tally finally heard how slurred Shay's words were. She was drunk. Maybe that was why she was acting so strangely. But she had called the others "the Smokies." She wasn't one of them anymore.

"You go to parties, Shay? While everyone here is locked up?"

"Well, I guess so," Shay said defensively. "I mean, they'll all get out once they turn. Once Cable gets over her stupid power trip." She looked at the unconscious form on the floor and shook her head. "She's going to be in a bad mood tomorrow, though. Thanks to you two."

The sound of complaining metal came from the detention room. Tally heard more voices.

"Of course, sounds like no one'll be around to see it," Shay said. "So how are you two doing, anyway?"

Tally opened her mouth, closed it, then managed to answer. "We're . . . good."

"That's great. Listen, sorry I was such a pain about all that. You know what uglies are like." Shay laughed. "Well, of course you do!"

"So you don't hate me?"

"Don't be silly, Tally!"

"I'm glad to hear that." Of course, Shay's blessing was meaningless. It wasn't forgiveness, just brain damage.

"You did me a big favor, getting me out of that Smoke place."

"You can't really believe that, Shay."

"What do you mean?"

"How could you change your mind so quickly?"

Shay laughed. "It took exactly one hot shower to change my mind." She reached out and touched Tally's hair, tangled and knotted from two weeks of camping out and riding all day. "Speaking of showers, *you* are a total mess."

Tally blinked. Hot tears were forcing themselves into her eyes. Shay had wanted so much to keep her own face, to live on her own terms outside the city. But that desire had been extinguished.

"I didn't mean to . . . betray you," she said softly.

Shay glanced over her shoulder, then turned back and smiled. "He doesn't know that you were working for Dr. C, does he? Don't worry, Tally," she whispered, putting one elegant finger to her lips. "Your ugly little secret is safe with me."

Tally swallowed, wondering if Shay had found out the whole story. Maybe Dr. Cable had told them all what she'd done.

A buzzing sound came from beside Dr. Cable. On the work tablet she had been carrying, a request light blinked with an incoming call.

Tally picked up the tablet and handed it to Shay. "Talk to them!"

Shay winked, pushed a button, and said, "Hey, it's me, Shay. No, I'm sorry, Dr. Cable's busy. Doing what? Well, it's complicated . . ." She muted the device. "Shouldn't you be rescuing people or something, Tally? That is the point of this little trick, right?"

"You'll stay here?"

"Duh. This looks bubbly. Just because I'm pretty doesn't mean I'm *totally* boring."

Tally brushed past her and into the room. Two doors had been ripped open, David's mother and another Smokey freed. The two were dressed in orange jumpsuits, with stunned and sleepy looks on their faces. David was working another door, his powerjack thrust into a small slot at floor level.

Tally saw Croy's face peering wide-eyed through one of the tiny windows, and planted her powerjack under his door. It whined to life, and the thick metal screeched as it bent upward. "David, they know something's up!" she called.

"Okay. We're almost done here."

Her jack had wrenched a small gap in the metal, not big enough. Tally reset the tool, and the metal groaned again. Her days of pulling up railroad ties soon paid off, the jack tearing a hole the size of a doggy door.

Croy's arms appeared, then his head, his jumpsuit ripping on jagged spurs of metal as he wriggled. Maddy grabbed his hands and pulled him through. "That's everyone who's left," she said. "Let's go."

"What about Dad!" David cried.

"We can't help him." Maddy ran into the hall.

Tally and David shared an anxious look, and followed.

Maddy was dashing down the hall toward the elevator, dragging Shay by the wrist behind her. Shay stabbed the tablet's talk button and said, "Wait a second, I think she's just coming back now. Hold please." She giggled and muted the device again.

"Bring Cable!" Maddy called. "We need her!"

"Mom!" David ran after her.

Tally looked at Croy, then down at Dr. Cable's crumpled form. Croy nodded, and they each took a wrist, dragging the woman along the slick floor at a trot, Tally's grippy shoes squealing.

When the party reached the elevator, Maddy grabbed Dr. Cable by the collar and pulled her up to the eye-reader. The woman groaned once, softly. Maddy carefully pried open one of her eyes, and the elevator *pinged,* its doors sliding open.

Maddy tugged off the doctor's interface ring and dropped her to the floor, then pulled Shay inside. Tally and the other Smokies followed, but David stood his ground. "Mom, where's Dad?"

"We can't help him." Maddy yanked the tablet away from Shay and cracked it against the wall, then pulled David in against his protests. The doors closed, and the elevator asked, "Which floor?"

"Roof," Maddy said, the interface ring still in her hand. The elevator began to move, Tally's ears complaining at the swift ascent.

"What's our escape plan?" Maddy snapped. The glazed look was completely gone from her eyes, as if she'd gone to sleep last night expecting to be rescued this morning.

"Uh, hoverboards," Tally managed to answer. "Four of them." Realizing that she hadn't done so yet, Tally adjusted her crash bracelets to call them in.

"Oh, cool!" Shay said. "You know, I haven't been boarding since I left the Smoke?"

"There's seven of us," Maddy said. "Tally, you take Shay. Astrix and Ryde, double up. Croy, you go alone and throw them off the track. David, I'll ride with you."

"Mom . . . ," David pleaded, "if he's pretty, can't you cure him? Or at least try?"

"Your father's not pretty, David," she answered softly. "He's dead."

GETAWAY

"Give me a knife." Maddy held out her hand, ignoring the shocked look on her son's face.

Tally scrambled through her knapsack. She passed her multiknife to Maddy, who pulled out a short blade and cut a piece from the arm of her jumpsuit. When the elevator reached roof level, its doors slid halfway open and groaned to a halt, revealing the uneven hole Tally had torn to gain entry. They slipped through one by one and ran for the edge of the roof.

A hundred meters away, Tally saw the hoverboards cruising across the compound, called by her crash bracelets. Alarms were ringing all around them now. If by some magic the Specials hadn't noticed the escape so far, the riderless boards had tripped the wire.

Tally spun around, looking for David. He was stumbling along at the back of the group, half in a daze. She caught him by his shoulders. "I'm so sorry."

He shook his head. Not at her, not at anything in particular.

"I don't know what to do, Tally."

She took his hand. "We have to run. That's all we can do right now. Follow your mother."

He looked into her eyes, his face wild. "Okay." He started to say more, but the words were drowned out by a noise like huge fingernails scraping metal. The hovercar door was fighting against the nanotech glue, setting the whole roof shuddering.

Maddy, last out of the elevator, had jimmied its door open with a powerjack. Its voice kept repeating, "Elevator requested."

But there were other ways onto the roof. Maddy turned to David. "Glue down those hatches so they can't get out."

His gaze cleared for a moment, and he nodded.

"I'll get the boards," Tally said, turning to dash for the edge of the roof. When she reached it, she jumped into space, hoping her bungee jacket still had some charge.

After one bounce, Tally was on the ground running. The boards sensed her crash bracelets and sped toward her.

"Tally! Look out!"

She looked over her shoulder at Croy's shout. A squad of Specials was headed toward her across the compound, an open door behind them at ground level. They ran inhumanly fast, covering the ground with long, loping strides.

The boards nudged her calves from behind, like dogs ready to play. Tally leaped up, teetering for a moment with one foot on each pair of sandwiched boards. She'd never heard of anyone riding four boards at once. But the closest cruel pretty was only a few strides away.

Tally snapped her fingers and rose swiftly into the air.

The Special jumped, amazingly high, the fingers of one outstretched hand just brushing the front edge of the boards. The contact set them wobbling beneath Tally. It was like standing on a trampoline while someone else jumped on it. The other Specials watched from the ground below, waiting for her to fall.

But Tally regained her balance and leaned forward, heading back toward the building. The boards picked up speed, and seconds later Tally leaped off onto the roof, kicking one pair of hoverboards to Croy. He pulled them apart while she separated the other two.

"Go now," Maddy said. "Take this."

She handed Tally a swatch of orange fabric, a small bit of circuitry visible on one side. Tally noticed that Maddy had cut pieces from the forearms of all the jumpsuits.

"There's a tracker in that cloth," Maddy said. "Drop it somewhere to throw them off."

Tally nodded, looking around for David. He was running toward them, his face set into a grim mask, the tube of glue crushed and empty in his hand. "David—," she started.

"Go!" Maddy shouted, pushing Shay onto the board behind Tally.

"Um, no crash bracelets?" Shay said, her feet unsteady. "This is not my first party tonight, you know."

"I know. Hold on," Tally said, and shot away from the roof.

The two of them teetered for a moment, almost losing their balance. But Tally steadied herself, feeling Shay's arms wrap tightly around her waist.

"Whoa, Tally! Slow down!"

"Just hang on."

Tally leaned into a turn, sickened by the sluggishness of the board. Not only was it carrying two, but Shay's wobbly moves were freaking it out.

"Don't you remember how to ride?"

"Sure!" Shay said. "Just a little rusty, Squint. Plus a little too much to drink tonight."

"Just don't fall off. It'll hurt."

"Hey! I didn't ask to be rescued!"

"No, I guess you didn't." Tally looked down as they soared over Crumblyville, skipping the greenbelt to head straight back toward the river. If Shay hit the ground at this speed, she'd be worse than hurt. She'd be dead.

Like David's father. Tally wondered how he'd died. Had he tried to escape the Specials, like the Boss? Or had Dr. Cable done something to him? One thought stuck in her mind: However it had happened, it was her fault.

"Shay, if you fall off, take me with you."

"What?"

"Just hold on to me and don't let go, no matter what. I'm wearing a bungee jacket and bracelets. We should bounce." Probably. Unless the jacket pulled her one way and the bracelets the other. Or Tally's and Shay's combined weight was too much for the lifters.

"So give me the bracelets, silly."

Tally shook her head. "No time to stop."

"Guess not. Our Special friends are going to be royally pissed." Shay clung tighter.

They were almost at the river, with no sign of pursuit behind them. The nanotech glue must have been putting up quite a fight. But Special Circumstances had other hovercars—the three they'd seen leave earlier, at least—and regular wardens had them too.

Tally wondered if Special Circumstances would call for help from the wardens, or whether they'd keep the whole situation a secret. What would the wardens think of the underground prison? Did the regular city government know what the Specials had done to the Smoke, or to Az?

Water flashed below her, and Tally dropped the swatch of orange cloth as they turned. It fluttered away, down toward the river. The current would take it back toward the city, in the opposite direction of their escape route.

Tally and David had agreed to rendezvous upriver, a long way past the ruins, where he had found a cave years before. Because its entrance was covered by a waterfall, it would shelter them from heat sensors. From there, they could hike back to the ruins to retrieve the rest of their equipment, and then . . .

Rebuild the Smoke? Seven of them? With Shay as their honorary pretty? Tally realized that they hadn't made plans beyond tonight. The future hadn't seemed real until now.

Of course, they still might all be caught.

"You think it's true?" Shay shouted. "What Maddy said?"

Tally dared a glance back at Shay. Her pretty face looked worried.

"I mean, Az was fine when I visited a few days ago," Shay said. "I thought they were going to make him pretty. Not *kill* him."

"I don't know." It was hardly something Maddy would lie about. But maybe she was mistaken.

Tally leaned forward, skimming the river low and fast, trying to leave the cold feeling in her stomach behind. Spray struck their faces as they hit the white water. Shay had started to ride properly, leaning with the slow arcs of the river's bends. "Hey, I remember this!" she shouted.

"Do you remember anything else from before your operation?" Tally yelled over the roar of water.

Shay ducked behind Tally as they struck a wall of spray. "Of course, silly."

"You hated me. Because I stole David from you. Because I betrayed the Smoke. Remember?"

Shay was silent for a moment, only the roar of white water and the rushing wind around them. Finally, she leaned closer, her voice thoughtful in Tally's ear. "Yeah, I know what you mean. But that was all ugly stuff. Crazy love and jealousy and needing to rebel against the city. Every kid's like that. But you grow up, you know?"

"You grew up because of an operation? Doesn't that strike you as weird?"

"It wasn't because of the operation."

"Then why?"

"It was just good to come home, Tally. It made me realize how crazy the whole Smoke thing was."

"What happened to biting and kicking?"

"Well, it took a few days to sink in, you know."

"Before or after you became pretty?"

Shay went silent again. Tally wondered if you could talk somebody out of their brain damage.

She pulled a position-finder from her pocket. The coordinates for the cave were still half an hour away. A glance over her shoulder didn't reveal any hovercars, not yet. If all four boards took different routes to the river, and all of them dropped their trackers in different places, the Specials were going to have a confusing night.

There were also Dex, Sussy, and An, who'd promised to tell every tricky ugly they knew to go for a ride tonight. The greenbelt would be crowded.

Tally wondered how many uglies had seen the burning letters in New Pretty Town, how many of them knew what the Smoke was, or were coming up with their own stories to explain the mysterious message. What new legends had she and David created with their little diversion?

When they reached a calmer part of the river, Shay spoke up again. "So, Tally?"

"Yeah?"

"Why do you want me to hate you?"

"I don't want you to hate me, Shay." Tally sighed. "Or maybe I do. I betrayed you, and I feel horrible about it."

"The Smoke wasn't going to last forever, Tally. Whether you turned us in or not."

"I didn't turn you in!" Tally cried. "Not on purpose, anyway. And the whole thing with David was just an accident. I didn't mean to hurt you."

"Of course not. You're just confused."

"*I'm* confused?" Tally groaned. "You're the one who . . ." She trailed off. How could Shay not understand that she'd been changed by the operation? Not just been given a pretty face, but also a . . . pretty mind. Nothing else could explain how quickly she'd changed, abandoning the rest of them for parties and hot showers, leaving her friends behind, just as Peris had so many months ago.

"Do you love him?" Shay asked.

"David? I, uh . . . maybe."

"That's sweet."

"It's not *sweet*. It's real!"

"Then why are you ashamed of it?"

"I'm not . . . ," Tally sputtered. She lost concentration for a moment, and the back of the board dipped low, sending a sheet of water up behind them. Shay whooped and held tighter. Tally gritted her teeth and took them a bit higher.

When Shay had stopped laughing, she said, "And you think *I'm* confused?"

"Listen, Shay, there's one thing I'm not confused about. I didn't want to betray the Smoke. I was blackmailed into going there as a spy, and when I sent for the Specials, it was an accident, really. But I'm sorry, Shay. I'm sorry I ruined your dream." Tally felt herself crying, the tears driven backward by the wind. The trees rushed past in the darkness for a while.

"I'm just glad you two made it back to civilization," Shay said softly, holding on tight. "And I'm not sorry about what happened. If that makes you feel any better."

Tally thought of the lesions on Shay's brain, the tiny cancers or wounds or whatever they were, that she didn't even know she had. They were in there somewhere, changing her friend's thoughts, warping her feelings, gnawing at the roots of who she was. Making her forgive Tally.

"Thanks, Shay. But no, it doesn't."

NIGHT ALONE

Tally and Shay made it to the cave first.

Croy arrived a few minutes later, without warning, he and his board hurtling through the waterfall in a sudden explosion of splashing and cursing. He tumbled into the darkness, his body rolling across the stone floor with a series of sickening thuds.

Tally scrambled from the back of the cave, a flashlight in one hand.

Croy shook his head and groaned. "I lost them."

Tally looked at the entrance of the cave, the sheet of

water a solid curtain against the night. "I hope so. Where's everybody else?"

"Don't know. Maddy told us all to go different ways. Since I was flying solo, I went all the way around the greenbelt first to get them off track." He laid his head back, still panting. A position-finder fell from one of his hands.

"Wow. You went fast."

"You're telling me. No crash bracelets."

"Been there. At least you had shoes on," Tally said. "Did anyone chase you?"

He nodded. "I held on to my tracker as long as I could. Got most of the Specials to follow me. But there were a whole bunch of hoverboard riders in the belt. You know, city kids. The Specials kept getting us confused."

Tally smiled. Dex, An, and Sussy had done their work well.

"Are David and Maddy okay?"

"I wouldn't know about okay," he said softly. "But they got off right after you, and it didn't look like anyone was following them. Maddy said they were heading straight for the ruins. We're supposed to meet them there tomorrow night."

"Tomorrow?" Tally said.

"Maddy wanted to be alone with David for a while, you know?"

Tally nodded, but her heart wrenched inside her. David needed her. At least, she hoped he did. The thought of him dealing with Az's death without her made the icy feeling in her stomach drop a few more degrees.

Of course, Maddy was there. Az had been her husband, after all, and Tally had only met the man once. But still.

She sighed. Tally tried to remember the last words

she'd said to David, and wished they'd been more comforting. There hadn't even been time to hold him. Since the invasion of the Smoke, Tally hadn't been separated from David for longer than that hour in the storm, and now she wouldn't see him for a whole day.

"Maybe I should go to the ruins. I could hike out there tonight."

"Don't be crazy," Croy said. "The Specials are still out looking."

"But just in case they need anything . . ."

"Maddy said to tell you no."

Astrix and Ryde showed up a half hour later, coming into the cave more gracefully than Croy, but with their own stories of running from hovercars. The pursuit had been confused, the Specials overwhelmed by everything that had happened that night.

"They never even got close," Astrix said.

Ryde shook his head. "They were all over the place."

"It's like we won a battle, you know?" Croy said. "We beat them in their own city. Made them look like fools."

"Maybe we don't have to hide in the wild anymore," Ryde said. "It could be like when we were uglies, playing tricks. But telling the whole city the truth."

"And if we get caught, Tally can come and rescue us!" Croy shouted.

Tally tried to smile at their cheers, but knew she wouldn't feel good about anything until she saw David again. Not until tomorrow night. She felt exiled, shut out from the one thing that really mattered.

Shay had fallen asleep in a small crevice after complaining about the dampness and her hair, asking when they were going to take her home. Tally crawled back to where her friend lay and snuggled up next to her, trying to forget the damage that had been done to Shay's mind. At least Shay's new body wasn't as painfully skinny; she felt soft and warm in the damp cold of the cave. Cradled against her, Tally managed to stop shivering.

But it was a long time before she fell asleep.

She woke up to the smell of PadThai.

Croy had found the food packets and purifier in her knapsack and was making food with water from the fall, apparently trying to placate Shay.

"A little escape was one thing, but I didn't know you guys were going to drag me all the way out here. I'm through with this whole rebellion thing, I've got a wicked hangover, and I really need to wash my hair."

"There's a waterfall right there," Croy said.

"But it's cold! I'm so *over* this camping-out bogusness."

Tally crawled out into the big part of the cave, every muscle stiff, every rock she'd slept on imprinted on her. Through the curtain of the waterfall, dusk was falling. She wondered if she'd ever be able to sleep at night again.

Shay was squatting on a rock, digging into the PadThai, complaining that it wasn't spicy enough. Bedraggled, in dirty party clothes, her hair stuck to her face, she was still stunning. Ryde and Astrix watched her silently, a bit awestruck by her looks. They were two of Shay's old friends who'd run away to the Smoke the time she'd chickened out, so it must have been months since they'd seen a pretty face. Everyone seemed willing to let her go on complaining.

One thing about being pretty, people put up with your annoying habits.

"Morning," said Croy. "SwedeBalls or VegiRice?"

"Whatever's faster." Tally stretched her muscles. She wanted to get to the ruins as soon as possible.

When darkness fell, Tally and Croy crept out from behind the waterfall. There was no sign of Specials in the sky. She doubted anyone was searching this far out. Forty minutes from the city on a fast board was a long way.

They gave the all-clear, and everyone rode farther upriver, to a place where the river's course twisted closer to the ruins. A long hike followed, the four uglies sharing the load of boards and supplies. Shay had stopped complaining, settling into a pouty, hungover silence. The walk seemed easy for her. Her wiry fitness from hard work at the Smoke hadn't faded in two weeks, and the operation actually firmed up a new pretty's muscles, at least for a while. Although Shay announced once that she wanted to go home, heading back on her own didn't seem to have entered her mind.

Tally wondered what they were going to do with her. She knew there was no simple fix. Maddy and Az had worked for twenty years to no avail. But they couldn't leave Shay like this.

Of course, the moment she was cured, her hatred for Tally would return.

Which was worse: a friend with brain damage, or one who despised you?

They reached the edge of the ruins after midnight, and boarded down to the abandoned building where Tally and David had camped.

David was waiting outside.

He looked exhausted, the dark lines under his eyes visible even in starlight. But he embraced Tally the moment she stepped from the board, his arms tight around her, and she hugged him back hard. "Are you okay?" she whispered, then felt idiotic. What was he supposed to say to that? "Oh, David, of course you're not. I'm sorry, I—"

"Shhh. I know." He pulled away and smiled.

Relief flowed through Tally, and she squeezed David's hands, confirming the realness of him. "I missed you," she said.

"Me too." He kissed her.

"You two are just so cute," Shay said, combing her hair with her fingers after the windy ride.

"Hi, Shay." David gave her a tired smile. "You guys look hungry."

"Only if you have any non-bogus food," Shay said.

"Afraid not. Three kinds of reconstituted curry."

Shay groaned and pushed past him into the crumbling building. His eyes followed her, but without any of the awe still in Ryde's and Astrix's faces. It was as if David didn't see her beauty.

He turned back. "We finally got some luck."

Tally looked into his lined, fatigued face. "Really?"

"We got that tablet working, the one Dr. Cable was carrying. Mom was yanking the phone part out so they couldn't track us through it, and she got it to display Cable's work data."

"About what?"

"All her notes on making pretties into Specials. Not just the physical part"—he pulled her closer—"but also how the brain lesions work. It's everything my parents weren't told when they were doctors!"

Tally swallowed. "Shay . . ."

He nodded. "Mom thinks she can find a cure."

HIPPOCRATIC OATH

They stayed at the edge of the Rusty Ruins.

Occasionally, hovercars would pass over the crumbling city, threading a slow search pattern across the sky. But the Smokies were old hands at hiding from satellites and aircraft. They placed red herrings across the ruins—chemical glowsticks that gave off human-size pockets of heat—and covered the windows of their building with sheets of black Mylar. And of course the ruins were very large; finding seven people in what had once been a city of millions was no simple matter.

Every night, Tally watched the influence of the "New Smoke" grow. A lot of uglies had seen the burning message on the night of the escape, or had heard about it, and the nightly pilgrimages out to the ruins slowly increased, until sparklers wavered atop high buildings from midnight until dawn. Tally, Ryde, Croy, and Astrix made contact with the city uglies, starting new rumors, teaching new tricks, and offering glimpses of the ancient magazines the Boss had salvaged from the Smoke. If they doubted the existence of Special Circumstances, Tally showed them the plastic handcuff bracelets still encircling her wrists, and invited them to try to cut the cuffs off.

One new legend towered above all the rest. Maddy had decided that the brain lesions couldn't be kept a secret anymore; every ugly had the right to know what the operation really entailed. Tally and the others spread the rumor among their city friends: Not just your face was changed by the knife. Your personality—the real you inside—was the price of beauty.

Of course, not every ugly believed such an outrageous tale, but a few did. And some sneaked across to New Pretty Town in the dead of night to talk to their older friends face-to-face, and decided for themselves.

The Specials sometimes tried to crash the party, setting traps for the New Smokies, but someone always gave a warning, and no hovercar could ever catch a board among winding streets and rubble. The New Smokies learned the nooks and crannies of the ruins as if they'd been born there, until they could disappear in a heartbeat.

Maddy worked on the brain cure, using materials salvaged from the ruins or brought by city uglies willing to borrow from hospitals and chem classes. She withdrew from the rest of them, except for David. She seemed particularly cool to Tally, who felt guilty for every moment she spent with David, now that his mother was alone. None of them ever talked about Az's death.

Shay stayed with them, complaining about the food, the ruins, her hair and clothes, and having to look at all the ugly faces around her. But she never seemed bitter, only perpetually annoyed. After the first few days she didn't even talk about leaving. Perhaps the brain damage made her pliant, or the fact that she hadn't lived in New Pretty Town for long. She still remembered them all as friends. Tally sometimes wondered if Shay secretly enjoyed having the only pretty face in their little rebellion. Certainly, she didn't do any more work than she would have in the city; Ryde and Astrix obeyed her every command.

David helped his mother, searching the ruins for salvage, and taught wilderness survival tricks to any ugly who wanted to learn. But in the two weeks after his father's death, Tally found herself missing the days when it had been just the two of them.

Twenty days after the rescue, Maddy announced that she had found a cure.

"Shay, I want to explain this to you carefully."

"Sure, Maddy."

"When you had the operation, they did something to your brain."

Shay smiled. "Yeah, right." She looked across at Tally, wearing a familiar expression. "That's what Tally keeps telling me. But you guys don't understand."

Maddy folded her hands. "What do you mean?"

"I *like* the way I look," Shay insisted. "I'm happier in this body. You want to talk about brain damage? Look at you all, running around these ruins playing commando. You're all full of schemes and rebellions, crazy with fear and paranoia, even jealousy." Her eyes skipped back and forth between Tally and Maddy. "That's what being ugly does."

"And how do you feel, Shay?" Maddy asked calmly.

"I feel bubbly. It's nice not being all raging with hormones. Of course, it kind of sucks being out here instead of in the city."

"No one's keeping you here, Shay. Why haven't you left?"

Shay shrugged. "I don't know. . . . I'm worried about you guys, I guess. It's dangerous out here, and messing with

Specials isn't a good idea. You should know that by now, Maddy."

Tally took a sharp breath, but Maddy's expression didn't change. "And you're going to protect us from them?" she asked calmly.

Shay shrugged. "I just feel bad about Tally. If I hadn't told her about the Smoke, she'd be pretty right now instead of living in this dump. And I figure eventually she'll decide to grow up. We'll go back together."

"You don't seem to want to decide for yourself."

"Decide what?" Shay rolled her eyes, looking at Tally to confirm what a bore this was. The two of them had plowed through this conversation a dozen times before, until Tally had realized there was no convincing Shay that her personality had changed. To Shay, her new attitude was simply the result of growing up, moving on, leaving all the overheated emotions of ugliness behind.

"You weren't always this way, Shay," David said.

"No, I used to be ugly."

Maddy smiled gently. "These pills won't change the way you look. They'll only affect your brain, undoing what Dr. Cable did to the way your mind works. Then you can decide for yourself how you want to look."

"Decide? After you've messed with my brain?"

"Shay!" Tally said, forgetting her promise to remain silent. "We're not the ones messing with your brain!"

"Tally," David said softly.

"That's right, *I'm* the one who's crazy." Shay's voice took on the tone of her daily round of complaining. "Not you guys, who live in a broken-down building on the edge of a dead city, slowly turning into freaks when you could be beautiful. Yeah, I'm crazy all right . . . for trying to help you!"

Tally sat back and crossed her arms, silenced by Shay's words. Whenever they had this conversation, reality became a little unhinged, as if she and the other New Smokies might really be the insane ones. It felt like Tally's horrible first days in the Smoke, when she hadn't known whose side she was on.

"How are you helping us, Shay?" Maddy asked calmly.

"I'm trying to get you to understand."

"Just like you did when Dr. Cable used to bring you by my cell?"

Shay's eyes narrowed, confusion clouding her face, as if her memories of the underground prison didn't fit in with the rest of her pretty worldview.

"I know Dr. C was horrible to you," she said. "The Specials are psychos—just look at them. But that doesn't mean you have to spend your whole lives running away. That's what I'm saying. Once you turn, Specials won't mess with you."

"Why not?"

"Because you won't make trouble anymore."

"Why not?"

"Because you'll be *happy*!" Shay took a couple of deep breaths, and her usual calm returned. She smiled, beautiful again. "Like me."

Maddy picked up the pills on the table in front of her. "You won't take these willingly?"

"No way. You said they're not even safe."

"I said there was a small chance something could go wrong."

Shay laughed. "You *must* think I'm nuts. And even if those pills work, look what they're supposed to do. From what I can tell, 'cured' means being a jealous, self-important, whiny little ugly-brain. It means thinking you've got all the answers." She crossed her arms. "In a lot of ways, you and Dr. Cable are alike. You're both convinced you've personally got to change the world. Well, I don't need that. And I don't need those."

"Okay, then." Maddy picked up the pills and put them in her pocket. "That's all I have to say."

"What do you mean?" Tally asked.

David squeezed her hand. "That's all we can do, Tally."

"What? You said we could cure her."

Maddy shook her head. "Only if she wants to be cured. These are experimental, Tally. We can't give them to someone against her will. Not when we don't know if they'll work."

"But her mind . . . she's got the lesions!"

"Hello," Shay called. "*She* is sitting right here."

"Sorry, Shay," Maddy said mildly. "Tally?"

Maddy pulled aside the Mylar barrier, stepping out onto what the New Smokies called the balcony. It was really just part of the top floor of the building, where the roof had entirely collapsed, leaving sweeping views of the ruins.

Tally followed. Behind her, Shay was already talking about what was for dinner. David came out a moment later.

"So, we give her the pills secretly, right?" Tally whispered.

"No," Maddy said firmly. "We can't. I'm not going to do medical experiments on unwilling subjects."

"Medical experiments?" Tally swallowed.

David took her hand. "You can't know for sure how something like this will work. It's only a one-percent chance, but it could screw up her brain forever."

"It's already screwed up."

"But she's happy, Tally." David shook his head. "And she can make decisions for herself."

Tally pulled her hand away, staring out over the city. A sparkler was already showing on the tall spire, uglies come to gossip and trade. "Why did we even have to ask? *They* didn't get her permission when they did this to her!"

"That's the difference between us and them," Maddy said. "After Az and I found out what the operation really meant, we realized we'd been party to something horrible. People had had their minds changed without their knowledge. As doctors, we took an ancient oath never to do anything like that."

Tally looked into Maddy's face. "But if you weren't going to help Shay, why did you bother finding a cure?"

"If we knew the treatment would work safely, then we could give it to Shay and see how she felt about it later. But to test it, we need a willing subject."

"Where are we ever going to find one? Anyone who's pretty is going to say no."

"Maybe for right now, Tally. But if we keep making inroads into the city, we might find a pretty who wants out."

"But we *know* Shay's crazy."

"She's not crazy," Maddy said. "Her arguments make sense, in fact. She's happy as she is, and doesn't want to take a deadly risk."

"But she's not really herself. We *have* to change her back."

"Az died because someone thought like that," Maddy said grimly.

"What?"

David put his arm around her. "My father . . ." He cleared his throat, and Tally waited in silence. Finally he would tell her how Az had died.

He took a slow breath before continuing. "Dr. Cable wanted to turn them all, but she was worried that Mom and Dad might talk about the brain lesions, even after the operation, because they'd been focused on them for so long." David's voice trembled, but it was soft and careful, as if he didn't dare put any emotion into the words. "Dr. Cable was already working on ways to change memories, a way of erasing the Smoke forever from people's minds. When they took my father for the operation, he never came back."

"That's awful," Tally whispered. She gathered him into a hug.

"Az was the victim of a medical experiment, Tally," Maddy said. "I can't do the same thing to Shay. Otherwise, she'd be right about me and Dr. Cable."

"But Shay ran away. She didn't want to become pretty."

"She doesn't want to be experimented on, either."

Tally closed her eyes. Through the Mylar shade, she could hear Shay telling Ryde about the hairbrush she'd made. For days she'd proudly shown the little brush, made of splinters of wood shoved into a lump of clay, to anyone who would listen. As if it were the most important thing she'd ever done.

They had risked everything to rescue her. But they had nothing to show for it. Shay would never be the same.

And it was all Tally's fault. She'd come to the Smoke, and had brought the Specials, leaving Shay an empty-headed pretty, and Az dead.

She took a deep breath. "Okay, you've got a willing subject."

"What do you mean, Tally?"

"Me."

CONFESSIONS

"What?" David said.

"Your taking the pills won't prove anything, Tally," Maddy said. "You don't have the lesions."

"But I will have them. I'll go back to the city and get caught, and Dr. Cable will give me the operation. In a few weeks, you come and get me. Give me the cure. You've got your subject."

The three of them stood there in silence. The words had poured out of Tally of their own accord. She could hardly believe she'd uttered them.

"Tally . . ." David shook his head. "That's crazy."

"It's not crazy. You need a willing subject. Someone who agrees *before* they become pretty that they want to be cured, experimental or not. It's the only way."

"You can't give yourself up!" David cried.

Tally turned toward Maddy. "You said you're ninety-nine percent sure these pills will work, right?"

"Yes. But the one percent could leave you a vegetable, Tally."

"One percent? Compared to breaking into Special Circumstances, that's a breeze."

"Tally, stop it." David took her shoulders. "It's too dangerous."

"Dangerous? David, you can get across into New Pretty Town no problem. City uglies do it all the time. Just grab me out of my mansion and stick me on a board. I'll come with you, just like Shay did. Then you cure me."

"What if the Specials decide to change your memory? Like they did my father's?"

"They won't," Maddy said.

David stared at his mother in surprise.

"They didn't bother with Shay. She remembers the Smoke just fine. Az and I were the only ones they were worried about. Because we'd been focused on the brain lesions for half our lives, they figured we'd never shut up about them, even as pretties."

"Mom!" David cried. "Tally's not going anywhere."

"And besides," Maddy continued, "Dr. Cable wouldn't do anything to hurt Tally."

"Stop talking like this is going to happen!"

Tally looked into Maddy's eyes. The woman nodded. She knew.

"David," Tally said. "I have to do this."

"Why?"

"Because of Shay. It's the only way that Maddy will cure her. Right?"

Maddy nodded.

"You don't have to save Shay," David said slowly and evenly. "You've done enough for her. You followed her to the Smoke, rescued her from Special Circumstances!"

"Yeah, I've done a lot for her." Tally took a breath. "I'm the reason she's like this, pretty and brainless."

David shook his head. "What are you talking about?"

She turned to him, taking his hand. "David, I didn't come to the Smoke just to make sure Shay was okay. I came to bring her back to the city." She sighed. "I came to betray her."

Tally had imagined telling her secret to David so many times, rehearsing this speech to herself almost every night, that she could hardly believe this wasn't just another nightmare in which the truth was forced from her. But as the reality of the moment sank in, she found the words spilling out in a torrent.

"I was a spy for Dr. Cable. That's how I knew where Special Circumstances was. That's why the Specials came to the Smoke. I brought a tracker with me, "

"You're not making any sense," David said. "You fought when they came. You escaped. You helped rescue my mother . . ."

"I'd changed my mind. And I never meant to activate the tracker, honestly. I wanted to live in the Smoke. But the night before the invasion, after I found out about the lesions . . ." She closed her eyes. "After we kissed, I accidentally set it off."

"What?"

"My locket. I didn't mean to. I wanted to destroy it. But I'm the one who brought the Specials to the Smoke, David. I'm the reason why Shay is pretty. It's my fault your father's dead."

"You're making this up! I'm not going to let you—"

"David," Maddy said sharply, silencing her son, "she's not lying."

Tally opened her eyes. Maddy was looking at her sadly.

"Dr. Cable told me everything about how she manipulated you, Tally. I didn't believe her at first, but the night you rescued us, she'd just brought Shay down to confirm it."

Tally nodded. "Shay knew I was a traitor, at the end."

"She still knows," Maddy said. "But it doesn't matter to her anymore. That's why Tally has to do this."

"You're both crazy!" David shouted. "Look, Mom, just get off your high horse and give Shay the pills." He reached out his hand. "I'll do it for you."

"David, I won't let you turn yourself into a monster. And Tally's made her choice."

David looked at them both, unable to believe any of it. Finally, he found words. "You were a spy?"

"Yes. At first."

He shook his head.

"Son." Maddy stepped forward, trying to hold him.

"No!" He turned and ran, tearing the Mylar shade down and leaving the others inside speechless; even Shay was shocked into silence.

Before Tally could follow, Maddy took her arm in a firm grip. "You should go to the city now."

"Tonight? But—"

"Otherwise, you'll talk yourself out of it. Or David will."

Tally pulled away. "I have to say good-bye to him."

"You have to go."

Tally stared at Maddy and slowly realized the truth. Although the woman's gaze held more sadness than anger, there was something cold in her eyes. David might not blame her for Az's death, but Maddy did.

"Thank you," Tally said softly, forcing herself to hold Maddy's gaze.

"For what?"

"For not telling him. For letting me do it myself."

Maddy shook her head, managing a smile. "David needed you these last two weeks."

Tally swallowed and stepped away, looking at the city. "He still needs me."

"Tally—"

"I'll go tonight, all right? But I know that David will be the one who brings me back."

DOWN THE RIVER

Before leaving, Tally wrote a letter to herself.

It was Maddy's idea, to put her consent in writing. That way, even as a pretty, unable to comprehend why she would ever want her brain fixed, Tally could at least read her own words and know what was about to happen.

"Whatever makes you feel better," Tally said. "As long as you cure me, no matter what I say. Don't leave me like Shay."

"I'll cure you, Tally. I promise. I just need written consent." Maddy handed her a pen and a small, precious piece of paper.

"I never learned penmanship," Tally said. "They don't require it anymore."

Maddy shook her head sadly and said, "Okay. You dictate, and I'll write it."

"Not you. Shay can write it for me. She took a class, back when she was trying to get to the Smoke." Tally remembered the scrawl of Shay's directions to the Smoke, clumsy but readable.

The letter didn't take long. Shay giggled at Tally's heartfelt words, but she wrote them down as directed. There was something earnest in the way she put stylus to paper, like a littlie learning how to read.

When they were finished, David still hadn't come back. He'd taken one of the hoverboards in the direction of the ruins. As she put away her things, Tally kept glancing at the window, hoping he would return.

But Maddy was probably right. If Tally saw him again,

she would just talk herself out of this. Or maybe David would stop her.

Or worse, maybe he wouldn't.

But no matter what David said now, he would always remember what she had done, the lives she had cost with her secrets. This was the only way Tally could be certain that he had forgiven her. If he came to rescue her, she would know.

"So, let's get moving," Shay said when they were done.

"Shay, I'm not going to be gone forever. I'd rather you . . ."

"Come on. I'm sick of this place."

Tally bit her lip. What was the point of giving herself up if Shay was coming too? Of course, they could always snatch her away again as well. Once the cure was proven to work, they could give it to anyone. Or everyone.

"The only reason I've been hanging around this dump is to try to get you to come back," Shay said, then lowered her voice. "You know, it's my fault you're not already pretty. I messed up everything by running away. I owe you."

"Oh, Shay." Tally's head began to spin. She closed her eyes.

"Maddy always says I can go anytime. You don't want me to go back all alone, do you?"

Tally tried to imagine Shay hiking to the river alone. "No, I guess not." She looked at her friend's face and saw a spark in her eyes, something real ignited by the idea of going on a trip with Tally.

"Please! We'll have a blast in New Pretty Town."

Tally spread her hands. "Okay. I guess I can't stop you."

They rode together on one hoverboard. Croy came along on

another, to take the boards back when they reached the city's edge.

He didn't talk the whole way down. The other New Smokies had all heard the fight outside, and finally knew what Tally had done. It must have been worse for Croy. He had suspected, and she'd lied to him face-to-face. He was probably wishing he'd stopped Tally himself before she'd had a chance to betray them all.

When they reached the greenbelt, though, he forced himself to look at her. "What did they do to you, anyway? To make you do something like that?"

"They said I couldn't turn, until I'd found Shay."

He looked away, staring at the lights of New Pretty Town, bright in the clear cold of a November night. "So you're finally getting your wish."

"Yeah. I guess."

"Tally's going to be pretty!" Shay said.

Croy ignored her and looked at Tally again. "Thanks for rescuing me, though. That was some trick you guys pulled off. I hope that . . ." He shrugged, and shook his head. "See you later."

"I hope so."

Croy stuck the boards together and headed back up the river.

"This is going to be the best!" Shay said. "I can't wait for you to meet all my new friends. And you can finally introduce me to Peris."

"Sure."

They walked down toward Uglyville until they found themselves in Cleopatra Park. The earth was hard underneath their feet in the late autumn chill, and they huddled close against the cold. Tally wore her Smoke-made sweater.

She'd wanted Maddy to keep it for her, but she'd left her microfiber jacket behind instead. City-made clothes were too valuable to waste on someone going back to civilization.

"You see, I was already getting popular," Shay was saying. "Having a criminal past is the only way into the really good parties. I mean, no one wants to hear about what classes you took in ugly school." She giggled.

"We should be a hit, then."

"Duh. When we tell everyone about your kidnapping me right out of Special Circumstances headquarters? And how I talked you into escaping from that band of freaks? But we're going to have to tone it down, Squint. No one's ever going to believe the truth!"

"No, you're right about that."

Tally thought of the letter she'd left with Maddy. Would *she* even believe the truth in a few weeks' time? How would the words of a fugitive, desperate, tragic ugly look through pretty eyes?

For that matter, what was David going to look like after she'd been surrounded by new pretty faces twenty-four hours a day? Would she really believe all that stuff about ugliness again, or would she remember how someone could be beautiful even without surgery? Tally tried to picture David's face, but it hurt to think of how long it would be before she saw him again.

She wondered how long it would take after the operation, before she would stop missing David. It might be a few days before the lesions completely took hold of her, Maddy had warned. But that didn't mean it was her own mind, changing itself.

Maybe if she decided to go on missing him, no matter

what, Tally could keep her mind from changing. Unlike most people, she *knew* about the lesions. Maybe she could beat them.

A dark shape passed overhead, a warden's hovercar, and Tally instinctively froze. The city uglies had said there were more patrols out these days. The regular authorities had finally noticed that things were changing.

The hovercar halted, then settled softly onto the earth next to them. A door slid open, and a blinding light popped on. "All right, you kids . . . oh, sorry, miss."

The light was on Shay's face. Then it flicked across to Tally.

"What are you two . . . ?" The warden's voice stumbled. Didn't this beat everything? A pretty and an ugly taking a stroll together. The warden came closer, confusion all over his middle-pretty face.

Tally smiled. At least she was causing trouble to the end.

"I'm Tally Youngblood," she said. "Make me pretty."

Scott Westerfeld is the acclaimed author of numerous best-selling novels for teens, including the UGLIES sequence; *Uglies*, *Pretties*, *Specials* and *Extras* published by Simon and Schuster. His other teen novels include *The Midnighters Trilogy*, *Parasite Positive*, *Last Days* and *So Yesterday* which was named an ALA Best Book for Young Adults.

Scott was born in Texas and now he and his wife, Justine, alternate summers between Sydney, Australia and New York City. Visit Scott's website at www.scottwesterfeld.com.